THEIR GUN

or so they assu⋯⋯⋯⋯ ⋯⋯⋯ ⋯⋯⋯⋯ ⋯⋯ rip-
ped through his position. But then they heard him
cry out. Spike felt a cold hand grasp his heart.

"He's alive!" Sol was near panic. "We can't
leave him down there!"

"We're not!" Spike unhooked his webgear and
slipped his gun in the crook of his arm. "I'm going
down there after him."

Sol pleaded to go. He'd left the gunner down
there. He'd bring him back.

Spike spoke harshly, his head still pressed against
the cool black earth. "You obey orders, or I swear
I'll press charges against you. I have the best
chance of bringing him back. Cover me."

Spike crawled slowly in the direction of the gunner's voice. A hail of bullets from the surrounding
jungle was mere inches from his head. . . .

MAJOR DONALD E. ZLOTNIK (Ret.) was a Green
Beret, paratrooper, and F-4 Phantom flyer in Vietnam,
and was awarded the Soldier's Medal for Heroism as
well as the Bronze Star. He is the author of five
previous novels.

FIELDS OF HONOR #1

✕✕✕✕✕✕✕✕✕✕✕✕✕✕✕✕✕✕✕✕✕✕✕✕✕✕✕✕✕✕✕

THE MEDAL OF HONOR

Donald E. Zlotnik,
Major, Ret., U.S. Army Special Forces

Ø

A SIGNET BOOK

SIGNET
Published by the Penguin Group
Penguin Books USA Inc., 375 Hudson Street,
New York, New York 10014, U.S.A.
Penguin Books Ltd, 27 Wrights Lane,
London W8 5TZ, England
Penguin Books Australia Ltd, Ringwood,
Victoria, Australia
Penguin Books Canada Ltd, 2801 John Street,
Markham, Ontario, Canada L3R 1B4
Penguin Books (N.Z.) Ltd, 182–190 Wairau Road,
Auckland 10, New Zealand

Penguin Books Ltd, Registered Offices:
Harmondsworth, Middlesex, England

First published by Signet, an imprint of Penguin Books USA Inc.

First Printing, November, 1990
10 9 8 7 6 5 4 3 2 1

 REGISTERED TRADEMARK—MARCA REGISTRADA

PRINTED IN THE UNITED STATES OF AMERICA

PUBLISHER'S NOTE
This is a work of fiction. Names, characters, places, and incidents either
are the product of the author's imagination or are used fictitiously,
and any resemblance to actual persons, living or dead, events, or
locales is entirely coincidental.

ARMY REGULATIONS (AR-672-5-1
Section II, Criteria

2-6. Medal of Honor

The Medal of Honor is awarded by the President in
the name of Congress to a person who, while a member
of the Army, distinguishes himself conspicuously by
gallantry and intrepidity at the risk of his life above
and beyond the call of duty while engaged in action
against an enemy of the United States; while engaged
in military operations involving conflict with an opposing
foreign force; or while serving with friendly foreign
forces engaged in an armed conflict against an opposing
armed force in which the United States is not a
belligerent party. The deed performed must have been
one of personal bravery or self-sacrifice so conspicuous
as to clearly distinguish the individual above his
comrades and must have involved risk of life. Incon-
testable proof of performance of the service will be
exacted and each recommendation for the award of this
decoration will be considered on the standard of
extraordinary merit.

(extract from the military regulation)

CHAPTER ONE

✪✪✪✪✪✪✪✪✪✪✪✪✪✪✪

DRIED BLOOD

November 27, 1967
14:20 hours

She scurried over the rain-soaked leaves between sections of the rotting trunk, trying to minimize the time spent exposed to the hated sunlight. Her brood of colorless young clung tightly to her back as she pushed against the loose bark of the dead tree with her large pincers and squeezed under the protective cover. As she did, one of her young was scraped off, falling onto a cushion of decaying bamboo leaves. A brace of red ants instantly appeared from under the leaves and attacked the unprotected creature.

Spike Harwood watched the large scorpion as she disappeared. Since daybreak he had been watching everything that moved around his hidden position in a thick stand of young bamboo. Spike's hearing and vision had been honed to an exceptionally high level after a night alone in the jungle.

He heard a soft crunch of damp twigs and leaves across the small clearing. He responded automatically by whipping the barrel of his riot shotgun in the direction of the sound and waited for its source to appear.

A volley of 105mm artillery shells whistled over his head and exploded prematurely in the treetops two hundred meters farther up the side of the hill. Spike ignored them. He had become perfectly tuned to the jungle and the battle that was raging around him. A helicopter passed over his position, flying only a few meters above the tree canopy. Spike blinked slowly when he heard the distinctive sound of a Chinese 12.7mm heavy machine gun thump out its death song. The helicopter's jet engine changed pitch and Spike heard the Huey crash in the trees. Unconsciously he pressed against the ground, waiting for the sound of the explosion to reach him. Trees crashing against one another echoed through the jungle, but no explosion followed.

The thick vegetation across the clearing from Spike parted slowly. He saw the worn tip of a round bayonet emerge, followed by the flash suppressor of an AK-47. An NVA soldier in a dirty uniform cautiously stepped out from the undergrowth and looked back over his shoulder. He beckoned with his head to an unseen comrade and then slowly scanned the area in front of him. He paused for only a second when his eyes spotted the bamboo that sheltered Spike, and then he continued his sweep.

Spike eased the stock of his pump shotgun up against his cheek as soon as the enemy's gaze had passed his position. He lined the front bead of his sights up on the sweat-stained tunic. Rarely during jungle fighting had Spike actually been able to see his target, and he felt the seconds-long visual contact with his prey begin to bother him as he kept waiting. The NVA soldier could be the point man for a much larger force, and Spike didn't want to give away his position by firing unless he was forced to. Another NVA soldier joined the first one in the small clearing and knelt next to his comrade. Spike used one of his free fingers to ease off the shotgun's safety. The second NVA spread a worn map on the ground and turned it so that its top pointed north. The first one continued to scan the borders of the clearing while his comrade tried to locate their position. Spike guessed that they were separated from their unit and decided that he would take both of them out.

Just then a long burst from an M60 light machine gun filled the clearing. Spike could see the vegetation quiver from the hidden weapon. The two NVA died instantly.

The jungle became silent.

Holding the rest of his body rigid, Spike slowly turned his head in the direction the machine gun had fired from. As he did, a bamboo leaf grazed the cold sore in the corner of his mouth that had developed into a jungle ulcer the size of a quarter. A burst of agony flashed through Spike's brain. He pressed his lips tightly together, trying to ignore the pain and concentrate on the problem facing him. The machine gunner would be jumpy after firing on the NVA and would kill him without hesitation.

Spike waited. He felt his stomach growl and his testicles move in his scrotum as they tried drawing up closer to his body. The slight movement brought another volley of pain. A bacterial infection had spread throughout his groin area, and the skin on his scrotum was peeling off in large strips. Spike had been in the jungle for six weeks without having the opportunity to shower or even wash in a stream. Lying prone on the bamboo leaves, he tried to remember the last time he had eaten, but promptly dismissed the subject from his mind. The fact was, he was starving. Drops of sweat ran down the side of his face and touched the festering ulcer. The new wave of pain was the final straw. He didn't care anymore.

"Yo, Skysoldier!" Spike whispered loudly. Whoever had fired the machine gun would certainly hear him.

There was a long pause before a voice across the clearing answered: "Paratrooper?"

Spike, knowing that the operator of the M60 was being extremely cautious and what he said next would probably decide if he lived or died, hissed, "All the way!"

The reply was instantaneous. "Spike?"

The bamboo rustled and two paratroopers appeared.

One of them carried the machine gun with a long belt of ammunition hanging over his left shoulder, and the other soldier carried a new M16. The machine gunner spoke: "It's good seeing you, Spike! I thought they got you when they overran the platoon yesterday."

The other soldier kept his M16 pointed at Spike just in case. He wasn't trusting anyone or anything.

Spike shook his head. "No, Sol, I was lucky, I guess." He nodded over at the nervous black soldier. "Who's he?"

The machine gunner shook his head slowly. "His name is Dudley. Talk about bad luck. He came in yesterday morning with a resupply chopper, less than an hour before the NVA hit us."

The black paratrooper realized that they were talking about him and tried grinning. "Man, this is some sorry shit."

Spike nodded and smiled back at the new replacement before addressing the machine gunner: "I found a wounded paratrooper back there. Let's go get him before I forget where I left him."

Sol nodded his head toward the dead NVA. "What about them?"

Spike curled his upper lip. "Fuck 'em."

"What about the company?"

"I saw the captain trying to form a perimeter with about thirty men right before we got cut off."

"Let's get going." Sol laid the belt of ammunition over his left shoulder and rose to a combat crouch. His M79 grenade launcher bouncing against his back felt uncomfortable, but he wasn't about to throw it away.

"Do you know where we're at?" the black paratrooper whispered from his position a few meters away.

Spike shook his head and looked over at the machine gunner. "Naw, do you, Sol?"

Sol shook his head. "No. Somewhere on Hill 875, I guess."

"This is a big fucking hill." Spike shifted his gaze

back across the clearing, where the dead NVA soldiers lay. "One of them was looking at a map when you zapped them." He rose to a crouch. "Cover me. I'll be right back." He unlocked the bayonet under his shotgun barrel and flipped it open.

"He crazy?" Dudley asked, pointing his M16 at Spike's back.

Sol nodded as he watched Spike scuttle across the small clearing. "We're all probably fucking crazy for being here."

Spike reached down with one hand and picked up the NVA map without taking his eyes off the wall of thick brush before him. He felt danger somewhere nearby, but he couldn't locate it.

A third NVA soldier rushed out from his hiding place with his bayonet pointed directly at the center of Spike's back. Sol saw the sudden charge, but there was nothing he could do. In the same instant Spike caught the movement in his peripheral vision and instinctively turned to face the challenge with the barrel of his shotgun. Just as the NVA's bayonet was about to plunge into Spike's chest, Spike fell backward to the ground. The NVA's bayonet passed over Spike's head, and he used the sole of his jungle boot to kick the rifle away. In another split second the NVA's forward momentum forced him onto Spike's bayonet. The butt end of the shotgun smashed against the ground from the force of the man's body impaling itself. Spike saw the enemy soldier's eyes widen in surprise, and then his mouth opened and closed twice in a silent protest before Spike booted the NVA in the groin and catapulted the now dead soldier over his head.

The whump! of the NVA's body hitting the ground made the black paratrooper, who had been covering Sol's rear, turn around. "Shit! Where the fuck did he come from?"

Sol shook his head slowly and sighed. He had been sure that the NVA had Spike. "Who in the fuck knows? Keep your eyes open. They're all over this fucking hill."

Spike searched the dead NVA soldiers for any additional papers, but found nothing. He opened their packs and saw that the soldier he had just killed had a plastic bag of cooked rice mixed with some kind of meat. Removing the food, he jogged the short distance back to Sol and Dudley's hiding spot in the bamboo.

"Fuck, I thought he had you." Feeling guilty, Sol added, "I couldn't open fire . . . it happened so damn fast."

Spike just nodded and held up the bag of food. "Hungry?"

"Hell, yes." Sol scooped a handful of the still warm rice out of the large plastic bag and looked over at Dudley. "Want some?"

The black paratrooper shook his head. He had been on the hill less than twenty-four hours and wasn't really hungry. Spike shrugged and wolfed down a half-dozen handfuls of the rice before slowing down.

"What's your first name?" Sol whispered over to the black paratrooper. He found his comment almost funny. He had spent the whole night alone with the man, and he didn't even know his first name.

"Everhart Dudley." The black paratrooper glanced at Sol out of the corner of his eye.

"Dud." Spike smiled. "Do you mind if I call you Dud?"

"You can call me anything you damn well please if you can get my ass off this hill alive."

"You got yourself a deal." Spike's smile was much more reassuring to the new replacement than it was to Sol.

Spike moved close to Sol and whispered, "A chopper just went down over there." He nodded with his head in the right direction.

"Yeah, we heard it go down too." Sol glared over at Spike like he didn't want to hear what was coming next.

"I think we should check it out. I didn't hear an explosion or anything."

"Probably." Sol shifted the M60 a little to his left to cover the area where the NVA soldiers had emerged. "But I think we should stay here and wait for somebody to show up from the Third Herd."

The look Spike gave him was enough of an answer. They both knew that the 173rd Airborne Brigade was fighting for its ass, and there wasn't anybody left to act as a relief force.

"All right, let's go," Sol said, relenting.

Spike led the way through the jungle, followed by Sol and then Dudley. Spike smelled the burning jet fuel and hydraulic fluid before he saw the crashed chopper. The pilot had tried pulling the Huey out of its fatal crash and had succeeded in gliding sideways through the trees until the airframe of the chopper came to rest against the huge trunk of a towering mahogany tree. Branches from smaller trees had broken through the Plexiglas and had killed both the pilot and the copilot. The door gunner on the side of the aircraft acting as the plow blade had died almost instantly when the chopper had smashed into the trees. But the gunner on the opposite side was still alive, with his legs pinned up to his waist under the airframe. He saw Spike the same instant Spike saw him.

"Oh, shit! Man, am I glad to see you!" the gunner said, twisting his head back to look upside down at his rescuers.

Spike held a finger up to his lips, signaling for the man to be quiet, as he approached and knelt down. He laid his hand on the airframe and instantly withdrew it. The green metal was still fiery hot.

The door gunner read the expression on Spike's face and risked speaking again in a whisper: "There's a fire on the other side of the chopper, and it's getting pretty hot under here." Sweat dripped off the young soldier's chin.

"We'll get you out of there," Spike said confidently, which was exactly what the door gunner needed to hear.

"Please, hurry," the gunner said fearfully.

Spike tried pushing the airframe with his shoulder to test how heavy it was. He didn't even budge it.

Sol had quickly appraised the situation. "We'll need a log to pry up the airframe."

Dudley saw a thick branch that had been broken off the mahogany tree during the crash. He picked it up and Sol helped him shove it under the edge of the chopper's cab. Even after both of them threw all of their weight on the branch, though, the chopper moved only a fraction of an inch.

Spike covered them as they tried freeing the trapped door gunner and kept glancing over at the growing flames.

"It's really starting to hurt!" the gunner hissed, panic in his voice. "Oh, shit! Don't let me lie here and roast to death!"

Sol rammed the branch deeper under the airframe, and both of them threw their weight harder onto the lever. The chopper tilted a couple of degrees, but the extra effort succeeded only in pouring out the remaining fuel in the ruptured fuel tank. Flames leapt higher on the other side of the chopper.

The young door gunner screamed.

"Hang in there, guy!" Spike reached over and grabbed the soldier's shoulders, but had to back away from the intense heat.

"I'm burning up!" the gunner screamed hysterically. "Please! Don't let me roast to death!"

"We won't. There's a bigger log over there that all three of us can get a hold of. We'll have you out of there in a couple of seconds!"

Spike sternly nodded back at the jungle in the direction they had come from. Sol picked up his M60 and started walking away. Dudley didn't understand what Spike was really saying. He could see that there wasn't any log nearby that was larger than the one they had been using. Spike frowned and nodded for Dudley to join Sol. The black paratrooper hesitated and then obeyed.

Spike stood directly behind the trapped gunner's head and whispered, "Don't worry, buddy. I won't let you burn to death."

"Thanks, man," the gunner, rasped, unable to turn his head far enough to see what Spike was doing.

Spike removed his pistol from its holster and took a step closer so that he wouldn't miss and fired at the top of the young man's skull.

Dudley heard the shot and jumped. Sol grabbed him as he turned back toward the chopper site. "Keep moving."

"He shot that kid!"

"Yeah, or we could have stayed there and watched him slowly roast to death." Sol swallowed hard to clear his throat. "Not much of a choice."

When Spike rejoined them back in the bamboo thicket bordering the clearing, Dudley refused to look at him. Sol pressed his lips together and shrugged. He understood. By this time Spike was blinking back tears. The fact that he had done the right thing still didn't make it any easier.

Sol, trying to get his mind off the helicopter gunner, changed the subject. "We need to find some water."

Spike nodded in agreement. "I'll go."

"Man, you look like you could use a rest," Dudley said apologetically, feeling bad about blaming Spike for what he had done.

"Naw, I could use the exercise." Spike folded back the bayonet on his riot shotgun and wiped the coagulated blood from the NVA soldier on his torn jungle pants.

"Where are you going?" Sol frowned. He hadn't remembered passing any streams on their way up the hill.

Spike handed over the NVA map. "I picked out a couple of likely spots nearby off the map." He pointed to a steep ravine about a hundred meters away. "There might be some trapped water in there, or I might be able to find a bomb crater with water in the bottom of it."

"Here." Dudley handed Spike his inflatable one-gallon water bag. It was brand-new and smelled like it.

Spike tried grinning, but the cold sore in the corner of his mouth split again, causing a fine line of blood to run down his chin. "Thanks. Are you guys going to wait here for me?"

"There's nowhere else to go." Sol frowned, pissed off. "Do you think that I would leave you out here alone?"

"If you have to make a choice, do it." Spike didn't wait for a reply. He meant what he said.

The jungle stillness was interrupted occasionally by the sound of small-arms fire, but the noise that kept the animals and insects quiet was the constant artillery fire and the air strikes farther up the hill and to the west. Spike advanced slowly, pausing frequently to listen and eyeball the surrounding jungle. The fight over the last twenty-four hours had been a patternless green hell, and he had as much to fear from stumbling on his fellow paratroopers as he had from the NVA.

The day before had started as a routine one for the whole battalion. For over a month they had been working the highland jungles surrounding the Dak To Valley without finding any sign of the North Vietnamese Army. Because of this, all four of the companies in the battalion had become lax and hadn't put their listening posts out very far from the company perimeters. That had allowed the NVA units to sneak within rifle range of the American paratroopers before being detected. About an hour after noon, the NVA hit Spike's company where his platoon was holding the perimeter. It had been a panicked slaughter on both sides. The surprise attack from the NVA had caught most of the airborne company sitting out in the open next to their foxholes. Spike escaped the initial attack because he had slipped down on the bottom of his foxhole to take a short nap right after lunch. He reacted instinctively to the automatic-weapons fire and waited until the heavy weapons had stopped firing, which signaled that the NVA were right on top of the American positions. Then he raised his head above the lip of his foxhole. He located a mass of NVA soldiers and chucked two M26 grenades at them. He then slipped on his rucksack and scrambled from his foxhole, which had turned into a death trap. The surrounding ground was littered with dead and dying paratroopers. He crawled past his dead platoon leader, Lieutenant Alsop, and the platoon's radio operator. Loud static was coming over the radio. Spike continued crawling until he reached the safety of the jungle, and then he stopped to fight.

He had a commanding view of the defensive position his infantry company had cut out of the jungle. The sight he was looking at was not a pleasant one. The NVA were swarming the hill like an army of red ants. He noticed his company commander trying to rally a small group of survivors, and he spotted some of his buddies slipping away in the jungle and somehow that sight made him feel a little better. But during the nightmare that followed, Spike would not see another live American paratrooper until the next day.

The sound of an incoming artillery round brought Spike's attention back to what he was doing. He had been daydreaming and that was dangerous. The artillery round exploded thirty meters away on the opposite side of the tree Spike had taken cover behind. He saw a black-and-green jungle boot sticking out from under the loose, dead ground cover, and then it disappeared.

Spike cupped his hands around his mouth and whispered loudly, "Skysoldier?"

The leaves rustled and a paratrooper crawled out from under the debris. Looking around, he couldn't locate Spike hiding in the shadows, so Spike stepped forward just enough to be seen and the soldier scurried over to him.

Spike saw that the trooper was so afraid that he wasn't even focusing his eyes. When his mouth opened,

Spike slipped his hand over the man's mouth and shook his head. The scared paratrooper understood and remained quiet.

Spike led the way through the jungle for another fifty meters before stopping. Then he noticed that the man with him didn't have his weapon or any of his combat gear. Not asking any questions, Spike handed the trooper his pistol. Tears filled the soldier's eyes as he gripped the weapon in both hands.

The sound of a Phantom jet making a low-level pass forced both of them to duck lower. Spike leaned as close to the man's ear as he could and whispered, "Water?"

A puzzled expression was replaced with a knowing look, and the paratrooper nodded and pointed back in the direction that they had come. He had passed a small stream earlier.

Sol didn't hear or see Spike and the new paratrooper approach until they were almost on top of him. Anger flashed in his eyes and he could feel his hands shaking. He had been taken by surprise even though he had been listening intently. The damp earth was cushioning almost all of the normal sounds any animal might make, and it looked as if it was going to rain again before dark.

Spike handed the gallon container of clear water to Dudley and tossed Sol his now full canteen. Spike had taken his time down at the stream drinking his fill of the cold water. Sol and Dudley accepted the new man without any questions. Spike offered him some of the NVA rice, and the paratrooper nodded his thanks and ate with the same fury that Spike and Sol had earlier.

Sol gave Spike another knowing look. The jungle surrounding them must be full of lost and wounded paratroopers who were hiding until a relief force could be airlifted in to rescue them. The problem was that the NVA were beginning to reorganize teams to sweep the surrounding jungle battlefield.

"I'm going back out there to look for some more of our guys," Spike whispered into Sol's ear. "You get these guys organized into some kind of a perimeter and keep a watch for my return, OK?"

Sol stared at Spike and then nodded his head in approval. He knew that once Spike had decided to do something, there was no way he would change his mind.

Dudley merely glanced at Spike as he disappeared into the jungle. He was getting used to seeing him slip off by himself. Sol pointed to where he wanted Dudley to cover their small perimeter, and then he sent the new man over to the dead NVA to recover their weapons and ammunition while he covered him with the M60.

Spike listened intently to the unusual quiet of the highland jungle. The battle was forcing all of the native creatures into hiding. He decided to return to the bivouac area where his company had been attacked and search the area for wounded and hiding paratroopers. He knew that he had traveled only a couple hundred meters during the night. He didn't want to get too far away from the company site because he knew that the brigade staff would saturate the area surrounding the company's position with artillery and air strikes once they realized that the company had been overrun.

Spike heard them talking before he saw them. Five paratroopers were grouped near the base of a wild banana tree, arguing about what they should do. Move back down Hill 875 and try to link up with another airborne company or stay in hiding until someone came to rescue them. Realizing that even a whisper carried farther than he had suspected, Spike wondered if he and Sol had made as much noise back in the bamboo thicket. Spike checked the area carefully for any NVA before calling out softly to the five men.

"What the fuck?" The leader of the group fumbled for his M16 lying on the ground, but he knew that if

Spike had been an NVA, all five of them would already have been dead.

Spike exposed part of himself and waved. The other man lowered the barrel of his M16. Spike motioned for the five men to join him. As the paratroopers rushed toward him, dragging their rucksacks behind them on the ground, Spike saw that one of the rucksacks had a folded radio antenna sticking out of it.

The leader of the group was about to yell at Spike, but was halted by the hard look Spike gave him and by the finger Spike shoved against the man's chest. Spike leaned over and cupped his hand around the leader's ear. "If I had been an NVA soldier, you would have bought the farm back there." Spike pointed at where the team had been sitting, out in the open, and the leader could see for himself how stupid it had been. Spike kept scanning the area as he whispered into the leader's ear, "I've got some men hidden a couple hundred meters from here—A slight movement in the jungle arrested Spike's attention. A foot-long lizard scurried off a branch onto the ground. Spike continued, "We'll link up with them as soon as we sweep this area for more of our guys."

The leader shook his head violently and cupped his hands around Spike's ear. He spoke too loud even with a cupped whisper. "No! We aren't going back there!"

Spike pulled the man's hands down and glared into the scared eyes. He grinned and patted the paratrooper's shoulder and then slowly winked. The act brought a lot of confidence back to the terrified men. Spike risked being heard by the NVA, but decided that it was worth it to communicate loud enough so that all five of the men could hear him: "Paratroopers don't leave their wounded on a battlefield."

The simple comment brought instant shame to the small team. All of them had been indoctrinated with the airborne tradition of never leaving their buddies behind during a battle. Nodding his head in the direction he was taking, Spike started crawling toward his company's old perimeter. One by one the five-man team followed him, with the ex-leader taking the rear. Leadership had been dropped on him suddenly because he was the senior man, not because he had wanted it, and he was relieved that the responsibility for making decisions that involved other men's lives was being taken from him by the new man.

Spike paused when he reached the edge of the old company defensive perimeter. He didn't recognize where he was and took a couple of moments to orient himself. He located the captain's foxhole and figured from there until he located his old platoon area. He was standing almost halfway around the perimeter from it.

At the sound of a low, pain-filled groan, Spike lifted his chest a few inches off the ground, trying to locate where the sound had come from. He was instantly sent back down to the earth by the stutter of a Russian RPD light machine gun firing less than twenty meters to his right. The paratrooper who had crawled up next to him started slipping back into the dense jungle, but Spike grabbed his shoulder. He then signaled with his hand for everyone to freeze in place. Spike watched where the bullets from the RPD impacted, and he calculated that the gunner was shooting from a foxhole located inside the old perimeter. Spike rolled over onto his side, handed his shotgun to the ex-leader, and then placed his dirty finger over his lips. The man's eyes widened as he realized that Spike was going to crawl over to the NVA machine gun. Spike removed a hand grenade from his webgear and pulled out the safety pin before he started inching forward through the thick bamboo, holding down the safety lever of the grenade with his thumb. Timing his movement with the bursts coming from the machine gun, he covered the distance that separated them quickly.

A whispered Vietnamese phrase reached his ears,

and then he heard the gunner changing ammo drums. He arched his back, but still couldn't see the enemy. Spike realized that it would be impossible to throw the grenade in the thick stand of bamboo and wished now that he hadn't pulled the pin. He looked around at the jungle growth surrounding his head and saw a thin vine. Slowly he wrapped it around the safety handle of the grenade and laid it on the ground. For several seconds Spike kept his eyes on the safety handle, watching for the slightest movement. The vine was doing the job. Spike backed off and reached for the K-Bar knife on his hip.

The NVA gunner spoke to his comrade and then opened fire again. Spike pushed the bamboo aside and saw the two soldiers lying side by side on the edge of the clearing. Four empty drums were scattered in the bamboo around them. The assistant gunner held a fresh drum in his hands while his comrade sprayed the American positions with automatic-weapons fire.

Using the loud spatter of fire to cover his movements, Spike charged from behind them and knifed the assistant gunner first. He immediately withdrew the knife and quickly thrust it in the other's side. The NVA grunted, reaching out instinctively for Spike's knife hand. The two of them grappled in the bamboo for what seemed like hours to Spike. Bamboo stalks clicked against each other, and then the NVA soldier rolled Spike over on his back. Saliva dripped from the corners of the gunner's mouth and filled the indent between the protruding neck cords of Spike's throat. The NVA dug his dirty fingernails into Spike's cheek, drawing blood. Spike concentrated all of his energy into the muscles of his knife hand and thrust at the same time the rest of his body collapsed. The knife sunk deep into the NVA's heart, and he dropped down dead on top of Spike.

Long seconds passed before Spike regained enough energy to push the NVA gunner off him. He checked the RPD machine gun and saw that it had an almost full drum of ammunition. Spike took a couple of deep lungfuls of air before calling out. "Skytrooper!"

The reply was instantaneous. "Watch out for that NVA machine gunner! He's got us pinned down!" The call came from one of the inner perimeter foxholes.

"He's dead!" Spike called back to the unseen paratrooper.

There was a pause and then a different voice answered from a foxhole a dozen meters away. "Thank God."

Using the barrel of the RPD, Spike pushed the bamboo aside. "How many of you are left?"

"Is that you, Harwood?"

Spike recognized his company commander's voice. "Yes, sir."

A head cautiously appeared above the edge of the captain's foxhole. He checked the whole perimeter out before speaking. "I think that machine gunner was the only one left." The captain paused and scanned the immediate area around him to make sure that there weren't any more NVA snipers nearby. The fight had turned him into a quivery mass of paranoia.

"Are you alone, sir?"

"No . . ." The captain risked exposing his shoulders above the edge of the foxhole, and he felt the hair tingling on the back of his neck in expectation of an NVA sniper's bullet.

Spike could see heads slowly popping up over the edges of the foxholes circling the perimeter, except for the section where the NVA machine gunner had covered. The captain stood up and Spike could see the blood covering his left side.

"All right, men, move out to the north. Let's get the fuck out of here!" The captain staggered and took a couple of steps before he dropped to his knees on the wet clay soil.

A sergeant appeared from a nearby foxhole and dragged the captain in behind him. "Spike?" the sergeant asked.

"Yeah?"

"Are you alone out there?"

"No. I've got five troopers with me."

"Good. I think you got the last NVA. He's been the only one shooting at us, and he's done a damn good job of keeping us pinned down all morning." The sergeant paused to catch his breath. "Do you have a radioman with you?"

"Yeah."

After ten seconds had passed, Spike realized that they were all too scared to expose themselves. Spike knew that they had to do something before the NVA got their shit together and attacked the company position again. Figuring that the NVA had taken as bad an ass-kicking as his company had—they would have been policing the battlefield by now, otherwise—Spike took a deep breath and slowly stood up.

"Don't any of you weak-dicked paratroopers shoot me," he commanded in a loud, firm voice and stepped out from the protection of the jungle, carrying the RPD in his hands. He walked casually between two foxholes and glanced down inside at the dead bodies. "All right. Get your skinny asses up and out of there, and start acting like United States paratroopers."

Slowly camouflage-covered helmets appeared around the perimeter. The five-man team stepped out of the jungle behind Spike. The ex-leader was carrying Spike's shotgun in one hand like a pistol and his own M16 in his other hand.

Spike made a quick head count: twenty-nine. A number of wounded who could still fight but couldn't walk sat up, and Spike could see the tops of their helmets.

"Is he the only officer left alive?" Spike asked the platoon sergeant, looking down at the unconscious captain.

"I think so. That fucking NVA machine gunner had us all pinned down. He must have killed a dozen troopers since dawn . . ." The sergeant's hatred was raw. He had been helplessly trapped at the bottom of his foxhole.

"How in the hell did he get that advantage over you?" Spike looked back at the critical high ground the NVA machine gunner had held.

"Stupidity on our part!" The sergeant glared at Spike. "You can bet your sweet ass that I'll never be caught like that again."

Spike recognized the sergeant as the second platoon's senior NCO. "Have you seen Lieutenant Alsop?"

"I don't think there are too many of your platoon still alive. The NVA came through your platoon's sector and swept through the rest of the company like a fucking nuclear bomb going off."

The captain opened his eyes. "A radio. I need a radio . . ."

The radioman from the first platoon stepped forward and handed the captain his horn.

"What are you going to do, Captain?" Spike frowned.

"I'm going to call in so many fucking air strikes around us that the fucking ants won't survive!"

"You can't do that, sir."

The captain lowered the handset from his ear. "Why not? The jungle is still full of NVA."

"Sir, we still have men out there." Spike knew that he would personally blow the captain away before he would allow him to call in air strikes on Sol and the other guys still hiding in the jungle.

The sergeant bailed Spike out. "Sir, he's making sense. A lot of our men escaped into the jungle during the attack."

"Fuck them! They were cowards and ran!" The captain started raising the handset back to his ear.

Spike felt the heat coming up from his stomach. "Are you calling *me* a coward, Captain?"

The West Point football star glanced up at the young buck sergeant, and for the first time that day he really saw him. Spike had blood caked on the side of his face where the NVA gunner had clawed him. "No, you did a good job, Sergeant Harwood."

Ignoring the captain's praise, Spike said, "I know where four more of our guys are at. I'm going back to get them and bring them here."

"No!" The captain's voice echoed against the wall of jungle that surrounded the clearing. "*I* give the orders around here, and we can't afford to lose any more men through stupidity!"

The platoon sergeant glared at the captain. The only one who had been stupid so far had been him. He had selected the position. "Sir, let Harwood go back and bring our men in. He knows where they're located and can pull it off quickly."

There was a long pause and then the captain relented. "OK, but hurry back. I'll give you one hour and then I'm going to circle this fucking area with napalm." The captain's eyes lost their focus and the fear lurking just underneath shone through. During the beginning of the attack up Hill 875, a five-hundred-pound bomb had accidently broken loose from one of the F-4s that had been strafing the hill and landed on the assembled battalion commander and staff. He had just missed attending the commander's call because he had felt sick, and thus he knew he was the senior officer left alive in the whole battalion. It was up to him to make decisions. He was a West Point-trained officer and he had dreamed of being in situations like this—a battalion under fire in combat—and he was in command as a captain. The problem was that he wasn't back at West Point dreaming anymore. This was for real and he was terrified.

Spike was about to say something when the platoon sergeant spoke first. "Go ahead, Harwood, and get our men. The captain is delirious from the pain and don't know what he's saying . . . Right, sir?"

"I am not!" The captain tried getting to his feet, but he was gently pushed back down into the foxhole. The sergeant pulled the handset out of his fist.

"Rest, sir." The sergeant's voice carried an open threat. "There ain't going to be anything called in until all of our men have been accounted for or until the gooks attack again." Then he nodded for Spike to leave.

Spike hesitated and then started shuffling away. The pain had returned to his crotch, and the little energy that he had gained from the rice had been all used up in his struggle with the NVA machine gunner. Spike hobbled a couple of meters into the jungle, where no one could see him, and dropped in exhaustion to his knees. He felt the tears of frustration welling up in his eyes, and he fumbled for the chain around his neck. He pulled on the thick gold chain until he could feel the comforting medallion. He closed his eyes and rubbed the gold Saint Jude's medal between his fingers.

He needed help.

CHAPTER TWO

✪✪✪✪✪✪✪✪✪✪✪✪✪✪

CHILDREN'S BLOOD

She moaned and thrust her hips up when she felt the boy's muscles contract and his face press against her neck. She felt the warm semen splatter onto her stomach. All of the boys she knew pulled it out and climaxed on her stomach.

Spike was sitting with his back against the worn couch the two teenagers were having sex on. He glanced from the brand-new TV over to the window, which was covered with a sheet of thick, opaque plastic. A strong wind outside was causing the plastic to snap and flap. Spike recalled how the window had been broken and frowned unconsciously. He gently rubbed the thick five-inch scar on the face of the four-year-old boy who was snuggled securely between his legs. The child reached up and rubbed the back of Spike's hand and then pulled Spike's arm down across his skinny chest.

"It's getting fucking cold in here," commented a ten-year-old sitting in an overstuffed chair a few feet away, but he was ignored by everyone else in the room. It was always cold in the boys' bedroom of the old house. Welfare didn't pay for much heat.

Spike's thoughts drifted back to a year and a half earlier, when the window had still had glass in it. A homeless orphan, he had been staying at his friend

Eddie Cruz's house next door when Ted had run over screaming that his brother-in-law had thrown the baby through his bedroom window. Glancing outside, Spike saw Ted zipping up his pants. Ted seemed near death himself from fear as Spike slipped on his Levis and dashed across the dirt yard to the cyclone fence that separated the two properties. The toddler was lying in one of the ruts in the driveway. He was covered with blood and was wearing only a filthy pair of training pants. A huge beer belly filled the space of the broken window.

Spike felt a shiver go up his spine as he recalled the incident. He had been scared as badly as Ted, but he knew that if he didn't do something, the baby would bleed to death. The fatman turned away and screamed back over his shoulder at his wife, who was trying to push her way past him and get to her baby. She was only seventeen and small for her age. With one arm the fatman threw her across the room and left the broken window to take out his rage on her instead of the three-year-old. Seeing his chance, Spike picked up the baby. Ted handed him his T-shirt to use as a pressure bandage and Spike wrapped it around the boy's cheek to stop the bleeding. Spike carried the boy in his arms as he ran the two miles to the hospital on Huron Street.

The child sensed that something was wrong by the tension in Spike's leg and stomach muscles. He turned around and straddled Spike's stomach with his legs. The tiny hands pressing on each of his cheeks brought Spike back to the present. The child was staring at him with a worried look.

Spike smiled. "It's OK, Peter. It's OK."

The small boy laid his head next to Spike's neck and fell asleep lying on his chest. Spike could smell the child's dirty hair and made a mental note to give him a bath when they had a chance, maybe in the morning when old fat-ass went to work. No one in the house would dare getting undressed to shower when he was home because he was crazy enough when he was stoned or drunk to tear a door down so that he could beat someone's ass. Getting caught naked in a shower was dumb. You couldn't run away.

Spike scratched the child's back and heard him sigh gently in his sleep.

"You guys are going to make him queer." The girl who had just finished screwing Ted leaned up on one elbow. "You know that, don't you, Spike?"

"He isn't going to be queer as long as there are women like you around, Kimberly."

"I'm not kidding. When guys hold guys like that when they're little, they turn out to be queers."

Peter sighed again and snuggled closer to Spike's secure-sounding heartbeat. "We'll risk him being queer."

"Do you want some before I get all dressed again?" Kimberly asked Spike matter-of-factly.

"Naw, I don't want to disturb Peter."

"Now he's turning *you* queer." Kimberly didn't like being rejected and used one of her demasculating tones to coax Spike up on the couch.

"Not hardly, Kimberly." Spike wasn't about to be cajoled by a fourteen-year-old street slut. He had been having sex since before he could climax and had heard every line a whore used to hook a john.

"Come on up," Kimberly called sweetly. "We haven't messed around in a couple of days."

Spike looked over at the ten-year-old. "Hold Peter for me, will you?"

The kid shrugged and went back to watching television. All of the furniture in the bedroom was stuff that other people had thrown out and they had picked up off the street before the garbage trucks could haul it away. The couch served as Ted's bed and the over-stuffed chairs were shoved together at night and used as a bed by the ten-year-old and Peter. The three-hundred-dollar television was one of three sets in the house, and they all had been stolen and given to the fatman as payment for a long overdue drug debt. He was the marijuana king of four square blocks of the neighborhood.

"I'll hold him," Ted offered, tucking his shirt down into his pants. He sat down next to Spike and took his nephew in his arms. Peter struggled feebly to stay with Spike, but gave up quickly when he felt the warmth of his uncle's body.

Spike slipped up on the couch with Kimberly. She immediately slipped her hands down the front of his Levis and wrapped her hand around his penis. "You aren't even hard yet!"

The ten-year-old glanced casually over at Spike and Kimberly. He twisted his lips tightly together and wondered what they thought was so great about playing with their stuff all of the time.

"Did you expect me to have a hard-on, holding the baby?" Spike asked, disgusted. "I think that you can work it up for me." He could already feel his pride expanding in her hand.

"Maybe . . ." She giggled and started stroking him.

"I don't want a hand job." He reached down and unbuttoned the front of his Levis and rolled over on top of the girl. She cooperated and pulled up the long-tailed shirt she was wearing; her Levis were already down from Ted's bout earlier.

"Damn!" Spike rolled back off her. She hadn't wiped Ted's semen off her stomach. "Clean that stuff off first."

"It's no big deal."

"Clean yourself up or forget about it."

Kimberly used a corner of the folded blanket to wipe herself, and then she reached for Spike again. The two teenagers spent the next five minutes having sex. Spike had just finished and rebuttoned his pants when the bedroom door flew open and Ted's fat brother-in-law filled the doorway.

"What are you kids doing up here? Fucking again?"

"Naw, Carl! We're watching television!" Ted's voice

was automatically filled with humiliation. He had
learned the hard way that his brother-in-law would
beat his ass if he even thought that Ted hated him.
Fear was the only thing the fatman wanted from anyone smaller than himself.

"Kimberly, have you been fucking these no-dicked
punks?"

"Come on, Carl. I save myself for real men."

Spike saw the effort she made to fake a smile. He
slowly maneuvered himself closer to the plastic-covered
window for a quick escape if the fatman decided that
he was going to be his night's entertainment.

Carl glanced over at Spike and tried grinning. "You—
who are you again?"

"Spike."

"Yeah, Spike. You like my kid, don't you?" The
question could have many meanings.

"Sure, he's a nice kid."

"Good. Take him with you when you leave." The
fatman dropped down on the couch next to the girl.
"Now!"

"Sure, Carl."

"Get your faggot ass out of here!" He waved his
hand at all three of the boys.

Kimberly tried smiling, but she hated it when the
fatman forced her to have sex with him. She would
have to tell him constantly how big his thing was. She
smiled at the thought. Even Ted, who had just turned
fifteen, had a bigger one than the fatman.

"See you later, Kimberly." Spike nodded over at
the girl. "Let's meet over at the laundromat when
you're finished here."

"Sure, Spike." Kimberly knew what Spike was doing.
He was warning Carl that *somebody* was going to see
her after he had finished with her. Carl liked to beat
his women.

The Army captain looked out his window down at
the sparse Saturday morning traffic on Saginaw Street.

He raised his coffee mug to his lips and sipped the hot liquid. The coffee felt good against his cold teeth. He had just finished running his daily five miles and it was cold outside.

"Captain, you're going to freeze your balls off running out there in weather like this."

"Probably, Sergeant. But the other option is not to run and then I'll get fat."

"So?"

"There's a war going on, if you haven't forgotten."

"That's right. You're one of those . . . those . . . whatcha-ma-call-its?"

The captain smiled at the good-natured ribbing he was getting from his senior recruiting sergeant. "Try 'paratrooper,' you old fat 'leg.' "

"Now, there you go again, Captain, getting personal and calling people names."

"A leg is a leg, and there's only one way to change that." The captain stood up and walked over to the windows. Large snowflakes were smashing against the warm glass and turning almost instantly to drops.

"You ain't going to get me to go airborne." The sharp-looking black sergeant shook his head, wearing a grin. "I've survived twenty-one years in this man's Army without doing anything really dumb and I don't plan on falling apart now." Suddenly he grew more serious. "Why did you decide to go airborne?"

The captain crossed his legs and placed them on the corner of his immaculate desktop. "I didn't have much of a choice, Top. I was assigned to the Inspector General's office in Washington, and was absorbing massive doses of Army politics." He looked at the sergeant and shook his head slowly. "I learned more about the internal workings of the Army in two years' working there than most people learn in a thirty-year career."

"So what has that got to do with going airborne?"

"It was my only honorable way out of the assignment, and believe me, Top, you didn't want to piss one of those generals off."

"So you went to jump school to get out of a Pentagon assignment early?"

"Bingo. And then I volunteered for a tour of duty in Vietnam." The captain chuckled and looked out of the window at the small group of kids walking along the unshoveled sidewalk. One of the boys was wearing only a blue jean jacket, and the others were almost as badly dressed for the winter weather. The first boy, walking in the center of the group, was carrying a small child on his shoulders, who was the only one of the group who looked warm. The captain turned to face the sergeant. "Top, do we have any money in petty cash?"

"Yes, sir, a couple hundred dollars."

"Hire those kids to shovel the sidewalks, will you, please?" The captain tapped his knuckles on the window and pointed down at the boys. The sound didn't carry very far and he beckoned with his hand at the boys.

Ted glanced up at the office building and saw the man beckoning to them. "Spike, there's some guy waving at us."

"Where?" Spike turned slowly on the mushy snow so he wouldn't slip with Peter on his shoulders.

"Up there in that window." Ted pointed to the office building. "What do you think he wants?"

"You got me. Come on." Spike started walking away.

"Don't you want to find out what he wants?" Ted asked, hurrying to catch up.

"Naw, let's go over to the stadium before it gets too late. We might be able to find some cans to sell." Spike started increasing his pace on the white mush.

"There's some Army guy calling for us to come over there." Ted grabbed Spike's arm and stopped him. "Maybe they want something?"

"We're all too young to join the Army," Spike said,

seeing the black sergeant standing next to the curb on the other side of the street.

"Kids! Come here for a minute!" the NCO yelled, cupping his hands around his mouth.

"Let's see what he wants." Spike looked both ways before jogging across the street, followed by Ted and his ten-year-old brother.

"How would you kids like to earn ten bucks apiece?" the sergeant asked, smiling.

"Doing what?" Spike asked cautiously.

"Shoveling snow." The sergeant pointed to the wide sidewalk that went around the building on two sides.

"Ten for each of us?" Ted asked.

The sergeant looked at the four-year-old and smiled. "Everyone but him."

"Me too?" Ted's brother asked, not expecting to be included.

"If you can handle a shovel."

"Sure!" A smile lit his face.

Spike looked over at Ted. "What are we going to do with Peter while we're working?"

The sergeant answered the question. "He could come inside and wait while you guys work. I promise we won't recruit him."

Spike grinned and nodded his head in agreement. Ten dollars apiece was a lot more money than they could make collecting aluminum cans. And even then, the odds were that they would have to fight someone to keep them before they could sell them.

The sergeant led the way into the office complex and showed the boys where they could get the shovels. He took Peter from Spike and carried him into the recruiting office. A Marine sergeant laughed and pointed at the crusty old sergeant and the child. "Getting desperate for recruits there, grunt?"

"He's got a higher IQ than you Marines. And he's probably stronger already than half of the Corps."

Spike looked up to see who the sergeant was talking to and noticed the Marine's colorful dress uniform.

"How old are you, son?" the Marine asked Spike.

"Sixteen."

"When do you turn seventeen?"

"Christmas Day."

"Come on back and see me then, and I'll get you into the Corps."

"I'll think about it." As Spike picked up his shovel and exited through the door, he spied a man wearing sweatpants and a sweatshirt.

The sidewalk was easy to shovel because the snow was only a couple of inches deep so far, and Spike wondered why they wanted to waste their money hiring boys to shovel the snow. Then he shrugged and kept working. Easy money was easy money.

He looked up at the bank of windows and saw Peter staring out at them. The man who had been wearing the sweatsuit was standing next to him, wearing an Army uniform. Spike paused and waved at Peter, who laughed and waved back.

After they had finished, the Army sergeant invited the three boys up to the recruiting offices, where two large bags of McDonald's hamburgers and french fries waited for them, along with large paper cups of hot chocolate. Ted and his little brother dug in while Spike checked to make sure that Peter was all right.

"Is he your little brother?" the Army captain asked. "That's a nasty scar he's got."

Spike nodded over at Ted. "He's his nephew."

"Oh, baby-sitting today?"

Spike smiled but didn't answer.

"I'm Captain Hanson. And that's Master Sergeant McClure. He bought the food for you guys."

Spike looked over at the black sergeant. "Thanks."

McClure smiled, signaling that it was no big deal.

"Do you kids live around here?" Captain Hanson asked, sipping his cup of coffee. Ted stopped attacking his second hamburger and glanced over at Spike. The captain caught his look.

"Down the street a ways." Spike removed the lid

from his cup of hot chocolate and held the cup out for Peter to pick the marshmallows off the top. "Has he eaten anything?" Spike asked, nodding down at Peter.

"Some hamburger," McClure answered.

Spike lifted the top off his hamburger and removed the pickles before offering it to the child, who reached over and started devouring the food.

"Aren't you going to eat?" Hanson asked, watching Spike closely. He had already observed that he was not only the natural leader of the small group but also the one who was taking care of the child.

"Maybe later." Spike saw that the bags were empty.

"Why don't you eat this hamburger?" McClure handed Spike the hamburger and fries that Peter had barely touched because the hamburger still had the pickles on it and he had made the unknown error of putting catsup on the fries.

Spike nodded his head and took the offered food. He had to hold back to avoid making a fool out of himself. The fact was, he was so hungry that his eyes ached.

The captain left the children in the main office to eat and went back into his private office to make some telephone calls. He felt good about hiring the kids to do the sidewalk. It was one of those little things that made his days a little brighter. The year he had just spent fighting in Vietnam had made some really big changes in his personality. Before, he could have cared less about a bunch of street kids, but now he went out of his way to help them. He had learned while he was over in Vietnam that it was the nation's street kids who were fighting the Vietnam War, and on more than one occasion they had saved his ass in combat. He owed street kids, and when Doug Hanson owed, he always paid back with interest.

"Thanks for the job and the food," Spike said, sticking his head into the open doorway and waving at the captain. "We have to be going now."

Captain Hanson nodded and continued listening to one of his Royal Oak recruiters telling him about

exceeding their monthly quotas for the Secretary of
Defense's 100,000 Program, which was meant to pull
in that number of recruits. They would be mostly
poor, low-IQ-rated teenagers off the inner-city streets.

Spike boosted Peter onto his shoulders and led the
way across the street toward Ted's house. He paused
when he reached the sidewalk and looked back at the
office building. The captain sat behind his desk with
his legs crossed over one corner and waved when he
saw Spike looking up at him. Spike waved back and
turned to face the driving snow, which had turned into
sleet. He pulled up his shirt collar and then used the
small boy's legs to keep his neck warm as he carried
Peter on his shoulders.

"Where are you going?" Ted yelled above the howl
of the wind.

"Back to your house, I guess."

"Carl said he doesn't want you back there again
today." Ted had to yell louder above the wind. "Where
are you going?"

"Probably over to Kimberly's garage tonight." Spike
closed his mouth to keep the cold sleet from attacking
his teeth and lowered his head against the wind.

Captain Hanson flipped through the two-week pile
of telephone messages stacked on his desk. After
two weeks of meetings at the recruiting region's headquarters, he was glad to be back at work. "Is there
anything important in this stack of papers, Sergeant
McClure?"

"Nothing that can't wait, except for your appoint-
ment for the Oakland County Children's Village volunteer program this afternoon."

"Oh yeah, I forgot about that." Hanson picked up
the memo that outlined the process by which he would
select one of the boys at the juvenile facility to work
with. He had offered to work with juvenile delin-
quents and would have to take two weeks of necessary
social-services classes before he could be assigned his

first case. "I don't know if I like this idea of selecting one boy out of three." Hanson waved the program synopsis in his hand. "What happens to the two unselected kids? They must feel like shit."

"Who set up this kind of a program for kids?" McClure said, agreeing with Hanson's line of thinking. It was a shitty way to deal with kids who had already had a lifetime's worth of rejection.

"Social Services. The counselors say that it works out better this way. And matching children with their volunteers is easier."

"They are the professionals, but my gut feelings tell me that even though the kids are in a juvenile center, they need people around them who care about them," Sergeant McClure noted. He had been raised poor, but there had been a lot of love in his family.

"As long as the Social Services types do their job and don't try to do mine, we'll get along just fine."

Spike reached back and pulled the piece of carpet over his shoulders and huddled closer to the small Coleman stove. He had set it up in a corner of the old wooden garage, and then he had made a small tent out of the roll of mildewing carpet that had been left on the dirt floor. He used a small piece of carpet left over for a cape. Spike had seen a movie on television where a buffalo hunter had wrapped himself up in a couple of buffalo robes and had sat out a storm in the middle of the prairie. He smiled to himself because at least he had the walls of the garage to keep out the cold wind.

When the garage door creaked, Spike turned to see if Ted or one of the other kids had braved the blizzard to visit him. He could use some company. It had been two days since the storm had hit the Detroit metro area and almost everyone was staying indoors. Spike shivered as a cold gust of snow and ice particles blew into the garage through a large crack between the poorly hung doors. No, Spike decided, no one had come. Only a fool would be out in such weather. He got up from his seat on a plastic soda case and picked up the piece of cardboard that had blown down and stuffed it back in the crack in the door. The wind howled.

"Shut the fuck up!" Spike yelled back through the crack and kicked the door. He was mad because he had been trapped inside the foul-smelling garage for so long and he was starving. The ten dollars he had made shoveling snow earlier in the week was long gone.

The garage door shook and the piece of cardboard fell back down on the dirt floor.

"Damn!" Spike got back up again to stuff the insulation back in the crack.

"Spike! Open up!" Kimberly's voice barely carried above the howl of the wind.

Spike kicked the two-by-four brace away from the door and pulled it open just wide enough for the girl to squeeze in, followed by about a ton of blowing snow. All of the heat that had been in the garage was sucked out in an instant.

"Oh, is it cold out there!" Kimberly said, shivering.

"Why did you come out here?" Spike asked, brushing the snow off her coat collar. The garage was less than fifty feet from her back porch, but it looked as if she had walked across town. Her cheeks were red and snow was piled up in her hair and on her coat.

"Brought you something to eat." Kimberly removed her hand from underneath her coat and held out the folded grocery bag for Spike.

"Thanks! I'm starving." When he opened the bag and saw the thick turkey sandwiches with gobs of mayonnaise dripping out of them, he cried, "You're a sweetheart."

"I know." Kimberly reached into the side pocket of her coat and pulled out a long-necked bottle of Pabst Blue Ribbon beer. "Sorry. We're out of Cokes. Besides, my mother would notice a missing Coke, but my dad loses count of his beers." She reached into her other pocket and pulled out two more beer bottles.

"Thanks, Kim. I would rather have had Coke, but beer is fine."

"It's freezing in here!"

"Yeah, come on, let's go in my tent, where it's a little bit warmer." Spike lifted the flap of the tent he had built in the corner of the garage and bent over to lead the way inside. There was barely enough room for the two of them, but the tent heated up fast with the two bodies filling the interior.

"This place smells like dead things." Kimberly wrinkled her nose in the dim light.

"Yeah, the carpet is rotting, but you get used to it after a while." Spike bit into what seemed like a fantastically delicious sandwich and leaned back against the cold wooden wall.

Kimberly reached over and unbuttoned the front of Spike's Levis. He was wearing two pairs of pants and a pair of gym shorts for underwear, and he had to push his back against the wall so that he could lift his hips high enough for her to pull his trousers down. Finally Spike's erection broke free of the layers of clothing. It had been almost a week since he had had sex. Kimberly stroked his penis a couple of times and then leaned over and slipped the head of it into her mouth. Spike ate the sandwich and sipped the beer while Kimberly gave him head. He came violently, before the sandwich was finished.

"That was quick, big boy," Kimberly said, stroking Spike's fading erection.

"It's been awhile." Spike reached over and opened another beer.

"You'd better button up before he freezes on you." Kimberly smiled and took the beer out of Spike's hand. She rinsed her mouth out before swallowing a little. She didn't like beer.

"Thanks again." Spike gave her a satisfied leer.

"Anytime, Spike." Her voice changed. "You know that I really like you a lot."

"I like you too, Kim . . ."

"You're the kind of guy a girl could marry."

"Kim, you're fourteen and I'm only sixteen!"

"Peter's mother was thirteen when she got pregnant and she was married when she was sixteen."

"Yeah, but I want to make something out of my life so that I can take care of my woman."

Kimberly snuggled closer to Spike. "Do you think that I'm a slut, Spike?"

Spike's answer was too quick. "No, you just express yourself differently, is all. You're looking for someone to love you, just like everybody else is."

"Is that why little Peter loves you so much?"

"Yeah. But I love the little guy too."

"If you make me your woman, Spike, I won't mess with anybody else. I promise."

Spike hugged the skinny girl with one arm and drained the bottle of beer. He was starting to feel a little better. It only took a couple of beers to get him buzzing. "Let me think about that offer. You know, it might be tough for you. I mean, you have sex with a guy like some people say hello."

Kimberly started laughing. "You're right about that, Spike. I don't mean anything by it, but I like having sex. Lots of it." Kimberly looked toward the garage door and watched the snow blowing in through the crack. "I like seeing the happy look on a guy's face when he's finished. It makes me feel like I have something worth giving."

Spike gave Kimberly a tight hug. He understood that she was searching for love and the only thing she had to offer in return for it was her body.

"I've got to go." Kimberly slipped out of the small carpet tent. She went over to the doors and looked back at Spike's smiling face framed in the tent entrance. His face was dirty and his dark brown hair was matted against his forehead, but he was still the best-looking kid in the neighborhood. "I love you, Spike."

He left the tent and went over and kissed her softly on her lips. "I love you, too, Kimberly."

A strong gust of wind forced her to move and exit the garage. She hurried back to the house. Spike watched her until she entered the back door and then stepped outside the garage to urinate in a snow drift. He shivered and pulled the door shut behind him. The two beers were making him feel warm. He lowered the flame on the Coleman stove and opened the last beer on the Coca-Cola opener nailed to a nearby two-by-four strut.

Even with the beer's glow, he started feeling lonely. Kimberly filled his thoughts. She was a whore, if that was all you wanted to see in her. But Spike had seen through the front displayed for everyone to see. She was a hurting little girl who desperately wanted someone to love her. Sex was just a tool that she used to get close to boys. She knew that sex made the boys happy and they always came back for more. She didn't care what people said behind her back. She gave love and someday she would get it back.

It started getting cold again inside the tent. Spike pulled the flap shut and turned up the small stove before curling up on the piece of carpet. The beers had made him sleepy. He pulled the cape up over his shoulders and curled up into a tight ball to keep as much of his body heat under the rug as possible.

Something woke Spike with a start. He didn't know how long he had been sleeping. He lifted his head up off the hand that he had been using for a pillow and listened. The garage door opened and closed. He heard a deep voice.

"He said the kid was in here."

Spike tugged the carpet closer over him and waited.

Another voice answered, "Maybe we have the wrong garage. Christ, is it cold in here! No damn kid is going to be staying out here all night." The tone of the man's voice changed as he turned his back toward Spike's tent. "Come on. Let's get out of here."

"Just a minute. What's that back there in the corner?" The first voice sounded close to his tent, and Spike drew his legs up and rolled over so that he could make a break for the door if the two men tried messing with him.

The flap of the tent opened slowly. Spike felt a rush of cold air against his face.

"There's nothing in here but a pile of old rotting carpet . . . and a Coleman stove that someone has left burning." The tone of the man's voice changed to one of caution. Spike felt his carpet cape being pulled back. "Here he is!"

Spike jumped up and dodged around the first police officer. He couldn't avoid the second one, though, who was blocking the doorway.

"Hold it right there, kid." The huge black policeman held Spike by one hand and held his other hand on the butt of his holstered service revolver. Spike struggled to break free, but the officer wrapped his arms around him from behind.

"Motherfuckers!" Spike tried kneeing the black cop. "Perverted motherfuckers! Leave me alone!"

"A foul-mouthed punk!" The black cop slapped Spike's face. "You'd better shut the fuck up, boy, before we really put a boot up your ass!"

Spike tried spitting at the cop, but the police officer wrestled him down on the oil-stained ground and put his knee against his chest. "Where do you live, boy?"

"Fuck you!"

"Tough, huh?" The cop reached behind his back and removed his chrome-plated handcuffs from their leather case. The other cop helped his partner roll Spike over and they cuffed his wrists.

"Why are you doing this to me? I haven't done nothing wrong!"

The officers lifted Spike off the ground and stood him up. "Trespassing and trying to torch a garage. We have a complaint from the owner of this garage and we saw the fire ourselves."

"That's a Coleman stove. I was trying to keep warm."

"Looks like a fire to us," the officer said, looking over at his partner. "Right?"

The big black man smiled and nodded in agreement. "You should learn not to fuck with your friendly police force, boy." He pushed the garage door open, and Spike could see the red-and-blue lights flashing on top of the police cruiser parked a couple of feet down the alley. He twisted, ignoring the pain from the handcuffs, so that he could look back at Kimberly's house, and saw her watching through a steamed-up window. The outline of her father filled the space behind her. Spike could tell by the way Kimberly was standing that she was being forced to watch the policemen haul him away.

"Get your ass in there." The first cop placed his hand on Spike's head and shoved him down on the backseat in the cruiser.

Spike instantly became nauseous from the overheated interior of the car and from the food and beer he had drank. "I'm going to be sick . . ."

"Yeah, kid, we've heard that one before." The black cop slipped behind the wheel and looked back at Spike through the thick Plexiglas window.

"I mean it." Spike leaned forward on the seat.

"If you throw up in my car, you little bastard, I'll make you eat it again," the white cop warned, tapping the Plexiglas with his nightstick.

Spike looked up at him and threw up against the Plexiglas. Small pieces of turkey and saturated bread stuck to the window and slid down the glass.

"You little cock-sucking bastard!"

Spike heard the front door open and then the back door opened and he was yanked out of the car and pushed down in the snow. The coolness of the snow felt good against his face until he felt the first kick.

After the beating, Spike was barely aware of being

driven to some unknown destination, then rough hands pulled him out of the police cruiser. Spike's right eye had already swollen shut and his left eye was about to close on him. He tried focusing and could only make out a bright red door that he was being led up to. He blinked his left eye and saw the small sign stuck on the door: "CHILDREN'S VILLAGE DETENTION—INTAKE."

On the right side of the door was a smaller sign that read: "TO OPEN—TURN DOORKNOB ON RIGHT—PULL DOORKNOB ON LEFT" Spike sighed to himself. He had thought that he was seeing double when he saw the two brass doorknobs.

"Get in there, you smelly little punk!" The black cop shoved Spike into another overheated area.

Spike heard a metallic voice coming over a speaker and the white policeman answering: "He tried to burn down a garage and resisted arrest."

A door lock clicked and Spike was led into another room. He could hear a voice far away telling him to undress. He fumbled with his jacket, but his fingers didn't work very well. Someone roughly helped him. Spike heard a couple of voices talking to each other as they searched his clothing for drugs.

"Come on, boy, you need a shower before we can in-process you any further. You stink to high heaven."

Spike could barely see out of his good eye as he was led down a cold hallway. It seemed that things were either broiling or freezing in the county-operated building. He was stopped three times before his guide told him to remove his gym shorts and get into the shower. Spike fumbled with the knobs and felt the water strike his chest. It felt great. He hadn't had the opportunity to shower in a couple of weeks, and the massaging hot water felt fantastic after spending so much time out in the cold and the whipping he had just received.

"All right, kid. You've been in there for a half hour. Get out!"

Spike whirled around. The voice was a woman's. He used his hand to lift one swollen eyelid and saw a woman sitting on a desk chair across from the juvenile facility's shower stalls. Another woman was standing next to her, smiling at him. A male guard stood with his hands on his hips, sneering.

"Let's go, boy."

Humiliated by standing naked before a pair of women, Spike threw the bar of soap. It hit the smiling woman on the cheek and she screamed in pain. Spike looked around the shower stall for anything else that could be used for a weapon. The male guard reached him first and wrestled him down onto the floor.

"You little punk! That is going to cost you!" the fat guard grunted as he struggled to keep Spike's face down against the tile floor. Blood seeped from between Spike's teeth and mixed with the water running down the center of the drain. "Boy, you're in the Children's Village now, and we don't take that kind of conduct from you punks!"

Spike had heard about the Village from some of his friends. It had a horrible reputation for beating kids. They had flowers growing around the buildings to make them look homey, and in the wintertime they would spend a lot of money to make each one of the buildings look Christmasy. But the place was a pit and the J Building that Spike was in was the worst facility of them all.

"You shouldn't have thrown that bar of soap at your social worker. Now she's going to have to write a report on you."

"Fuck you!"

"What did you say, punk?" The guard mashed Spike's face harder against the floor drain.

"Fuck you . . . fuck you . . . fuck you!" Spike screamed hysterically. "Fuck you!"

A senior social worker had come in and was watching Spike from a safe distance. He looked over at the pair of guards. "He's probably tripping on some drug. Write him up as a drug entry."

Spike's eyes focused on the man in the suit as they

dragged him naked down the hallway to the waiting cell. "I didn't do anything!"

The man looked down the hall after the naked sixteen-year-old. "Sure, kid, sure."

Spike had been locked up in the J Building basement's drug-detention center for three days and had no way of knowing that the Army captain he had met earlier was following the director of the Oakland County Children's Village into her office, which was located directly over his cell.

The director paused at the corner of her gray metal desk and drummed her fingers on the edge. She didn't like the military and liked even less having to host an Army captain. If the county executive hadn't personally ordered that she satisfy the officer, she would not have allowed him to visit. In that case, however, her superior was in a political battle with the probate judges over who would control the Children's Village, and she was smart enough to play both factions against each other to survive.

"Well, Captain . . ." She took a seat behind her desk and crossed her legs. She enjoyed the power of being the director of one of the largest youth facilities in the state of Michigan. She had over fifty men working for her and almost as many women. She smiled and tilted her head to one side. "What can we do for you today."

"I've been scheduled for a tour of the Village, and I believe that I'm supposed to be assigned to a boy today," Hanson said, scanning the room. He noticed that the knickknacks on the wall and especially the photographs showing the director with a number of powerful politicians. He also noticed that she was wearing exactly the same plastic smile in each one.

"I'll personally give you the tour. I think that you'll enjoy seeing how we run things here, especially with your military background. I have a well-disciplined staff and the children respond well to them." The woman patted her hair self-consciously, but immediately caught herself. "What is this new program the Army is working on? It's called McNamara's 100,000?"

"The Secretary of Defense has decided that the Army will recruit a hundred thousand young men who otherwise wouldn't be eligible for enlistment. Most of them will be juvenile offenders."

"Such as?" she asked, playing him along. She had a lot to protect and McNamara's program was threatening her power base. The Children's Village was designed to hold two hundred and fifty-seven children, and her budget and staff levels depended on keeping her beds full. "Isn't the program designed to recruit troubled children off the streets?"

"Some of them will probably be eligible. Why?" Hanson was no fool, and he sensed that she was trying to manipulate him.

"Oh, I'm just curious. We deal with some children here who could use a little military discipline."

"You don't use discipline here?" Hanson smiled.

"Oh, for gosh sakes, no!" She stood up and smoothed out the front of her skirt. "We're not allowed to touch a child, unless it is to restrain them." She tried smiling, but it was futile. "We're starting to get a large number of children admitted on drug charges." A thin smile appeared on her lips. "You don't recruit children with drug problems, do you?"

"Sorry, that we don't do." Hanson sensed that he had just given the woman the information she was looking for.

She raised and lowered her eyebrows. "Well, Captain, come on and get your tour of our little village."

A leader of men for a number of years, Captain Hanson could see that she ruled the staff with an iron hand. He could also see that the fledgling woman's liberation movement was way ahead of its peers here. As they passed through the different buildings on the grounds, the female social workers and guards were extremely friendly with the director, but the male workers and guards were reserved.

The director paused outside of H Building. "I would say that we have the best protection program for neglected and abused children in the state."

"You have one of the biggest budgets, don't you?" Hanson couldn't help saying. "Like they say in the Army, ma'am, money talks, bullshit walks."

She glanced at him out of the corner of her eye. "Money does help us develop good programs. I agree with that." She looked at her watch. "I think that about wraps up our tour."

"Fine, you do have a very good operation and I am very impressed with the efficiency displayed by your people." Hanson glanced down the hallway as they walked. "Where do I meet the social worker who is going to introduce me to the children? I guess they offer three kids and I get to pick one of them. Right?"

"You don't sound too pleased." She showed her claws through the tone of her voice.

"I don't like the idea of selecting a child. I became a volunteer so I could help kids. The way I look at it, two kids end up getting hurt."

"Who knows? Maybe the child that you select will be the loser." She regretted making the comment the instant the words had passed her lips.

"That could be the case . . ." Hanson's voice dropped. "Do I have to select one of the three today?"

She realized that she might have screwed up politically. There was no doubt in her mind that the county executive would call the Army captain later that afternoon, and she wanted the officer on her side when he left the facility. "In your case, Captain, you can pick any child we have here at the Village."

"Thank you." Hanson looked out the window at a group of boys playing football. One of the older boys was holding down a smaller one while his friend stuffed snow down his pants. A burly guard started running toward the boys. Hanson could hear the boy's screams of revenge and the laughter of the others.

The director parked the state-owned car in front of the main offices that occupied the ground level of the J Building. Three boys were shoveling the sidewalks in front with a guard watching them closely. Hanson noticed that the guard turned his back to the director as she approached so that he wouldn't have to speak to her.

She held the door open for Hanson. "And that completes our little tour of my operation."

"Thanks, I must say that you run a very tight ship here." At that moment Hanson's gaze rested on a steel door on the far side of the lobby. A uniformed guard sat behind a chest-high counter, and a well-dressed woman stood near a tough-looking teenage boy who was crying. Hanson could see that the boy wanted to run back through the main doors, but restrained himself. "What's that over there?" Hanson pointed at the guarded door.

"Oh, that's the entrance to our J Building detention facility." Her voice changed to a professionally happy tone. "We've got to have a place to secure the really bad ones that we get in here from time to time."

"May I tour it?" Hanson looked down at his watch. "We still have a half hour before I'm due to meet the three boys for the selection process."

She glanced nervously at the closed door and then over toward her office. "Wouldn't you rather have a cup of coffee instead?" She smiled, not wanting him to see the dirty underside of the facility. Normally only social workers and court officials were allowed in the J lockup facility.

"I'm all coffeed out."

"I don't want you to think that we are trying to hide anything, but the boys we have locked up down there are some really tough characters. Lots of drug abusers and even a murderer or two." She paused. "We even have a pyromaniac. He tried burning down a garage and a house with people sleeping inside, and then he attacked two police officers and some of our staff." She glanced over at the captain. "He's quite ill."

"I'm not afraid of a kid with matches," Hanson snorted, taking a step toward the steel door. "Can we finish my tour?" He was being pushy, but for a reason. During the conference at his regional headquarters, he had been assigned the mission of evaluating youth-detention facilities and writing a regional report that would go to the Pentagon. The top brass were very concerned about McNamara's 100,000 Program's intention of recruiting juvenile offenders and inner-city blacks.

She gave in. "Sure, but just remember that all of the children in J lockup are troubled, and some of them require special restraints."

"I understand. We have stockades in the military too." Hanson followed the director through the steel doors and noticed immediately the strong smell of disinfectant. "Have they just mopped the hallway?"

"Constantly. Some of these boys are animals and they urinate through their cell bars at the guards," she said, disgusted. A female guard greeted her with a smile that her mouth didn't seem accustomed to. As the woman unlocked the last door before they entered the J lockup area, Hanson heard a boy screaming at the top of his lungs.

The director increased her pace down the hallway, trying to make the tour as quick as possible. But Hanson took his time and glanced into each one of the small bullet-proof glass windows of the cells. Only one of them was empty. They reached the end of the room lockups and Hanson could see a row of standard jail cells with bars. All of them were occupied.

"These are the really bad children," she announced, nodding toward the cells.

"Do you keep the girls separate?" Hanson asked, noticing that the inmates were all boys.

"They're all over in A Building South. We don't have any really violent girls."

"Never?"

"When we have the rare case, we have a quiet room in A Building where we can lock her up until she calms down."

"I noticed that there aren't any toilets in the rooms or cells. Where do the kids go to the bathroom?"

"We've learned through experience that you can't trust the juveniles with toilets. They stop them up and then flood their cells." She stopped walking and looked back at the captain. "So we've removed the toilets from their cells. They are taken out on an individual basis to go to the bathroom."

Hanson smiled. Now he knew the reason for the strong smell of disinfectant. The boys were urinating and probably defecating on the floors of their cells and rooms. Hanson recalled his weeks of training in a mock POW camp. The guards had had total control over him. They would use their control to even torture him when he had to go to the bathroom, and they had loved humiliating the POWs by making them beg. He could understand why the juveniles would urinate from their cells at the guards.

The sound of a shower running caught Hanson's attention, and he glanced over at the two shower stalls at the end of the wide hallway. A boy was soaping down with his back to the female guard watching him shower. As the director and Hanson approached her from behind, the guard cried, "Don't use any of that soap on your wimpy little cock!" She cackled and crossed her arms over her chest. "And hurry up!"

Shocked, Hanson looked over at the director. Her face was bright red. The boy looked back over his shoulder and saw the Army captain and the hated director. He turned around and casually rubbed the soap in his pubic hair and started washing his penis with exaggerately slow strokes.

"Get him back in his cell!" the director yelled, livid

with anger. "And I want to see you in my office as soon as you finish with him!"

The guard looked like a whipped dog. She realized that she had made an unforgivable error in front of a visitor.

Hanson took the time to look around the area while the director chastised her guard and the boy dug through the cardboard barrels next to the showers for a clean pair of underwear. Hanson stepped over and looked down in the two barrels that were placed side by side. One of the barrels contained hundreds of pairs of BVD shorts and the other barrel contained white tube socks. The boy selected only a pair of underwear.

"Don't you wear socks?" Hanson tried smiling.

"I haven't earned the privilege," the teenager hissed.

The director noticed Hanson talking to the boy and explained, "He's suicidal and isn't allowed to wear anything except undershorts in his cell."

The boy rolled his eyes, but didn't reply. He knew the consequences of mouthing off to the dragon lady.

Captain Hanson looked over the teenager's shoulder as the boy was being led away to his cell and saw a thin boy staring at him through the bars of his cell. Wearing only a pair of BVDs, the youth had his hands wrapped around the rusty bars. Hanson could see that the teenager's cell was the worst because it was so close to the showers. The steam had rusted everything in the cell, including the steel sleeping platform hung from the wall. The pallet was covered with a thin mattress, which was the only furniture in the cell. Hanson stared at the boy's face. He had two black eyes, and bruises marked his chest and arms. As the boy turned away and sat gingerly on his cot, Hanson could tell that he was recovering from a severe beating.

The director led Hanson to the exit door and signaled for the guard on the other side to unlock it. Hanson looked back over his shoulder and then walked back to the worst cell, where the teenager sat holding his head in his hands.

"Son?" Hanson waited until the youth turned to look at him. "Haven't we met before?"

"Naw, I don't know you, mister."

Hanson had been having trouble placing the youth because of the discolored eyes, but as soon as he spoke, he knew that it was the kid who had shoveled his office sidewalk. "Yeah, we've met. A couple of weeks ago."

The boy shrugged and went back to looking down at the floor.

"He's our pyromaniac," the director told Hanson as she joined him.

Hanson waited until they were back in her office before asking, "You said I could have any child in Children's Village under the volunteer program, right?"

"Yes, except children confined here for murder," she said absently still thinking about the incident of the guard in the shower.

"I'll take the pyromaniac."

She whirled around to face the captain. "You've got to be kidding. That boy is one of our worst cases. He's beat up our guards!" She shook her head. "I'm sorry, he's too violent to be allowed into the volunteer program."

"You told me that I had my choice."

"Anyone except him."

Hanson knew he had the upper hand and pressed her. "I don't understand why you have female guards in an all-boys facility. I mean, for most people, it's embarrassing to have someone of the opposite sex watch you take a shower—or worse yet, go to the bathroom."

"We have a functioning equal-opportunity policy here in the Children's Village, and that includes performing all of the assigned guard duties, no matter how difficult it is for the women." Even as she spoke, she was reconsidering the captain's request. Maybe letting him have the pyromaniac was a good idea. The boy was totally uncontrollable and would make the

Army officer look like a fool if he ran away. That would end the officer's snooping around the Village. "Fine, you can take the boy. He might just open your eyes to how difficult it is for us trying to work with his type of offender."

"Thank you, very much." Hanson crossed his legs and leaned back in his chair. "Do you think that your people can have him ready to go in a half an hour?"

She hid her sneer with her hand. "So soon?"

"Yes. The program outline states that we are supposed to have a four-hour session with our selected child on the first day."

"You can wait in the lobby. I'll have him processed and sent out to you." She pushed the intercom switch on her desk and spoke to the senior staff member in J Building.

"Thanks, ma'am. I enjoyed the tour. It was very informative." Hanson picked up his cap and looked down at the red, white, and blue glider patch sewn on the side of it. He looked back over his shoulder at the director and smiled before leaving her office. Fighting the North Vietnamese was much easier than dealing in bureaucratic politics. He didn't hold anything against the woman; she was only trying to survive in her world.

Hanson waited in the lobby for an hour, writing down notes for his report, before the steel door opened and the fat guard from J lockup escorted the boy over to the sign-out desk.

"Do you really want to assume responsibility for this kid?" the guard mumbled. "He's more trouble than he's worth."

"I'll sign for him." Hanson picked up the pen attached by a cord to the sign-out log book. The guard behind the desk slipped a multicopy preprinted form over for him to sign and tore out the yellow copy.

"Keep that with you as long as he's in your custody. When he runs away, call the sheriff's number there on the bottom of the paper."

"He won't run away," Hanson said, pausing to read the kid's name before folding the paper and tucking it in his pocket.

"Have him back here by five for supper or he'll go hungry tonight. We don't have room service."

Hanson looked at the pair of guards. There was little doubt in his mind who should be locked up and it wasn't the children. Reading the boy's name off the form, he said, "Come on, Spike. Let's get out of here."

Spike zipped up the county-issued jacket when they stepped outside. The overheated cell he had been sitting in for the past two weeks had destroyed his resistance to cold weather.

Hanson paused next to the olive-drab Army sedan and unlocked the door for Spike. Looking up at the row of large office windows, he saw the director pointing her finger at the female guard who had been harassing the boy in the shower. Just then she looked out the window and saw Hanson watching her. Hanson smiled and waved. He put his hand on Spike's shoulder as the boy slipped onto the front seat. "Where do you want to go?"

Spike didn't reply. All the same, sensing that the man was trying to be friendly, he reached over and unlocked the driver's door.

Hanson sighed when he slipped behind the steering wheel. He had plenty of information already to enter in his report to the Pentagon. "How about visiting your old neighborhood?"

Spike looked at the Army captain out of the corner of his eye and shrugged again, like he really didn't care.

"Fine, but you'll have to show me the way."

Spike nodded his head in agreement.

Captain Hanson stopped the sedan in the parking lot of Wisner Stadium. "I've got to run over to my office for a couple of hours. Can you meet me back here by three?"

Spike looked over in surprise. "Are you going to let me take off by myself?"

"Sure. Why not?"

"The rules say that a volunteer has to stay with a kid from J Building at all times."

"We're going to bend the rules a little. I trust you."

Spike stepped out of the sedan and leaned over to look back inside at the captain sitting behind the wheel. "What if I don't come back?"

"Well, Spike, I'll be the only one who will be disappointed. They plan on your running away."

Spike scowled and slammed the door. He jogged across the slush-filled street and disappeared into the shadows between two dilapidated houses.

Hanson watched the boy disappear and sighed. He was probably screwing up by allowing the kid to take off by himself in his old neighborhood. But if he was going to win the boy over, the child would have to trust him.

Spike waited in the shadows and watched the Army captain pull away. Then he smiled and pulled up the collar on his jacket.

CHAPTER THREE

✪✪✪✪✪✪✪✪✪✪✪✪✪✪✪✪✪✪

BLOOD BROTHERS

Captain Hanson put the telephone on its receiver and looked at his watch. He was already a half hour late in meeting Spike, but he couldn't hang up on the recruiting commander. The general was going to present Hanson's recruiting outfit with the annual best company award and had called personally to congratulate him. Then the conversation turned to Hanson's visit at the juvenile facility and the general became very interested in his captain's firsthand experience. The whole military chain of command was very concerned with the Secretary of Defense's new program, worried that it was going to fill the enlisted ranks with gang members and troubled youths who would be hard to discipline.

"Sergeant McClure?"

"Yes, sir!"

"Take the rest of my calls for the afternoon. I'm late in picking up my new charge from the Children's Village."

"How's it going, sir?"

"We'll see when I get back to Wisner Stadium."

"How's that, Captain?"

"I was supposed to pick him up there a half hour ago."

Hanson hurried out of the office and out to his sedan. The cold engine had a hard time turning over, and he almost wore the battery out before the engine caught.

A light snow was falling when Hanson turned into the snow-covered parking lot next to the school. There weren't any other tire tracks in the fresh snow. He pulled to a stop next to the school and looked across the street for Spike.

"Shit," Hanson cursed under his breath. "He's gone."

Spike brushed the snow off his pants legs and watched the Army sedan in the parking lot below him. He sat curled up on the top step of the outside stairs that led into the converted school. The wind wasn't so bad there and he had been waiting for almost an hour.

The wipers on the car rubbed against the windshield, sending a scraping sound out over the parking lot. It was starting to get dark out. Hanson wiped the inside of the window with his gloved hand and tried looking back toward the stadium. He had trusted the kid and was going to look foolish going back to the Village to report the boy missing. He turned off his engine and stepped out into the snow. He figured he would wait a couple more minutes, but first he wanted to walk back to the rear of the building to see if Spike was waiting there by some chance.

Spike watched the captain walk around the building and disappear. He was gone only a couple of minutes and reappeared. Spike remained on top of the stairs. He blended into the dark shadows perfectly.

Hanson reached for the car door and at the last possible second, he saw the outline of someone sitting on top of the stairs. He smiled to himself. The boy was very smooth.

"Are you coming, Spike?" He opened the door and waited.

Spike stood up and brushed the accumulated snow off his jacket and pants. He was also smiling. He had almost fooled the Army paratrooper captain.

"Are you hungry?"

"A little." Actually, Spike was famished.

"Let's stop at a restaurant on our way back." Hanson looked over at the boy and without thinking he brushed the snow off Spike's hair.

"Sounds good to me," Spike said, accepting the fatherly gesture.

"Did you see the little guy?"

"Yeah." The tone in Spike's voice revealed more than he wanted the captain to know about his feelings.

"You spent all of that time with him?" Hanson asked, trying to spark a conversation.

"Naw. His father doesn't like me, so I could only talk to him through the window."

"You must be cold."

"Not much."

"That's a long time to be outside."

"I wasn't outside all of the time."

"Oh?"

"I got laid."

Hanson grinned and looked over at the sixteen-year-old. The teenager had made the comment so matter-of-factly that he thought the boy was lying. But no, he could tell that Spike had spoken the truth. "You've got a girlfriend?"

"Not exactly. She just likes to fuck."

"Oh, I see." Hanson had been raised in the fifties, and sex had been talked up a lot by teenagers, but they rarely scored. "Now I know why you're so hungry."

"Yeah." Spike slid down in the seat and stared out of the window as they drove down Oakland Avenue back toward the Children's Village. The captain didn't know just how close he had come to running away. Spike knew that they would never have found him if he had wanted to stay hidden, but at the last moment he had changed his mind. "I froze my balls off waiting for you. I thought Army guys were on time."

"Sorry about that. Normally I am." Hanson reached over and punched Spike's arm lightly. "Thanks for waiting for me."

"No problem," Spike said, continuing to stare out of the window.

While eating, the two talked for almost an hour, taking their time. The teenager opened up quickly to the honest, open-hearted soldier. He felt very comfortable talking to the man. Spike had learned early living on the streets of Pontiac to size up a person quickly. Spike laughed when Hanson asked him about being a pyromaniac and explained what had really happened in Kimberly's garage and during his inprocessing session at the juvenile facility.

"You mean that you'd been living in a garage since I saw you over by the recruiting office?"

Spike nodded, taking a bite out of the double cheeseburger. He swallowed the food before he answered, "Yeah, but it's not as bad as it sounds. I had a Coleman stove and some old carpeting to wrap around me."

"What is this story about you beating up some cops?"

"Shit! They kicked my ass and then those cunts at the juve were getting their jollies off watching me shower."

"I saw that happening when I toured the Village with the director."

"Yeah, the female guards get their kicks out of humiliating the little guys. It doesn't bother most of us older guys, but the twelve- and thirteen-year-olds have heart attacks."

"I can understand that. When I was that age, I didn't even like my parents coming into the bathroom when I was taking a shower." Hanson finished his coffee and added, "Why doesn't it bother you?"

"I won't give the bitches the satisfaction." A dark look crossed Spike's face. "Mendez—that was the guy you saw—he does a hip-grinding act that really pisses the bitches off. Personally, I think it gets those old cunts hot."

Hanson shook his head. The kids had a right to be upset. It was ironic that a combat-experienced paratrooper captain had more compassion for the kids than a college-trained social-services professional did.

Once back in the car, Captain Hanson turned into the side street that went past the state police station and pulled up in front of J Building.

Spike looked out the window, using his hand to wipe the fog away. "What time is it?"

"Quarter to five."

"You mind waiting out here till five?" Spike looked over at the captain. "I don't want to go in there until I have to."

Hanson saw the fear in the boy's eyes. "Sure, I enjoy talking to you."

A long silence ensued. A couple of times Hanson started to say something, but decided against it. Spike was trying to get out something that he was holding inside of him, and he needed a little time. Finally he broke the silence. "Why are you bothering with me?"

"I owe some people. Maybe through kids like you, I'll get to pay them back," Hanson said, his voice thickened.

Spike was puzzled. "Why don't you just pay *them* back?"

"I would if I could, but none of them are around anymore. A couple of them died fighting in Vietnam." Hanson lifted the paper coffee cup to his lips and took a long sip. "And when I was your age, there were a couple of older men who came into my life during times when I really needed someone."

"Where was your dad?"

"My parents divorced when I was three. I never knew my father and my mother never remarried. She put me in the Big Brother program so that I could have some adult male companionship."

"I've heard about them. There's a Big Brother office here in Pontiac." Spike looked out the window at a flock of Canadian geese. "One of my teachers tried getting me to join them."

"Why didn't you?"

Spike drew an arrow with his finger on the window and then used the cuff from his jacket to wipe it out. "Sorry, I made a mess on your window."

"It's all right." Hanson leaned the back of his head against his window and felt the cool glass. "So, why didn't you join? Did your father get jealous?"

Spike smiled and then quickly hid it. "I don't have a father."

"Everybody has a father and a mother, Spike."

"Not me. My mother got knocked up by some guy when she was living out in California." His eyelids formed narrow slits. "I don't have a father."

"Why aren't you living with your mother?"

Spike shrugged in response. "I do sometimes, but I don't like the drugs or any of the assholes that are always over there trying to fuck her." Spike glared at the captain to warn him not to push it any further. "And they don't like me hanging around. It makes them feel guilty, I guess."

"We've got a lot in common, Spike—no fathers, mothers, who are, uh, doing their own thing."

"Yeah," Spike said softly.

Hanson sensed that Spike didn't want to talk about his parents anymore. "Are you with a gang?"

Spike shook his head and twisted his mouth before answering. "I don't wear anyone's colors. I've got my friends."

"That's pretty risky, isn't it?" Hanson knew from his recruiting in the area that gangs controlled the streets.

Spike grinned, more to himself than in response to Hanson's question. "They think that I'm a crazy motherfucker."

"Oh?" Hanson asked, encouraging him to go on. "How's that?"

"One of the Aztecs was fucking with me and I bricked him."

Hanson stiffened a little in his seat. "Bricked him?"

"Yeah. He kicked my ass at school with his buddies

watching, and I followed him over to his woman's house. I waited on a nearby garage roof in the alley behind her house until he left and I dropped a cinder block on his head when he passed below me. He was in the hospital for two months."

"You could have killed him."

Spike shrugged.

"Didn't the rest of his gang come after you?"

"They tried fucking with me at school, but I went crazy on two of them during my English class."

"You fought two gang members at school?"

"No, I went loco on them. I threw a couple of chairs and did a lot of screaming and foaming at the mouth and stuff." He glanced at the captain and smiled. "You see, I knew that they were going to make a big scene at school in front of a lot of people so their honor wouldn't be fucked with. So I picked the time and place. I put a little white toothpaste inside a scrap of paper and had it in my shirt pocket. When they started fucking with me in class, I slipped the toothpaste in my mouth and mixed it with spit until it looked like foam. Then I stood up and started my act, foaming at the mouth and screaming a lot of shit at them."

"Smart, Spike. Everyone thought you were having a fit."

Spike nodded in agreement. "It worked. The Aztecs still think I'm fucking nuts and respect my independence. I was only expelled from school for two days." Spike looked at the captain after checking the main doors of the Children's Village to see if any of the guards were watching them. "I'd better be getting inside now."

The sedan became abuptly quiet.

"Yeah. I guess you had better go." Hanson looked down at his watch. "It's two minutes to five. We'd better check you in on time or they'll raise hell."

Spike got out of the car and walked straight over to the double doors without stopping to wait for the captain to walk with him. He didn't want the guards watching to think that he liked the man because they would use that against him the next time they wanted to punish him. He touched the cold handle on the door and shivered. He wanted to turn around and run away as fast as he could, but the guard on duty beckoned for him to approach the desk. He was the same one who had been on duty when Spike had checked out.

"Empty your pockets on the counter." Then the guard turned to Hanson and barked, "Sorry, but you'll have to leave now so that we can in-process him."

"Sure," Hanson snapped, refusing to let the guard intimidate him. He looked at Spike. "I'll stop by to visit you tomorrow. Do you need anything?"

Spike was shocked. "I, uh . . .no, nothing." He wasn't expecting to see the captain again, especially so soon. He had heard from other kids in the juvenile facility about the volunteer program, and most of the other volunteers kept to the minimum of four hours a week with their assigned kid, and that was usually on Saturdays. There had never been a maximum time limit set.

"Well, be good, and don't give them a reason to keep me from seeing you."

Spike, emptying his pockets for the guard onto the stainless steel tray he was holding, smiled and his face lit up from the inside. "I will."

Master Sergeant McClure flipped through his Rolodex card file and hummed a Southern Baptist hymn to himself. He was starting to get the old Christmas spirit and changed the tune in mid-chord to "Jingle Bells."

Hanson looked up from the report he was reading. "Do you call that music, Top?"

"I just love Christmas up here in the North." McClure turned his chair around so that he could see out of the window. "All this snow makes Christmas special."

"It's the commercial hype," Hanson chuckled.

"Naw, it's the snow—and the fact that we are about five months ahead of our recruiting goals." McClure shook his head slowly. "This is the first time I've ever been ahead of next year's goals."

"We can thank McNamara for that." Hanson ran his finger down the list of entrance-exam scores next to the new inductees' names. Few of the scores were high enough to allow enlistment without a waiver. "All we're really getting are the poor kids off the streets and some minority gang members. The middle- and upper-class families are tucking their sons away in colleges with deferments to protect them from the draft."

"Somebody has to fight the war," McClure said evenly. "Poor folks have been fighting America's wars since the beginning. It's supposed to be equality for all in a democracy, but if you believe that, then you'll believe that airplanes can fly backward. The poor people fight the wars and then they end up getting shat on when they get home 'cause all of the jobs are taken by the ones who didn't go and fight."

"You've got a point there, Top. But at least the military gave them a chance. I know a lot of young kids who got their heads screwed on right during their enlistments, and some of them have even used the GI Bill to get a college education."

McClure pressed his lips together. "If they can survive the war."

"It used to be that the officers at least were from wealthy families," Hanson noted, flipping the pages of the report. "But that ain't the case anymore."

McClure looked up, his curiosity aroused. "What do you mean by that, sir? Aren't you a West Pointer?"

Hanson huffed under his breath. "Hell, no, O.C.S! I'm one of those dumb street kids who made good, if that's what you want to call it." Seeing that the sergeant was interested, Hanson continued. "You see, what happened was that during the Korean War the Army shipped over a whole graduating class of second lieutenants from West Point directly to the front lines. About fifty of them were killed and it went down in West Point history as a massacre. The class has been recognized ever since for their great sacrifice."

"I'm not following you, Captain," McClure said, leaning back in his chair.

"The Vietnam War is being fought almost entirely by poor kids. The key word, Top, is 'fought.' West Pointers and a few rich brats are over there, but they get assigned to secure staff or high command advisory positions, where their risk of seeing action is minimal." Hanson was warming to one of his favorite subjects. "Let me explain. You see, when I was working in the Inspector General's office out of the Pentagon, we had access to all kinds of studies, facts, and figures. It takes a little detective work, but once you piece together a couple Army policies, you'll see what I'm driving at. First, let's look at the Army's officer promotion policy. Time-in-grade from second to first lieutenant had been dropped to exactly one year."

Sergeant McClure nodded his head in agreement.

"Now, there is a new policy that has come out of the Pentagon, especially for the Vietnam War, that states: all regular Army commissioned officers—"

McClure interrupted, "All the West Pointers."

"That's right. They're all commissioned into the Army Regular."

"I'm lost again, Captain. What's the big difference? A gold bar is a gold bar to an enlisted man."

Hanson shook his head. "Only to an enlisted man. Let me get back to my story. With one year time-in-grade required for promotion from second to first lieutenant *and* the new policy that all regular army officers must spend one year in the States before being shipped to Vietnam—"

McClure saw what Hanson was driving at and his coffee cup dropped hard on the table, sending some of it splashing across his desk. "Shit! So regular Army officers end up going to Vietnam as first lieutenants."

"Right."

"And first lieutenants are assigned as company executive officers, and they stay back in secure base areas and run the administration and supply for the company in the field."

"Bingo," Hanson said, impressed by how fast McClure put the puzzle together, since most enlisted men didn't follow officer politics. "And the high-risk assignments are *second* lieutenant assignments as platoon leaders or as forward observers with the artillery."

"And that's how the Pentagon, which is run by West Point officers, protects their precious second lieutenants from getting zapped too early in their careers."

Hanson smiled and added, "And we end up having a couple generations of West Point officers who have technically gone to war, but haven't really experienced it. That's a dangerous combination."

"That's fucked, sir!" McClure exclaimed. Just then he looked up and saw a man wearing a pair of wire-rimmed glasses with yellow lenses. What was this hipster doing here? "Can I help you, sir?"

"Yes, you may," the man said softly, visibly nervous being in the recruiting office. "I'm looking for a Mister Hanson."

"*Captain* Hanson is sitting over there." McClure nodded with his head.

"Thank you." The young man adjusted his glasses and walked directly to Hanson's desk.

"Can I help you?" Hanson asked, using his airborne-command voice.

"Yes, you can. We need to talk in private."

"I'll take a walk, sir." McClure left his desk and rolled his eyes as he left the room.

"We can go into to my office if you would feel more comfortable."

"No, this is fine. I don't have very much time and I'll get right to the point."

"Do you want to enlist?" Hanson asked, gently mocking the man.

"No." Fire flashed from the man's eyes, warning Hanson that he hadn't come to be played with. "I'm a caseworker over at the county courthouse. Spike Harwood is one of my assigned cases."

"Is there something wrong with Spike?"

The social worker raised both of his hands as a shield. "No! That is, there's nothing wrong with Spike that we can't work out together."

"We?"

"I've been informed that Spike has refused to cooperate with his assigned psychologist, and frankly, Captain Hanson, the staff over at the Children's Village is blaming you."

"Me?"

The man lit a Kool cigarette. "They say since you have become his court-appointed volunteer, he has stopped cooperating with the staff."

"Do you believe that?"

The social worker smiled. He had been working with social-services agencies for too long not to have figured out what was going on. It was obvious that the captain posed some kind of a threat to the Village staff, and this was the classic way for a volunteer to be taken off the access list. He blew out a long column of blue smoke and looked directly at the captain, now sitting on the edge of his chair. "No."

"Good," Hanson said, relaxing.

"Did you tell Spike not to talk to his psychologist?"

Hanson slapped the top of his desk. "Have you talked to Spike about it?"

"Not yet. I've just found out."

"As soon as Spike told me what had happened, I reported the incident to the director. His psychologist is a woman, you know." Hanson sipped his coffee and then looked down inside the cup. The bottom was filled with floating coffee grounds. "I picked Spike up one day after his session with her and he seemed very uptight about something. I asked him if he wanted to talk about it and he just shook his head. I didn't push the issue, but after we had something to eat, he started opening up. He told me that he had done everything that I had recommended. He had taken all of the psychological tests and had cooperated with all of the staff, except"—Hanson shook his head—"with that female psychologist. I had told the director earlier that Spike would not respond well to a female in a position of authority over him—"

"You picked that up quickly. Did you know that his mother left him and went out to California to join a hippie commune?" The social worker watched for Hanson's reaction.

"No, I didn't."

"Go ahead, continue."

"She disagreed with me and said that the children were assigned to case psychologists based on availability and not on the child's sexual preferences." Hanson pointed at the court caseworker. "Do you know what her first question to Spike was?"

"I can only guess," he said, stubbing out his cigarette.

"First of all, she told him that she was a mother of three teenage boys and that she needed to know the answers to some personal questions. Spike said that was fine. And the first question out of her mouth was: How many times a day do you masturbate?" Hanson's voice rose. "Can you believe that shit? I mean, asking any sixteen-year-old a question like that?"

The caseworker's eyebrows flickered. "I think the timing was poor, but the question is a common one in therapy, especially if they feel the child has a sexual adjustment problem." He held up his hand to stave off Hanson's retort. "But you're right, that should never have been brought up right off the bat. What did Spike do?"

Hanson chuckled. "Naturally, he shut up and refused to answer her. So she wrote up that 'document' you're holding, stating that the boy refuses to cooperate."

"Is something striking you as humorous?" The

caseworker didn't find anything funny in Hanson's statement.

"It's what Spike asked me in the car." Hanson shook his head. "You know, as sexually aware as those street kids are, sometimes they can be so damn naive. He looked right at me and asked, 'Captain, do people beat off more than once a day?' " Hanson started laughing. "The kid's question was so damn innocent that I had to laugh." He wiped his eyes with the back of his hand. "Christ, it's a wonder all of the kids in those facilities aren't totally screwed up when they come out."

"Well, you see how it turns out when only one side of the story is recorded." The caseworker pointed at the folder. "They can destroy a kid all in the name of therapy."

"How can I get this report removed from Spike's files?" Hanson asked, leaning back in his swivel chair. "None of this crap is true."

"That's one of the problems with the system. All of these reports are connected with a juvenile case and therefore are confidential, except when they want to use them." The caseworker looked down at the floor. "It sure isn't very American, is it?"

"Gestapo tactics in our Social Services system. I never thought I'd see the day." Hanson leaned forward in his chair and called, "Sergeant McClure!"

McClure appeared too fast back in the office. Obviously he had been eavesdropping on the conversation.

Hanson nodded at the thick file the court caseworker had laid on the desk. "There's no way that Spike could even get in the military service with stuff like this"—he glanced over at the approaching sergeant—"if they supplied it to a recruiter."

"Only you could sign a waiver for him," the caseworker stated, reaching the main purpose of his visit.

Hanson agreed immediately.

"You're going to have to move fast and have everything ready so that the day after Christmas, when he turns seventeen, you can ship him out." The case-worker smiled. "I know Spike's probate judge very well, and he'll sign the release from the Children's Village so he can join the Army. Personally, I think that old guy likes the kid."

Hanson looked over at his sergeant. "What do you think, Top? Can we process his paperwork in ten days?"

"Does an owl shit through feathers?" McClure smiled. "He'll be in-processed and ready to go, or I'll be one dead nigger."

"You don't have to make it so personal, Top." Hanson smiled.

"We can sign for him from the Children's Village the day after Christmas and have him on military standby until the induction center down in Detroit opens up the following Monday. It will be all legal and proper." McClure looked up from thumbing through Spike's file. "This is some bad shit, Captain."

"I know." Hanson looked at the caseworker. "Why would they do this to a kid?"

"Spike's case is one of the worst ones I've ever seen. That's why I've risked coming here and talking to you on my own. I think that you're the real reason they have worked so hard to break Spike."

"Me?"

"You're a threat to them. First of all, you're the representative of the military system that is threatening their paychecks with the government's 100,000 Program. It's going to do exactly what it was designed to do—that is, empty juvenile-detention facilities across the nation of seventeen- and eighteen-year-olds." The caseworker's voice became aggressive. "Remember, when you're in the social-services business, employees and caseloads are combined to establish a budget for the department, and in a bureaucracy that equates to *power*."

"This is some sad shit." Hanson felt totally helpless.

"It's reality, my military friend. The kids don't

amount to very much except as pawns to base a budget on." The caseworker crossed his legs, and Sergeant McClure refilled his coffee cup. "Thank you, Sergeant."

"We owe you a free cup of coffee." McClure wasn't exaggerating. "Excuse me, sir, but I've got some work to take care of."

"Sure, Top, go ahead." Hanson returned his attention to the caseworker. "I've noticed that my presence isn't really wanted out at the Village. I try to stay within the rules and work with the social workers out there, but whatever I do seems to be the wrong thing."

The caseworker nodded his head, understanding exactly what was going on. "You probably won't understand. Spike was a hard-core case before you came on the scene. And then in a matter of a couple of weeks, you had him acting like a kid who was raised in Bloomfield Hills, with table manners and all." The caseworker pointed his finger at the captain. "That, my friend, makes you too dangerous to have hanging around their facility. Anyone who can turn troubled kids around that fast is a threat to the whole juvenile system. You see, we make our livings off failures.

"Don't forget that we're talking about college-trained professionals. If *they* can't reach a troubled kid, they damn sure don't want you doing it." The caseworker bit his lower lip and added, "Change that to *we* don't want you doing it. I'm a part of this fucking system."

For the first time Hanson realized just how difficult it must have been for the man to come and show him Spike's file. "I'm grateful for what you've done."

"What is important right now is helping Spike escape from this system." He lowered his head. "I'm personally against the Vietnam War and I've even participated in a couple of student protest marches over at the University of Michigan. But after I started working in the juvenile services . . ." He sighed. "At least they'll have a chance, even if they have to go and fight in Vietnam. Staying here, they'll just end up as human fodder to keep the system running."

Hanson leaned forward over his desk. "What do you recommend that we do?"

"We have to get Spike out of here first of all, and then we concentrate on recruiting as many seventeen- and eighteen-year-old kids out of the Village as possible. I can help you by working from inside the system. I have access to extensive files on all of the kids, as you've seen. We can select those who have the best chance of making it in the military." He grinned more to himself than at Hanson. "I can't believe that I've turned into a closet Army recruiter."

"I appreciate what you're doing for us."

"Listen, Captain," the caseworker said, standing up and preparing to leave. "That bitch screwed over a lot of very good people to get that directorship at the Village. And now she is screwing over a lot of kids. It'll take her awhile to figure out what we're doing, and by then it'll be too late to stop us. If I know the county executive—and I do know his type—he'll fire her ass!" The caseworker's expression changed and he studied Hanson for a couple of seconds before picking up the file on Spike and tearing out over half of the pages and then handed them to Hanson.

"What's this?" Hanson asked, reading the labels.

"When I came here, I didn't know what to expect from you. I figured that if you turned out to be a horse's ass, I'd leave here and put Spike's file back in the record room." He smiled. "What the hell, you might as well keep this poison-pen garbage."

Hanson's face lit up. "Thanks! Thanks a lot."

"No problem, partner."

"Partners!" Hanson heartily shook the caseworker's hand.

Top McClure's wife spent two days getting ready for their guests. Originally she had planned to spend the Christmas holiday alone with her husband, since all of their children were grown up and spread out around the country. When he had come home from work and asked her if she would mind hosting a bunch of Pontiac street kids for Christmas dinner, she had not only agreed, but enthusiastically decorated their small apartment with all the Christmas ornaments they had in storage.

"Well, woman, you've done yourself proud," McClure said, standing in the doorway with his hands on his hips. He inhaled a deep lungful of sweet Christmas smells coming from the kitchen. "They should be arriving soon." He looked at his watch. "I told the captain that we'd be ready for them by noon."

"Top, do you really think everything is all right? I've never entertained white folks before on Christmas." She scanned the room, looking for anything that might be out of place.

"My love, everything is fine. And as far as white folks go, they ain't much different than us black folks. Besides, these are little white folks, and they don't much care who makes the Christmas cookies. You've met Spike before and the other kids are just friends of his—a four-year-old named Peter and his brother, Spike's girlfriend of sorts, named Kimberly, and I think the captain said that the little boy's mother might come along. She didn't know if she could come because her husband's in prison and might call her today. But anyway, we have enough food in case a couple of spare kids show up. You know Captain Hanson. He might find a stray kid in a snow drift somewhere on his way over here."

She started laughing. She loved kids and missed her grandchildren during the holidays. McClure winked at his wife and smiled.

The door buzzer anounced the arrival of their guests. McClure opened the door and smiled at the group in the hallway. Merry Christmas, sir," he said, shaking hands with Hanson.

"Merry Christmas, Sergeant McClure. It was sure nice of you and your missus to do this for us."

"Bachelors need somewhere to go on Christmas

Day . . .and God knows, we've had our share of crowds for the holidays."

After removing their shoes in the hallway, the kids entered the apartment cautiously. None of them had ever lived in such a fine apartment before and didn't know what to do. Peter's mother was almost as shy as her little son.

Mrs. McClure broke the ice by asking the girls to help her in the kitchen, and the boys were sent to find something worth watching on the TV in the living room. Peter wouldn't leave Spike's side.

"Come on over to the bar and fix yourself a drink, Captain. I made some nonalcoholic eggnog for the kids." McClure looked over at Spike and grinned. "How about showing the other kids how to make it, Spike? With cinnamon on the top." McClure made the first cup to show Spike how.

Spike made the first cup for Peter, who drained it in one long gulp and handed the cup back for a refill.

"I think he likes it." Hanson laughed and followed McClure over to the mahogany bar that was imported from the Phillipines. "I appreciate your doing this, Top."

"I'm not going to say it again. We are the ones who should be thanking you. We would have just sat around here all day moping, waiting for our kids to call us long-distance."

The sound of children laughing came from the living room, where Mrs. McClure was telling them a story about Christmas angels.

Spike watched everyone enjoying themselves and felt a warm feeling for the first time in ages. He glanced over at the captain. The man had filled a void in his life as a father figure. Looking over, Hanson caught Spike staring at him and smiled. There was nothing phony about the way he felt toward the boy.

Peter's mother approached the two men at the bar. "Captain Hanson, thanks for inviting me and my kid to join you for Christmas. Since my husband was arrested . . .I . . ." She started crying.

"Now, now . . ." McClure looked over at his wife for help and she came quickly to the rescue. He waited until the women had gone into the kitchen before adding, "Santa Claus left some stuff in the bedroom."

"Did you have any problem finding the right gifts so late?" Hanson had given McClure the money to buy presents for all of the kids, but he was worried that everything might have been sold out in the stores.

"Nothing we couldn't work out." McClure winked. "I think Santa should make his appearance after we eat."

Hanson nodded his head in agreement. "Oh, Top, I forgot to tell you earlier. I received my orders for Vietnam last week."

McClure paused in the doorway and looked back over his shoulder. "So soon after your last tour?"

"I volunteered. No sense in wasting what I learned the first year over there by staying behind a desk."

"Which unit?"

"The Third Herd." Hanson held his glass up as a toast. "The 173rd Airborne Brigade!"

McClure shook his head and said as he disappeared into the kitchen, "I should have known you would go back to an airborne unit."

Hanson saw Spike standing in the doorway and tried to smile. "You're going into the Army next week and I'll be leaving for Vietnam. How about that?"

Spike nodded his head to hide his unhappiness. He didn't want the captain to go back to the war. He had been staying with Hanson since the caseworker had gotten his probate judge to release him to the military, and for the first time he had felt part of a family.

"So you approve?"

Spike forced a grin and shrugged, trying to act like he didn't care that much.

The women served the turkey dinner and the kids ate so much that the McClures thought they would run out of food before they stopped eating. Then Santa appeared and brought gifts for all of the kids and a special birthday present for Spike—a pair of airborne jump boots.

"You'll need those boots when you get to jump school." Hanson glanced over at McClure, who rolled his eyes. "I couldn't stand it if you were a 'leg.' "

"Give the kid a break, Captain." McClure laughed and sipped from his glass of bourbon.

Hanson went back over to the bar to refill his glass and beckoned for Spike to join him. He poured himself a drink and then a half finger in another glass for Spike. "You'll need that for a toast."

"Thanks, Doug." Spike had started calling the captain by his first name a couple of weeks earlier.

"But before we go back in the other room, I have something else for you. The boots were meant as a joke." Hanson reached into his pocket and removed a long, flat jeweler's case. "Here."

When Spike opened the box, he looked up at the captain. "It's sharp."

"It means a lot to me. The medallion is a Saint Jude's medal. It was blessed at his shrine in Chicago." Hanson had to stop and swallow because he was becoming emotional. "Once you go into the Army, you'll need someone looking out for you. It's a ten-*baht* chain from Thailand and it's real gold. I got it when I was stationed in Vietnam on my last tour. We bought the chains to use as bribes in case we were captured by the VC. As you can see, I didn't need mine."

"Can you hook this for me?" Spike held the chain and the gold medal up for Hanson to hook around his neck.

"Sure." Hanson hooked the locking clasp and squeezed Spike's shoulders. "You'll make a decent paratrooper once they put a little muscle on you."

Spike glared back at the captain. "Decent, my ass! I'll make the best paratrooper ever to wear jump wings."

"We'll see. Come on, they're waiting for us," Hanson said, leading the way back to the living room.

"Well, they're back." McClure stood up. "It's time for a Christmas toast." He held his glass up. "Everyone get your glasses."

The children poured eggnog in their glasses before forming a circle around the fireplace.

McClure nodded at Hanson. "I think the captain should make the toast."

"It's your home, Top."

"Please, Captain, do me the honor."

Captain Hanson thought for a second and then glanced at Spike. "To those who have fought . . .to those who have fallen . . .to those who continue to fight." Hanson drained his glass and bit the edge off. The fragment cut his lip. He squeezed the glass in his hand and threw it into the burning fireplace. McClure followed suit and threw his empty glass after the captain's. The children all watched wide-eyed, puzzled by the wartime ceremony. Nevertheless, they sensed that something important had just occurred.

Seeing the blood at the corner of Hanson's mouth and the cut on his palm, Spike used the edge of the fireplace to break his glass and he threw all but one piece in the fire. He then used the sharp fragment to cut a small gash in his palm.

He walked over and laced his fingers with Hanson's. Then he raised both of their hands over their heads. "Blood brothers."

Hanson smiled. "Blood brothers!"

A young warrior had been born.

CHAPTER FOUR

✪✪✪✪✪✪✪✪✪✪✪✪✪✪✪✪

BLOOD WINGS

Spike sat in front of the leased Greyhound bus, next to the folding front doors. He liked watching the highway through the huge windshield and the seat afforded him a perfect view. The driver kept looking back over his shoulder at the rowdy group of soldiers sitting in the back of the bus, passing a fifth of Seagram's Seven around. The whole bus load had graduated from advanced infantry training and were heading for Fort Benning, Georgia, and the Army's airborne school.

The driver said to Spike, "Do you think you can calm them down a bit back there?"

Spike had been selected as the trip leader by the replacement-center commander because he had already been promoted to private first class. Spike had not only been the honor graduate in his basic class, but in advanced infantry training as well. Because of this, he had been recommended for a program designed to identify potential leaders early and promote them to sergeant (E-5) out of their training cycle before sending them on to Vietnam. The regular NCOs hated the accelerated-promotion program and called the selectees "Shake 'n' Bake" NCOs.

The soldier holding the bottle saw Spike coming down the aisle toward his group and smiled. He had

hated Spike since their first day together in basic training and was constantly trying to draw him into a fight.
"Well, looky here who's coming to the back of the
bus—our leader, Private First Class Harwood."

Spike stopped near the soldier's seat. "Beems, the
driver wants you guys to hold down the noise or—"

"Or what?" the drunk soldier asked, slurring his
words.

"Or you'll have to stop drinking back here." Spike
turned to leave.

"What if we refuse to do either?" Beems pointed
the bottle at Spike. "What the fuck are you going to
do about it?"

"I'll have the driver stop the bus and throw you
off." Spike smiled. "And report you AWOL when we
get to Fort Benning."

"Throw me off?"

"Well, I'll ask you to leave first."

"Listen to this shit!" Beems yelled belligerently.

Spike's hand moved so fast Beems didn't have time
to react. The bottle was snatched out of his hand and
shoved under his neck, making him gag and fall back
in his seat. Spike leaned down, keeping the pressure
against Beems's throat. "I've had enough of your shit,
fella." He withdrew the brown bottle and carried it to
the front of the bus, where he pulled open the folding
door and threw the half-full bottle out on the side of
the road.

The driver smiled and nodded at the young soldier.
He hated driving trainees to Fort Benning because of
the trouble they caused, but this trip was going to be a
piece of cake with the young leader onboard.

Spike leaned his head against the seat's neckrest
and reached over to his jacket on the next seat and
removed the letters. He reread the one from Captain
Hanson first. The captain was with the 173rd already
and had been given a company command with the 2nd
Battalion. Hanson sounded cheerful in the letter, but
Spike could tell that there was a lot left unsaid be-

tween the lines. The second letter, from Master Sergeant McClure, had been typed on the recruiting command's stationery. McClure and his wife had "adopted" the Butts family after meeting them at Christmas. Spike held up the Polaroids so that the dome lights in the bus shone on them. Sergeant McClure had Peter sitting on his desk in his office and Ted was drinking a Coke in the background. The second picture showed Mrs. McClure holding Peter up against her chest and they were looking out at the camera, cheek to cheek. Spike slowly went through the package of photographs, feeling good that someone was looking after Peter. He couldn't have found a better family to watch over him.

"Pictures of your family?" asked someone from the seat behind him.

Spike turned around and saw a soldier who had been in one of the other companies in his AIT battalion. "Sort of . . . just real good friends."

"He's a cute little dude," the soldier said, pointing at Peter.

"Yeah."

"Is that a scar on his face?"

"Yeah, he had an accident. Fell through a window." Noticing that the soldier's seat partner was sleeping, Spike said, "Why don't you come up here so we don't wake him up?"

The soldier came forward and took the seat next to the window, where Spike had stacked manila envelopes containing the group's records. "My name is Bob O'Toole."

"Spike Harwood." They shook hands.

"Is Spike your real name?"

"Yeah. My mother thought that I should have a tough-sounding name because my father was . . .not around much."

"It's a tough name, all right." The soldier sighed and leaned back in his seat. "You nervous about jump school? My gut is rolling already and we haven't even arrived yet."

Spike looked over at the blond-haired soldier and sized him up. He liked the guy's bluntness. "Yeah. Everyone's a little scared about things they don't know anything about. I think the sergeants will tell us what we need to know—just like back in basic and AIT."

O'Toole nodded his head in agreement. "Remember that story back on the infiltration course? About the guy who ran into a rattlesnake halfway through and jumped up and was cut in half by a machine gun?"

Spike grinned. "It was a cottonmouth in my company. I bet that story has been around to scare trainees since World War II."

"Probably." O'Toole sighed again. "My dad was a Ranger in World War II. He was captured by the Germans at Anzio and escaped. That's why I have to make it through airborne training and get into a paratrooper unit in Nam."

"I don't think you'll have any trouble there," Spike said, tucking his pictures back into his jacket pocket. "The 101st and the 173rd are both taking a lot of casualties and replacements are needed right now."

"How do you know that?"

"A friend of mine is a captain over there. He just wrote me a letter about what is going on." Spike patted his jacket pocket.

O'Toole changed the subject. "Do you think they'll make me a platoon leader or a squad leader when we get to Benning?"

The question threw Spike off balance and he turned, trying to read O'Toole's expression. "Why? Does it make a difference to you?"

"No, but I was a platoon leader in basic and in AIT. They made me the honor graduate at AIT. I was hoping that I could get a leadership position in airborne school so that I can write back to my dad that I was selected a leader throughout my training."

"Yeah? I was my company's honor grad too."

"Really?"

"Yeah, let's make a deal. Whoever gets picked for a leadership position, he'll pick the other guy as his assistant. That way we'll both have someone we can rely on."

O'Toole held out his hand. "It's a deal."

The airborne school cadre were all lined up, waiting for the bus to unload at the transportation docks. They had been through this process before and worked as a well-organized team that would have won an Academy Award if they had been making a film for Hollywood.

Spike stepped off the bus, carrying the records under his arm. He reported to the senior cadre NCO and handed the records over. The sergeant just pointed to a bench where Spike could set the package down. Then he nodded for Spike to fall back in ranks.

The group of airborne cadre stood quietly and watched the soldiers unload from the bus. As Beems stepped off, he glared at Spike and whispered in his ear, "I owe you an ass-kicking!"

Spike didn't change the blank expression on his face. He knew that the airborne cadre were sizing up the new trainees. "Get your baggage." The command was given in a very low tone of voice, but with authority.

Spike turned around and helped the driver unlock the baggage compartments under the bus, and O'Toole helped both of them stack the duffel bags and suitcases in a neat row so that the other men could easily find their gear.

The senior cadre adjusted his black baseball cap and said, "Pick up your gear and fall back in ranks."

Spike could see that the rest of the NCOs had taken up positions around the edges of the formation. "O'Toole, come with me."

O'Toole didn't know what Spike was up to, but followed along with his duffel bag thrown up on his shoulder. Spike walked over to the head of the formation and dropped his bag onto the ground. The rest of the new airborne trainees were falling in at the rear of the formation, which was closer to the bus, with less distance to carry their gear.

"What's going on?" O'Toole whispered.

"I think they're going to start fucking with us."

"Are you sure? They haven't even yelled yet." O'Toole glanced over at the senior sergeant and saw him smiling. "They seem like all-right guys."

"It's just like in basic and AIT—a game." Spike reached down and pulled his duffel bag closer to his legs.

One of the junior cadre started the game off. "All right, you bunch of fucking legs. Pick up your gear!"

"Sarge!" Beems called to the senior cadre NCO.

The sergeant smiled and sauntered over to the soldier in the center of the tight formation. Catching the reek of whiskey, he asked, "Yes?"

"Sarge, I've got too much to carry in one trip." He looked down at the duffel bag and the large suitcase next to his legs.

"What you can't carry, you lose," the sergeant screamed, an inch away from Beems's face.

"Right face!" the senior NCO barked. "Double time . . . march!"

The formation staggered and buckled as the baggage-laden troops began running. The NCOs started screaming and running around the formation. O'Toole looked over at Spike and smiled. Spike had called the shot perfectly. One of the NCOs ran up behind Spike, who was running in the front right corner of the formation, and barked, "You set the pace! I don't want any girlish leg bullshit either! You run at an airborne shuffle!"

"Yes, Sergeant!" Spike threw his duffel bag over his shoulder and started a slow shuffle. Most of the formation, having seen the sergeant talking to Spike, followed suit when he lifted his duffel bag to his shoulder, instead of trying to carry their gear at their sides.

After the senior cadre NCO had run up behind

Spike and O'Toole and told Spike to turn a few times, Spike realized that they were running in a large square. They had been shuffling for about twenty minutes when they started catching up to the men who had dropped out of formation. The sergeants attacked the dropouts like vultures and harassed them until they got back in. Spike heard one of the NCOs approaching from his rear, and then the sergeant laid into one of the men behind him.

"You still drunk, soldier?"

"No, Sergeant!" It was Beems, and Spike heard the pain in his voice from having to carry both of the heavy bags.

"You smell drunk."

"I had an accident, Sergeant." In trying to talk, Beems lost his breath and gagged.

The sergeant screamed in his ear, "If you fall out of this formation, you're out of my jump school. Do you hear me?"

"Yes, Sergeant!"

The NCO increased his pace and ran across the front of the formation to select another trainee to harass.

Spike glanced over his shoulder and saw that Beems was about ready to give up. "O'Toole, move over and let him come up between us."

O'Toole obeyed, easing over into the next rank. The heavy bags everyone was carrying made the formation more of a mob than a legendary airborne running formation. Spike waited until Beems got between them and then reached down to grab the handle of his suitcase. "Let's share it between us."

The sobering drunk glared at Spike. "I'm still going to kick your ass, Harwood."

"Fine, but you won't be able to do that if they throw you out of jump school." Spike lifted the suitcase and took most of the load. He had already concluded that the guy was a talker and not a doer.

The sergeant in charge saw what Spike was doing

and made a mental note. The whole purpose of the baggage run was to observe the new troops under pressure and select the trainee leadership for the three-week school.

The formation had dwindled to about a third of the men when they turned a corner and Spike saw the loading docks where the bus had stopped. The senior cadre stopped them in exactly the same spot they had started. One of the soldiers in the center of the formation bent over and vomited. The smell of the partially digested food caused another soldier to throw up too. Within a matter of seconds, a half dozen of the trainees were heaving their last meals.

"This is fucking disgusting!" the airborne sergeant cried. He had jumped onto the cement loading dock and was rocking back and forth on the wooden four-by-twelve beam bolted to the cement to protect the trucks that unloaded there. Spike could see the sunlight reflecting off the toes of the highly shined jump boots. "You people are disgusting!"

One of the junior NCOs went over to a soldier throwing up all over his duffel bag and screamed in the man's ear, "Stop it! Stop it right now . . . Swallow!"

The young trainee tried obeying and gagged before gushing out the remainder of a partially digested hero sandwich.

"Whenever you legs have finished fertilizing our asphalt, we can give you your barracks assignments," the senior sergeant noted, continuing to rock back and forth on the edge of the dock.

Spike caught his slight smile. The sergeant was still acting out the preplanned game. "You are the sorriest group of trainees this airborne school has *ever* been challenged to train. The Department of the Army must think that we can work fucking miracles." The NCO scanned the formation—he was waiting for the stragglers to catch up—and then continued, "I have friends fighting for their asses in Vietnam. With airborne units, of course. And you barf bags are what I'm going to have to send them for replacements."

Spike couldn't hide his grin any longer. The sergeant was obviously reciting a well-rehearsed speech to keep their attention, while his assistants policed the stragglers and got them back into the formation.

"You!" The senior NCO hopped down off the loading dock and landed inches from Spike's face. "You have a mouth functioning problem?"

"No, Sergeant!"

"What was that unnatural position your mouth was in?"

"I don't understand, Sergeant."

"This!" The NCO used his thumbs to pull Spike's mouth back in a smile and then let go.

"That's a smile, Sergeant."

"A what?"

"A smile, Sergeant."

"Is that something you do before you fuck a girl?"

"Sometimes, Sergeant."

"Does that mean you like me?"

"Yes, Sergeant!"

"Did all of you hear that?" The NCO whirled around and yelled over at one of his assistants. He turned back and put his nose less than an inch away from Spike's and yelled in his face, "Do you want to fuck me?"

"No, Sergeant!" Spike barked, maintaining his composure.

"Well, smiling leads to liking and liking leads to fucking." The sergeant pointed at the ground. "Drop and give me fifty, soldier." He spun around on his heel and stalked off while Spike gutted out the push-ups.

A half dozen of the junior cadre started yelling for the trainees to pick up their baggage again. A collective sigh came from the formation as the men lifted their gear and got ready to start running again. The NCOs led the men across the street to the training company's barracks and had them put their gear up on their bunk beds.

Harwood and O'Toole teamed up for a double bunk near one end of the open squad bay.

"Shit, our barracks were right here all of the time and they had us running all over this fucking training post carrying our gear," O'Toole complained, plopping on the lower bunk next to Spike. The mattresses were all *S*-rolled on the bunks, and two sheets with two olive-drab blankets had been tossed on top of each mattress and capped with a pillow cover.

One of the cadre appeared at the end of the squad bay. "Check your bedding and make sure that you have everything. Change into a fatigue uniform and be ready to fall out in ten minutes."

"Oh, shit," O'Toole said, pulling his duffel bag off the top bunk and fumbling with the combination lock. "Fuck, I forgot my combination!"

"Relax. We've got plenty of time." Spike unlocked his duffle bag and removed the set of fatigues that he had placed on top, having assumed at AIT that they would be required to get into a work uniform at Benning. Spike was fully dressed when looked over at O'Toole, who was frantically searching for a belt.

"Fuck! I can't find a damn thing!"

"Here." Spike tossed O'Toole's spare belt with a highly polished buckle and one of his spare Ranger hats, which were required for airborne training because they were soft and could be folded up and put into a pocket.

"Thanks, man."

"Come on, let's get going," Spike said, leading the way down the steps to the exit door.

The senior barracks sergeant was waiting outside with two assistants, and he noted that Harwood and O'Toole were the first ones out of the building. Spike saw thick white lines painted on the asphalt about eight feet apart with black numbers painted on them about five feet apart. He guessed that they were supposed to fall in on the numbers and led O'Toole over to one of the white lines.

The NCO watched Spike and smiled. "What are you doing out here so early?"

"We got dressed early, Sergeant." Spike said, answering for both of them.

"You don't do that in an airborne training company, soldier."

"Yes, Sergeant."

"Well?"

"Well, what, Sergeant?"

"Well, as long as you're out here early—making your buddies look bad—drop!"

O'Toole and Harwood immediately fell forward into the prone push-up position.

"Knock out some push-ups until every single other guy is out here in formation."

Spike started in a slow rhythm and O'Toole matched him. They had done sixty push-ups before the formation seemed complete. The senior NCO yelled for the barracks to be checked for stragglers, and O'Toole dropped on his face against the asphalt. Spike hit seventy-four push-ups and collapsed next to his friend.

The senior NCO put his jump boot on Spike's hip pocket and leaned down to whisper, "Is that all the push-ups you can do?"

Spike nodded and answered. "Yes, Sergeant."

"You ain't going to make it in my school." The sergeant pushed down with his boot. "Seventy-four push-ups ain't enough."

Eyes wide, the whole formation glanced over at the two on the asphalt. Most of them couldn't do twenty-five good airborne push-ups in a row.

The NCO glanced over at one of his assistants and winked. He had been very impressed with Harwood's and O'Toole's efforts. He beckoned for the sergeant to come over and whispered in his ear, "Make Harwood a line NCO."

The sergeant looked over in surprise. "He's only a PFC."

"I can see that."

"The trainee officers are going to be pissed."

The sergeant glared at his new assistant. "Who runs this company—fucking trainees or us?"

The young sergeant looked down at the tips of his boots. "Us."

After a week, the training company was looking sharp when they made their early morning runs. The sound of their boots on the pavement sounded like claps of thunder.

The officers stepped out of the side door of the mess hall, led by a tall, well-built captain who paused near the sidewalk and waited for his eleven lieutenants to catch up.

"Sir," asked a short, stocky lieutenant, "do you think that the training battalion commander will do something about this Harwood kid?"

"We'll know at roll call this morning," the captain said in a clipped manner, as if he didn't want to waste any energy on the junior man. He then led the officers over to the formation area, where the enlisted airborne trainees were waiting for them. Among the only privileges the officers enjoyed over the enlisted men during the three weeks of training were eating in the officers-reserved portion of the mess hall and joining the formation after the enlisted men had already fallen in and taken most of the harassment from the instructors.

"The battalion commander is here," the same stocky lieutenant announced.

"I can see him," the captain retorted nervously. He had been the one who had complained to the senior airborne staff that it was not right for an enlisted man to be a stick leader during airborne training when there were officers available. The company senior instructor had given a private first class command of eighteen men, forcing the officers to double up in the other jump sticks.

The battalion commander watched the captain approaching and then looked over at the young soldier who was the cause of all the telephone calls he had made over the last three days to the post's commanding general.

The captain saluted the lieutenant colonel. "Captain Maynard reporting, sir."

The battalion commander returned the salute. "At ease, Captain. You've got quite a working network in the Army."

"Of what, sir?"

"The name Maynard carries quite a bit of weight in some circles," he noted, glancing at the captain.

"Quite a few generations of us have been soldiers, sir," the captain said, smiling.

"I've heard," the commander said dryly, and if the captain had been paying attention, he would have caught it. "How many generations of Maynards have graduated from West Point?"

"Five, sir." The pride in his voice was extreme.

"How many of those generations earned their way?" The words cut like a knife through the frosty morning air.

"All of them, sir."

"Well, your father did a good job during World War II, but that was with the armor units, not infantry."

Captain Maynard stared at the lieutenant colonel, trying to decipher what he was saying. He didn't like the tone of voice the officer was using. When Maynard was growing up, his father had had a hundred lieutenant colonels working for him, and as a teenager young Maynard had had full-bird colonels catering to him, trying to win his father's favor.

The battalion commander continued, "I made a few telephone calls yesterday after you made your request known." He smiled briefly. "It seems that since your father retired last year, the center of power at the Pentagon has shifted back to the infantry from the armor branch."

"What does that have to do with my request, *Lieutenant Colonel*?" Arrogance dripped off the last two words of the captain's reply.

"We should keep everything in its right perspective, shouldn't we—*Captain*?" The battalion commander smiled again. "You can address me as 'sir.' "

Maynard's face turned bright red. His father had been one of the most powerful generals in the United States Army, and he was not used to lieutenant colonels talking back to him.

"Back to your request. I checked with the post senior staff and they all agree that it is unusual for a private first class to command a training jump stick, but it isn't against any Army policy as long as he doesn't have any trainee officers directly under his command. I don't think he does?" The lieutenant colonel was enjoying the game he was playing with the arrogant young officer.

"I would not have an enlisted man serving in a leadership position higher than my officers in a company that I command, sir."

"You don't command anything here, Captain. We allow you to act as a trainee leader during jump school because you are an officer. But you're still a trainee trying to earn your blood wings just like everyone else—including the enlisted men."

"Sir!"

"I recommend that you fall back in formation."

"Sir, I demand to see the commanding general."

"There are quite a few officers in the chain of command between you and the CG."

"I don't care sir. I'll see all of them. I want to talk to the general."

"Fine. In fact, I'll save you a lot of time and allow you to see him directly—this morning, if you like."

Maynard sensed that something was wrong and backed off a little. "I can wait until after training, sir."

"I'll give you a second chance to reconsider your request to see the general, and I recommend that you call your father first."

At Maynard's look of confusion, the battalion commander tapped his swagger stick against the starched crease of his trouser leg. Twisting his neck against the coolness of his silk camouflage scarf, he grinned, showing all of his teeth. "Ask your father if he knows a

Major General Keith Holt. He's the commanding general of the infantry school.''

"What does he have to do with my father?"

"They were cadets together at West Point, and I don't think they liked each other very much."

Captain Maynard swallowed hard. He whirled around and strode off to join his circle of junior flunkies, who were in awe of him because his father had been a four-star general.

The first two weeks of airborne training went by fast for Harwood and O'Toole, and their trainee jump stick won every company award. O'Toole, assistant stick leader, led the stick through the PT test with flying colors, setting a stick average of 478 points out of a possible 500. O'Toole had scored a perfect 500, while Spike picked up a score of 491.

Captain Maynard was livid. It was looking like Harwood's jump stick was going to beat out the officer-led sticks for the training cycle's award for best stick in the company. Maynard swore that wasn't going to happen and even accused some of the school cadre of letting Harwood's stick beat them during training competition. It had been a very stupid move because it had turned the training cadre against him. The only good thing that had happened during these two weeks was that he had recruited an enlisted ally in his war with Harwood—the soldier who had gotten drunk on the bus.

"He's looking over here again at us, Spike." O'Toole was nervous around the officers. "I really think he's trying to screw you."

"Naw, he's just being an officer. I think he's jealous that our stick is kicking ass during the training exercises."

"Do you think we should let one of the officer sticks beat us?" O'Toole started laughing when he saw the look on Spike's face. "I was just kidding."

"Don't even kid about shit like that." Spike hurried

up the steps that led to the parachute-landing-fall practice deck. "Come on and get this drill started before one of the instructors jumps on our asses." Spike set up on the edge of the four-foot-high platform for a left-sided fall and jumped off when the sergeant gave the command. O'Toole followed him while Spike got at the end of the line and waited for his turn again.

Captain Maynard watched Spike's troops sail through the drill without having to be corrected once by an instructor. That will soon change, he thought, grinning as he waited next to the suspended "agony swings." The harnesses were used to train paratroopers to prepare for landing and to control the suspension lines on their T-10 parachutes. The exercise was called "suspended agony" by the trainees because the leg straps cut into a soldier's crotch after a few minutes of hanging from the harness. Harwood's stick was due to rotate to the harnesses as soon as they had finished PLFs.

Spike emerged from the sawdust pit where they had been practicing PLFs and reported to the trainee company commander: "Sir, Stick Nine is ready for training."

Maynard slowly returned Spike's salute. "Rig your men up, trainee. Have each man get a partner. I'll be yours."

"Yes, sir," Spike said, surprised by the officer volunteering to team up with him.

O'Toole paused a second when he passed Spike's harness. "Watch out. I think he's going to fuck with you."

Nodding, Spike hooked the nylon straps between his legs through the leg loops and then locked the metal female clasps to the center chest plate. He adjusted the straps and spread his legs like a bowlegged cowboy to adjust his pride between the straps. It didn't matter how well the straps were positioned—eventually they hurt—but nobody wanted to get a nut caught under one of the straps and then have his partner hoist him up. The instructors would harass the poor bastard the rest of the day if he had to be lowered again to readjust his leg harness. Like they said, a man couldn't jump back into an aircraft once he jumped out.

The senior cadre noticed the captain teaming up with Harwood and kept his eye on the pair.

Captain Maynard smiled and grabbed hold of the rope that would hoist his partner off the ground. "You rigged, Harwood?"

"Almost, sir. Just let me make a couple of adjustments." Suddenly Spike felt the rope snap tight, so his toes barely touched the ground. He dropped with all of his weight in the harness. "Sir, the sergeant hasn't blown his whistle yet. We haven't started."

"You have, Harwood."

Spike shook his head, glad that he had adjusted his harness before the captain had grabbed the rope. The guy was an asshole. Spike looked over and saw the instructor staring at them. A professional paratrooper, he knew what the captain was doing and blew his whistle for the rest of the trainees to hoist up their partners.

"How are you riding up there, Private Harwood?" Maynard sounded like a fat second-grader who had finally been given the chance to torment the most popular kid in class.

"Starting to hurt, sir." In fact, Spike felt fine, but he wanted the captain to think he was in pain.

"Got a nut caught?" Maynard grabbed a hold of Spike's leg and pulled down hard.

"Naw," Spike said, grinning.

When the whistle blew again, the trainees released the ropes and their partners dropped into the sawdust pits. "Change partners!"

Maynard beckoned for one of the lieutenants to come over. "You can go back to your buddy, Harwood."

The senior instructor appeared out of nowhere. "Not so fast, Harwood. You stay with the captain."

Maynard glared at the sergeant, but didn't dare disagree.

The sergeant helped the trainee captain rig his harness and handed him his leg straps through his spread-apart legs. Maynard slipped the second strap through the leg loop and was starting to lock the chest plate when the instructor grabbed the loose strap and yanked it tight. Just as the wide strap slapped against the captain's scrotum, he felt someone pulling up on the rope. A junior instructor had joined in. Maynard's testicles were both caught under the strap.

The captain gasped for air and groaned, "Drop me! *Drop me!*"

"What's that, Captain?" Leaning forward as if to hear better, the senior instructor grabbed Maynard's leg and placed all of his weight against it. "Something wrong, sir?"

"Ahhh!" Maynard screamed. "My nuts!"

"Oh, you want to come back down?" The instructor looked over at the NCO holding the rope. "Drop him, please. His nuts are caught under the harness." The NCO let go of the rope and the captain crashed into the sawdust pit. The senior man bent over, making it look as if he was helping Maynard loosen his leg straps, and whispered so that only Maynard could hear him, "Don't you ever try fucking with one of my students again—sir!"

Spike saw the look in Maynard's eyes as the sergeant whispered, and he knew that somehow he had made a dangerous enemy.

O'Toole slipped his tray onto the table and went over to the milk machine. He returned carrying a glass in each hand, chocolate in his right and plain in his left.

"Thirsty?" Spike asked, holding a heaping forkful of spaghetti in front of his mouth.

"I just don't want to have to stand in line again." When O'Toole had sat down, he said, "That was some nasty shit the captain tried pulling on you this afternoon. Everybody's talking about it."

Spike shrugged. "I don't know what I did to piss him off."

"He's just an asshole." O'Toole drank a full glass of milk and sat the empty glass down. "The sarge said some officers are like that, but when they get their asses over in Vietnam, they learn to respect enlisted men—real quick!"

Spike abruptly changed the subject. Maynard wasn't worth getting bent out of shape for. "I'm glad we're having spaghetti tonight. We're going to need all of the energy we can get for tomorrow." He broke a piece of garlic bread and covered it with butter.

"Are you scared?"

"A little. I think everyone's scared a little during jump week."

"I hope we have good weather and don't have to sit in the ready shed all day."

"Yeah." Spike looked over and saw Beems staring at him. "You'd think that guy would be tired of fucking with me by now."

O'Toole turned around in his seat and flipped him the finger.

"Watch out or he'll put you on his list of people he's going to whip," Spike noted sarcastically, returning his attention to his food.

A trainee dropped his tray next to the open seat at Spike's table and sat down. O'Toole glanced at the univited guest and then ignored him. There were no reserved seats in a training mess hall. The trainee started cating, smacking his lips so loud that the trainees from nearby tables looked over at him. When he pushed his chair back from the table and started shoveling the food into his mouth, O'Toole said, "Let's go." He removed a few pieces of bread from his tray and stood up. Agreeing with his buddy, Spike left the table.

Beems grinned and watched the two soldiers leave the mess hall. Then the man who had been eating like a pig picked up his tray and joined his buddy, laughing.

The next morning the barracks lights went on at four o'clock. Waking up, Spike instantly remembered

that this was the day for their first jump. Excitedly he
grabbed his shaving kit and towel and hurried toward
the showers before the rest of the platoon got moving.
O'Toole was already drying off when he set his gear
on the bench.

"You're up early."

"I woke up at three and couldn't go back to sleep."

"You should have woken me up."

"Shit, you need your beauty sleep."

Spike shaved and brushed his teeth in the shower.
He dried off quickly and pushed his way out of the
now crowded latrine. Beems was standing at the top of
the stairs, waiting to get in, when Spike stepped out of
the open doorway wearing only a towel wrapped around
his waist. Beems elbowed Spike in his side, knocking
the wind out of him.

"Something wrong, Harwood?"

Spike looked up and dropped his shaving kit. He
had taken enough of the man's crap and was going to
fight him even if it meant getting thrown out of jump
school. Suddenly a hand grabbed Beems by his shoulder and spun him around. "You report to me before
breakfast formation!"

Beems hadn't seen the black cap standing around
the corner of the stairs. "Yes, Sergeant!"

When he fell out for the breakfast formation, Spike
saw Beems doing push-ups in the dark with the senior
NCO's shadow looming over him.

"I wouldn't let him bother me if I were you," a
voice said from behind him.

"I'm not"—Spike tried recognizing who was standing in the shadows and made out the shape of a figure
wearing a baseball cap—"Sergeant." He assumed the
owner of the voice was one of the cadre.

"You'd better get over to breakfast." The voice
wasn't familiar, but Spike obeyed anyway and set off
at a run. He was just reaching the line outside of the
mess hall when O'Toole caught up to him. "What was

the battalion commander talking to you about?" he asked.

Spike was surprised. "Nothing much." All through breakfast, though, he puzzled over why the lieutenant colonel had said that to him.

How had he known about Beems and him?

The parachute hangar smelled of mothballs and burned jet fuel. Through the partially open doors Spike saw four C-130 cargo airplanes. His company was standing in line, drawing their T-10 parachutes and the B-4 bags to carry them in once they had landed on the ground.

"I shouldn't have eaten so much for breakfast," moaned O'Toole. "I've got to shit."

"There's a latrine over there." Spike motioned with his head. "Go ahead and I'll hold your place in line."

O'Toole broke ranks and ran over. The senior instructor ignored him as he kept his eye on Captain Maynard and his group of officer flunkies. He could see that Maynard was overacting to hide his fear and smiled. The first of the five jumps required to win blood wings was always the hardest. Most of the trainees were afraid of the night qualification jump, but that was actually one of the easiest ones. It just sounded scary.

Spike kept looking over his shoulder for O'Toole as he neared the riggers issuing chutes. He was next in line and O'Toole still hadn't come back.

"Issue me two chutes—my buddy's in the latrine."

"You'll get two—a main and a reserve."

"Make it four then."

The rigger was about to say something sarcastic when the senior black cap nodded for the rigger to do what Spike said.

O'Toole blushed when he joined Spike in the rigging area. "Fuck, I had diarrhea."

"Probably just a case of butterflies," Spike said as he handed O'Toole his chutes and B-4 bag.

"Do you think so?" O'Toole said, worried that he would have the runs once they boarded the aircraft.

"Sure of it. Here." Spike handed O'Toole a couple of antacid tablets. "They'll settle your stomach."

"Thanks, man."

The senior airborne instructor mounted the wooden platform in the center of the hangar and raised a hand-held megaphone. "Listen up!" He waited for the excited hum to die down before continuing. "Stick Nine has been selected as the honor stick for this training class." He paused to let the surprising announcement sink in. It was the first time that an enlisted-led stick had won the honor. "Stick Nine will be the lead stick jumping today, and Private First Class Harwood will be the first man out of the door."

"Spike, we did it!" As O'Toole reached over to pat Spike's shoulder, the B-4 bag he was holding in the center of his chest slipped down.

"O'Toole, hold your bag in place so that I can hand you your leg straps," Spike barked, trying to hide his excitement over winning the honor stick by concentrating on getting his buddy suited up.

O'Toole pulled the gray B-4 bag back under the emergency-release plate on his chest and reached down between his legs for the strap Spike was handing to him. He locked the two leg straps to the release plate and slipped in the safety pin.

Spike stepped around to his front to pound the chest plate with his fist to insure that it wouldn't accidently release the four straps that held the main parachute on O'Toole's back. Once he was satisfied, he held up O'Toole's reserve chute so he could thread the wide cloth belt through the loops. Spike pushed against the reserve chute so O'Toole could attach the two snap links to their D-rings on his harness.

"Put your hands on your head." Spike slipped the strap through the buckle and O'Toole grunted. He laced the waist strap back halfway through the buckle and formed a quick release so that all O'Toole would have to do is pull on the tab and the strap would let go. Then he could detach the reserve chute and get to the quick-release plate on his chest and out of the main chute harness when he landed.

"It's too tight," O'Toole murmured, bending forward to adjust the harness straps between his legs.

"Don't forget that the opening shock will loosen your whole harness."

"Yeah. And by then my nuts will be numbed for life." O'Toole wiggled a little to make a few minor adjustments.

"Help me into my chute." Spike pulled his main over his shoulders and turned his back to O'Toole so that he could lift up on the bottom of the chute and then hand him his leg straps between his legs.

"I should have let you suit up first. This is fucking torture," O'Toole growled, feeling the chin strap of his helmet rubbing against his neck.

Spike placed both of his hands on his reserve parachute attached across his stomach and sighed. He was rigged and ready to make his first parachute jump. He thought that he would be scared, but actually he was only excited and looking forward to boarding the aircraft.

"Line up for your rigger's check. Stick nine in the front." The senior instructor laid the megaphone on the platform and jumped down to the cement floor. He was personally going to check Spike's stick. He had made over a thousand static-line jumps and was one of the best master blasters at Benning.

Captain Maynard glared at the instructor as he passed. "I should have been first jumper," he wanted to shout.

Spike raised his hands and placed them on the top of his helmet with his legs spread comfortably apart. The NCO black cap checked the safety pin in the reserve chute and patted the side of Spike's reserve. Spike turned so that the sergeant could check his waist buckle, and the black cap patted him again without saying a word. Spike turned his back to the instructor and felt the NCO checking his static line.

"Here." The sergeant handed Spike the snap link on his static line over his shoulder. Spike hooked the link to the front of his reserve handle and felt a sharp slap on his rear.

Spike shuffled over to the opening in the huge doors and waited until each man in his stick had been personally checked by a jump master. Then one of the junior instructors ran to the front of the stick and waved for them to follow him. Hearing the roar of the C-130 engines, Spike followed up the tail ramp. They boarded in reverse order so that Spike took the nylon mesh seat closest to the side jump door, O'Toole next to him.

The aircraft filled quickly. The paratrooper trainees had practiced boarding a wooden mock-up C-130, and the process was smooth and disciplined. As Maynard passed by, he glared down at Spike. He smiled and that made the officer even more angry. Spike locked his seat belt and checked to see if all of his men had buckled themselves in. Seeing that a couple of them looked terrified, Spike balled his fist and gave them the power sign, which helped them relax a little.

The C-130 taxied out onto the runway, and Spike coughed as the wheels left the ground. The thought going through his mind was that he would not be inside of the plane when it landed.

Turbulence shook the aircraft as it banked to line up for its pass over the drop zone. Spike watched the senior jump master's face for a sign that he should get ready. In reply, the NCO winked, and for the first time Spike realized that the instructor liked him. The sergeant then pointed at the side jump doors and yelled something to his assistants. They unlatched the doors and opened them. A loud roar created by the engines and the wind rushing along the airframe filled the interior of the aircraft. A couple of the trainees crossed themselves and whispered Hail Marys.

The jump master, holding both of his hands against his headset, went over to the side door where Spike was sitting. He leaned out to locate the drop zone and check the wind direction on the ground, indicated by a purple smoke grenade set off by the ground crew. He pulled back inside and yelled something. No one could hear what he said, but the red jump lights went on and the sticks understood that the jump master was giving the command for them to stand up.

Spike automatically went through the list of jump commands that they had rehearsed for the past two weeks, and reached up to grab the steel cable that ran the length of the aircraft. He hooked his static-line snap link onto it and yanked down hard to insure that it had locked shut. Then he slipped the safety cotter pin in place.

He was facing the jump door when he heard the jump master yell the words that he would never forget as long as he lived:

"Stand in the door!"

As Spike started inching forward, Captain Maynard appeared out of nowhere and hooked up in front of him to take the lead position in the open doorway. Spike saw the hatred in his eyes, but he remained calm and looked over at the jump master, whose face was red with anger. The red light went off and the green go light flashed on. The pilot had given the command that they were in a jump position over the drop zone. Because it would last only a few seconds, the jump master didn't have time to make any corrections and slapped Maynard's rear. "Go!"

For the first time since he had stolen Spike's place, Maynard looked down at the ground. Seeing tiny trucks and ambulances 1,250 feet below, he froze.

"Go!" The jump master hit Maynard again on his rear.

Maynard looked over at Spike, fear contouring his face.

"Go! Go!" The jump master cried, seeing the starboard stick members disappearing through the opposite door.

Spike shuffled forward and shoved the back of Maynard's parachute, pushing him out of the way. Pausing for a split second, Spike looked at the jump master and winked. Then he jumped.

"Airborne!" His excited scream was lost on the wind. He counted slowly in his mind: one thousand-one, one thousand-two, one thousand-three, one thousand-four, one thousand-five, one thousand-six, and felt a sharp tug on his harness as his parachute silk caught the wind and flared open. He spread his risers apart and checked his camouflage canopy for any holes or tears before checking for any paratroopers who might be on a collision course with him.

The C-130s disappeared in an instant, leaving the sky filled with hundreds of open parachutes. Hearing the instructors working the DZ below calling to jumpers to slip either to their right or left to avoid midair collisions, Spike was surprised how clearly their voices traveled upward.

"I love it!" Spike heard O'Toole cry from somewhere above him and he smiled. The fear of the unknown was gone, replaced by a tremendous exhilaration. He wanted to float on the breeze that lifted his parachute for the rest of the day.

He reached up as high as he could on his right riser and pulled down to slip past a nearby paratrooper who was staring down at the rapidly rising plowed drop zone. Spike could see the large numbers on the back of the soldier's helmet and the tape bar that signified an officer. It was Maynard.

The minute-long descent was over far too soon for Spike and O'Toole. Spike glanced over and saw that his friend was hanging spread-eagled and yelled to him, "Put your feet together and prepare for landing." Spike himself had already assumed the proper landing position and stared straight ahead so that he wouldn't anticipate the landing and tighten his muscles. His toes touched the soft, sandy soil, and he rolled over and then back up on his feet. He undid his side strap and pulled the safety pin out of his quick-release link and turned the dial so that he could hit the pressure pad with the palm of his hand and release all four of his harness straps simultaneously. The instant the strain was removed from the parachute risers, the main canopy started flapping in the soft ground breeze. Spike ran around the billowing silk and collapsed it. Grabbing the apex, he started folding up the lightweight material so that he could stuff it into his B-4 bag. He had completed the whole maneuver and flipped the gray bag over his shoulders almost before he realized that he had landed safely. All of the long hours of training had paid off perfectly.

"Spike!" O'Toole ran to catch up to his buddy as he headed toward their assigned DZ pickup point. "I love it! Airborne!"

Spike smiled. "Yeah, I had a hard-on all the way down."

"Bullshit," O'Toole said, glancing at the front of Spike's fatigue pants.

"Get away from me." Spike started laughing. "Yeah, man. I loved it too. Scared me at first when we were in the door, but once my chute opened, I was all right."

"Scared you a little? I thought I would shit my pants when the jump master opened our door and the wind roared in."

"Four more jumps to go and we got our wings," Spike said, adjusting the bag on his shoulders.

"I wish it were four hundred more." O'Toole wiggled his hips like a little boy who has to urinate.

Spike saw Maynard running toward the bushes, unbuckling his pants as he ran. "Looks like the captain has to take an emergency shit."

"Wait until the jump master gets a hold of his ass! I bet they'll throw him out of jump school for what he pulled up there."

Spike watched the captain disappear in the brush. "Don't hold your breath." He didn't know much about the captain, but he sensed that he had some powerful sponsors.

O'Toole turned around and looked up at the last of the paratroopers floating on the wind. "Shit, it doesn't last very long."

"Once we get to a regular unit, we're supposed to jump with the new steerable chutes and can these old T-10s," Spike noted, hefting the load on his shoulders again to flex his muscles. "We'll jump the steerables at three thousand feet, maybe four, and that'll give us a long time in the air."

"I can't wait. I really do love this shit, Spike!" O'Toole started a slow jog toward the cattle trucks and started singing softly: "I wanna be an airborne ranger/Living a life of blood and danger . . ."

Spike shook his head and smiled. O'Toole was like a kid who had just gotten his first piece of ass. "Wait up for me, asshole."

O'Toole laughed and started running faster, working off the excess adrenaline coursing through his veins. "Catch me, you leg motherfucker! Five bucks I beat you in!"

Once aboard the open-bed cattle truck, Spike hopped on top of the stack of B-4 bags stuffed full of used parachutes. He had been placed in charge of the detail taking the chutes back to the rigger sheds to be repacked for their next jumps. Feeling the warm breeze drying the light sweat covering his face, he leaned back against the gray bags and watched the tall loblolly pines sticking up through the stands of scrub oak flash by.

A column of M551 Sheridan airborne-assault vehicles, heading out to the ranges to fire their 152mm main guns, passed Spike's truck going in the opposite direction. The armor convoy sent up huge, billowing dust clouds in its wake. The rest of Spike's detail started complaining about the dust, but nothing was going to bring Spike down from his good mood. He let the wind brush the dust off his face and smiled to himself. He could feel the grit covering his teeth and leaned way out over the side panels to spit. His thoughts turned to Captain Hanson and he smiled. He couldn't wait to write him about his first jump. He knew that he had come a long way in a short time. Only a few months ago he had been locked in a drug-rehabilitation cell in the Oakland County Children's Village. Now he was a paratrooper in the United States Army. He shook off his disbelief. It had been a very lucky day for him when he had walked by the recruiting station, carrying Peter. If it hadn't been for Captain Hanson, he would still be walking the streets in Pontiac. It had been Captain Hanson's encouraging letters from Vietnam that had pulled him through basic training and advanced-infantry training, and it had been his fear of letting the captain down that had compelled him to achieve every honor that was available to him.

Spike smiled. He might have come a long way, but there was still a lot of unexplored road left ahead of him. The Army only saw one color—green—and they judged a man based on what he could produce and not on his family background or what kind of trouble a guy had gotten into before he had joined up.

The truck pulled onto an asphalt road and turned left toward the main base area and Fort Benning. Spike reached into his rear pocket and opened the Army manual on Russian-made small arms. The pocketsized field manual had cost him ten dollars, but it was worth it. The supply sergeant who had sold it to him had wanted fifteen, but had lowered the price because Spike was such a good customer. He owned every manual on *Lessons Learned* in Vietnam and had a better library in his footlocker than most company training rooms. He studied constantly, even during ten-minute breaks. It had started out casually and then it had become a consuming desire, especially when he received a letter from Captain Hanson that mentioned a piece of equipment he was using in Vietnam. Spike wanted to know everything about Vietnam and the special tactics being developed over there.

Spike and his detail were released back to their barracks and given the rest of the day off to prepare for the next day's two jumps. Spike happened to glance over at the captain and his flunkies when he hopped from the truck, and was met by hateful stares.

The incident in the C-130 was never brought up again, but Captain Maynard and all of the officers were scheduled to different aircraft from Spike's for the remaining jumps.

Later that week, Spike stood in line on the drop zone and waited for the battalion commander to reach him with his set of blood wings. As he idly watched a pair of Hueys maneuver around the edge of the DZ and land somewhere behind a stand of scrub oak, his thoughts weren't on the awards ceremony, but on what would happen the next day. He had turned down his leave and had asked for a direct assignment to Vietnam. He needn't have worried. Their orders had come in the day before and almost all of the enlisted men were headed for Vietnam as replacements to the 101st Airborne Division or the 173rd Airborne Brigade. Spike smiled. He had lucked out and was being assigned to the 173rd, along with O'Toole. He hoped that he would have a chance to see Captain Hanson when he got over there.

"PFC Harwood," the battalion commander said, pausing in front of Spike. Instantly he came out of his reverie and stiffened to attention. "I'm very impressed with your leadership." The bluntness of the statement caught Spike off guard, and he didn't know how to reply. The lieutenant colonel pinned a set of silver jump wings above Spike's left breast pocket. "Congratulations— paratrooper!"

"Thank you, sir."

The battalion commander reached back and the

senior black cap handed him a set of buck sergeant stripes. Using safety pins, the commander attached the stripes to Spike's sleeve. "Maybe we should change that congratulations to sergeant."

Spike looked down at the gold-and-green stripes, at a total loss for words. He had known that they were going to send him to the Shake 'n' Bake program, but he hadn't expected stripes so soon, especially jumping over corporal.

"It took a little doing and a letter from Major General Holt, but we pulled it off. I must say that you've been one of the best trainee leaders we've ever had pass through this course, and I'm proud to have been your battalion commander."

O'Toole summed up the collective feeling of the enlisted men standing nearby: "Hot shit!"

CHAPTER FIVE

✪✪✪✪✪✪✪✪✪✪✪✪✪✪✪

COMMIE BLOOD

Wilting from the searing heat, accompanied by what seemed like one hundred percent humidity, Spike sat in the shade next to a long plywood and tin hootch. He was wearing all new jungle fatigues with the issue wide-brim green hat. Even the clerks smiled when they passed him because his gear identified him as a newcomer to Vietnam.

"Sarge?"

Spike stood up and nodded his head at the private. The soldier didn't look like a paratrooper. He wore a wide leather watch band and a half-dozen strands of hippie beads around his neck. "Yes, trooper?"

"I've been sent over to take you to get your weapon."

"Thanks." Spike picked up the rest of his gear and followed the soldier back to the supply hootch. "Are you with one of the line units?"

The soldier shook his head. "No, I'm in supply." He glanced over his shoulder and stared at Spike's stripes. "You made buck sergeant fast."

"Yeah." Spike left it at that and followed the private into the large general-purpose tent that had been stretched over a two-by-four frame and a cement floor. The flaps covering the entrance were pulled back, and a large floor fan was operating at full speed, trying to pull the hot air out of the canvas oven. Behind the plywood issue bench, a staff sergeant looked up from the porn magazine he had been reading and instantly frowned when he saw the seventeen-year-old wearing buck sergeant stripes. "What the fuck do you want?"

"A weapon," Spike snapped, tired of being treated like shit because he had busted his ass and earned three stripes in training.

"Whose fatigue jacket do you have on?" The sarcasm was accentuated as the sergeant reached down to adjust his erection.

"Play with yourself on your own time. I came here to get a weapon and some ammunition—not watch you jack off," Spike growled, not about to take any crap.

"You cocky little shit, you're talking to an NCO."

"I am a noncommissioned officer myself, as you might have noticed."

"A fucking Shake'n'Bake."

"Do you want to try to shake my ass?" Spike shouted, spoiling for a fight.

"What's going on here?" a first lieutenant called, stepping through the entrance.

The staff sergeant fixed his jaw. "Nothing, sir. We were just about ready to issue this here 'sergeant' a weapon."

The lieutenant grinned. "You look too young to be wearing those strips, Sergeant."

Spike didn't trust himself to answer civilly and looked down the row of weapons in their secured racks.

"The lieutenant's talking to you, Sergeant," the supply NCO threatened, slapping his open palm down hard on the makeshift counter.

Spike glared at the NCO and slowly turned to look over at his company executive officer. He had had his fill of harassment about his rank and wasn't about to start off his assignment with the company by being bullied. "I'm seventeen years old, sir, and I've earned every stripe on my sleeves."

"I don't doubt it." The officer laid his .45-caliber pistol on the counter. "There's something wrong with the safety on this weapon, Sergeant."

"No problem, sir." The NCO opened a footlocker and handed the officer a pistol still wrapped in its original shipping foil.

The officer paused before leaving the tent. "Which company in the battalion have you been assigned to, Sergeant Harwood?"

"Bravo Company, sir."

"Good. I'm glad to have you. I'm the executive officer for Bravo. If there's anything that I can do for you while you're still in the rear area, just ask. That's what we're here for."

Encouraged by the man's friendliness, Spike ventured to ask, "Sir, do you know where Captain Hanson is assigned?"

The officer paused in the entrance and slowly turned around. "Do you know him?"

"Yes."

"He's with Alpha Company at Dak To."

"Isn't Bravo Company there also?" Spike asked. He had heard some of the clerks talking about the units when he had been in-processing.

"Yes, two whole battalions will be out there before the end of the week. It's funny you mention Captain Hanson. I just heard that his company is in a big firefight at the north end of the valley." The officer smiled. "You just might get a chance to meet him sooner that you think. Bravo Company is being assembled to reinforce Alpha."

"I just might. A chopper is due to fly me out to Dak To later this afternoon."

The officer looked over at the supply sergeant. "Issue him one of those new shotguns we just received, if he wants one."

"But, sir, I'm holding them for . . ." the supply sergeant protested, reaching for a new M16. He had already made plans to sell the shotguns to a couple of NCOs.

"Issue him one if he wants it!"

"Yes, sir."

The lieutenant left the tent.

"You *don't* want a shotgun, right?" the staff sergeant said, handing Spike the M16.

"I don't know. Let me look at one."

"They're locked up."

"Well, you heard the lieutenant. Let me see one."

The sergeant's face flushed as he headed to the rear of the tent and uncovered the case of new riot shotguns.

Spike was smiling as he left the tent. For the first time since he had arrived in Vietnam, he had had a chance to strike back at the people who had been teasing him. He really didn't want the riot shotgun and preferred an M16, but he figured that he could have some fun with the smart-assed NCO.

"We just got these in from the States and are supposed to issue only one per platoon for tunnel work and village sweeps. If you take it, you'll be the one in your platoon who has to crawl into the tunnels." The NCO was partially telling the truth, but he was trying to scare Spike into not taking the weapon.

Spike racked the pump shotgun open and then checked out the attached bayonet that folded under the barrel. He liked the feel of it in his hands. "Five rounds?"

The sergeant nodded and reached under the counter for a box of shotgun shells. "They've issued a new fleshette round for it that's better than buckshot."

Spike picked up the round and hefted it in his hand. "Give me a box of ammo and I'll test it back at the battalion range."

"You *don't* want to take the shotgun."

"Maybe not, but I want to test it first." Spike took the box of shells and left the tent with the shotgun held down in a German carry at his side. The battalion had built a small rifle range at the back of the perimeter, where new replacements could zero and test-fire their weapons.

Spike loaded the shotgun and laid it down on a sandbag. Walking fifty feet down the range, he propped up a four-foot square of plywood for a target. When he returned to his weapon, he noticed that he had drawn a small crowd of spectators. He didn't need an audience, but there wasn't much he could do to run them off, so he tried to ignore them as they took up seats on the nearby bunkers.

The first round kicked harder against his shoulder than he had anticipated and a third of the fleshettes missed the target. Spike laid his weapon down and walked down to check his target. The small steel darts had penetrated the plywood at different depths, but the effect was sobering. The fleshettes would be devastating against a human target, especially at night when visibility was limited. He was beginning to like the idea of carrying a shotgun.

"Nice spread," a friendly voice noted. "That should work well in the jungle."

"Yeah," Spike said, trying to pull one of the darts out of the wood with his fingers. He couldn't budge it.

"Try this." The paratrooper handed Spike a black-bladed fighting knife.

"Thanks." Spike dug the fleshette out of the layered wood and looked at it. "I sure wouldn't want to get hit with one of these."

"Me neither. I've heard about fleshettes for the 105mm howitzers, but not for shotguns."

"American innovation."

As Spike returned to his shotgun, the soldier followed him. "Is that yours?"

Spike smiled. "Yep."

The wind blowing through the open doors of the chopper made the ride enjoyable. Spike sat next to the door gunner and watched the jungle landscape slip by below them. Seven other replacements were riding in the same chopper to the Dak To site, where the 173rd Airborne Brigade was building what would soon be its forward operations area. The 2nd Battalion was already in place around an old Special Forces camp, securing the area while the engineers built the fighting bunkers and dirt berms to protect the headquarters element.

Spike noticed the fear in some of the replacements' eyes, but he himself was happy as hell. There was an excellent chance that he would be able to spend a couple of hours with Captain Hanson before getting sent out to where his company was patrolling, and he was dying to see the look on his mentor's face when he saw the sergeant stripes.

A twin-barreled 40mm anti-aircraft gun mounted on an M48 tank chassis opened fire to the west of the chopper, and Spike saw the tracer rounds streak parallel to the ground at a target on a dark green mountain. The sound of the weapon was lost in the roar of the wind surrounding the helicopter. Spike turned his attention back to the path the aircraft was taking. They were following the course of the Vietnamese highway that ran the length of the wide, lush valley. Spike didn't know the name of the road, but he could see the small outposts that lined the important supply route.

The helicopter's rotor blades changed pitch, and the aircraft gained altitude to fly over a particularly dangerous stretch of the highway before entering the Dak To area. The pilot pointed down at a heavily bombed spot on the side of a steep hill and spoke to his copilot over the intercom set that Spike was also patched in to.

"That's where the 173rd got in a fight yesterday."

"Bad?" The copilot's voice shook from the vibration of the chopper.

"I hear they lost twenty-four KIA and a couple dozen wounded."

"What about the NVA?"

"You know those reports are bullshit. They reported killing a hundred and four and saw blood trails leading back into the jungle . . ." The pilot glanced over at his friend. "Probably four NVA dead and one wounded deer."

Pushing the earphones tighter against his head so that he could hear better, Spike pushed the intercom button and asked the pilot, "Do you know the unit that got in that fight?"

The pilot sheepishly glanced over his shoulder at the young buck sergeant, who had been given an intercom headset because he was the senior passenger onboard the aircraft. "No, except that it was the 173rd." The chopper banked to the left and started descending for a landing. "They've only got a small headquarters element down there and two companies so far—I think Alpha and Bravo."

"Thanks." Spike knew then that it had to have been Alpha Company that had tangled with the NVA because his own company was standing guard in the new base area being built.

The helicopter landed softly in the center of the helipad constructed to one side of the new runway the engineers were cutting out of the jungle. Each end of the small strip the Special Forces camp had built for small Caribou aircraft was being lengthened to be able to handle C-130s.

The first one off the chopper, Spike paused just long enough to remove his small rucksack from under the seat and left the chopper area bent over so that the rotor blades wouldn't take his head off. A sergeant first class waiting for the replacements to disembark waved for Spike to join him back far enough away from the chopper so that the red clay dust wasn't blowing in his face.

"Sergeant Monk," the NCO said, holding out his hand.

"Spike Harwood," Spike replied, shaking hands.

"Welcome to Dak To forward support base," the

NCO said neutrally, having noticed that Spike was too young to be anything except a rapid-promotiom NCO. He didn't agree with the Stateside promotion policy, but then again, he didn't like senior NCOs finding jobs in the rear areas so they didn't have to hump the jungle as platoon sergeants and squad leaders. "Which company are you assigned to?"

"Bravo."

Monk looked Spike over solemnly. Why assign a teenage buck sergeant to a line airborne infantry outfit and an experienced NCO like himself to a headquarters operations slot? He had made it known to everyone who would listen that he wanted a field assignment. He had been trained to lead infantry troops in combat, and that was what he wanted to do. The battalion commander had instead decided that he was too valuable for field duty and had assigned him to the headquarters. "They have a command post set up over there on the far side of the runway. Wait here until I get the rest of the replacements taken care of, and I'll show you how to get over there."

Spike dropped his rucksack next to a pile of sandbags and took a seat. Monk directed all of the other replacements to their respective units and then returned. "C'mon, Harwood, it's time that you saw your new home."

Spike picked up his pack and slung his shotgun over his shoulder. He had found an empty Claymore mine-carrying pouch to use as an ammo bag for his shotgun shells and had it slung over his right shoulder. As they walked, the bag bounced gently on his left hip. "By any chance, do you know a Captain Hanson?"

The senior NCO stopped and turned slowly around. "Why?"

"He's a friend of mine from back in the States. You could say that he recruited me."

Monk took a long look at the young sergeant before adding, "How close a friend?"

"Pretty close." Spike said, beginning to get irritated.

"Best friend?"

"He's like a dad to me." Spike wanted to take back the words as soon as they left his mouth. The sergeant might be the kind of NCO who hated officers and would use the information to screw him in the future.

A look of deep pain filled the sergeant's eyes. "I know Captain Hanson, real well. He's a fine officer who takes damn good care of his men—probably to a fault." The last part of the sentence was added after the NCO had swallowed hard. "We'd better hurry if you want to see the captain before he . . . he leaves."

"He's here?"

"Yeah, over by the runway." The NCO started hurrying toward the sound of bulldozers and heavy equipment expanding the runway, and Spike had to run to catch up, along a path that had been cleared through high elephant grass.

The NCO stopped. "He's over there."

Spike turned to look where the sergeant was pointing. Some distance away, next to an airmobile D6B tractor, four paratroopers were sitting on their helmets, but he could see that none of them was Hanson. "Where?"

The NCO wouldn't look at him. "Ask one of those troopers. They're from his company."

As Spike approached, one of the paratroopers looked up. Spike saw the weariness and pain in the man's eyes, and then he saw the row of dark green rubber bags. "Can you tell me where Captain Hanson is?"

"He's the third body bag from the end." The paratrooper went back to scratching something that only he understood in the red laterite dust at his feet. "Don't open the bag."

Spike's eyes widened as the full impact of what was going on hit him. The four men were waiting to load dead paratroopers on a Medevac chopper. He approached the long row of body bags and counted as he passed the lumpy containers, stopping at the foot of the third one. He saw the graves-registration tag attached to the handle and bent over to check the name. It was the captain. Spike put his rucksack down gently next to the row of dead troopers so that he wouldn't disturb the dust. He could see that a fine film of red laterite had already coated the body bag.

Sergeant Monk stood in the distance and watched the young buck sergeant kneeling in front of the dead captain. It was a hell of a way to be welcomed to his new unit, but Monk knew that Harwood would have never forgiven him if he hadn't told him before the captain's body was shipped back to the mortuary.

Spike knelt in front of the body bag for a long time, letting his mind wander back to Pontiac and the first time that he had seen the captain in the upstairs window. It seemed like a century ago, yet it had been less than a year. He could feel a stinging sensation on his face as he looked down at the lump inside of the death container and he blinked his eyes. The stinging wasn't caused by sleet, like the icy rain of that night last November, but from the particles of clay that were being blown through the air by the departing helicopters.

The four-man detail kept glancing over at Spike, not knowing what they should do and at the same time feeling that they should do something. They ended up doing nothing, which was for the best.

Spike took a deep breath and bent down over the body bag. He had to know for sure. He located the zipper and started to unzip the bag.

"I wouldn't do that if I were you, Sergeant." The paratrooper who had spoken earlier started to stand up, but after seeing the look on the Spike's face, he decided that the young NCO could see for himself.

Spike pulled the zipper down slowly. Hanson's head was turned to one side, and Spike could see that a bullet had hit his mentor's lower jaw, removing half of his face. Spike continued pulling the zipper down until the bag was completely open. Captain Hanson had been hit at least a dozen times at close range by an automatic weapon.

As Sergeant Monk started walking over, he saw that the young airborne sergeant was holding one of the captain's hands, staring into the open eyes of the dead man.

"Do you want to wait here until the chopper comes?" Monk asked, penetrating Spike's numbness.

Spike nodded and then in a husky voice said, "Yes, please. We're blood brothers." He squeezed the captain's bloody hand.

The senior NCO nodded, not trusting his voice anymore, and waved for a couple of the detail men to pop smoke for the arriving helicopters.

Spike stayed with Captain Hanson until the last moment and then walked him over to the chopper as they loaded his body. As he did, Sergeant Monk noticed something in the young sergeant's mouth. It looked like a medal attached to a gold chain around his neck. As one of the detail men rushed off into the elephant grass to vomit, Spike stared blankly at the departing choppers.

"They'll take good care of him." That was all that the sergeant could think of saying to Spike.

Spike nodded. "Where's my company's CP?"

The NCO pointed across the runway to the top of a sandbag bunker. Spike picked up his gear and walked directly across the wide strip. The sergeant stood with the rest of the detail and watched the small teenager.

"There goes one cold motherfucker," one of the detail men noted.

Sergeant Monk nodded in agreement. He had been in Vietnam for almost twenty months and hadn't seen a display of such cool before. The captain's body had already started to bloat from the heat, and the wounds he had received were gruesome. When Spike had reached into the body bag and held the dead officer's hand, Monk had wanted to throw up himself.

Spike dropped his steel-framed rucksack next to the entrance of the company command post and ducked to enter the sandbagged structure.

"Can I help you, Sergeant?" asked a voice from the back of the bunker.

"Yes, I'm assigned to Bravo Company," Spike said, blinking his eyes to adjust to the dark interior.

"Don't you address officers as sir?" The voice carried an inquisitive tone.

"Yes I do, sir, when I can see them." Spike blinked again. "It's really bright outside."

"Sorry about that, Sergeant. I've been in here most of the day and forgot." The captain approached and held out his hand. "I'm Captain Whitmore, your CO."

Spike shook hands and looked around the bunker. A staff sergeant sat near a row of field telephones, and a second lieutenant was sitting in a corner drinking a cup of coffee.

"We'll have to wait until the first sergeant gets back from making his rounds of the perimeter before assigning you to a platoon, but I'm almost sure it will be with the First," the captain said, returning to the corner where the lieutenant was sitting. "Tell me a little bit about yourself."

"Sergeant Harwood." Spike put his shotgun down against the wall.

"Sergeant Harwood, eh? Where are you coming from?"

"Airborne school, sir."

The lieutenant rolled his eyes. "Directly from jump school?"

"Shit!" the captain cried disgustedly.

"Something wrong, sir?"

"Yes! But not with you—just the fucking system that ships raw trainees directly to a fucking war!" This kid was way too young, he thought, to be leading an infantry fire team. "Well, we won't have very long to get to know each other. I've only got three weeks left in-country."

Spike grinned his congratulations, but his thoughts returned to Captain Hanson and he wished that the two captains had switched places.

The entrance light was blocked as a huge black sergeant entered the bunker.

"How does it look out there, Top?" the captain asked, marking a map with a blue grease pencil.

"Excellent. They've got all of the roofs on their fighting bunkers and are sandbagging their alternate positions. We should be in very good shape by dark." The company first sergeant dropped his gear next to his field desk and sat down.

"We have a new NCO," the captain said dourly, pointing at Spike.

The sergeant took his time looking the teenager over before speaking. "Welcome to Bravo Company, 2nd Battalion 503rd Infantry—Airborne."

"Thanks, Sergeant."

"We're short an E-5 in the First Platoon's third squad." He glanced over at the two officers. "Do you have any disagreement with that, Lieutenant?"

The officer shook his head.

"Fine. I'll take him back out there and introduce him to his platoon sergeant as soon as I call in my report to battalion." The first sergeant removed his company fire plan from his clipboard and laid it out on his desk.

"I can take him, Sergeant," the lieutenant said, picking up his ammo belt and gear as he stood. Spike started to follow him out of the bunker, but once outside the lieutenant stopped and turned back to face Spike. "Look." He pointed with his weapon-free hand at the seven-inch centipede trying to find an opening into Spike's rucksack.

A shiver went down Spike's spine as he used the butt end of his shotgun to smash the poison arthropod.

"Those bastards are all over the floor of this valley. Saturate all of your gear with insect repellent. It helps to keep them away." The lieutenant paused and looked Spike over in the daylight. He couldn't help shaking his head. "This is the shits."

"What's that sir?" Spike could see that the officer was in his late twenties, maybe even thirty. Most second lieutenants were in their early twenties, and some Officer Candidate School graduates were as young as eighteen.

"You and me together in the same platoon—a baby sergeant and an over-the-hill second lieutenant."

"That might be good, sir."

"How's that?"

"What you don't know, I might be able to help you with," Spike said, tired of being dismissed because of his age.

First the officer grinned and then he broke out in a wide smile. "That might work, Sergeant." He started walking down a narrow trail that led through the chest-high grass. "Come on and meet your fire team."

"Did you receive a direct battlefield commission, sir?" Spike asked, talking to the lieutenant's back as they walked in single file.

"No, OCS. I was a staff sergeant and my old CO asked me if I wanted to go. It's a good opportunity with the rapid-promotion policy and all. I might be able to make captain, maybe even major, before I retire." He stopped and looked back. "That is, if I live through this shit."

Spike, seeing the first two-man bunker out on the perimeter over the lieutenant's shoulder, asked, "How many men do I have in my team?"

"Two right now—Makino, a M60 machine gunner, and Levin, a blooper operator and ammo bearer for the machine gun." The lieutenant pointed to the machine-gun position. "You'll have to dig your own hole over there." He indicated a spot he wanted Spike to occupy on the perimeter. "We weren't expecting you or I would have had them dig a three-man hole."

"That's fine, sir. I still have a few hours of daylight left." Spike dropped his rucksack where the lieutenant wanted the foxhole dug and followed him over to meet his men.

Levin was sitting outside the covered foxhole, taking a drink of warm water from his canteen, when he saw the lieutenant and a new buck sergeant approaching from their rear. "Hey, Makino, we've got company."

The Japanese-American soldier stuck his head out of the foxhole and whispered under his breath, "Fuck! I hope he's not our new fire-team leader."

"Probably is," Levin chuckled. He looked up and grinned at the approaching lieutenant. "Hello, Lieutenant Alsop. We're ready for the night and any NVA sappers they want to send against us."

Spike could tell by Levin's tone that the lieutenant was respected. He adjusted his shotgun on his shoulder and took a deep breath to calm himself. He was a little nervous because he knew how important the first meeting was with the men he was expected to lead in combat.

"I want you to meet your new fire-team leader, Sergeant Spike Harwood."

"Shit!" cried the man inside the bunker.

Lieutenant Alsop frowned. "Get your ass out here, Makino."

The paratrooper stuck his head out of the foxhole and brushed the sweat out of his eyes with the back of his dirt-caked hands. "Sir, I've got a lot of work to do before it gets dark out. We haven't put out our final protective fire stakes yet." Makino refused to look at the buck sergeant.

"Fine, get back to work." Alsop looked over at Spike. "You're home."

Spike left the two men and went back over to his rucksack and removed his folding shovel. He marked out the shape of the two-man foxhole he planned to dig and started removing the sod. He wanted to give the two paratroopers in his fire team time to adjust to the idea that they had a leader.

"As Makino came out of the foxhole, he looked over at Levin. Levin knew what the specialist fourth-class machine gunner was going to do and held out his hand to stop him. "Let it rest, Makino. He's not to blame."

"They ain't going to give us a fucking punk as a fire-team leader." Makino strode over to where Spike was digging and put his hands on his hips before speaking. "What in the fuck do you think you're doing?"

Spike waited before answering. "Digging a foxhole."

"Didn't they teach you Shake 'n' Bake's that you're supposed to take care of your men first?"

"You don't look like you're having any problems digging your foxhole."

"I need help in setting out my FPF stakes." Makino added mockingly, "You know what they are, don't you?"

"Yep." Spike knew that he was being baited.

"Well, are you coming?" Makino kicked out with his foot and sent a freshly dug dirt clod flying through the air. The mud ball landed against the side of Spike's head.

He had had enough.

He dove and caught Makino by surprise around his knees and knocked him to the ground. Spike was on top of the small man in seconds and had landed three blows against Makino's face before he could recover. Arching his back, Makino bucked Spike off to one side and then sprang up on his feet and assumed a karate fighting stance.

Spike could hear Levin comment in the background: "Oh, shit."

Makino attacked.

He hit Spike a half-dozen times before Spike realized that he had fucked up big time. Kick after kick rained on his legs and arms. It was now just a matter of protecting himself the best that he could from the blows. He caught the heel of Makino's boot and flipped him backward on the ground. Spike had a lot of street sense in fighting and put up a decent defense, but his offensive attack was over.

"What in the hell is going on here?" Lieutenant Alsop cried. He had heard the paratroopers in the nearby bunkers cheering on the fight and had come to investigate. Spike was bleeding from the corner of his mouth and couldn't straighten up completely.

Levin answered for the two of them as they both struggled to catch their breath: "Makino is showing our sergeant a couple of karate patterns, sir."

Alsop glared at the machine gunner, who was breathing hard between swollen lips. There was no doubt that Makino would have destroyed Harwood if he hadn't come along to break it up. "Save your energy for digging holes. Don't forget the NVA are out there." He pointed to the jungle and turned around, leaving the three paratroopers to work out the problem. Alsop had figured that something like this was going to happen, especially because Makino had been passed over for promotion to buck sergeant by Battalion only the day before.

Without a word Spike started setting up the final protective fire stakes for the machine gun. When he finished that job, he went back to digging his night position.

Sergeant Monk stepped out of Bravo Company's CP. Looking up, he saw the sun was setting behind the mountain ridge and inhaled. He could smell rain coming. The first sergeant's voice followed him out of the bunker: "Thanks for the information, Monk."

One of the company radio operators left the bunker and ran toward the perimeter with the news that he had just heard Monk tell about the new buck sergeant opening the captain's body bag.

Spike sat alone in his foxhole and listened to the night sounds coming from the jungle a hundred meters away. It was so dark out that he couldn't see anything and had to depend on his ears for any sign of an enemy approaching the barbed wire and booby traps in front of his position. He tried adjusting his seat in the foxhole, but all of his muscles were sore and his legs and side throbbed with pain.

Makino felt like shit as well. He wasn't feeling the effects of the fight; he had been far more sore after a karate match. What was making him feel bad was the body-bag story. The dead captain must have meant a lot to Harwood. Makino had heard about the captain from some friends in Alpha Company. He was a man everyone had respected.

Nearby, Levin held his soft jungle cap up to his face so that he could hide a drag from his cigarette. He hated late-night perimeter guard because it was so difficult to stay awake. He tried squinting his eyes to see better. Hearing Makino moving around in the dark, he asked, "You all right, Makino?"

"Yeah, man, I'm fine." After a pause he added, "I feel like shit about Harwood."

"Yeah, that was some heavy shit. Do you think he actually was holding the captain's hand? I mean, that's weird, man!"

Makino, a fifth-degree black belt in Korean karate, was a very tough paratrooper and didn't allow the war to break through his emotional defenses, but he knew what the right thing to do was and did it. "I'm going over to see the sarge." He didn't wait for Levin to answer as he crawled out of the fighting hole.

Spike heard someone crawling up from his rear and waited. The noise was so quiet that the man obviously knew what he was doing in the darkness. Spike felt for the butt of his shotgun lying on the sandbags that lined the edge of his foxhole.

"Sarge?" The voice was barely above a whisper.

Spike hesitated, not being accustomed to being addressed as a sergeant, and then realized the voice was calling him. "Here."

The body stopped at the edge of the foxhole. "Sarge, Makino here . . . I-I just want to apologize."

The jungle sounds filled the void.

"It's a long story, but I was jealous when I saw you were a buck sergeant. I was passed over yesterday—"

"Accepted." Spike spoke the single word softly, suppressing a groan from the pain in his side.

"Some people call me Yuk. My first name is Yukinari, but it's too hard for some of you round-eyes to pronounce . . . so you can call me Yuk if you want to . . ."

"Thanks, Yuk."

"Do you want me to stay here with you the rest of the night?" Makino knew that the first night in on the firing line was bad enough, let alone being alone in a foxhole.

"I'm fine. I'll see you in the morning." Spike took a deep breath. "I apologize too. I shouldn't have started that fight, and if I'd known you're a karate expert, I would have just blown your ass away!"

Makino chuckled. "Later, Sarge."

Spike, hearing the man crawl away, used the back of his hand to wipe the tears off his cheeks. He had been sitting in the dark thinking about Captain Hanson. He had held all of his emotions inside, not letting any of the men in the company know how he really felt. A street kid, he had trained himself all of his life to hide what he was truly feeling so that no one could take advantage of him. The person most people saw wasn't Spike.

Captain Hanson had been different. He had been tough, but also kind and compassionate. The captain had seen right through Spike's defensive barrier, one of the few people who had ever tried.

The tears flowed freely down Spike's cheeks in the dark. He didn't sob. He had too much self-control to break down completely—but at the same time he thought about shoving the barrel of his shotgun down his throat and pulling the trigger. He regretted not having ever told the captain that he loved him. Even though Hanson wasn't much older than a brother to him, he would always consider him as his dad.

"Sergeant Harwood?"

Spike swallowed to clear his throat and wiped his face with his sleeve before he answered. "Yes, sir."

Lieutenant Alsop had been walking in a low crouch, blending in perfectly with the elephant grass. "I thought that you could use some company out here for a while."

"Naw, I'm fine, sir." No matter how hard Spike had tried to conceal it, a slight quaver slipped out of his voice.

"Sergeant Monk told me what happened today out on the runway." Alsop paused and listened to the night sounds before continuing. "That's some heavy shit to handle on your first day out here."

"I'm fine, sir," Spike protested, fighting hard not to start crying again.

"Bullshit." Alsop dropped into Spike's foxhole. "Don't pull that tough-guy crap with me, paratrooper. This is Vietnam and out here we see each other naked. We smell it when one of our men shits his pants during a firefight, we see it when someone pukes . . . and if you're good, you *feel* it when one of your men is hurting inside." Alsop automatically paused, listening to make sure the insects were still calling to each other out in the jungle. "You're hurting inside, Harwood and I just want you to know that I give a fuck."

"Th-th-thanks, sir. It was a bit rough finding him all fucked up like that . . . in-in a body bag. I-I was really looking forward to seeing him again . . ." This time Spike couldn't hold back the tears or the sobs.

Lieutenant Alsop sat silently on the edge of the foxhole and pulled guard for his sergeant. Spike curled up on the bottom of his hole and grieved so hard that he thought he was going to die. Time passed without being counted in minutes, only in pain.

Spike finally gained control of himself. Feeling foolish for allowing the lieutenant to catch him off guard like that, he sipped from his canteen and splashed a little water over his face. "I wonder who's going to bury the captain. He was a street kid and didn't have any family left."

"The Army will take care of him, Sergeant Harwood."

"Do you think they'll tell me where he's going to be buried?" Spike asked, finding that he felt much better after letting it all out.

"I promise you, we'll know exactly where they put him to rest." Alsop picked up his rifle. "I've got to check the rest of the platoon. Do you think you'll be all right now?"

"Yes, sir."

"No more thinking about suicide—promise?"

Spike's head jerked around. In the dim light of a flare on the far side of the perimeter, he saw the lieutenant's shadow. "How—how did you know?"

"Like I told you, a good leader senses when his people are hurting. Man, you should have seen your face when you left the airstrip."

"It was that obvious?"

"Like you said, Hanson was like your dad."

"Sir, you won't tell the rest of the men that I started bawling, will you?"

"Never happen, paratrooper. It stays between the two of us. Maybe someday you can pay me back in kind."

"Thanks, sir."

Later that night, Spike found himself dozing off. He felt guilty about it, but the fight and the emotional strain had been too much for him. All of a sudden he heard a faint sound of metal rubbing against metal and he bolted upright. He tried visualizing what could have made the sound. There was no wind and the heavy rains that had threatened all night long had never come. He listened and heard the soft sound again. He went over every possible item out in front of him that could have made the sound and finally centered on the barbed wire rubbing against an engineer stake. He listened again to confirm it. Spike was very good at recognizing sounds during the night from living in scary old houses all of his life.

The sound reached him again, but this time a soft scraping accompanied it. Certain something was trying to get through the perimeter barbed wire, he reached for his shotgun. Could it just be an animal? He would look foolish in the morning for having fired his shotgun and alerting the whole base camp. Spike hesitated. He didn't need a reputation of being a scared teenage buck sergeant. When he listened again for the sound, though, this time he heard someone crawling directly toward his foxhole.

Groping in the dark, he felt with his hands for the small stakes he had shoved into the ground in front of his position. He had gotten the idea from placing the machine gun's fire stakes, but these stakes were aligned so that he could rest the butt of his shotgun between two prepositioned sandbags and rest the barrel atop a stake. He had nine of the stake-and-sandbag positions around the front of his foxhole. Spike selected the position pointing toward the sounds. Pushing off his safety, he gently squeezed the trigger.

The explosion echoed in the jungle and then the perimeter became extremely quiet. For a moment Spike felt like a fool: there had been nothing out there. Then a voice called from the bunkers to Spike's right and was answered by a stream of green tracers—a machine gun, he realized—coming from the jungle.

Spike reacted instantly. Ignoring the enemy machine gun, which was out of range for his shotgun, he fired three more fleshette rounds in the direction of the barbed wire.

Makino opened fire, answering the enemy light automatic weapon. Within a minute the artillery battery started firing illumination rounds and lit up the barbed wire so that the paratroopers could see. It was filled with NVA sappers.

Spike dropped back into his foxhole and reloaded his shotgun. He was too busy to be scared. He popped up again and saw two targets. He fired twice and dropped back down again, but this time after he shoved two shells back in his weapon, he unlatched his bayonet. He raised his head slowly and saw that Makino had locked his machine gun on its rightmost FPF stake and was firing short bursts down the fire lane. The machine gunner to his right had done the same thing, and the two streams of M60 bullets crossed just outside the barbed wire. The captain ordered the company to fire their "final protective fires." The disciplined paratroopers obeyed and formed an interlocking wall of small-arms fire by placing the barrels of their weapons on the special stakes they had carefully placed in the ground in front of their fighting holes. Sergeant Monk and Lieutenant Alsop had spent most of the afternoon walking around the perimeter selecting lanes of fire for each of the positions and marking the depressions in the ground for mortars and artillery rounds to cover. The order for the final protective line fires was used only as a last resort before being overrun, or when the enemy surprised a base camp and the officer in charge needed time to decide what to do. A well-planned FPL was almost impossible to break through, and even if they did, the casualties for the attacking force would be very high. Alsop and Monk had done their job well.

The NVA sapper attack caught at the barbed wire was decimated. They couldn't withdraw and they couldn't attack. The slaughter of the North Vietnamese company lasted less than ten minutes.

Hearing someone running to his rear, Spike whirled around to see if it was an NVA soldier, but saw the captain and his lieutenant running from the command bunker to the perimeter. A RPG-7 round came from the treeline and exploded short of the Makino and Levin's bunker. Spike had seen where the round had come from in the jungle, but knew that his shotgun wouldn't be effective at that range. Instead he scurried out of his foxhole and crawled over to where Levin was firing his M79 grenade launcher.

"By that clump of banana trees to your left front, a hundred and twenty-five meters. NVA rocket launcher!"

"Gottcha." Levin adjusted his sights and fired a high explosive round. When it seemed to fall short, he fired the second round. The RPG-7 didn't fire again.

"Brief me," The captain ordered, out of breath.

Spike briefed him as to what had happened and pointed to the dead NVA soldiers in the perimeter wire. "I think the attack is over."

Lieutenant Alsop gave Spike a wide-eyed stare and smiled. The young buck sergeant had already earned his pay on his first night on the perimeter. "Let's wait until first light to police the battlefield," he suggested to the captain.

"Fine. But keep up the artillery fire so that the NVA can't come back for their dead. Illumination too."

"Yes, sir." Alsop then spoke into the handset of the PRC-77 radio he had carried out of the bunker with him. "Redleg 6, fire mission, over."

Spike popped out of his foxhole as the first rays of light streamed through the dark green jungle. Makino covered Spike and Levin as they went down the barbed wire and checked the NVA bodies for documents. Spike counted five sappers who had been killed by fleshettes.

Levin shook his head. "Five—that's pretty good for a rookie sergeant."

Spike looked over at the blooper operator and smiled. "Rookie?"

"Well, not anymore."

Spike went back to searching the NVA bodies. One of the sappers moved and tried lifting his hand holding a Russian-made pistol.

"Watch out!" Levin cried, lowering his M79 grenade launcher, which had an anti-personnel round in its chamber.

"Don't shoot him." Spike raised his hand and stepped on the barrel of the NVA pistol. "He's a prisoner of war."

Levin shook his head. He couldn't believe the calmness of Spike's reaction. "A what?"

"A P.O.W." Spike tugged the pistol out of the severely wounded NVA's hand and looked back at the row of bunkers. "Medic!"

CHAPTER SIX

✪✪✪✪✪✪✪✪✪✪✪✪✪

MONTAGNARD BLOOD

The battalion officers were assembled in the brigade's forward command bunker, waiting for the arrival of their battalion commander from the rear, where he had been briefed on the upcoming operations order for the Dak To area. Sergeant Monk was changing a burnt-out light bulb over the map that depicted the area surrounding the base camp in a 1:25,000 scale. All friendly positions had been plotted, including the Special Forces' Civilian Irregular Defense Group companies of Sedang tribesmen, who were positioned along the Laotian and Cambodian borders where they intersected with South Vietnam. The tri-border area had long been a communist stronghold from which they assembled and attacked the valley villages.

Sergeant Monk had used a yellow Magic Marker to color in all of the valleys that ran east and west across the center of South Vietnam, from the tri-border area to the coast. The yellow showed up the valleys clearly and explained why the North Vietnamese had always used that invasion route into the south through the high jungle mountains.

"You've done a fine job with that map, Sergeant," said Captain Whitmore. "Even I can see why the Dak To Valley is so important."

"Thank you, sir," Monk said, busy checking the electrical cord that ran the length of the bunker and outside to the 10kw generator. "By the way, how's that new buck sergeant working out? I hear he was the one who caught the NVA sapper attack before they got through the perimeter wire."

"Yes, I have to give Harwood credit for that, but I'd say that it was a case of beginner's jitters more than anything else," said Whitmore.

"Whatever. I owe him my ass because I know where the first satchel charge would have been tossed." Monk swept his hand around the bunker. "Command bunkers draw sappers like honey draws bears."

"You a country boy, Sergeant Monk?"

"Maine, upstate." In stepping outside to check the generator for fuel before the briefing started, Monk heard the battalion commander's chopper landing and stuck his head back inside of the bunker. "The commander has arrived."

Lieutenant Colonel Yates, followed by a captain, debarked the command helicopter. The chopper had a AN/ASC-6 communications central installed behind the pilot's seat so that the battalion commander could control all of his companies on the ground from the aircraft. It was one of the most modern communication networks in the war.

"Sir . . ." The captain hurried to catch up to the senior officer. "Do you think I should meet my men first?"

"No, I want to introduce you to the battalion staff at this briefing. Whitmore can take you out to the perimeter afterward to meet the company."

"Fine, sir." The captain, carrying his brand-new rucksack by one strap over his shoulder, was wearing a new set of jungle fatigues with all of the identification patches sewn on the jacket.

Sergeant Monk, watching the two officers approaching, knew right off not only that the lieutenant colonel's companion was new, but also a West Pointer, just by the way he walked and by the fact that he was being given the command of a highly coveted airborne infantry company during his first six months in-country. Monk shook his head as he slipped back into the bunker before the officers got too close and he would have to salute them.

"Attention!" Monk called the bunker occupants to their feet when the senior officer stepped through the doorway.

"At ease, gentlemen." The battalion commander strode over to the map and motioned for the new captain to take a seat next to the radios. "I have only a few minutes here and then I have a meeting with the brigade commander. First, I want to tell all of you how pleased I am over the outcome of the firefight Bravo Company had last week." He looked at Captain Whitmore as he went on, "You've ended your command on an excellent note, and I have personally recommended you for a Silver Star for valor."

Whitmore blushed. He hadn't done anything except call for the company to fire their final protective fires and directed a few air strikes and artillery from the command bunker. He knew that he didn't deserve the third highest award a soldier could get for valor in combat.

"Sir?"

"Yes, Whitmore?"

"Sir, have you processed the award recommendations that I sent back to the rear for my men?" Whitmore asked, trying to shift the attention away from himself to where it belonged.

"We'll get to them in due time, Whitmore. First, I want to make sure you officers are taken care of."

Whitmore stiffened in protest. The battalion commander had just ignored the presence of Sergeant Monk and the enlisted radio operators in the bunker.

"I'd like those looked at, sir, before I leave so I can present the awards myself."

"Well, Whitmore . . ." Yates's mouth formed the

condescending staff officer's neutral smile he had developed during his years assigned to the Pentagon. Captain Whitmore was the only R.O.T.C.-commissioned officer still commanding a company in his battalion, and Yates was personally happy that the man was DEROSing back to the States. "Now that you've brought that topic up, I might as well handle it before we get into the upcoming operational briefing." The senior officer looked over at the captain who had arrived with him. "Gentlemen, I would like to introduce the new Bravo Company commander. Captain Eugene Maynard will be assuming command as of today. Captain Maynard is the number-one graduate of the class of '65." The lieutenant colonel smiled again. "He is also the son of General Maynard, who happens to be a very good personal friend of mine."

Maynard smiled and stood up. "Thank you, Colonel Yates, I am very happy to have been selected to command an airborne company, especially with the famous 173rd."

Captain Whitmore looked over at his platoon leaders. He still had a week left in the field, so what did the commander have planned for him?

The briefing took less than an hour. Yates covered the brigade's operation plan for the 2nd Battalion, which essentially directed the unit to conduct platoon-sized patrols to the west side of the Dak To area of operations and the Tumerong Valley. The brigade commander had been chastised by General Westmoreland personally for having all of his infantry inside of the barbed wire and for not conducting any offensive patrols. Westmoreland favored his airborne units and watched over their welfare like a protective mother hawk: he didn't want them concentrated in camp like sitting ducks.

"Are there any questions?" Yates inquired, placing his hands on his hips with his index fingers stretched along the top of his pistol belt. He wore camouflage patches on his jacket, but the silver oak leaf on his collar caught the light from the bright bulb. No hands went up. "Good. I wish all of you good hunting out there in the jungle. So far the 2nd Battalion has the highest enemy KIA rate in the brigade. We can thank our Captain Whitmore's company for that."

Whitmore blushed again.

"One hundred and thirty-nine NVA regulars were killed in action in one night, and only two paratroopers were wounded. That is an excellent show for Bravo Company." Yates looked over at Maynard. "I hope you can top that score, Eugene."

"I'll do my best, sir." Maynard beamed back his acceptance of the challenge.

"Whitmore, take Eugene out to meet his men and then come back here. You'll be flying out with me."

Whitmore was shocked. He hadn't expected to be replaced so soon. "Yes, sir."

"I want to be out of here in two hours," Yates ordered, returning his attention to Sergeant Monk's map.

Outside, Captain Maynard picked up the rucksack and rifle he had put down next to the bunker's entrance. "How about showing me my tent so that I can put this gear away first?"

Whitmore looked hard at the rookie captain before answering. "We don't have tents. I stay in the company CP, with my field first sergeant and radio operator."

"Oh? You share your quarters with enlisted men?" Maynard asked, upset.

"It's more like they're sharing their quarters with me. They're the ones who built it."

Whitmore led the way out to the perimeter, thinking about the award recommendations that he had sent back to brigade headquarters. At least he would have a chance to push the awards through the administration staff now that he had a couple of free days before leaving for the States. Once they reached the perimeter, he turned to face Maynard, "Here's where

the NVA sappers tried penetrating through our wire.
That bunker over there was almost taken out by RPG
fire, and that foxhole over there was where they were
first detected by one of our men. We learned from
that fight that you need flares and booby traps *in*
your barbed wire to stop them. NVA sappers are
damned good." Whitmore nodded for Maynard to
follow him. "Come on and I'll introduce you to the
buck sergeant who was responsible for saving our asses
that night."

Maynard followed reluctantly. He didn't want to
meet any of the enlisted men until he had a chance to
talk to his platoon leaders and establish his standards.
He believed in a strong chain of command and thought
that the lieutenants were the ones who communicated
with the enlisted men, not the company commanders.

Approaching the foxhole from the rear, Whitmore
saw the sergeant sitting on the edge of the hole, clean-
ing his shotgun. Listening posts had been put out
along the edge of the jungle to prevent any surprise
attacks or snipers. "I think you'll like this young sergeant, Eugene. He's a hard worker and I've put him in
for a Silver Star. He killed five of the sappers by
himself during the fight."

A tinge of jealousy flashed through Maynard. He
had dreamed of becoming a war hero in Vietnam, and
somehow he felt cheated when he heard Whitmore
praising a sergeant. "That sounds great. I hope all of
my paratroopers are as tough as him."

Whitmore stopped and looked back again at the
West Pointer. There was something about him that he
didn't like at all. "You get all kinds of paratroopers in
a unit—brave ones and cowards. It takes good leadership to turn the cowards into heros."

"I'll take the brave ones," Maynard said sarcastically, "and you can take the cowards with you when
you leave. I was bred to be a soldier."

Whitmore paused a couple of feet behind the young

sergeant. Captain Maynard looked out over the barbed wire at the quiet jungle and frowned. They were going to have to cut the thick growth back at least a hundred more meters.

"Captain Maynard, I'd like you to meet Sergeant Harwood," Whitmore said proudly.

Spike felt his breath catch in his throat as he turned around and locked eyes with Maynard. The captain's face turned bright red from surprise and anger.

"Have you two met before?" Whitmore asked, looking at Spike.

"Yes, sir, we were in the same jump school class together. Captain Maynard was our trainee company commander." Spike kept a tight mask on his emotions, but inside his stomach was churning.

"That's nice, but it's a little ironic that the first person you've met in your new command is a friendly face," Whitmore remarked, trying to ease the tension he was feeling between the two men.

Spike felt his chest tighten. "You're our new company commander, sir?"

Maynard recovered quickly and sneered. "Yes . . . yes, I am, Sergeant."

"Oh, fuck . . ." Spike whispered under his breath.

"What did you say, Sergeant?" Maynard asked, on the attack.

"Oh, fine, sir. Just fine."

By now Captain Whitmore had realized that their association in jump school had not been a friendly one. "Come on, Eugene, and I'll show you the rest of the perimeter—"

"We'd better get back to the CP. I've got things to do before it gets dark," Maynard said, cutting Whitmore off.

"Fine with me." Whitmore held out his hand for Spike to shake. "It was a pleasure serving with you, Sergeant. I just wish I had had you with me my whole tour."

"Thanks, sir." Spike shook hands with his old company commander, but his gaze remained riveted on the back of Maynard's head.

"Bad first meeting?" Whitmore asked when Maynard was out of hearing distance.

"The worst, sir." Spike loaded his shotgun and checked the safety.

"I'll be back in the rear area for a couple of days. Do you want me to try to get you transferred to another unit?"

"Naw, that wouldn't work, sir. Besides, I've sort of gotten used to Yuk and Sol already." Spike nodded toward the M60 position, where the two paratroopers were both taking a early afternoon nap before going out to one of the listening posts with Spike.

"Fine. But if it gets too bad, don't hesitate to ask for some help." Whitmore added sincerely, "I owe you."

"Naw, sir. We're even."

"I owe you. You saved my command from being wiped out." Whitmore patted Spike's shoulder. "You know, I've recommended you for a Silver Star."

"Thanks, sir."

"The recommendation is up at Brigade being processed. I wasn't supposed to mention it to you, but I want you to know directly from me about how I feel. I wanted to be here to give it to you, but . . ."

"But you'd be stupid to stay here if they're going to let you go back early." Spike kept his eyes on the disappearing Maynard.

"Well, I've got to make a sweep of the perimeter and tell the rest of the company good-bye."

The battalion commander was waiting impatiently in the bunker by the time Whitmore returned. He had to wait a little longer. As Whitmore grabbed his rucksack out of the command bunker, he took an extra minute to say good-bye to his radio operator. They had been through a lot of firefights together and had become very close. In fact, Whitmore had formed so many close relationships in this unit that he knew a part of him would remain when he left.

Yuk and Sol weren't asleep, as it turned out. They waited until the two captains were out of sight and then walked over. Sol sat on the edge of Spike's foxhole and dangled his feet inside. "What was that all about?"

Spike shrugged. "Captain Whitmore brought our new CO by."

"So, what's he like?" Yuk asked.

"I don't know how he'll treat the company, but I've got a feeling that I'm in for some serious shit." Spike slapped the stock on his shotgun. "Damn! Of all the companies in Vietnam, he has to end up commanding this one."

"Don't worry, Spike, if he fucks with you, we'll frag his ass."

"Bullshit! We aren't going to pull any of that leg crap." Spike picked up his Claymore bag and checked to see how many rounds he had left. Resupplying his shotgun was going to be a problem. "I'm going to see if I can catch up to Captain Whitmore before he leaves and see if he can scrounge up a couple of boxes of fleshette rounds for my shotgun."

"Don't forget that our platoon is going out on patrol in an hour and then set up listening posts for tonight." Sol looked out at the green wall surrounding the base camp. The jungle could be hiding anything.

Spike spotted Captain Whitmore walking toward the helicopter next to the battalion commander and Captain Maynard. He hesitated and then decided that the shotgun shells were more important than his pride. Spike ran over, holding his shotgun down at his side. When Whitmore saw Spike jogging toward him, he took a couple of steps back down the path.

"Sir, sorry to bother you, but I was wondering if you could send me back a couple of boxes of fleshette rounds for my shotgun."

"Sure, Spike. What gauge?"

Spike smiled, not wanting to embarrass the captain. "Twelve." All riot shotguns were twelve gauge.

"Consider it done."

"Thanks, sir." Spike turned to leave.

"Hold it right there, Sergeant," Lieutenant Colonel Yates said, joining them. "What in the hell kind of weapon are you carrying?"

Spike held up the issue shotgun. "A riot shotgun, sir."

"Who in the hell authorized that weapon in my battalion?"

"Sir . . ." Whitmore said, trying to direct the commander's attention to him.

"I'm asking the sergeant, Whitmore."

"They're new in-country, sir," Spike said boldly, looking the lieutenant colonel directly in the eye, making him nervous. "I believe that the issue is going to be one per platoon to be used for clearing huts and tunnels."

"Why haven't I been briefed on this?"

Spike didn't know the answer and looked at Captain Whitmore for help.

"We received the message about a month ago, sir, out here in the companies." Whitmore looked over at Maynard, including him as he went on, "Sergeant Harwood is the man who discovered the NVA sappers, sir. He killed five of them with that shotgun."

"Oh?" Yates said, taking a new interest in the young NCO.

"Yes, sir. I've recommended him for a Silver Star," Whitmore said, wanting to make sure that the senior officer was aware of the recommendation because enlisted awards had a way of getting lost.

"Very good, Sergeant. Very good."

Spike didn't smile at the praise. He had pegged Yates as an older version of Maynard.

"I have to get back to the brigade headquarters." Yates said, turning to leave.

"Sir, when are you going to move the battalion CP forward to Dak To?" Whitmore asked, before he realized that he wasn't the Bravo Company commander anymore.

Yates glared at him and snapped, "That really isn't any of your damn business, Captain." He strode away angrily.

Maynard ran around to the far side of the chopper so that he could talk to the lieutenant colonel without Whitmore or Harwood hearing him. He cupped his hands around his mouth and spoke loudly, above the sound of the chopper engine, in the senior officer's ear. Spike saw Yates glance over at him a couple of times and nod his head in agreement with what Maynard was saying. Then Yates patted the captain's arm and smiled as he boarded the helicopter.

Spike saluted and Captain Whitmore saluted back and then gave Spike the thumbs-up sign as the chopper banked away over the tops of the triple-canopy jungle and disappeared.

Sol and Yuk were waiting for Spike when he got back to the perimeter. "What did he have to say?" Sol asked, holding up his camouflage makeup stick for Spike to use.

"Not much. Whitmore is going to get me some more ammo. And Maynard and the battalion commander are already busom buddies."

"Hold still—let me put that on you, you're making a fucking mess." Sol used the grease stick of dark green makeup to darken Spike's cheeks with and a lighter color to highlight the dark areas of his face. "We leave in twenty-five minutes. Lieutenant Alsop has given our fire team the point."

Yuk stuck some grass in the elastic camouflage band surrounding Spike's helmet and added a few leafy twigs to break up the outline of his helmet.

"Let's go," Sol said, slapping Spike's shoulder and picking up his M79. "I still think we should frag the fucker."

*   *   *

Lieutenant Alsop moved his platoon out of base camp after briefing them on their patrol's mission. They were assigned a Montagnard village about ten thousand meters northwest of the airstrip. Since the NVA sapper attack, the whole battalion had been taking turns running platoon-sized patrols out as far as ten clicks—or ten thousand meters—from the base camp to keep the NVA from setting up mortar positions near the runway and firing on incoming aircraft.

The patrol moved swiftly through the high elephant grass that covered the valley floor, but once they reached the lower slopes of the mountains, thick stands of young bamboo blocked their way. Lieutenant Alsop decided that in order to maintain stealth, they would use a Montagnard trail that ran parallel to a narrow stream coming down from the high ground. The tactic was dangerous, but then, they were *looking* for a fight.

Spike advanced on the point with Yuk and Sol backing him up with the M60 machine gun. They were moving about two hundred meters ahead of the rest of the platoon—an unusual tactic that Spike had talked the lieutenant into letting him try. Spike figured that the three of them could handle any trail watchers they ran into. Also, the extra distance between them and the platoon would allow for an early warning if they ran into a force worth engaging. And if they ran into an NVA bunker system, the point element could withdraw without making contact. At first Lieutenant Alsop hadn't liked the idea because it put the point element in an extremely dangerous position, but the three paratroopers were certain that they could handle themselves, and the pair of URC-10 radios that Spike had scrounged up finally convinced the lieutenant that he should try the tactic. The URC-10s were hand-held radios that had only two channels and a range of about a half mile in the jungle. Spike carried one in his pocket and the lieutenant carried the other one.

In single file, the three-man point moved like shadows down the narrow Montagnard path, Yuk following close enough behind so that he could constantly keep Spike in view. Wherever Yuk's eyes went, the barrel of the M60 followed automatically. Sol carried his M79 down low, with an anti-personnel round in the chamber. He wore a specially made vest with pockets all over the front that held forty more rounds for his grenade launcher. Most of the ammunition Sol carried was high explosive, but he had a wide selection of fleshettes, smoke, white phosphorus, and two very-hard-to-get tear-gas projectiles.

Suddenly Spike paused and raised his right hand. Yuk dropped to one knee, alert but not alarmed. The fire team had made up their own hand and arm signals. When the point man raised his right hand, it meant: stop, take cover, and listen. When he raised his left hand, it signaled danger. Sol turned around to cover their rear and Yuk covered Spike with the machine gun.

Spike had stopped because the path had reached an intersection with a wide trail that he didn't remember seeing on the map. As the point element waited and listened, they heard the rest of the platoon coming up behind them. Spike held the small radio up to his mouth and whispered. "Blue. Yellow, over."

Lieutenant Alsop, who had been walking with the URC-10 held up to his ear, replied "Go, Yellow."

"Path intersects a wide trail. Stop the patrol and wait while we check it out, over."

"Roger, Yellow. Standing by." Alsop signaled for the platoon to take a break along the sides of the path.

Spike tucked his radio into his jacket pocket and eased out onto the trail in a battle-ready crouch. He noticed that the damp earth along the path was marked by hundreds of small footprints made by both bare and sandaled feet. Spike dropped to one knee and studied the bare footprints. They were very wide and

short without any arch in them whatsoever. Spike
assumed that they had been made by Montagnard
tribesmen, who always went barefoot in the jungle.
The sandal marks had tire patterns on the soles. Spike
had seen those before for sale in local Vietnamese
villages that lined the highway from Saigon to Danang.
The sandals were made out of worn tires and actually
were very comfortable and durable in the damp jungle.

Spike signaled for his team to move forward cautiously up the trail. Soon they reached a sharp curve
cut around the edge of a ridge line on the mountain,
and Spike approached with extreme caution.

Loud voices and laughing echoed around the bend
just before Spike reached it. His left hand flew up in
the air and formed a fist before going straight out to
his side: danger, take cover!

Yuk slipped into the thick jungle, blending with it
instantly. Less than three feet from the path, he
crouched. Spike had disappeared, but Yuk had noted
the place on the trail where he had been standing and
knew approximately where he was. Sol paused for a
second and looked down the path before stepping into
the jungle. He moved off the trail about fifteen feet
until he could get a clear view of a tiny portion of the
path running downhill.

Spike pushed the switch on his URC-10, hoping that
the lieutenant was listening because he didn't have
time for a long message. He whispered two short
words. "Danger. Hide!"

Lieutenant Alsop had been at the ready and instantly alerted his platoon.

The jungle became silent as the Americans waited
for the voices to round the bend. Spike's view was
very limited, and he was starting to edge closer to the
trail when an NVA soldier called out to one of his
comrades from less than four feet away. The wide-
leafed plant in front of Spike shook as an enemy point
man stepped off the trail and let the four-abreast formation of NVA soldiers pass by.

Yuk caught a glimpse of the NVA soldiers wearing clean, pressed khaki uniforms and tan pith helmets, and wished that he had hidden deeper than three feet into the jungle. He glanced down at his black M60 machine gun and wondered if it could be seen from the trail.

Sol heard the NVA approaching their position, but couldn't see anything up the trail. He had to wait until the point element of the NVA unit reached his narrow tube of vision through the thick vegetation. A couple of moments went by and then the whole area at the end of his green tunnel was filled with NVA soldiers walking casually down the trail with their weapons carried comfortably over their shoulders. Sol automatically started counting the files of men as they passed.

Spike felt the sweat dripping from his nose. He prayed the NVA wouldn't stop for a break. He could smell their body odor as they passed, and he easily heard the cadence of their breathing. When one of them spoke, it sounded like a cannon going off.

Lieutenant Alsop and his platoon heard the NVA unit passing along the trail about a hundred meters away. He was tempted to open fire on them, but decided against it until he knew what his point element's situation was.

Spike waited a good half hour after the last NVA had passed his hiding place before stepping back out onto the trail. He slipped around the curve in the trail and peered up it for a couple hundred meters before going back and assembling his fire team. He could see that Yuk and Sol had been sweating too.

Sol beckoned for Spike to come over. As Spike watched up the trail and Sol watched down, Sol put his lips almost against Spike's ear and whispered, "I counted two hundred and eight."

Spike's eyes widened. The better part of an NVA battalion had just passed within three feet of them. He whispered back to Sol, "Platoon," and beckoned for Yuk to follow.

Alsop had been staring up the path hoping that Spike would appear when the NVA voices had gone. The sight of Spike caught him by surprise and he almost opened fire.

Spike nodded at his platoon leader and joined him next to the path. He felt safe enough to whisper. "Large NVA unit just passed us on the trail. Sol counted over two hundred of them. They were dressed in clean khakis and carried AK-47s, RPDs, and RPGs. I think I caught a glimpse of a 12.7 heavy machine gun strapped to a bike."

Alsop looked worried. He had heard the NVA as well and knew that they must have felt very secure on the trail to have been talking so loud.

"What do you want to do?"

"Let me call that information back to the base camp and see what the captain wants us to do."

Spike nodded and joined his team back at the point. Yuk offered Spike a drink of water as he dropped next to him. "Close shit."

Spike nodded his head in agreement. They had been very lucky. He closed his eyes to rest them and realized that he wasn't scared. In fact, he was enjoying it. He opened his eyes and glanced over at Yuk to see if the machine gunner had noticed what he was thinking. Yuk was chalking camouflage on his machine gun. Spike grinned and looked over at Sol, who had been watching him.

Spike winked.

When Lieutenant Alsop came up, the look on his face gave away what was on his mind. "The captain wants us to go to the village."

Spike gave a curt nod and left the lieutenant to take the point again. Yuk and Sol followed him. No one in the platoon had to be told that silence from now on was essential.

Once around the curve, the trail straightened out and dipped into a narrow crevice where water dripped down the bare, rocky face of the mountain. A few thick vines had found a perch on the rocks, but the vegetation was sparse, affording no cover for an NVA ambush. Spike slipped through the crevice quickly, ready to disappear into the jungle at the slightest sign of NVA soldiers.

The afternoon slipped by very fast for the point team as they moved down the trail toward the Montagnard village. There was no doubt in Spike's mind that the NVA unit had passed through the village or very close by.

A pair of Montagnard hunters was the first sign that they were near the village. They saw Spike before he saw them and stood waiting for him to approach.

"VC?" Spike asked the older-looking Montagnard. The old man looked blankly, not understanding.

Sol spoke to the man in fluent French. "Have you seen any North Vietnamese soldiers?"

The old man nodded and pointed back down the trail they had just covered. The old man was smart. He had to have guessed that the Americans had seen the large NVA unit.

"Is your village nearby?" Sol asked, pointing up the trail.

The old man answered in broken French, "There are no VC in our village. Go, leave us alone."

"How far away is your village?" Sol asked, using the barrel of his blooper for emphasis.

The old man pointed with his crossbow that it was just over the ridge.

"Come." Sol invited the two hunters to join them.

Spike called back and informed the lieutenant that they were approaching the village and had picked up two Montagnard hunters.

The village had been built within the past few years. Montagnards were slash-and-burn farmers who cleared a plot of jungle, cultivated it for a few years, and moved on to another location when the soil gave out.

The village had been marked on the map as belonging
to the Sedang tribesmen.

Lieutenant Alsop and the rest of the platoon caught
up to the point element before they had entered the
village. Using Sol as an interpreter, he was assured
that there were no NVA in the village. The elder
begged that the soldiers not burn their houses and eat
their children. Sol explained to the tribesmen that
Americans did nothing of the sort, but the old man
just nodded his head as if he knew better. The NVA
had told him many times that Americans were canni-
bals and loved the tender flesh of young children. He
looked at the large white-skinned men and then at
Yuk, who had skin like the North Vietnamese. He
would wait and see what they ate before allowing the
hidden children to return to the village. In fact, the
reason they had stayed on the trail talking to the
Americans was so that the women would have time to
hide the children in the jungle.

"Search the village in two-man teams." Alsop waved
for the small platoon to spread out and sweep the
huts. He wanted to complete his assigned mission and
get the hell out of there as fast as possible. The large
NVA unit could return at any time, and his platoon
wasn't strong enough to fight them and win without
taking severe casualties.

Spike, waiting in the shade with his fire team as the
rest of the platoon swept the village, noticed that a
small Montagnard woman feeding her pigs kept looking over at them and then fearfully glanced at a middle-
aged Montagnard man wearing a short tribal black
waistcoat and knee-length loincloth. The man kept
moving from hut to hut, staying out of the way of the
Americans but yet always near them. Then Spike noticed that the other Montagnard men kept their distance from him, but he couldn't figure out why, except
that the Yard could be the chief or a VC sympathizer.
Picking up a piece of rice straw and slipping it between
his teeth, Spike puzzled over the villagers' skittishness.

There was something different about the Montagnard man that he couldn't quite put his finger on. He looked from the man over at the woman feeding the pigs and caught her staring at him. This time fear was written all over her face.

Lieutenant Alsop joined Spike in the shade. "This is fucking making me nervous."

"Me too."

"What do you say, Sergeant Harwood?" At that moment Alsop saw where Spike was looking and frowned. "Is something wrong?"

Spike shook his head. "Naw, nothing important . . ." The man's feet: it hit him like a singing telegram. He remembered the wide footprints without arches in the damp earth along the trail that were made by the Montagnards. The man's feet were normal and arched. He was used to wearing shoes!

The Montagnard girl, seeing the thunderstruck expression on Spike's face, reacted quickly. If the spy was discovered, her whole village would be burned to the ground and the hostages the North Vietnamese had taken would be murdered. She picked up a basket of ripe bananas and hurried over to the Americans lounging in the shade of the longhouse. All the while the NVA spy watched her keenly.

"Please, do not show that I am talking to you," she said in French, offering the bananas to Alsop. She looked into the lieutenant's eyes, hoping that he spoke the language. Sol's back was turned on the NVA spy when he answered the woman, "I speak French."

She kept her back turned as well as she bowed and offered Sol some of the bananas. "If you kill him, they will return and kill all of us."

Sol smiled and nodded his thanks for the small bunch of bananas. "Is he an NVA?"

"Yes . . ." She paused. "They have fifteen of our people as hostages."

"We won't betray you."

"Thank you." She kowtowed and left.

Sol quickly related the conversation to Alsop.

"What do you think, Lieutenant?" Spike asked as he casually watched the NVA spy move across the center of the village.

"We'll leave the village and set up an ambush on the trail. I have a feeling that he'll take off to warn his comrades as soon as we leave."

Lieutenant Alsop waited until the platoon had finished searching the village and then called back to the company CP that the village was clean and they were moving on to their alternate objective, a night ambush site.

The platoon was relieved when they had left the village, for everyone had sensed a death trap. Alsop called his squad leaders together and briefed them on the ambush site: a length of the trail near the village they had just covered. He had the squads place their Claymore mines to cover the long kill zone with the last pair of Claymores at each end of the ambush site, pointing up and down the trail. Alsop figured the kill zone was long enough to cover a column of NVA of company size, if they were traveling close together at night.

Spike and his team were given the southernmost end of the ambush, where any NVA unit coming from the village would have to pass them completely before the trap was sprung. Alsop knew that Spike's men had the willpower to wait. Yuk fixed two fire lanes for his M60 in a slight bend in the trail. He would be able to fire up the trail for almost the complete length of the kill zone, and he could cover about twenty feet down the trail before it curved again. It was an excellent site for an automatic weapon. Sol liked the position, too, because he could fire his M79 without having to fear premature detonation against brush. Spike took a covering position for the M60 to protect it in case the NVA discovered it during the fight and tried flanking it.

Night fell quickly. A few birds called to each other and then they also became quiet as the insects took over in the darkness. Feeling for his rucksack in the dark, Spike positioned it so that it pointed in the direction of the predetermined assembly area: in the event any member of the platoon was separated during the fight they would go there and be picked up when the whole unit pulled back. It was a tactic he had learned in AIT from instructors who had recently returned from Nam.

Spike liked sitting alone in the dark jungle without anyone to interfere with his concentration. He had developed a way of tuning out everything around him that wasn't important. When he had pulled his first night jungle patrol, he had tried seeing everything in the dark and was exhausted before midnight. He had learned quickly that as the light faded in the jungle, his senses of hearing and smell and touch took over and his optic sense rested. It was like going into a trance but being extremely alert.

After hours of waiting, the sound of sandaled feet reached him, and he froze. It was a single person walking rapidly from the village. The beam of a flashlight filtered through the thick vegetation. Spike closed one of his eyes to protect his night vision and watched the shadow of the NVA spy slip past his position. Lieutenant Alsop, of course, wanted the man to pass safely through the ambush.

Pulling back the piece of green cloth tape that covered the crystal of his Army issue watch, Spike saw it was two o'clock. He replaced the tape and slipped back into his trance.

A few false alarms followed. An hour later, something big came up to the edge of the trail and paused. Spike heard it sniffing, and then it huffed and went crashing off to the side of the trail. Though Spike failed to identify that animal, he knew damn well what the next one was. Some time later, a small animal scurried across the trail and then something heavy slithered along the ground a few meters to his rear. It was a large snake. Spike listened intently, relaxing only when the snake moved back into the jungle.

Spike heard Yuk checking the dust cover on his M60 and then he heard Sol shift his position. Both of the sounds were barely audible, but Spike was tuned into anything that created a sound within a hundred meters of where he sat. His nylon poncho liner was wrapped over his shoulders to keep the early morning chill off his damp fatigues, which his body heat was slowly drying.

Spike checked the time again and noticed that it was already past four. The NVA spy had had plenty of time to link up with the unit that they had seen earlier and return to the village. Spike relaxed a little in the dark. It would start getting light out in about an hour.

Just as he was beginning to come out of his night trance, Spike heard a soft crunching. It slipped along the trail, followed by another one. Spike was sure these were men, and he turned his head so that he faced the source of the sound and estimated the distance. Yuk had heard the soft noise also and had shifted his position slightly. Spike counted the NVA soldiers as they passed his position. Because there were only four and they were traveling very slowly along the trail, he guessed that they were the point element of a larger force and he hoped that the lieutenant wouldn't open fire too soon. If he did, his fire team wouldn't have a chance in hell of escaping because the rest of the NVA unit would curl the edge of the American ambush, Spike's fire team first and foremost.

Alsop saw the NVA approaching the center of the kill zone through the Starlight scope he had been using all night. He had just been issued the night-seeing device that day, and he was amazed at how clearly he could see everything, even in the dead of night. He watched the four NVA soldiers advance cautiously, keeping to the edge of the trail.

The point man stopped often and peered into the jungle as if he could actually see in the dark. What disturbed Alsop the most, though, was the point man sniffing continually. "Christ," Alsop thought, "I hope none of the men are smoking." There and then he promised himself that if he survived the night, he would insure that none of his men ever smoked again during a night position in the jungle.

Soon Spike heard the rest of the NVA unit coming up the trail. He felt his stomach sink and a sudden urge to defecate. He squeezed the cheeks of his butt tightly together, trying to concentrate on the enemy. The last thing that he wanted to do was shit his pants.

Yuk placed the barrel of his M60 against the small stake that he had shoved into the ground to mark his leftmost limit. Beyond that, he would be firing into his own platoon. He knew that once the lieutenant detonated his Claymores, all hell would break loose and he needed to maintain a reference point from which to open fire. The fire fan for his M60 was only a few degrees wide, but it covered a critical fifty-meter length of the trail. Any NVA soldiers not killed by the Claymore mines would be cut down in a deadly crossfire by his machine gun and the rifles from the platoon.

Sol swallowed hard. The numbers of the force of NVA—outnumbering the platoon by at least four to one—passing their position was terrifying. Desperately he tried to recall what type of round he had in his blooper, but his mind refused to cooperate. Instead his thoughts bizarrely latched onto the huge Passover celebration his father had conducted right before he had left to go into the Army. Sol ground his teeth and forced himself to concentrate: it was a white phosphorus round in his M79. He sighed, relieved that he had remembered. If he had fired that like a fleshette round, the trajectory of the heavier projectile would have been too low and he would have probably killed Yuk. Just then Sol frowned, wondering if the vivid image of his father conducting Passover was a sign that he was going to die.

The exploding Claymores made Yuk jump even though he had been expecting them. The blasts of hand grenades followed, which along with white phosphorus rounds lit up the kill zone. Yuk could see khaki-clad bodies flying everywhere and opened fire with his M60. He held it down to short six-round bursts and swept the trail for about thirty seconds and then turned to face back down the trail just in case all of the NVA hadn't been trapped in the ambush. It was a smart move, for his first burst caught two NVA soldiers trying to flank the ambush position.

As ordered, Spike waited before detonating the two Claymore mines that faced directly down the trail. The explosions killed a dozen NVA instantly.

In all, the ambush caught a complete company of NVA infantry in its kill zone, and of the few survivors none were capable of fighting.

What Lieutenant Alsop didn't know was that two more NVA companies were coming up the trail behind the first one and that Spike's Claymores had caught the front of the second company. Immediately the NVA battalion commander deployed his troops perfectly on both sides of the trail and started moving forward along each side. He had recognized instantly that his first company had walked into a well-executed ambush, but what he didn't know was which side of the trail the Americans were on.

Yuk heard them coming first and scooted around on the ground to bring his M60 to bear on the advancing NVA. He opened fire in controlled bursts, but when the muzzle flashes of the enemy became too numerous, he just held the trigger back and swept the jungle. He was causing a great deal of damage to the NVA advance, and the battalion commander instructed that one of his 12.7mm heavy machine guns take out Yuk's position.

Seeing two muzzle flashes to his left rear, Spike

realized that the NVA were trying to outflank the ambush. He fired three rounds and had moved around so that he could cover Yuk's rear when the 12.7 opened up. The overpowering thump above all the other noises of the battle sent a shiver down Spike's spine. No one could hide from a 12.7. It would chew its way through a tree trunk or shovel the dirt away from the front of a foxhole until its thumb-sized projectiles found its targets.

Yuk tried matching fire with the heavy weapon, but was outgunned. He saw a group of NVA trying to pass his position on the far side of the trail and took all five of them out of the fight. That's when he realized dawn had broken during the ambush. He had seen them.

He had lined up on a spot in which he had seen a lot of movement and started squeezing the trigger when a round from the 12.7mm machine gun splattered the side of his M60 and tore it out of his hands. Fragments of steel from the exploding M60 penetrated Yuk's face, sending streams of blood into his eyes. In the same moment he slipped into unconsciousness.

Immediately Sol turned Yuk's body over. Seeing his face covered with blood and then the destroyed M60, he assumed that Yuk had been hit in the face and was dead. Realizing the 12.7 had found the range, Sol pulled back to Spike's position.

"Where's Yuk?" Spike yelled above the sound of the battle.

"He's dead! Hit in the facc!" Sol was out of fleshettes and fired an HE round that hit the side of a tree and exploded. He removed his pistol and started firing at the moving khaki figures filtering through the jungle.

A bugle sounded somewhere to the south, and the NVA troops started withdrawing back down the trail. All the same, Spike knew that they were only going to regroup and attack again. They had left too many wounded and dead in the kill zone to leave them behind.

"Let's pull back to where the lieutenant is and find out what in the fuck is going on!" Spike said.

Alsop was on the radio, calling in artillery and air support. He was having a hard time trying to explain to the new captain that he was in the middle of a firefight and didn't have time to brief him on the ambush results. "Sir, stay off the air and let me talk to the artillery forward observer!"

There was a pause and the FO came on the line. Alsop gave him the coordinates for the artillery fire and the area where he wanted napalm dropped.

Spike waited for the lieutenant to get off the air before asking, "Do you want us to dig in or are we going to withdraw?"

Alsop looked over at his platoon sergeant, who was also waiting for instructions. "We're in pretty good shape right now, with only a couple of casualties. We'd better pull back just a little and dig in. I think they're coming back, but in force this time and I don't want them catching us running."

The platoon sergeant nodded his approval, and Spike left with Sol to dig a foxhole below the small ridge line Alsop had selected earlier for an alternate fighting position. All around them Spike heard other paratroopers frantically digging shallow foxholes.

The NVA commander had assembled his leaders and directed them to assault the American position before the jets arrived and started dropping bombs. He knew that if his battalion was going to survive, he had two options. They either had to press so close to the American positions that they were protected from the air strikes or else disengage immediately and disappear into the jungle. But he had too many wounded still trapped in the ambush kill zone to leave them.

Spike was the first to see the NVA returning and dropped his shovel to open fire. The perimeter then opened fire and brought the charge to a standstill. The NVA had achieved part of their objective, getting close enough to protect them from the American artillery fire falling to their rear, but now they were trapped between the American small-arms fire and the artillery.

A lull ensued in the fighting as the NVA commander assessed his situation. Assuming that he was fighting an American platoon, which meant there was a green lieutenant in command, he ordered his troops to maneuver around the edge of the ridge line and flank the American position. Here he made a fatal error, though, not knowing that Alsop was too experienced to fall for such a simple maneuver.

As Spike lay prone in his foxhole, waiting for the next NVA assault, he heard someone call:

"Spike! Sol!" The voice was Yuk's. "Where are you guys? I'm blind!"

Spike felt a cold hand grasp his heart. The voice was coming from below.

"He's alive!" Instinctively Sol started crawling forward before Spike grabbed him. They struggled for a couple of seconds before Spike could subdue him.

"Spike, Help me!" Yuk pleaded. He was answered by an NVA light machine gun.

"What are we going to do?" Sol was near panic. "We can't leave him down there!"

"We're not!" Spike unhooked his webgear and slipped his shotgun into the crook of his arm. "I'm going down there after him."

"No! I'm the one who left him and I'll be the one to go and get him!" Sol said, shoving Spike aside. The sound of his voice drew NVA small-arms fire, and both of them were forced flat against the ground.

With his head still pressed against the cool black earth, Spike growled, "You obey orders, or I swear I'll press charges against you. I have the best chance of getting him and bringing him back. You cover me." Not giving Sol a chance to argue, Spike crawled over the edge of his shallow foxhole and disappeared in the undergrowth.

Spike crawled only a few yards before he was met with a hail of small-arms fire from the surrounding jungle. He tried changing direction, but was pinned down whichever way he tried crawling. The only thing saving him from being hit was that he had crawled into a slight depression. If the NVA gunners couldn't hit him, though, their bullets were missing him by mere inches.

Seeing Spike's predicament, Sol tried getting the lieutenant to bring the artillery fire closer to their position to take some of the pressure off Spike.

For his part, the NVA commander had heard Yuk calling for help and led a two-man team out to capture or kill him before the Americans could rescue him.

Yuk called out again. "Spike! I can't see . . . I'm blind!"

"I'm coming, Yuk!" Spike screamed into the ground, not daring to raise his head even an inch.

The commander heard Yuk calling right in front of him. He pushed aside the bamboo and saw the American soldier lying next to the machine gun with blood covering his face. He smiled over at his comrade and slipped into the American fighting position.

"Is that you, Spike?" Yuk said, relieved. "Man, this is scary—"

The NVA commander wrapped his arm around Yuk's throat and used his knife to cut one of his ears off. As Yuk screamed, Spike jumped up and caught a round in his shoulder that sent him smacking back down against the earth.

The NVA commander turned Yuk's head to the other side and cut off his other ear. Yuk tried to protect himself with a karate chop, but was too weak from loss of blood to deliver an effective blow. The NVA cut Yuk's throat and stuffed his ears into his back pocket before slipping back to his position in the jungle.

"Yuk! Yuk!" Spike screamed, but received no answer. Two artillery rounds fell near Spike's position. Ignoring his wound, he used the explosions as cover to run forward. With his bayonet fixed, he hit Yuk's fighting position in a crouch. "Oh, my God!" he cried as he looked down and saw what they had done to his friend. His scream was so loud that Lieutenant Alsop lowered the handset from his ear and listened.

Sol jumped from his foxhole and yelled, "Airborne!" The cry sent the whole platoon charging down the ridge line. The unexpected assault threw the NVA into a panic, and they fled down the hill directly into the artillery fire. At first the NVA commander shouted at them to stop, but the retreat had become a rout. He had suffered a humiliating defeat, with only one set of ears to add to his trophy necklace.

Sol found Spike standing over Yuk's body. "Spike, it's me . . . Sol."

Spike's eyes were red and the look on his face was so ferocious that for a moment Sol feared for his own life. "Spike! It's me!"

Slowly Spike's eyes focused and he recognized his buddy. "They fucked with him," he whispered, gazing down at the mutilated body between his feet.

Sol felt like throwing up when he saw what the NVA had done to Yuk. Nausea, though, was soon replaced by a powerful surge of hatred.

As Spike started advancing down the trail after the retreating NVA, Sol's eyes widened. Had Spike lost his mind? "Where are you going?"

Spike paused for a second and looked back over his shoulder. "To find the commie motherfucker who took Yuk's ears."

As a light machine gun started chattering off to their left front, Sol hurried over and yanked Spike to the ground. "Later, buddy . . . later. We don't want to get too far out in front of our own lines."

Like an automaton, Spike obeyed and sat crumpled up on the layer of brown bamboo leaves. Sol could see that he was going into shock from his shoulder wound. "Lie down for a minute, Spike, and I'll try and find a medic."

"Why?" Spike's voice echoed in his own ears. "Are you hit?"

Sol felt like crying. Spike looked so young and pathetic lying on the jungle floor.

At a loud rustle behind them, Sol whipped up his weapon, not taking any chances. A squad of paratroopers broke out of the jungle. The sergeant stared at Sol and said, "What's up?"

"Still a few NVA running around, but the area is stable." Sol eyed the rest of the squad. "We need a medic."

The squad leader nodded at the man who had been bringing up the rear, and the medic rushed forward and started looking at Spike's wound. "He looks like he's going into mild shock."

Sol shrugged. "I can understand why."

"Let's get back up the hill," the medic said, looking at the sergeant. "I'm going to need some help."

CHAPTER SEVEN
✪✪✪✪✪✪✪✪✪✪✪✪✪✪✪✪✪✪

BLOODY, JUST BLOODY

The brigade surgeon tapped his index finger on the head of the new canvas stretcher in his tent. He knew that the logical thing to do was to order the young sergeant back to the hospital, but there was something about the look in the teenager's eyes that made him hesitate.

Spike sat on the dark olive-drab stretcher with his shirt off. His upper left shoulder had been bandaged and his left arm was in a sling. Although the armor-piercing round had punched a neat hole through his left lat muscle, it had done hardly any damage and he felt pretty good. The most noticeable part of the wound was the huge black-and-blue mark.

The doctor frowned before saying, "I know better than this, but I'm going to try to honor your request. But the first sign of that wound ulcering and you're going to be shipped back to a field hospital. Fair enough?"

Spike smiled and hopped off the stretcher. "Fair enough, sir."

"I want you to stop by my tent at least every other day until that wound closes. And before you go, I'd better give you another penicillin shot. Remember—no patrolling!"

Spike flinched when the doctor filled the disposable needle and held it up to the light to insure that there were no air bubbles in the plastic chamber. "All of you paratroopers are alike. You don't mind a hole in your body big enough to stick your finger in, but a simple shot makes you wince."

"I mind bullet holes, sir."

The doctor rolled his eyes and sunk the needle deep in Spike's arm.

Sol, who had been waiting for Spike outside the tent, slowly rose from his Vietnamese squat when Spike stepped into the bright sunlight. "What did he say?"

Spike grinned. "He's going to let me stay here."

"I think you're nuts, Spike," Sol said, balancing his blooper in his right hand. "You've got a ticket out of here and you should take it."

Spike sobered. "I told you I'm not leaving until—"

"That's stupid."

". . . until I find the bastard who took Yuk's ears."

Sol waved his weapon like a baton out across the dark green mountainside. "He could be anywhere out there. He could already be dead. He could have thrown the ears away."

Spike squinted and slivers of gold flashed in his dark brown eyes as he stared over the wide valley. "He's out there and I'm going to find him."

"You're crazy, Spike."

"Maybe . . ." Spike started walking toward the perimeter, where Bravo Company was pulling guard. The company was on a well-earned stand down for a week before they were due to go back out on patrols. They had most of the day off to sleep and work on their gear and pulled perimeter guard at night.

Captain Maynard watched Spike walk past the open entrance to his CP and ground his teeth. Lieutenant Alsop had credited the sergeant in his after-action report for exceptional leadership during the ambush. Grimacing at the thought, Maynard picked up his map case and exited the heavily sandbagged bunker. He was due to fly back to the brigade headquarters for a situation briefing with the commanding general. Bravo Company was the top combat company in the brigade, having recorded the most contacts with the NVA and capturing the most weapons. Maynard was being given the credit, but everyone in the company knew that it had been Harwood who had spotted the NVA spy in the Montagnard village. And it had been Harwood who had recommended that Lieutenant Alsop let the spy escape and set up the ambush. It had been Harwood who had fought a rearguard action that allowed the platoon to withdraw under heavy enemy fire. The whole brigade was talking about how Alsop's platoon had taken on a whole NVA battalion and only lost nine dead and eleven wounded. The NVA body count was still coming in from the other two companies who were still sweeping the jungle and finding NVA mass graves containing five to ten bodies each.

Maynard felt a migraine headache coming on as he slipped over the nylon seat in the helicopter. He thought about making peace with Harwood, but the thought passed quickly. That would make him look weak to the other officers. He had to put the enlisted lowlife in his place. But how?

Spike sat on top of his two-man bunker with his leg crossed Indian style. He took in a deep breath and held it in his lungs. He loved the sweet night air that came down the wide valley, so free of automobile exhaust and factory smoke that plagued his hometown. Pontiac was filled with General Motors foundries and auto-assembly plants. He hadn't known what really fresh air was until he had gone to basic training, and then he thought that there was something wrong with the air because it smelled funny.

As Spike slipped his poncho liner over his head and shoulders to keep the hordes of mosquitoes away, Sol snored in the foxhole beneath and mumbled something in his sleep to one of the tormentors in his dream. Spike thought about Sol Levin and the unbelievable wealth his family had. At first Sol hadn't talked about his family, but he had slowly relaxed and told Yuk and him stories about their private Lear jets and homes located around the world. Sol spoke of his father's wealth always as the butt of his jokes. When someone would complain about how poor they were, Sol would complain about how rich he was and how he had to suffer because of it. The jokes Sol made about wealth were really funny and Spike caught himself smiling just thinking about them. Especially the story Sol had told them about his family forcing him to fly with them to Aspen when he wanted to spend time screwing some loose gentile girl "from a poor section of Chicago" whom he had met in school. What made the story so funny was that the poor girl's family was only worth a mere ten million dollars, give or take a couple of million.

Sol stuck his head out the rear slit of their bunker. "Is it my turn yet?"

Spike looked at his watch. "Another hour."

Sol turned on his flashlight and looked for his gear in the bunker. The red lens filtered the light so that it would protect his night vision.

"I'm going to run over to the mess hall and bum some coffee. Where's your canteen cup?" Standing, Sol stretched next to the low bunker and rubbed the sleep out of his eyes.

"Black for me." Spike handed Sol his metal drinking cup. "If they have anything ready to eat, bring it back."

Sol disappeared down the path that led back to the brigade forward headquarters, where they had set up a mess tent. Spike went back to watching the barbed wire. He was depending on the trip flares and booby traps in the wire to warn him if the NVA tried to infiltrate the base camp, which was growing larger every day as more and more units arrived.

Spike glanced over his shoulder at the small D6B tractor and the pair of Caterpillar D7Es working through the night on the runway extension. The 4th Infantry Division was building a large base area in the valley, and the 1st Cavalry Division had sent its 1st Brigade and placed both it and the 173rd under the operational control of the 4th Division, which didn't make the air-assault troops very happy, but rumors were spreading that the 4th Division was going to be the controlling unit in the major battle that was developing. Spike didn't like the idea personally because it was just common sense that a leg commander would save his own men and use the paratroopers as bait or cannon fodder to protect his own division from taking too many casualties.

Daylight was breaking over the eastern ridge line of the valley when Sol returned carrying two canteen cups of steaming coffee and a napkin-wrapped package under his arm. "I had to wait for them to cook the bacon, but it was worth it," Sol said, handing Spike the greasy, great-smelling package.

"Thanks, man," Spike said, biting into the bacon and egg sandwich. "Good shit," he mumbled, holding up the remaining half.

"Eat with your fucking mouth shut," Sol said angrily. "Man, do I have to teach you everything?"

Spike gave Sol the finger and turned around to watch the perimeter wire as the darkness began to give way to the dawn.

"What's that?" Sol pointed to the tall trees bordering the base camp.

"Where?"

"In those trees . . ." Sol squinted, trying to focus on the strange shapes.

Picking up a small set of military binoculars in one hand, Spike checked their adjustment before holding them up to his eyes. The canteen cup dropped from his other hand as he used it to grasp the binoculars.

"What do you see?" Sol asked, worried.

Spike stared for a long time before answering him. "The hostages . . ."

"Who?" Sol asked, getting angry. "What in the fuck are you talking about? Hostages?"

"The fifteen Montagnard hostages."

Sol took the binoculars and held them up. "My God . . . oh, my God!"

Spike stared at the fifteen naked bodies dangling from the branches of the trees. Most of them were small children and they had been strung upside down by their ankles. Their chest and stomach cavities had been cut open so that their intestines were draped around their heads. "Go get the lieutenant," Spike said tonelessly.

Sol dropped the glasses on the sandbags and headed quickly toward Alsop's bunker. As he did, he noticed Captain Maynard boarding the battalion commander's helicopter, parked on the brigade's forward pad. That was new. Normally the captain would land next to the company command post and fill the foxholes around the perimeter with dust. "Maybe Maynard is finally beginning to realize that infantry privates are human," Sol thought. In the next moment, though, he remembered the bloated bodies hanging from the trees, and a hot ball of gas oozed up his throat, followed by his breakfast.

Alighting from the helicopter, Captain Maynard checked his uniform before entering the operations complex. The staff officers were crating their equipment for their move to the forward area at Dak To.

"Hey, Eugene!" One of the captains on the G-3 staff waved over at his classmate. "I hear that your company is really tangling with the NVA."

Maynard nodded his head humbly and smiled.

"I knew that you'd be the type to kick ass in combat. Like our TAC officer said about football and war—they're transferrable skills."

Maynard nodded his head in agreement. "I'll see you later, I've got to find my battalion commander. I've got a shit load of paperwork to take care of."

"He's in the back with the S-1—going over some awards for your company, in fact."

Lieutenant Colonel Yates was holding a stack of award recommendations in his hand and handing them individually to an elderly major when he saw Maynard approaching. "Speak of the devil," he said, smiling. "We were just going over some of your company's awards."

"Really? I'm glad that I got here in time to help."

"How's that?" Yates asked, signaling for the captain to take a seat near him.

"I want to have Sergeant Harwood's Silver Star recommendation pulled."

"Why?" Yates asked, mystified.

"I have heard rumors that the action is phony."

"Phony?" The old major who was the brigade's administrative officer frowned.

"Yes, I've heard from a couple of the platoon leaders that Captain Whitmore and Harwood made a deal to recommend each other for valor awards." Maynard didn't have to struggle to keep a straight face as he lied. He had mastered the art of lying boldly to survive West Point.

"Whitmore?" The major shook his head. "I have a very difficult time believing that."

"It's true," Maynard attacked, using his best hurt expression.

"Whitmore doesn't have a pending award for valor," the major said, staring Maynard right in the eye.

"Then . . . then he must have gotten cold feet and withdrew it."

"I have a tough time believing that also," the major replied sternly, not liking the inflection in Maynard's voice. "I've known Whitmore for years and he's established an excellent reputation for integrity."

"Are you calling me a liar?" Maynard challenged.

"Let's call it a case of being misinformed. You should go back and check your sources." The major smiled tightly. "You don't have a valor award pending, by some chance, do you, Captain Maynard?"

"Ahhh, well . . . as a matter of fact, I do," Maynard admitted, trapped.

"For what action? You haven't been with the brigade long enough to have been in a battle, have you?" Now the major was keen on a scent. He had been in Vietnam for eighteen months and had seen just about every trick that an officer could pull in the awards and decorations game.

"We had a big firefight and a night ambush . . . where . . ." Maynard looked over at Yates for help.

"Didn't Lieutenant Alsop command that *platoon*?"

"I command Bravo Company and I'm responsible for everything they do or fail to do!"

"I can't argue with that. But you still haven't answered my question. Wasn't it Alsop's platoon that engaged the NVA? And isn't Sergeant Harwood in that platoon?"

Yates, seeing the conversation was going against his junior contemporary from West Point, interfered: "Enough! I will not tolerate a staff officer harassing one of my company commanders."

"No one is harassing your man, Colonel. Just asking a relevant question is all," the major said, not backing off. "Please." He took the stack of awards out of Yates's hand and shuffled through them. "Ah, here it is—Captain Eugene Maynard, son of General Maynard—"

"We don't need your sarcasm, Major!" Yates's face was turning red.

"A Distinguished Service Cross, no less," he noted, reading the recommended citation. "Single-handedly attacked an NVA machine-gun bunker and wiped out the occupants?" The major looked at the captain.

Maynard looked at his commander. "Sir, I will not stand here and have my honor questioned."

The major continued, ". . . fought hand-to-hand with an NVA commander and wrestled him to the ground and thrust a bayonet deeply into the enemy's throat and then dragged a wounded soldier back to his friendly lines?" The major laughed. "This is fucking fiction."

"I've had enough of your accusations, Major!" Yates slammed his fist on the desk, drawing the attention of all the officers in the large room.

The major calmly shuffled through a stack of papers on his desk, taking his time finding the paragraph he was looking for. He spun the after-action report around so that the battalion commander could read it for himself, and then he pulled another after-action report out of the pile. "My job is to match facts in incidents like this, and if you read Lieutenant Alsop's report and plot his location, you will see that they were almost a thousand meters away from each other. There were no reported enemy casualties at Captain Maynard's location."

Yates responded by sorting through the stack of award recommendations and pulling the one for Harwood out of the pile. He deliberately took his time tearing the papers to shreds. "I support my company commanders . . . Major."

"Good. Now *support* them to the commanding general." The major's face showed his anger. "You had no right to destroy official documents."

The battalion commander then tore up the two conflicting after-action reports, knowing that the evidence they contained would destroy Maynard's career. They had just been shipped back that morning and he was banking on their not having been copied yet.

"Colonel, wait here!" the major cried, storming off to the commanding general's office. He returned within seconds. "Follow me, sir!"

The brigadier general looked like he didn't want to be bothered with such a petty matter, but his administrations officer had insisted. In a moment the general saw that Yates was very angry and that he was accompanied by a powerful four-star general's son.

The major briefed the general on what had occurred in his office, followed by Yates's rendition of the incident. Yates, a master politician, had calmed down completely and acted like the understanding senior officer who had witnessed a very unfortunate incident, in which the major had verbally assaulted the captain.

The general decided on playing it safe. The major was an over-the-hill officer who had been passed over for promotion three times and was on his way out of the Army. "Major, I really am embarrassed that you would accuse a fellow officer of misconduct on such a large scale." He raised his hand to cut off the major. "I don't want to hear any more about this incident, and you can pack your things. I've had enough of you going off half-cocked."

"You're relieving me?" the major said, shocked by the turn of events.

"Unless Lieutenant Colonel Yates will accept your apology." The general looked over at the battalion commander.

"Sir, normally I would, but in this case, my honor and my company commander's honor were questioned in front of enlisted men, and he must be punished to show them our innocence."

"Innocence?" the major spluttered, enraged.

"Enough!" the general shouted. "You are finished in this brigade, Major. Report back to the Saigon detachment and find yourself another job. You should be able to figure out the process by yourself."

Lieutenant Alsop stood next to Spike's bunker and looked through the field glasses. "Do you think they're waiting for us to go out there, Sergeant Harwood?"

"They could be. Or they could have booby-trapped the bodies."

"You could be right either way." Alsop lowered the field glasses. "That's sick."

Sol came up with the solution. "Call in napalm and burn the whole fucking jungle over there."

Lieutenant Alsop looked around the area. A napalm run would actually clear a little more of the jungle away. "Let's try it." He used the platoon radio to call back for the napalm strike.

The air strike was approved and within ten minutes a pair of Phantom F-4s made the pass, directed by a L-19 Bird-dog that circled a mile away, carrying the brigade's air observer. Paratroopers climbed on top of their covered foxholes and watched the fiery display. As a huge black cloud rolled back over the base area, a number of secondary explosions rumbled inside of the sound of the burning napalm.

Spike watched through the field glasses for only a couple of seconds to make sure that the napalm was on target. He had no desire to watch the bodies burn.

"Do you think the spy in the village is responsible?" Sol said from behind him.

"Probably." Spike lowered his binoculars.

Sol's voice dropped. "Did you see the girl?"

"I couldn't tell. The bodies were starting to swell from the sun."

"The NVA sure have guts," Sol snapped, starting to get angry.

Spike swallowed hard and jumped up on his bunker's roof. "We kicked your ass!" He formed a fist with his good hand and held it above his head. "Do you hear me, you communist motherfuckers? We kicked your ass!"

Sol looked at Spike as if he had gone crazy on him. "You all right, buddy?"

Spike looked back down at his partner and smiled. "I'm fine. We must have really kicked their asses during the ambush for them to pull that shit for revenge."

Not knowing how to answer, Sol nodded back toward the base area. "Come on. Let's go take a shower before the quartermaster shower point runs out of water."

Spike, though, remained standing on the sandbags and watched the black cloud rolling up in the still air above the jungle.

"Come on, Spike. Let's clean up," Sol insisted, trying to get Spike off the bunker.

Just then a single sniper round impacted against one of the top sandbags.

Spike cupped his hand around the corner of his mouth. "I killed your fucking friends, you mother-fucking commie!"

Three rounds were fired rapid-fire from the edge of the jungle. Spike remained standing in the open, daring the NVA sniper to try again.

"Get down from there, Spike!"

"Fuck them. They can't hit shit but women and kids," Spike said, glaring out over the barbed wire.

The NVA sniper, having adjusted his sights on Spike's chest after making a slight wind and elevation adjustment, started squeezing the trigger on his new Russian sniper rifle. In concentrating so hard, though, he failed to respond to the sound of the six 105mm rounds whistling in and was dead before he realized that he had been the forward observer's prime target.

Spike hopped down from the roof of the bunker. "Motherfuckers can't hit shit. He should have taken me out with his first shot."

"That's really comforting to know, Spike." Sol shook his head. "You're totally fucking crazy."

"Naw, I know they can't hit shit. They smoke too much dope."

Sol and Spike had their green field towels slung around their necks as they walked toward the showers.

The word had spread around the perimeter like wild-fire about what Spike had done. By the time the story had gone completely around the large base area, it had Spike insulting the whole NVA high command. He was becoming a legend in the battalion and he hadn't been in Vietnam for two months.

"Man, am I looking forward to a hot shower!" Sol said as they neared the two five-hundred-gallon black rubber tanks set up next to a small stream. A small gasoline-operated pump removed the water out of the stream and pumped it into the first black tank, where the water was purified and then transferred to the second tank, where it went to a heating unit. A quartermaster specialist directed them over to an undressing area, where benches had been set up and a stack of clean towels placed in the drying area. The showers were already full and there was a short line waiting to take their turns.

"You'll have to wait over there until these men are done," an airborne master sergeant said, pointing to a grassy area a couple hundred feet away. "We don't want to make too big of a target for NVA mortar crews."

A paratrooper standing in line sneered, "The NVA can't hit shit. Ask Sergeant Harwood."

Spike caught himself blushing. "We'd better do what the master sergeant recommends. Too many paratroopers in the shower area will make a nice target." He was turning to leave when he spied a naked body rushing toward him from the entrance to the shower tent.

"Spike!"

A smile broke out on Spike's face when he recognized the naked paratrooper. "O'Toole! What in the hell are you doing here?"

"When I got to Camp Alpha in Saigon, they changed my orders to the 1st Cavalry." O'Toole threw a couple of shadow-boxing punches at the air before adding,

"But I convinced them that I was a paratrooper and they decided to transfer me back to the 173rd."

"You convinced them?"

O'Toole threw a couple of jabs and then smiled. "Well, actually, I bribed one of the clerks. It cost me a hundred fucking dollars, and all that asshole did was take my records out of one pile and slip them in another one!"

"And you're here." Spike grinned. "It's really good seeing you again, O'Toole." Spike thought about Yuk and swallowed hard. He didn't like the idea of having another friend here, where the potential for being killed was so high.

"I'm with Alpha Company. Who you with, Spike?"

"Bravo." Spike turned and introduced Sol. "This is the best blooper man in Nam."

Sol smiled and shook hands. "He brags a lot."

O'Toole shook his head. "You don't have to tell me."

The master sergeant broke up the reunion. "Are you going to go back in there and finish your shower?"

"Yeah, Sarge." O'Toole started back toward the open shower entrance. "I'll look you up later, Spike."

"Where did you meet him?" Sol asked when O'Toole was out of earshot.

"Airborne school. He's a good man."

Eating from a paper plate, Captain Maynard glared across the field table over at the enlisted men. The brigade headquarters company had set up a small tent for the general's mess and had furnished it with dark green field tables and folding chairs. Any officer in the brigade was welcome to eat in the tent, but only invited guests were allowed to use the tin flatware and plates from the general's mess kit.

"What do you think about the new operations scheduled for tomorrow?" Maynard asked the Alpha Company commander.

"We'll see. I'm teamed up with Charlie Company, and we're supposed to sweep the back side of the mountain to our east."

"It sounds easy."

"It should be except for the humping along the ridges. I haven't busted my ass so much since Ranger school!"

Manyard looked down at the plate of greasy spaghetti. "It's better than this small-unit hunter-killer shit they have my company doing."

The Alpha Company commander shrugged. "It's all counted as time spent in-country. Besides, it's easy duty for the officers because you don't have to hump. You can stay in the rear."

Maynard swiped his paper plate off the table with the back of his hand. "What do you mean by that smart-assed remark?"

The Alpha Company commander looked up at Maynard, unfazed. Maynard had already established a reputation in the battalion for being a spoiled brat who would try to manipulate anyone to get what he wanted. "I meant what I said. You don't have to hump the jungle during a hunter-killer operation."

"Are you trying to imply that I volunteered my company for small-unit operations so that I wouldn't have to go out in the jungle?"

"You know, Maynard, I don't know what your fucking problem is, but you had better stick to fucking with enlisted men, because us officers aren't going to take your shit!" The Alpha Company commander picked up his plate and plastic fork and went to join two other officers at another table.

Over in the 1st Platoon, Lieutenant Alsop sat on a stack of sandbags and waited until all of the members of his platoon had assembled around him for their briefing. He kept count as they dribbled in from the mess hall and scowled. The platoon was down to

nineteen men, including NCOs, and they were waiting
for replacements to fill up the company.

"Is everyone here?" he asked, looking over at his
platoon sergeant, who nodded. "Good. I've got some
good news and some bad news."

The platoon groaned.

"The good news is that we're going to be left behind
to hold the perimeter while the rest of the company
sweeps the southern portion of the valley in hunter-
killer teams. The bad news is that there are only
nineteen of us and we're going to be spread real thin
along the perimeter." Alsop saw the men relaxing
after hearing the news. They had been in a couple of
tough fights and needed time to rest and get their shit
together again. "Captain Maynard selected us for perimeter guard duty because—"

"Because he wants to fuck with Harwood," one of
the paratroopers cut in.

"That was out of line, trooper!" Alsop cried. He
knew that the man was telling the truth, but he couldn't
openly support insubordination.

Spike's face turned red. He knew that the platoon
had been given a lot of dirty details because of his
popularity, but staying behind as perimeter guards was
a lucky break and not a punishment. "I don't know
about that. I'd rather sit on a bunker than hump the
jungle," he said, looking over at the paratrooper who
had made the comment. "Besides, what goes on between the captain and me doesn't affect you guys."

"Bullshit," the trooper snorted, not backing off.

"One more comment out of you and I'm going to
take some of your paycheck," Alsop said, cutting the
man off. "All right, get some sleep this afternoon and
we'll assign bunkers after supper."

The platoon broke up and went back to their fighting positions in groups of two and three.

Minutes later, Captain Maynard watched from his
CP and smiled as the company first sergeant headed
toward Lieutenant Alsop's foxhole. Maynard lit a thin

cigar and puffed on it, waiting for Alsop's reaction when the first sergeant told him that his platoon would unload pallets of ammo during the day and pull guard duty at night.

Alsop flung his helmet down on the ground and looked over toward the captain's CP. He could see the West Point officer leaning against the bunker with a cloud of smoke circling his head. The paratrooper in his platoon had been right: Maynard was screwing with the whole platoon to get cheap shots at Sergeant Harwood.

The battalion had been patrolling around the huge Dak To forward base area for three days without a single sighting of any North Vietnamese units in the whole valley. The senior generals down in Saigon were contemplating moving the combat units out of the Tumerong Valley to operational areas farther north, where there had been large NVA sightings.

Spike had heard the rumors along with the rest of the men staying in the base area. He was pissed because they had been working their asses off humping crates of small-arms ammunition and artillery rounds that needed to be rigged for helicopter lifts out to the units and artillery-support bases.

Spike stopped and untied the drive-on rag he had tied around his forehead. Wringing out the sweat, he retied it around his head. Sweat steamed out of his pores and he could feel it running down his back to the waistband of his fatigues. From the knees up, his trousers were stained dark from the body fluid he was losing under the hot jungle sun.

Sol looked over at his friend and frowned: Spike was working too hard. The hole the NVA bullet had made in his lat muscle had closed, but it was a vivid red around the edges. The wound could still break open and cause Spike a lot of additional agony. Sol knew that Spike was working harder than the other men because he felt responsible for the captain screwing with the platoon.

Sol called over, "Hey, take it easy. We've still got three hours before the lift ships arrive to haul this shit out to the field."

Spike stopped stacking the wooden crates and looked at the C-130 cargo airplane approaching the wide runway for a landing. "Fuck, this is hard work."

"Especially after pulling guard all night." Shaking his head, Sol sent a volley of sweat pellets across the dry wooden crates.

"Look at that stupidity." Spike nodded toward the runway.

Sol didn't understand what he was trying to tell him. "What?"

"They've been lining up those one-five-five powder canisters all day long next to the runway."

"So?"

Spike made room on top of the stack of boxes he was standing on. "Come up here where you can see better."

Sol hesitated and then climbed up the twenty-foot stack of crates and joined Spike. "So what?"

"Look . . ." Spike pointed at the long trail of canisters perfectly aligned along the side of the runway by the forklift operators. He moved his finger along the line and stopped when he reached the tip of his boots.

Sol understood. "Oh, shit!"

"Yeah, a fucking fuse." Spike gingerly sat on a sun-heated crate and waited a second for his sweat-soaked pants to cool off the wood before making himself comfortable. "Let's take a break."

Sol sat next to him. "Man, if the NVA could set that shit on fire, it would act as a fuse and travel right over here." He tapped the crate he was sitting on. "And boom! The whole fucking ammunition dump would go up."

The C-130 taxied over to the end of the line of powder canisters and lowered its rear ramp. The crew began unloading the pallets while the pilot let the engines idle.

"It looks like the Air Force is in a hurry," Sol said, smiling.

"Wouldn't you be, too, if you were carrying a full load of powder and ammo?" Spike hung his legs over the edge of the crate and stared at the dark green hill behind the base camp, trying to detect the locations of Alpha and Charlie companies. Maybe the Air Force pilot didn't have too much to worry about, he decided. Two airborne companies were patrolling the mountainside, the rest of the brigade was covering the valley, and the far mountains were being patrolled by the 1st Cav. NVA mortar or rocket crews would have a very difficult time sneaking in close enough to harass the runway.

Spike had no more thought this when a puff of gray smoke erupted near the center of the runway. A few seconds later a muffled explosion reached Spike and Sol.

"Fucking mortars!" Sol cried, dropping flat onto the crates.

Spike watched a second mortar round impact about a hundred meters to the left of the first one and realized that the C-130 was bracketed. Still, the large aircraft didn't move, for the crew in the cockpit couldn't hear the explosions over the sound of the engines. After a long pause four rounds exploded around the C-130 and burst into beautiful white flowers. The NVA were using white phosphorus. They *had* noticed the powder canisters lined up along the runway leading to the ammo dump, and they knew that the C-130 was unloading more ammo. The powder canisters would act as a fuse and the aircraft as the detonator. A second volley of burning white phosphorus rounds impacted, and three of the rounds hit the parked aircraft. There was a short delay and then the center of the airframe burst open.

"Come on, Spike! Let's get the hell away from here!" Sol screamed, already climbing down.

A M102 airborne 105mm battery instantly started firing counter-mortar fire and destroyed the NVA mortar position, but the damage from the suicide crew had already been done. The C-130 burned hot and had started igniting the row of powder canisters. Spike saw the forklift operators jump from their vehicles and start running from the extreme heat of the burning jet fuel. Events began happening extremely fast around the base area. Paratroopers ran for cover, expecting the ammunition aboard the C-130 to start exploding all over the runway.

Spike dropped off the stack of crates and ran bent over toward the burning powder canisters, which looked like giant firecrackers going off. He paused just long enough to pick up his sweat-soaked fatigue jacket he had left to dry out on a concertina-wire fence and slipped it on over his bare back before sprinting hard down the line of pallets toward an idling abandoned forklift. At two-hundred meters from the C-130 Spike could already feel the intense heat, and the forklift was parked another fifty meters closer to the aircraft.

Sol was screaming for him to get the hell away from the runway, but Spike ignored his friend's warning. He was intent on getting to the forklift. An exploding pallet of hand flares onboard the airplane sent a bright red fireball rolling up in the sky and a heat wave scorched Spike's eyebrows. He stopped running for a moment to turn his back to the fireball and then made a mad dash for the forklift. He could feel the heat sear his hands when he grabbed the steering wheel and touched the shifting lever.

Sol watched helplessly from the edge of the runway as Spike tried working the unfamiliar gears on the vehicle. Suddenly it jerked forward and Spike gunned the engine. The front blades rammed into a pallet of powder, pushing it back five feet out of line with the rest of the pallets. Spike backed up the forklift and repeated the process again and again, until there was a fifty-foot gap in the powder fuse that led to the huge ammunition resupply point at the end of the airstrip.

Spike felt the heat blasting through the back of his jacket and a sharp, stinging pain on his neck. He hurried to widen the gap so that the flames couldn't jump the breach he had made. When the gap was over a hundred feet wide he pointed the forklift back toward the ammunition dump and floored the gas pedal.

Sol met him before he reached the ammunition stockpile and jumped up on the side of the slow-moving vehicle. He grabbed the pipe cage that covered the top of the forklift and nearly let go because of the heat. Spike pointed the vehicle toward their side of the perimeter and drove over to their bunker line.

Captain Maynard had watched the entire incident from the entrance of his CP bunker. Sergeant Harwood's act of extreme courage had saved the forward base area from disaster. If the ammunition depot had caught on fire, it would have rendered the whole base area untenable. That would have necessitated evacuation and the NVA would have capitalized on the panic.

"You dumb shit!" Sol was furious. "That whole fucking airplane was filled with one-five-five pro-joes!"

"I couldn't let that fire reach the ammunition depot," Spike said matter-of-factly.

"Fuck you! Personally, I think that you want to fucking die!" Sol threw his pistol belt across the bunker and it hit a crate of M16 ammo.

Ignoring his friend's remark, Spike rubbed the back of his neck. "That stings."

"It should! You've had all of the hair on the back of your stupid fucking head burnt off!" Sol looked around the small bunker for their first-aid kit. "You fucking gentiles sure didn't get the brains when they were being passed out!"

Spike smiled. "You're right. You Jews were the first ones in line."

Captain Maynard leaned over and looked in the

fighting bunker. "Harwood! Levin! Get your gear and come with me!"

Spike looked at Sol: what was the captain up to now?

The C-130 wreckage was billowing black smoke, but the fire had been contained on the runway and would burn itself out before morning. A flight of gunships were working over the area where the mortars had fired from earlier. Artillery echoed all along the valley floor from defensive fires the units had selected earlier. The commander of the forward base area wasn't taking any chances on a sneak attack.

Spike caught up to the captain. "Sir, is something going on?"

Maynard paused long enough to glare at Spike and quip, "Yeah, 'something' is going on back up there on the mountain. Alpha and Charlie companies have tangled with a very large NVA force trying to sneak around Dak To. The NVA were staying close enough to our base area to miss our harassment and interdiction fire, yet stayed far enough away from our perimeter to evade listening posts. Alpha Company ran right into them on their way back down the mountainside."

Spike glanced up on the side of the mountain where the 105mm rounds were impacting. It was only a few thousand meters as the crow flies, but a good two days of humping through the jungle. Sol gave Spike an aw-shit look and shook his head.

Maynard stopped outside of the brigade's command bunker. "Harwood, you and Levin guard the entrance to the command bunker. The general is concerned that the NVA might have infiltrated the base camp during the explosions."

Spike glanced at Sol and raised his eyebrows. "Sir, it's still daylight—"

Maynard whirled on him. "You do what you're told!"

"Yes, sir." Spike waited until the captain had entered the bunker, which had eight layers of sandbags on the roof, and then he looked over at Sol. "Let's go up on top and watch the show over there on the mountain."

The sides of the large bunker were sloped and made for an easy climb to the top. Spike stacked a couple of sandbags on top of each other to make a comfortable seat. He laid his shotgun across his lap and pointed at a pair of F-4s streaking down the valley. "I don't think they're going to drop their loads."

"Why?" Sol asked, settling next to Spike.

"Too close."

The F-4s roared past the bunker without dropping their bombs. Spike had been right.

"The artillery battery is firing direct fire." Sol pointed at the six howitzers nearby. "See, there's the forward observer." An officer was standing on top of their fire-direction center bunker, adjusting the rounds against the side of the jungle-covered mountain less than two thousand meters away. The sounds from the big battle echoed down the slopes.

Spike felt a cold shiver ripple down his back, even though he was sweating profusely. The stubs of curled and charred hair still left on the back of his neck stuck out. Spike sensed that something was wrong on the side of the mountain. The firefight was lasting too long for a chance encounter with the NVA.

The NVA battalion trying to sneak around the Dak To base camp might have succeeded if it hadn't been for a freak order by the Alpha Company commander to his platoon leaders on their way back down the mountainside. After searching the reverse side of the mountain, he had told them that the last platoon back inside the base area wouldn't get any beer or showers. After not encountering any sign of NVA troop movement on their patrol, the company had spread out down the trail leading to the valley, with some of the men actually running down the hillside trails to be the first ones inside the safety of the barbed wire.

The 1st Platoon lasted less than five minutes after running into the first NVA company. Reacting fast, the 2nd and 3rd platoons managed to form a loose perimeter that slowed down the NVA advance enough for the company command to call in artillery fire on the fluid NVA positions. The direct-fire artillery gave the remaining paratroopers a chance to organize and fight back against the huge odds.

O'Toole volunteered to fight a rearguard action so that his platoon could escape back up the mountain and link up with the command element. He had become separated from the company by only a few hundred feet, but it might as well of been miles. He found a place where he could back up against a sheer cliff and fight until his ammunition ran out or Charlie Company could rescue him.

The Charlie Company commander ordered his company to assault down the trail behind Alpha Company and ran into a wall of tear gas—American tear gas.

Because of the fraggings of new men, the brigade commander had ordered that all tear-gas grenades and powdered tear-gas canisters be left in the field, for the paratroopers had developed a very effective method for handling officers and NCOs who functioned poorly in the field. They would warn them by chucking a tear-gas grenade into their hootchs during the night. The method got their point across, and it was much better than throwing fragmentation grenades and having to worry about murder charges.

The Alpha Company commander had his men chuck their tear gas before starting down the mountainside, figuring that the mountain winds would blow it away before Charlie Company had caught up to them. Unfortunately, most of the gas was trapped in a large depression on the trail and formed a solid barrier. Charlie Company was forced to break through virgin jungle in order to skirt around. The tear gas sealed Alpha Company's doom, but saved Charlie Company from running into a hasty ambush the NVA had set up on the trail for them.

Down below, Spike and Sol had returned to their bunker and had turned on their platoon's spare PRC-25 radio to Alpha Company's frequency. They watched the artillery rounds hit the side of the mountain and listened to the Alpha Company commander shouting to his platoon leaders.

Sol looked over at Spike with concern. "It sounds like Alpha is receiving some heavy shit."

Spike nodded.

The radio was turned down low, but the urgency in the voices of the Alpha Company radio operators told the story that was unfolding on the mountainside.

"Fuck!" A new voice was full of panic. "Captain! Everyone is dead! . . . Captain! . . ."

Static filled the airwaves before another voice came on the air. "Who are you?" It was a little calmer but still filled with fear.

"Mason! First Platoon! Where in the hell are you guys?"

"Where's your lieutenant, Mason?"

"I just fucking told you: everyone else is dead! I found . . . oh, God, they've found me . . ."

The radio went silent.

"Mason? Mason?"

Spike glanced over at Sol. It was worse than bad. Alpha Company was getting their asses waxed.

"They're not even using call signs on the radio," Sol said, looking down into his bunker at his weapon. "Maybe we should get our gear together. I think some deep shit has started to flow down in this valley."

Spike nodded his head in agreement. "I'm going to listen for a few more minutes."

The few minutes turned into hours. A half-dozen more paratroopers joined Spike around the radio and listened to the desperate voices of their comrades in Alpha Company as they were slowly hunted down and killed by the NVA.

Darkness fell early on the eastern side of the valley where the battle was raging. Spike saw the long shadows slipping down to the valley floor and knew that under the thick vegetation that visibility was almost gone. It would be almost impossible for a relief force to make it up there during the night, and it was obvious that Alpha Company had tangled with a much larger NVA force.

Charlie Company established a perimeter for the night about three hundred meters from Alpha Company's last known position, hoping that what was left of Alpha Company could infiltrate back to their positions during the night. Again the paratrooper officers had underestimated the NVA commander, but it really hadn't been their fault. The NVA battalion commander they were facing was one of the best leaders in the NVA division, and he had been personally selected by the NVA corps commander to take up the critical blocking position east of Dak To for the upcoming major offensive. The NVA battalion commander had fought against the French and was extremely good in the jungle. The pair of paratrooper captains he was facing were nothing more than children playing at war to him and had been easily outmaneuvered.

Up on the mountainside with his back against the cliff, O'Toole watched the darkness surround him. At first it had terrified him, but gradually he felt as if a comforting blanket was being drawn around him. From his hiding place O'Toole watched the NVA sweeping the battlefield, killing wounded paratroopers and stripping the dead of anything of value. He scanned the jungle floor and minutes before it became too dark to see, his gaze locked on the familiar shape of an M60 lying next to a large tree. The arm of a dead paratrooper lay over the stock of the weapon. O'Toole looked around before making a quick dash for it. Up close he saw a half-full belt of ammo still attached to the weapon. Still glancing all around for NVA, he paused long enough to check the dead trooper's rucksack for additional ammo and found two additional belts. Carrying the rucksack over one shoulder and the M60 by its carrying handle, he scuttled back to the cliff. He had dropped the rucksack just as the first NVA soldier broke out of the jungle.

O'Toole pulled the trigger on the M60 without aiming, and the bullets sprayed the jungle floor in front of the NVA without slowing him down. In the next moment O'Toole grabbed the front grip on the machine gun and took a better aim for the next burst. The NVA skidded to a halt. A surprised look crossed his face as he realized that he was dying. So far the NVA hadn't met much resistance, and the blood fever during the slaughter had replaced discipline.

O'Toole used the next couple of seconds to take up a good fighting position with the automatic weapon. He was protected from his rear by the cliff and from each side of his position by large hunks of fallen rock. The NVA would have to come at him from a fifty-degree fan to his front, and he could cover the whole area with the M60, until his ammo ran out.

Spike listened to the sounds echoing down the mountainside. The small-arms firing had died down to almost nothing. Every once in a while a short burst from an M16 or an AK-47 disrupted the early evening silence between volleys from the 105mm battery firing near Spike's position on the perimeter. The artillery M102 howitzers had been firing so much during the afternoon that the chambers of the weapons were so hot, the gunners didn't need to pull the lanyards anymore. The rounds would cook off within seconds after the breeches were closed.

Then, in the lulls between artillery rounds, Spike distinctly heard a lone M60 firing long bursts.

In the dim light filtering through the trees from flares dropped by an Air Force aircraft, O'Toole saw the NVA platoon charging his position. He held the trigger back and swept the area in front of him. NVA soldiers fell, only to be replaced by others. The M60 stopped shaking in his hands and O'Toole looked down to see what had gone wrong. There were no linked rounds to the left side of the weapon. Just as he reached back for his M16, he saw a pair of NVA soldiers approaching him from both sides.

"Airborne! Motherfuckers!" He selected the closest one next to him and fired.

O'Toole didn't feel the AK-47 rounds tear the back of his head off.

Spike thought that he had heard something on the wind and squinted at the dark side of the mountain. He sensed that something awful had happened, but he didn't know what.

The battle for Dak To had just begun, and only after eight hundred and sixteen American paratroopers died would it all end.

CHAPTER EIGHT

☒☒☒☒☒☒☒☒☒☒☒☒☒☒☒☒☒

BLOOD RUNS
UPHILL

November 17, 1967
19:00 hours

The North Vietnamese major general looked out over the valley that ran east and west out of the tri-border intersection into the Tan Canh–Dak To mountains. He had just arrived from North Vietnam with the 1st North Vietnamese Army Division.

One of the regimental commanders waiting for him to return to the bunker lit a Russian cigarette and offered the pack to a young colonel sitting next to him. The other officer shook his head and reached in his pocket for his own pack of Salem Longs.

"American cigarettes?" the older colonel snarled. The grimace made his face even more frightening to behold. The whole left side of his head had been horribly scarred from a napalm strike the year before in the jungle near the Parrot's Beak down south.

"Yes, I like their menthol taste," the junior colonel noted, not about to be intimidated by the old warrior.

"I don't allow my soldiers to use anything made by those pigs!" He hot-boxed his cigarette.

"Then you are a fool. The Americans carry canned food and supplies that are very hard to get out here in the jungle." The younger colonel smiled and held up the Salem. "Personally, I take great pleasure in knowing that an American soldier had to die for these cigarettes. My men removed them from his rucksack."

The major general entered the large underground bunker the division's engineers had just finished building, and the senior commanders assembled there fell silent. He took his time scanning their faces. Most of them were familiar, but a few of the faces were new. He saw a young lieutenant colonel standing against the dirt wall in back.

"What are you wearing around your neck?" the general asked, unable to make out what was on the man's gold chain.

"Ears, sir." The lieutenant colonel's voice was so deep that the general was surprised.

"Since when do officers of the People's Army commit atrocities?"

The 174th Regimental commander stood up to defend his favorite battalion commander. "Sir?"

The general slowly turned to look at the colonel.

"Sir, I have permitted him to wear those American ears as a symbol to our men. Lieutenant Colonel—"

The general cut him off. "I know who he is and if I'm not mistaken, this is not the first time there have been charges of atrocities made against him."

The warning given, the major general dropped the incident and returned to the front of the room, where a large battle map had been erected on a tripod. He looked over one more time at the battalion commander before starting his briefing and saw the sick smile on the man's face. The general knew that the man was a butcher, but in war it was those kinds of men who excelled on the battlefield, and they were in demand.

"I have risked assembling all of you together here because we are about to launch the largest offensive that we have ever attempted in the South Vietnamese highlands. The Americans patrolling the tri-border area have been coming too close to our major resupply depots in Cambodia and Laos. We have a twofold mission: drive the Americans from the borders and, if we can, cut South Vietnam in half." He looked out at the resigned faces watching him. There had been numerous attempts at dividing the south in the past two years and they had all failed miserably. Since the Americans had built up their forces and the Koreans had sent over their Capitol Division, everyone knew that it was now just a dream.

The scar-faced colonel stood up. "We have intelligence, sir, that the American pigs have fifteen battalions committed to that area, and they have all been put under the operational control of their 4th Division."

The general grinned. The old colonel always had the best intelligence on Americans and rarely was he wrong. He had been a Vietminh battalion commander when they had fought the French and had established espionage cells among the maids and janitors who worked on the French bases and in their villas. These same people now worked for the American high commands because they had perfect credentials. He had also infiltrated the bars and steam baths with his special agents. It had taken the old colonel twenty years to establish his organization and he even had mother-daughter teams working for him. The NVA general nodded slowly and asked the colonel, "Who is the American general commanding their 4th Division?"

"A major general named Peers. He is a graduate of their West Point."

"Is he aggressive?"

"Our Russian intelligence liaison says that he will fight, but our advantage is his staff. It is led by inexperienced combat officers. If we attack with vigor"—he looked at the regimental commander, who was still smoking the American cigarette—"and with determination, we should severely hurt the American effort to control Dak To."

The major general sensed the extreme dislike the old intelligence officer had for the Salem smoker. "We have four regiments of experienced soldiers against their fifteen combat battalions. The advantage is theirs in numbers, but goes to us in experience."

Everyone in the room knew what the general was saying. American field units were commanded by children—lieutenants and captains who were almost always fresh out of school. The NVA commanders in the field rarely had a problem defeating the Americans when their air cover and artillery couldn't be used. In the A Shau Valley, where air support was seldom supplied because of the dense fog and artillery was difficult to position because of the steep mountains and narrow valleys, they had never lost a one-on-one fight. Dak To was different, though, and they knew the Americans could bring their full support power against them. They would have to strike quickly with the Americans and then stay close so that they would be afraid to call in air and artillery strikes in on their own positions.

"General, when are we going to initiate this battle?" the commander of the 66th Regiment asked.

"We will start moving into position tomorrow. The 33rd Regiment will attack our objective from the south. You will attack with your 66th Regiment from the southwest and take Dak To." He looked back over his shoulder at the young colonel who smoked Salems. "The 174th Regiment will be held in reserve near"—he looked closely at his map—"Hill 875."

November 19, 1967
1330 hours

Maynard watched Yates as he questioned the Charlie Company commander about the battle that had taken place on the mountainside. The 4th Battalion had been assigned to bail out Charlie Company and sweep the area for survivors from Alpha Company. The whole 173rd Airborne Brigade had been shocked to learn that a full-strength American airborne company could be totally destroyed by the NVA. There had been only one survivor from Alpha Company, the forward observer, a Lieutenant Beusenal, and he wasn't expected to live. He had been found with both of his legs blown off and one of his arms so badly mangled that it didn't look like it could be repaired.

"You say that you couldn't get to Alpha because of tear gas?" Yates shook his head.

"Yes, sir. It's brigade policy not to return to a base camp carrying open tear-gas containers."

"I want you to forget what you've just said. Do you hear me?" Yates threatened. The brigade chief-of-staff was a classmate of his from West Point, and he knew that if the policy about the tear gas became known, it would end his classmate's chances for a star. The unofficial and disclaimed West Point Protective Association was functioning to protect its graduates, as it had been since the first class had graduated from its ivy-covered halls.

The captain looked over at Yates with a funny expression. "I've already stated that in my written report." He was trying to cover for *his* West Point classmate, who had commanded Alpha Company.

"You fucking idiot!" Yates screamed at the battle-weary captain.

The Charlie Company commander struggled to his feet. He hadn't slept in three days and was exhausted. Yates had had Maynard bring him over to the battalion CP as soon as the brigade staff had finished their debriefings with him. "Colonel, I'm beat . . . really tired. I've lost over half of my company and a lot of good friends from Alpha Company. Don't you ever call me an idiot again—until you get your ass out there and show us how it's done." The captain's voice was

soft from exhaustion and it was difficult for the proper
level of emotion to show through. He turned to leave
the bunker and added, "I'll bet everything that I own,
including my captain's bars, that the NVA battalion
commander was up there leading his men."

Yates's face turned white and then dark red. "I'm
going to have you court-martialed for that remark!"

"For what? For telling you that two of your companies were in the field together fighting for their lives
and you decided to command the action from the
brigade's rear area?"

"You are insubordinate!"

"Fine. Then court-martial me and the whole Army
will know what you didn't do." The captain left the
bunker without looking back, muttering in quiet fury,
"I don't know any battalion commander who lost a
whole goddamn company!"

Yates turned to Maynard. "I'll ruin that bastard
traitor's career!" The truth of the captain's words were
forcing him to lose control, and he broke a grease
pencil in half as his anger boiled over.

Captain Maynard left him alone in the bunker and
told the operations sergeant, who had gone outside to
have a cigarette, to keep everyone out of the CP until
the battalion commander had time to get himself together. Maynard made it sound as if the lieutenant
colonel was grieving for his dead paratroopers.

Sol saw the captain coming from the battalion command post and nudged Spike. "It looks like the big
debriefing is over early." They both had seen the
Charlie Company commander storming out of the CP.

"That had to be some heavy action up there." Spike
couldn't help looking back over at the charred battle
site. The Air Force had bombed the surrounding area
after Charlie Company had been extracted. Medevac
helicopters had spent a whole day hauling bodies
out of the jungle. Everyone inside of the base area
knew that the paratroopers had lost the engagement
because the choppers were flying the bodies to the

rear area so that no one would see the large number of their dead comrades. Alpha Company had been totally wiped out, and all of their radios and weapons had been captured by the NVA. Charlie Company had been rendered ineffective for combat, with less than a platoon-sized unit remaining. Replacements were being flown into the Dak To base camp directly from Saigon, and most of the rookie paratroopers hadn't even completed their initial in-processing training before being sent out to the perimeter.

1600 hours

The final sign that a big battle was brewing was shown in the urgency the high command placed on filling the 173rd Airborne Brigade up to full strength. Paratroopers who had been assigned to leg units throughout Vietnam were being sent to Dak To.

"I hear that they've already formed a new Alpha Company," Sol said, shaking his head.

"At least our company is back up to full strength now," Spike remarked, looking over at the replacements working on their gear. Some of them were digging new foxholes around the perimeter because there wasn't enough room in the existing holes for all of them. "It's a little scary. Somebody knows something that they're not telling us."

"About what?" Sol looked up from the thick-wire bore brush he was pulling through the barrel of his M79.

"They've even ignored our guys who are on R&R and assigned new troops to take their places . . . as if they don't want to wait a week until they return."

"A big motherfucker is brewing up there in those fucking mountains. I can feel it in the head of my dick," Sol said, watching the mist drifting over the treetops on the mountainside.

"The head of your cock can tell you if there are NVA nearby?" Spike started laughing so hard that tears welled in his eyes.

"It's not funny! I have a sensitive dick!"

"Go away! Get the fuck away from me!" Spike fell off his sandbag seat, drawing the attention of the rookie troopers working nearby. They didn't see what could be so damn funny about anything at Dak To. A C-130 was still piled up in a heap off to one side of the runway, and everybody in the whole world knew that the 173rd had just had their asses kicked.

"I'm serious, Spike. When the head of my dick itches, that means a fight is brewing. It happened on patrol right before the NVA sprung our ambush and again when you were talking to that kid named . . . O'Toole? Was that his name?"

Spike stopped laughing abruptly after hearing his jump school buddy mentioned. "Yeah . . ." The brigade was recommending O'Toole for the Medal of Honor. The relief force had found thirty-one dead NVA soldiers within twenty feet of his body, and before the sole survivor from Alpha Company had been Medevaced to a Stateside hospital, he had told members of the brigade staff about O'Toole's heroism. He had been lying hidden in the bamboo only a few meters away from O'Toole, but had been so badly wounded he couldn't move or even call out for help. Lieutenant Beusenal's story had spread throughout the whole airborne brigade and had reached Spike's company within hours after the staff had returned from the field hospital. The enlisted man's frequency on the PRC-25 FM band, which was normally the highest frequency setting on the radio, picked up the story and spread it to every unit in country.

"Sarge?" The nervous voice of a new replacement brought Spike back to reality. "How many magazines should I load up?"

"I'd have at least twenty loaded and carry four frag grenades on my webgear." Spike smiled to ease the paratrooper's obvious fear. "That way you won't have to bother loading magazines during a firefight."

"Do you think we'll run into any NVA on this patrol?" the man asked, his voice cracking.

"That's what it's all about, paratrooper."

"Yeah, but I just had a baby girl. I'd sure like to have a chance to see here once before—"

"You will. We're going out on a normal patrol, not a suicide mission." Spike slapped the man's shoulder with more gusto than he was feeling.

"Yeah, you're right, Sergeant." The paratrooper left feeling a lot better.

"Everyone is feeling it." Sol noted, wiping an oily rag over his weapon and tucking the cloth back in the side pocket on his rucksack. "It's as if a black cloud of doom is hanging over this valley."

"Is the head of your cock still itching?" Spike was about to break out laughing again when his attention was arrested by a figure coming down the path. "Well, looky who's coming to visit the troopies in their foxholes."

Sol didn't have to look up. He could tell by the tone in Spike's voice that it was their company commander.

Maynard walked behind Lieutenant Alsop, next to an engineer captain. As the trio stopped before Spike's two-man foxhole, Maynard said to the engineer officer, "This is the center of my company area on the perimeter. You can get by with occupying every other bunker, which should be enough to hold the perimeter if you come under attack."

The engineer captain, who was taking over this portion of the perimeter, looked out over the barbed wire and then over at Spike. "What do you have out there for booby traps?"

"Trip flares mostly, sir." Spike pointed at a pair of green wires running from the front of the bunker out to the barbed wire. "Plus, we have two Claymores per fighting position."

The engineer looked over at Maynard. "Are you going to leave the Claymores in place?"

"Sure, if you want them," Maynard said, acting like he was doing the captain a favor.

"We want them."

"Do you want me to have Lieutenant Alsop show you how to set up a defensive perimeter?" Maynard asked in a patronizing voice.

"You don't have to show me shit, Maynard. I've built four Special Forces A camps and I can do quite well on my own." The captain regarded his peer with contempt. "I think you'd better take a few lessons yourself. Your daddy can't help you out there in the jungle."

"Do I detect a hint of jealousy?" Maynard said, letting the comment pass.

"Of you?" The engineer captain turned on his heel and walked away down the row of bunkers and foxholes.

November 20, 1967
0810 hours

Alsop's face was grim as he approached his platoon sergeants. Brigade intelligence had received a report from an NVA reconnaissance sergeant who had recently defected from the 1st North Vietnamese Division. He had said that three infantry regiments and one artillery regiment were already in position around the valley with a mission to level the American base camp. The information had already been tested against two locations, and both times major contacts had been made with the NVA.

Lieutenant Alsop paused next to a bunker to get control of himself. He had been scared shitless during the briefing at battalion HQ, along with the rest of the lieutenants who were going to have to go out there and engage the NVA forces. Up to now Alsop had thought contact with a single NVA company was big-time stuff. He lit another cigarette and smoked half of it before starting off again to meet with his NCOs.

"What's the bad news, Lieutenant?" A staff sergeant who was acting as the platoon sergeant tried cheering everyone up with a cheerful tone in his voice.

"We're going back to the boonies in the morning," Alsop announced, picking up on the sergeant's tone of voice. "We move out by foot at first light and work our way over to our first objective . . ." He opened his pocket 1:50,000-scale map and spread it out in front of his sergeants in the failing light. "There's where we're going." He tapped the spot on the map that he had marked with a red grease pencil.

"Did you have to use a red grease pencil?" the staff sergeant cut in.

"It's the only one I could find at the time. Why?" Alsop asked, looking at his senior NCO out of the corner of his eye.

"It's a commie color and besides, it looks like blood," the sergeant said, spitting out a stream of tobacco juice.

Spike leaned over and pointed at the map. "Yeah. That arrow you drew there—it looks like blood running uphill."

"Stop with this shit!" Alsop felt a shiver ripple over his shoulders. "Just listen." He pointed with his finger. "We're going to take this ridge line over to this valley and then cut across here to the base of Hill 875."

"What's so important about Hill 875?" the staff sergeant asked, turning the map a little to get a better look.

"The whole battalion is going to link up at the base of the hill, and then we're going to assault up to the top. Alpha Company will be coming in by chopper."

"That sounds good." Spike leaned against his shotgun with one knee on the ground. "At least there's going to be a lot of us in the same area. There's safety in numbers."

Alsop caught himself before he said too much. Not wanting to scare his men, he kept to himself the reason why the whole 2nd Battalion was going to meet at Hill 875. The defector had also said that the NVA 174th Regimental headquarters was on the hill with an elite batallion defending it. "Have your men ready to move out at first light and carry enough C-rations and ammo to last for a week."

"A week, sir?" Spike frowned. C-rations were heavy to carry. Three days was the normal load of rations for an infantryman in the jungle, and if they planned on staying out longer, a resupply chopper would haul in more.

"Yes, the way things are going out here, I don't want to have to rely on any airborne resupply choppers."

Spike thought for a second and nodded, but he sensed that the lieutenant was holding back some vital information.

November 21, 1967
0530 hours

Morning brought a thick ground fog that reduced visibility to less than fifty feet. Spike liked the idea of having a blanket of fog to conceal their movement, but Captain Maynard, terrified of being ambushed, wanted to delay their departure until they could see better. When Alpha Company had been annihilated, Maynard had felt they had gotten what they deserved because they had dropped military discipline in the field and had acted like a bunch of schoolchildren by running back to the base camp for showers and beer. But now that he was going out on patrol, there was a different attitude developing in his West Point-trained military mind. He was beginning to realize that *luck* played a major role in war—a much larger role than the school from which an officer had been graduated.

Maynard's request for a delay, however, was over-ruled by the battalion commander. He was under strict orders to get his battalion into position around Hill 875 and destroy the NVA Regimental headquarters before it could slip back into Laos.

Spike's squad was given the point for the company formation, with his platoon acting as the reaction force. Spike removed his camouflage helmet and hooked it on his rucksack. After he had tied a drive-on rag around his forehead to keep the sweat out of his eyes, he told Sol to stay at least twenty-five feet behind him so that he could hear in the dense fog what was going on ahead of him. In fact, the whole platoon was inspected to insure that their gear didn't rattle as they moved.

Once on the move, Spike discovered that the wind was blowing up the valley from his rear, and he frowned. He would rather have had the wind coming toward him so that he could smell anything ahead. The company had been walking for over an hour when Spike stopped and sniffed: cigarette smoke. No, it was a cigar. He waved for Sol to come forward and whispered in his ear, "Some fucking idiot in our company is smoking a cigar. Have the lieutenant check it out."

Sol nodded and slipped back to the platoon leader. When Alsop smelled the strong odor, he wondered how Spike could have picked it up before he did. Alsop signaled for the platoon to take a break, and he slipped back down the line, looking for the culprit. He found him in the command element.

"Sir, you're going to have to put out your cigar."

"Is that why you stopped the whole company? Just to tell me to put out my cigar?" Maynard asked, livid.

"Sergeant Harwood can smell it way up at the point. If he can smell it, so can the NVA."

"Alsop, we have a whole airborne company with us, the toughest fighting men on earth. Are you afraid?" Maynard said loud enough for those surrounding him to hear. He was trying to instill a football-type fighting spirit in his men.

"Sir, why don't you talk to the Charlie Company commander about Alpha Company?"

Maynard looked around sheepishly and saw that everyone was watching him. He ground out his cigar under his boot.

Having won his point, Alsop left the captain temporarily satisfied. But as he went back to his platoon, he had a terrible premonition: this fool of a captain was going to get a lot of good men killed.

1505 hours

Spike dropped to one knee and listened. The fog had burnt off hours earlier, but the jungle was absolutely quiet except for a soft rushing of a mountain stream at the base of Hill 875. Sol covered Spike as he filled up their canteens after drinking from the stream.

Lieutenant Alsop moved up the ranks of his platoon to find out why they had stopped so early in the afternoon and saw Spike and Sol next to the stream. He joined his point element and drank deeply before whispering softly, "I think we're here."

Spike nodded in agreement, slightly irritated to have company. Captain Maynard had refused to relieve the 1st Platoon from the point, and Spike in turn had refused to give up the position as point man because there were too many new men in the platoon and he wasn't going to risk their lives recklessly. He had adjusted to pulling the point position so well that he wasn't comfortable in the jungle when he was surrounded by others. He liked being alone.

"I'll get the captain and see if he wants to lager here for the night." Alsop waved for Spike and Sol to hold their position until he returned.

A flock of wild birds flew overhead and landed for a few seconds in the trees over the company until they realized their mistake and flew off chattering to themselves.

The NVA battalion commander was raising his chopsticks to his mouth, when he heard the birds below his position on the hill. Frowning, he listened intently for any other sound, but heard nothing. All the same, something had startled them. He handed his bowl of fish and rice to his aide and reached for his pistol belt. A nervous tic in the corner of his eye assured him that there was something wrong down below. He always felt the twitch when there was danger nearby.

His sergeant reacted instantly without having to be told. He waved for his squad to gather their weapons and follow. The battalion commander personally reconnoitered for his unit, and he rarely allowed one of his officers to command the most dangerous position during a battle. He had established a reputation in the division as being a vicious warrior and earned the honored nickname Tiger-eater. Every man in his battalion knew him by sight and both respected and feared him and the personal totem he wore around his neck: a string of ears that he had personally cut off the heads of American soldiers he had killed. His special trademark was cutting off the ears before the man was dead.

1540 hours

Spike moved where Maynard pointed. They were going to establish a company perimeter around the narrow stream so that they had access to water during the night and until the rest of the battalion linked up with them. Spike advanced up the hill and established a one-man listening post. There was no need to waste any more men until everyone had dug a fighting position, and Sol was digging a two-man position for both of them. Sniffing, Spike thought he detected the pungent odor of *nuoc-mon*, a strong fish-based sauce the Vietnamese used with their rice dishes. The breeze shifted and the scent was gone. Had he really smelled the odor? Spike remained alert until he could be assured that it was only his imagination at work.

Then a soft scraping noise filtered down through the branches of the trees above him. Spike glanced up, but couldn't see anything because of the secondary growth.

He listened, but the sound didn't repeat itself. Spike felt sick to his stomach. He had drunk too much of the cold water too fast. To his rear he heard the sharp noises of shovels hitting small rocks, then soft thuds as the men threw the dirt from their foxholes. Flicking his head, he refocused his attention back up the hill. He was sure that the sounds wouldn't carry uphill much farther than where he was.

The NVA battalion commander led the squad of elite jungle sappers down the side of Hill 875. The battalion had been there for over a week now in the prepositioned bunkers. He had personally walked every square foot of the hill and could orient himself accurately without a map. Suddenly he paused. Was he hearing the scrape of shovels? He lowered himself to the jungle floor and listened intently until he was satisfied that there were soldiers below him digging foxholes. He looked over his shoulder and smiled at his squad.

Then he edged forward, his cape of camouflage parachute cloth making him almost invisible in the thick foliage.

Spike stiffened. It wasn't a sound; in fact, it was the absence of sound that made him freeze. He slipped his camouflage poncho liner over his head, leaving only a small opening to see through. So completely did he blend in with the vegetation that a family of monkeys swung from a nearby tree and started feeding off the semi-ripe fruit in the tree above. The leader of the troop kept looking down nervously, but it couldn't see anyone.

When the NVA commander saw the monkeys feeding nearby, he relaxed a little. Any clumsy Americans would have sent then scurrying through the jungle. His sharp hand signal brought the members of the sapper squad around him in a tight circle. He didn't speak, but pointed in the direction he wanted a man to go and gave a curt nod of his head. Now that he was getting close, he wanted his men to spread out and probe for the size of the American perimeter. He already knew that the unit had to be at least a company patrol, for after the great victory the week before, he knew the Americans wouldn't travel in the jungle unless they were in strength.

Spike held his breath.

The NVA had appeared out of nowhere. Spike blinked his eyes rapidly to insure that he wasn't just seeing things. The NVA made a sharp movement with his hand and four more soldiers appeared, forming a tight circle around him. Spike guessed from the camouflage that hid every part of their bodies that they were some kind of recon unit. He couldn't believe how quiet they were.

Suddenly he realized that if he could hear men digging below him, so could the NVA scouts. Spike could feel his palms sweating against the wooden stock and pump grip on his shotgun. He had already decided that he wasn't going to open fire unless they detected him.

The monkeys in the tree above him were alerted by their leader's bark and went scampering off in the jungle. The NVA battalion commander looked up, but wasn't alarmed. He knew that it was his unit that

had disturbed the feeding monkeys. He flipped back
his camouflage cape and removed his pistol from his
holster. Then he turned directly toward Spike.

A string of human ears on a gold chain riveted
Spike's attention.

An anger greater than any he had ever known over-
took him. Throwing off his poncho liner, he stood up
in a combat crouch. Too late the NVA commander
saw Spike emerge from the jungle twenty feet away
and raised his pistol. The first round of fleshettes
instantly killed him and two of the NVA sappers.
Spike racked the pump action on his shotgun and fired
again, killing the other two NVA before they could
bring their weapons to bear.

Spike had no way of knowing that he had killed an
NVA battalion commander because the man had traveled incognito. In any case, the only thing Spike focused on was the necklace of human ears. He reloaded
his shotgun without thinking and walked forward in a
crouch. Reaching down, he tore the string of trophy
ears from around the NVA soldier's neck. His hatred was
so consuming that he lost sight of the fact that he was
standing on an NVA-held hill with five dead enemy
soldiers at his feet. Instead he counted the ten pairs of
shrunken, sun-dried objects. Spike picked out a pair
that might have been slightly tan.

"Spike? You all right?" Sol hissed from behind.

Spike turned around slowly, holding the chain of
trophy ears up in the air, and spoke in a hollow, calm
voice: "I found Yuk's ears like I promised."

Up the hill, the NVA occupying the first ring of
hidden bunkers heard the rounds go off and took
positions behind their weapons. Patiently they waited
for the American fools to step into the camouflaged
fire lanes, which they had cut from the jungle so well
that it was difficult for anyone to see them until they
were in the kill zones. The executive officer for the
elite battalion expected his commander to return at
any moment from his reconnaissance. No one in the

battalion believed that the great Tiger-eater could be killed. Why, he had actually spat on an American colonel in Danang while the colonel's jeep had been stopped at a busy intersection.

The executive officer looked at his watch. There was still plenty of time for his commander to return. He smiled as he thought of a new set of bloody ears on his commander's necklace.

Down below, Spike stepped into a tiny clearing formed by four huge trees that blocked off all sunlight for anything below. "Spike, you don't look very good." Sol saw the twisted face of his friend and knew that Spike was freaking out on him.

There was no answer.

Sol signaled for the rest of the squad to take up positions around the clearing. The new replacements stared at the dead NVA being dragged into the perimeter. The soldiers were the first real enemy they had seen. And the superb camouflage alarmed even the veterans in the company.

"Spike, let's get the fuck out of here and go somewhere quiet," Sol said, extremely calm. He knew that his friend was going through some kind of personal crisis.

Spike didn't answer.

In his place— Spike had been unofficially appointed as the acting squad leader because there hadn't been any NCOs with the replacements—Sol signaled for the squad to take up defensive positions.

Spike dropped into a Vietnamese squat in front of the NVA commander's corpse and stared into the open eyes. Still in the grip of his hatred, Spike reached in his shirt for the gold medal that hung around his neck and slipped it into his mouth. He thought about Captain Hanson and Yuk and O'Toole, and he cried.

He sobbed so loud that his whole squad heard him from their fighting positions. Several of the new replacements looked back at Sol in confusion, but his glare kept them from saying anything.

Spike stopped crying suddenly and looked over at his friend with clear eyes. "Let's string them up."

"What?" At first Sol didn't understand.

Then it dawned on him. "Spike, we don't do that kind of shit."

"Not like the Montagnards were. We'll leave their uniforms on, but we'll string them upside down from the trees." Spike was back to normal. "Break out our supply of suspension cord."

Sol nodded and dropped his rucksack. Every paratrooper in the brigade carried a couple dozen feet of suspension cord in their packs. The extremely strong nylon cord was used for a variety of purposes by the paratroopers, like making poncho hooches in the jungle.

"Do you think Captain Maynard will get pissed if we drag the bodies back out in the jungle?" Sol said, glancing over at the captain, conferring with the battalion staff much farther down the hill.

"Fuck him. I want them hanging by their heels when their buddies come looking for them tonight." Spike pointed to a couple of trees with low branches up the hill just past the listening post.

The five NVA sappers were strung up by their ankles as Spike watched. He waited until his squad was finished with their ghastly detail and then took a flashlight out of his rucksack. Removing the red lens, he placed the light in the crook of a tree and aimed it so the beam shone directly on the face of the NVA commander.

"What are you doing, Spike?" Sol asked, worried about Spike's sanity.

"Setting up a booby trap for their friends." Spike removed a Claymore mine from his rucksack and pushed its spiked legs in the soft jungle soil. Then he crouched behind it to aim the anti-personnel mine to cover the clearing. He rigged the detonator so that if the NVA soldier was cut down, the Claymore would explode.

"Spike, are you going to leave your flashlight here?"

"Yeah." Spike smiled and turned on his flashlight. "We'd better get back to the perimeter."

A strong wind picked up as the Americans left the dead NVA soldiers, and they started swinging back and forth. Blood dripped down their arms and formed large drops at the end of their fingertips. The wind moving the bodies made the blood streak the jungle plants uphill and it looked as if their blood was running up the side of the mountain.

Lieutenant Alsop was waiting for Spike and Sol when they returned. The first thing he noticed was the gold chain with the ears in Spike's left hand.

"What happened up there? What was the shooting all about?" the lieutenant whispered, even though they were inside of the perimeter.

Sol answered for Spike. "An NVA recon party ran into Spike."

"Did they get away?"

Spike looked hard at the lieutenant. "No."

"How many? Christ, you should have called me sooner!"

"Five."

"What are you holding in your hand?"

"Ears."

"Ears?"

"Yeah, American ears. The NVA patrol leader was wearing them around his neck."

Alsop felt the can of C-ration franks and beans starting to come back up. "Shit, I think I'm going to be sick."

Spike dropped his hand down to his side and hid the macabre trophy against his pants leg.

"What are you going to do with them?" Sol asked, refusing to look at the gold chain.

Spike hadn't been thinking that far ahead and frowned. "Let's bury it, right now."

"Yeah."

"The gold chain too?" Alsop didn't know why he

asked such a stupid question, but the chain looked valuable.

Spike held the trophy back up so that the lieutenant could see it again. "Would you want to wear this chain?"

Alsop shook his head vigorously. "Bury it . . . now."

The NVA battalion executive officer knew that something was wrong when his commander didn't return by midnight. He knew the direction the sapper squad had taken and formed a small party of experienced soldiers to search for their battalion commander. Not only was a full moon rising, but the trip downhill would be aided by the pieces of reflective tape that they had placed on the uphill sides of the trees to mark the selected fire lanes.

The light from the flashlight, now dim, drew the NVA team to the clearing in the jungle. Though cautious, all of them had seen Americans using flashlights at night in the jungle, thinking that because they were inside of a well-defended perimeter that they would be safe. The executive officer was the first one to see the great Tiger-eater hanging by his ankles with the flashlight shining on his face.

Spike heard the Claymore mine detonate and smiled. He licked the cold sore that was beginning to form in the corner of his mouth and looked over at Sol's shadow next to him in the foxhole.

CHAPTER NINE

✪✪✪✪✪✪✪✪✪✪✪✪✪✪✪

AIRBORNE BLOOD

November 23, 1967
1330 hours

The incidents with the two NVA patrols confirmed that there was a major enemy force holding Hill 875. Captain Maynard alerted the battalion commander, and the rest of the 2nd Battalion, 503rd Infantry, closed in around the hill.

The new Alpha Company arrived in helicopters and formed a defensive perimeter around the battalion headquarters clement and the small ammunition dump. The battalion heavy-weapons section set up their battery of 4.2-inch mortars and began breaking out their ammunition. None of the men needed to be told that the enemy was close at hand. It almost seemed as if the wind itself was whispering the word "danger" over and over again.

Lieutenant Colonel Yates looked up from the map he had spread out on top of a pile of empty wooden ammo crates. He smiled when he saw the brigade chaplain approaching from the Huey that had just landed. "Morning there, Chaplain. Aren't you a bit forward of the rear area?"

The Catholic priest, who was serving in the Airborne Chaplain's Corps, smiled a friendly greeting. "I go where I'm needed."

"If that's the case, you'd better get on *top* of the hill

215

and administer to the gooks. But make it quick, because our first sortie of F-4s is about to arrive."

The chaplain ignored the sarcastic remark and went over to several mortar men breaking out ammo. Yates chuckled under his breath and adjusted the silk camouflage scarf he was wearing around his neck. The sun was beginning to warm the LZ.

A flight of four Phantom jets screamed by and released their loads of five-hundred-pound bombs against the side of the hill. A shock wave rolled down the slope and gently slapped Yates's face. He inhaled deeply and smiled. He loved the smell of burned gunpowder and explosives. It was a modern-day warrior's perfume.

The NVA regimental commander felt the roof of his bunker shake and dirt fell on his maps, but the fifteen feet of dirt on top of the bunker withstood the blast. The regimental staff ignored the exploding bombs and continued working. They had all been through air attacks before and knew that they were immune to everything except delay-fuse two-thousand-pound bombs dropped from B-52 bombers.

"Have the Americans started their assault yet?" the colonel asked, lighting another Salem from the cigarette he had already burning.

"No, sir."

"Remind our men that I want them to hold their fire until the Americans are so close they cannot disengage and they can't use their accursed artillery against us."

"Yes, sir, they have already been informed." The staff major knew that he didn't have to remind the infantrymen down in the bunkers, since their lives depended on close-in fighting tactics.

Lieutenant Alsop checked the magazine in his M16 and looked over at his men. He raised his arm and signaled for the skirmish line to start moving forward. Bravo Company had been ordered to start the assault up the hill five minutes after the fast movers had dropped their bombs and the artillery and mortar prep fires had stopped. The paratroopers left their foxholes slowly and started advancing in low crouches. All of them expected the NVA to open fire as soon as they cleared their holes. But the jungle remained quiet.

Spike moved slowly. No point element was needed because they knew the NVA was dug in around the hill. It was just a matter of advancing until they hit a bunker line. For that, each of the paratroopers had been issued one LAW rocket. Spike had his LAW slipped under the flap of his rucksack.

Sol squeezed the wooden stock on his M79 grenade launcher to prevent his hands from shaking. In his fright his thoughts slipped back to his father. There was absolutely no reason why he should be on the side of Hill 875 assaulting an elite North Vietnamese unit. His father had insured that there were no Levin names in the draft pool back in Chicago. In fact, wealthy Chicago names between the ages of seventeen and twenty-five had been totally immune to the draft lottery since the Vietnam War had started. Jokes were beginning to spread throughout the metro area that this was one lottery that rich people were extremely lucky in *not* winning. When Sol had found out that his father had donated over a million dollars to a certain charity whose chairperson was also the wife of the president of the Chicago draft board, he had become so angry that he had gone down and volunteered for the infantry. To cap it off, he had joined the paratroopers. Sol's father had disowned him the very next day. Sol had retaliated by naming the local draft board as beneficiary of his GI life-insurance policy.

A cough from a nearby trooper brought Sol back to the real world. He was shocked: how could he have been daydreaming during an assault? He looked to both sides and saw Spike and the replacement who just had a baby daughter. The rest of the company was hidden by the jungle.

The chatter of a single RPD light machine gun informed them they had reached the NVA bunkers.

Spike dropped to the ground and tried looking under the vegetation for any sign of a weapon firing. He saw nothing. As he rolled over, his eye caught a piece of silver reflector tape attached to the back side of a tree. The tape puzzled him until a paratrooper from his unit stepped out of the jungle into a narrow path that had been cut out of the thick ground cover. An AK-47 opened fire, instantly killing him.

"Fire lane!" Spike yelled, taking the risk of warning anyone else from making the same mistake. His cry was answered by fire from the bunkers less than fifty feet up the hill. In moments the whole company came under fire.

Captain Maynard called in the supporting artillery that had been standing by. When the first volley landed long, the company forward observer made a minor adjustment. The second volley landed near the bunkers, but did little damage. The NVA knew American strategy too well for that. A machine gun opened fire to Spike's left, sending a hail of death down a fire lane. Spotting it, Spike pulled the LAW rocket out of his rucksack. He left his rucksack in the brush and rolled over to the edge of the marked lane. He waited until the machine gun fired again and crawled out to the very edge of the lane. Spying plants at the far end of the lane quivering from the muzzle blast, Spike pushed the switch on the LAW. The rocket hit the bunker dead center and ignited the large ammo supply the NVA had stockpiled inside.

The destruction of this key bunker allowed a fire team to maneuver up the hill and use their LAWs to knock out a few more of the well-built structures. Slowly the paratroopers punched a hole through the first perimeter around the headquarters. Artillery was almost ineffective because the thick tree cover caused the rounds to detonate prematurely. The FO tried having the fuse set on delay and that tactic helped a little, but the rounds would ricochet off the trunks of the trees and it was a coin toss as to where they would land.

The battle for Hill 875 was rapidly turning into a purely infantry fight.

Watching the steady stream of wounded paratroopers coming down the hill, Lieutenant Colonel Yates smiled, proud of his battalion's progress. They were advancing ahead of the rest of the battalions in the brigade against their assigned objectives, and he was looking very good to the brigade staff.

The Catholic chaplain was administering last rites to a row of severely wounded paratroopers when an NVA platoon appeared out of nowhere. The surgeon looked up just in time to see the soldier who bayoneted him. One of the wounded men was still able to reach for his weapon and opened fire. He warned the battalion base camp, but paid for the warning with his life.

While Yates struggled with the flap on his holster, shocked that an NVA unit had breached his perimeter, the chaplain watched an NVA soldier walk down the row of wounded paratroopers and shoot each one in the head. He continued watching in total disbelief as an NVA soldier pointed his pistol at a paratrooper crawling toward him to attack him with his bare hands.

Just then the chaplain's gaze rested on an M60 machine gun that had been brought back off the hill with a wounded gunner. As if in a trance, he scooped the weapon off the ground. If the gunner had put the weapon on safety before he had been hit, the chaplain would never have figured out how to fire it. As it was, he pointed it at the laughing NVA soldier and pulled the trigger. The NVA soldier flipped backward over the bodies of the men he had already executed. The chaplain swung the barrel around and cut through an NVA squad. He started running toward the withdrawing NVA soldiers, firing the machine gun.

The lieutenant in charge of the CP security reaction force deployed his men in the perimeter gap the NVA had sneaked through and mopped up all of the surviving enemy.

Seeing them advance ahead of him, the chaplain

sank onto his knees and lowered the barrel of the hot M60 in the short grass. He could smell the grass burning and cried. He had killed.

Colonel Yates had watched the whole incident from where he still stood by the ammunition stockpile and realized that the aid station hadn't been the NVA platoon's objective. It had been the ammo he was standing near. Slowly it dawned on him that he was not chasing a bunch of VC peasants across rice paddies, but was engaged with a well-trained, professional army.

Spike took his time moving through the NVA bunker line. He checked out the bunker he had hit with the LAW and saw that there were no survivors. Using the front of the bunker for cover, he waited for Sol to break out of the jungle. As two paratroopers stepped into the fire lane and started moving towards Spike, he could see what easy targets they had made for the NVA.

"Airborne!" Spike yelled, waving for the troopers to join him. They looked shocked when they saw him and started running his way.

"Sarge, man, are we glad to see you. We thought we were lost." The replacement took a deep breath. "This is some heavy shit."

Spike nodded. "A little tougher than normal."

"What are we going to do?"

"Wait here until I can orient myself with the rest of the platoon. I think we're a bit ahead of them." Noticing the LAWs tucked under the flaps of the replacements' rucksack covers, he said, "Give me your LAWs and wait here for me." He pointed over the bunker. "The NVA are that way."

Sol broke out of the heavy cover only a few meters away from Spike. The heavy thuds of a 12.7mm machine gun sent both of them diving for cover, and a huge hunk of splintered wood flew through the air above Sol's head. "Shit!" he cursed into the damp earth against his mouth.

The NVA gunner had seen Sol exit from the jungle with the LAW strapped to his back. Knowing that the rocket could destroy his bunker, he lowered the barrel slightly so that the thumb-sized bullets could tear away the rotting log that the American was hiding behind.

Spike's reaction was instantaneous. He slipped his shotgun over his shoulder and flipped open the sights of one of the LAW rockets. The enemy machine gunner lowered the barrel of his weapon another three inches and marked his location for Spike with another long burst. Large hunks of the semi-soft wood flew through the air.

Sol knew that it would only be seconds before the heavy machine gun dug through the log and found his flesh, but to move even an inch either way would cause instant death. He started to recite an old Hebrew prayer of the dead that he didn't even remember he knew and then recalled his grandfather reciting it on his death bed.

Spike saw the barrel sticking out of the well-camouflaged bunker, took a quick aim with the LAW rocket launcher, and fired. The barrel of the machine gun swung all the way to one side of the firing port and stopped singing its death song. Spike jumped up and was running forward when he saw the barrel start returning to its firing position.

"Fuck!" In an instant he dove for cover. He removed one of his M26 fragmentation grenades from his webgear and pulled the pin. The bunker was only ten meters from his position. Spike approached the bunker from its side and chucked the hand grenade through the front firing slit after holding it live for a three count.

Sol waited until the machine gun had stopped firing before rolling over a dozen feet to his left. His rucksack forced him up off the ground and he cursed. It had been a dumb tactic, but luck was with him. The machine gun was silent.

Spike looked for another bunker, but couldn't see

any. A LAW rocket firing farther to his left told him that the rest of the platoon was also punching a hole in the NVA defense.

"I owe you a hero sandwich for that one, Spike!" Sol reached for his canteen to take a sip of tepid water and relieve his dry throat. "NVA are all over this fucking hill. I wonder if the captain knows what he's taking on?"

"I haven't seen him. Have you?" Spike said, removing his shotgun and scanning the jungle up the hill.

"Naw."

"Let's go back to where I dropped my rucksack," Spike said, leading the way back to the spot where he had left the two replacements.

Sol was the first one to spot the two NVA and killed the nearest one with an antipersonnel round from his M79.

Firing from the hip, Spike took out the remaining one. As he crept closer, he saw that the NVA had killed the two paratroopers and had been looting their rucksacks. "Fuck, they caught them from behind," Spike said, pointing down. From the position of the pair of dead troopers, who were facing up the hill, it was obvious they had failed to check their six o'clock position. A mixture of anger and guilt filled Spike. They had been new replacements and shouldn't have been left alone.

Seeing that Spike was bothered by the death of the troopers, Sol said, "It's not your fault."

Still upset, Spike reached for his gear. That's when he caught a slight movement out of the corner of his eyes. He swung his shotgun around and was ready to open fire when Lieutennt Alsop and his radio operator stepped out of the jungle in low crouches. Alsop looked relieved to see two of his platoon members.

"The captain wants us to pull back. The bunker line is too strong to break through," Alsop reported, dropping down to rest before heading back down the hill.

"Sol and I have already taken out two bunkers, so

there has to be a gap in their perimeter that we can exploit."

"Two?" Alsop asked, surprised.

"Yeah, Lieutenant. You're leaning against one of them." Sol smiled. Alsop hadn't even seen the perfectly camouflaged NVA bunker that he was resting his rucksack against.

Alsop rolled over to one side and looked into the dark firing port. "Hot shit! I didn't even see it!"

"This group of NVA mean business." Spike pointed to the slight, curving rise on the jungle floor. "It looks as if they've followed the contour with their bunkers . . . I heard a LAW going off in that direction," Spike said, continuing to scan the jungle with his shotgun barrel pointed. He didn't want a repeat performance of what had happened to the pair of replacements. "If we go back down this hill, Lieutenant, we're going to have to fight our way back through this same bunker line again in the morning."

"Yeah. And what about our dead and wounded?" Sol demanded, getting pissed.

"I'll call the captain on the horn." Alsop reached back and his radio operator placed the handset in his palm.

Maynard was lying in a slight depression with the company's field first sergeant and three more men from his headquarters element. He had called in artillery support for his platoons, but all of his platoon leaders had asked him to stop bringing it in so close because the rounds were hitting the trees and spraying them with shrapnel. The forward observer was trying to call in larger-caliber artillery from the 4th Division, but was having a problem getting through. It seemed as if everybody was fighting for their own asses.

Maynard's radio operator handed him the handset. "First Platoon, sir."

"Sky Dog eight, this is Six," Maynard said worriedly. Farther up the hill, Alsop looked around the jungle as he whispered, "Six, we've punched through the NVA bunker line."

"Where are you located?" Maynard knew that his 1st Platoon was somewhere on his right flank, but as soon as they had made contact with the NVA, he had lost communications with all of his platoon leaders.

Alsop checked his folded map and guessed his location. "I figure we moved two hundred meters up the hill before we made contact."

"I agree." Maynard ducked his head instinctively when a nearby M60 opened fire.

"Do you want to exploit this hole we've made in their line?" asked Alsop. He really didn't want to stay on the side of the hill, but if they were going to have to take the top, he didn't want to go back down and start all over again in the morning.

"Hold what you've got and pull your platoon together. I'll move my command element to your location . . . out." Maynard handed the PRC-77 secure-voice radio handset back to his radioman and looked over at his FO. "We're going to bust through the NVA line with the first platoon." He didn't tell the artilleryman that it had already been done.

Meanwhile, deep within his nearby impregnable bunker up the hill, the NVA regimental commander listened to his officers brief him. He nodded each time one of them had finished and finally tapped his map with a long fingernail. "We wait. Let them establish one of their night perimeters, and then we'll destroy them with a counter attack." He smiled. He knew that the Americans still had to penetrate two strong rings of bunkers around the hill before they could reach his headquarters, and even then there was a major avenue left by which to retreat back to Laos or Cambodia.

Captain Maynard linked up with Alsop and the 1st Platoon and called in all of the rest of his company to the position where the NVA perimeter had been broken. Fighting had all but stopped along the Bravo Company front as the NVA withdrew to their next line of defense.

Spike and Sol returned to the CP after making a

short reconnoiter up the hill. Spike hadn't wanted to go too far and make contact again with the NVA until the company had a chance to reorganize and the artillery forward observer could provide accurate mortar and artillery fire.

"What did you find?" Alsop asked, seeing that Maynard acted as if he wasn't interested in what Spike had found.

"A good place to set up a night lager site. About fifty meters up, there's a slight rise in the ground and then a depression before it starts going up again. It's a pretty good position to defend." Spike squatted, but then immediately stood up again when he felt a burning sensation in his crotch. He had contracted a fungus in the moist area between his legs where his fatigues pants held the sweat. Crotch rot was a serious problem in the jungle, especially when there wasn't an opportunity to shower or dry out.

"Is there something wrong with you, Sergeant?" Maynard asked sarcastically.

"Yes, sir, I picked up an infection," Spike replied calmly. He didn't need the captain fucking with him, not now on the side of Hill 875.

"Crotch rot won't get you out of the field."

"I haven't asked to leave the field, sir."

Alsop was getting tired of the captain always picking a fight with his sergeant. "Sir, Harwood and Levin are trying to brief us."

"We're staying right here for the night. I'll use the NVA bunker for my CP," Maynard retorted, eyeing the earth roof that would stop any artillery shell the airborne brigade had available.

"Go ahead, sir. The NVA know the exact location of that bunker, and I personally think they'll be coming back as soon as it gets dark out," Spike protested.

Maynard gave him a dirty look before he gasped from a sharp pain in his lower intestines. Using his fingers to gently feel for the exact locations of pain, he said, "I know that, Sergeant. But we're not going any

farther up this hill until I get conformation from the
battalion commander and we can link up with our
sister companies on our flanks.'' Maynard pointed to a
low spot in front of the old NVA bunkers. "We'll
form an oval over there with the company and use the
NVA bunkers for listening posts. Make the north side
of the perimeter tight and the back side just strong
enough to handle any sappers who might try to hit us
from the rear. The first platoon can hold the center,
facing north.''

"Do you have gut pain, Captain?" Alsop asked,
watching Maynard rubbing his side and lower abdomen.

"Dysentery. A bad case too." He felt like he had to
take a crap and looked around the area for a place to
unload.

"Sometimes when you change your diet a lot, it
causes a mild case of the runs." Alsop glanced over
and saw that Sol and Spike were smiling.

"What do you mean by that remark, Lieutenant?"
Maynard located a small stand of young bamboo a few
meters away and started moving toward it.

"You've been going back to the rear a lot. Switch-
ing from C-rations to regular food can screw up your
digestive tract.''

"I said I've got a severe case of dysentery!" Maynard rushed over to the bamboo and turned his rear
toward the thicket before dropping his pants and squatting down. He was embarrassed having to defecate in
front of enlisted men, but he wasn't about to wander
off in the jungle with so many NVA around. "What
are you staring at?''

Alsop reached over and turned Spike around so that
his back faced the captain. "Nothing sir, we've just
planned our positions." Alsop whispered under his
breath so that only Spike and Sol could hear him,
"What a fucking asshole!''

"Careful, Lieutenant, that's a West Point officer
who's the-son-of-the-son-of-the-son of a West Pointer."
Sol smiled.

"And none of those bastards have ever fought a fucking war." Alsop pointed at the NVA bunker line. "I don't like this shit one fucking bit, but then again, I don't want to move any farther up this hill today and run into some more shit. I guess we'll have to make do with what we've been given."

Bravo Company had suffered nine KIA and fourteen wounded during the assault. Charlie Company had suffered light casualties, but Alpha Company once again had received the most casualties when the NVA had made their swift counterattack against the base of the hill with the company they had hidden in the jungle for just that purpose. If the NVA had waited another day, they would have been much more successful because the battalion CP perimeter would have been much more relaxed. Alpha Company was rapidly picking up a reputation for being jinxed.

Lieutenant Colonel Yates finished talking to the brigade commander and smiled as he dropped the radio handset onto the wooden crate he was using for a temporary desk. The 4th Division commander was sending in two more battalions to support the attack on Hill 875. The NVA assault against his battalion perimeter had convinced the division staff that the enemy was determined to hold the hill. The general had decided that they would surround it completely and destroy the NVA regimental headquarters. The 4th Battalion, 503rd Airborne Infantry, and the 3rd Battalion, 8th Infantry, were assigned to close the door so that the NVA couldn't escape back into Laos. Little did the general and his staff know that the NVA 174th Regiment had no intention of leaving the hill.

Yates called his operations officer over. "I want all of the company commanders and staff here by 0600 tomorrow for a briefing." He grinned. Tomorrow he would take the hill and that would assure him a star on his collar. General Westmoreland was being briefed hourly on the battle for Dak To, and Yates's name had already been mentioned in association with Hill 875 and the NVA counterattack.

"Sir, do you think that it's a good idea to call the commanders back down the hill?" the major asked. He didn't like the idea of leaving the companies with platoon leaders in command when the NVA had already shown their strength and determination to hold the hill.

"I want to personally make sure each one of the commanders and my staff"—he glared at the major—"understood just how important tomorrow's assault is going to be for their careers."

The major rolled his eyes as he turned away. He couldn't think of too many officers who would be worrying about their careers as they sat in their foxholes on the side of the hill, except maybe for Maynard. But he was cut from the same cloth as Yates.

The night passed swiftly. Spike slept in catnaps, taking turns with Sol checking the platoon foxholes and reassuring the new replacements that everything was okay. Watching Spike making these rounds, Alsop made a pledge to himself that he was going to see that Harwood received a high decoration for what he had done so far during the fight. He didn't care if Maynard hated the sergeant, he would go over the captain's head if he had to. As Spike stopped at the edge of his foxhole and ran his hand down the front of his pants, Alsop saw the look of pain on his face.

"Medic," Alsop said, beckoning for the company's senior medic to come over. "Do you have anything with you for a bacterial infection?"

"For you, sir?"

"No, Harwood."

"Sorry, sir. I only have one tube of ointment left and the captain said to hold on to it."

"Go see Harwood. I think he's got a bad infection." Alsop pointed toward Spike's position. "If the captain asks what happened to it, just tell him that I took it."

"Yes, sir."

Spike looked up at the medic as he approached, sending up swirls of ground mist as he walked.

"Hey, Doc, looks like you've had a busy day," he said, concerned how the medic was handling the pressure having to take care of so many wounded. Most of the men who had been killed were kids little older than Spike.

"Good. How you doing?"

Spike shrugged. "Making it."

"The lieutenant said that you had some kind of infection," the medic said, setting down his aid kit on the edge of the foxhole.

"Nothing serious."

"Drop your pants." The medic unzipped the side pocket on his medical kit and removed a small tube of fungicide.

"I didn't know that you were that kind of guy, Doc." Spike grinned and remained sitting on the edge of his foxhole.

"Drop your pants, Spike," Sol commanded, leaving no room for Spike to argue.

"You too, Sol? Shucks, I really didn't know."

"Stop the crap and let Doc look at you."

Spike unbuttoned his filthy jungle fatigues and lowered them to his mid-thighs. He wasn't wearing any underwear.

Sol's breath caught in his throat. "Holy shit, Spike!" The skin on Spike's scrotum was peeling off in huge strips, leaving seeping sores. "Man, you should have seen a doctor days ago!"

"Yeah . . . and what would Captain Maynard have said?" Spike felt bad about hiding the infection, but he knew that the captain would have called him a coward if he was Medevaced out right before a major battle.

The medic curled his lip. "Sergeant Harwood, I don't think that this stuff is even going to begin healing that infection. This is the worst case I've seen."

Spike pulled his pants back up gently. The cool air on the sores had made them even more sensitive to the touch of the material.

"Try this anyway. It'll numb the sores and ease up the pain a little." The medic handed Spike the whole tube of ointment.

"Thanks," Spike said, accepting the medication. He could use something to ease the pain.

0600 hours

Lieutenant Colonel Yates watched his company commanders assembling at the base of the hill. The young captains looked extremely weary. He noticed that Maynard wasn't with them and then saw the Bravo Company, 2nd Platoon leader walking toward him. "Where's Captain Maynard?"

"He's sick, sir. He sent me."

Yates nodded curtly and then motioned for the officers to gather around. He had a tripod set up so that they could all see the drawing of Hill 875 and the positions the other battalions were taking up, surrounding the enemy headquarters.

"Gentlemen, I would like to congratulate you on your excellent showing during yesterday's fight. The Second Battalion, Airborne Infantry, made an excellent entry in the history books, and all of you will be rewarded for your support."

The battalion operations officer sat on a stack of mortar ammunition boxes with his arms crossed over his chest. He remained silent, but he noted the expressions on the faces of the officers who would have to continue the fight up the hill. They looked like a bunch of tired college jocks who didn't even know the rules for the game they were about to play. The major caught himself thinking about which ones of the assembled officers would die before the hill was taken and forced himself to think about something more pleasant.

A roar of jet engines filled the sky and Yates was forced to stop talking until the F-4 Phantom passed overhead. The jet was a part of a sortie that had just dropped their load on the top of Hill 875 and was banking to its left away from a known NVA anti-aircraft position.

The operations officer watched the jet approaching and frowned when he saw a five-hundred-pound bomb break loose from the rack it had been hung up on and fall straight toward their position. His eyes opened wide as it dawned on him that the bomb was going to land right on top of them. He fell forward off the ammunition crates in a futile effort to protect himself. None of the other officers saw it coming. One second they were gathered in a semicircle around the battalion commander's map, and the next instant they were all gone, with a shallow crater marking the spot.

The jet pilot continued his high-speed turn, not even noticing that he had lost a hung-up bomb from his wing.

The battalion sergeant major, now the senior man in the CP, looked out with disbelief at where all of the battalion's leadership had been standing only seconds earlier. A dull, loud humming filled his ears and a sharp pain followed. He didn't notice the blood running from his ears, and it was a few minutes before it dawned on him that he couldn't hear.

Captain Maynard blanched and his eyes lost their focus. He handed the black plastic headset back to his radio operator and whispered, "A bomb just wiped out the whole battalion command and staff."

"What?" The company field first sergeant couldn't believe what he had just heard. "All of them?"

"Every single one. I'm the senior officer in the battalion," Maynard said, feeling a deep fear growing inside him.

"What are you going to do?" the sergeant asked, seeing the fear in his captain's eyes.

"I don't know."

Lieutenant Alsop, who had overheard the conversation, instantly realized the extreme danger facing the whole battalion if the NVA decided to attack. "I'd call Brigade if I were you, sir."

The words cut through Maynard's haze of fear. "Yes, good idea. Radio operator, get on the brigade emergency freq!"

The young paratrooper didn't need to look up the numbers in his SOI. He had memorized every one of the brigade's frequencies, plus a number of air-to-ground freqs. He handed the set to the captain.

News of the disaster spread like wildfire around the company perimeter, and Spike saw that his men were near panic. They kept looking back down the hill as if they would run, given the slightest reason. "Sol, we've got to do something," he said, nodding down the line. "If a single round goes off right now, they'll run."

Sol responded by standing up and casually walking around the perimeter, stopping to talk to each of the paratroopers about minor topics. Spike left his bunker and went around the perimeter in the opposite direction, calming the men down and reasuring then that they could handle anything the NVA threw at them from their dug-in positions.

Maynard handed the horn back to his operator. "Brigade is going to fly in a new staff within the hour. I'm in command until then."

The brigade was shocked over the loss, but reacted instantly by assembling a battalion staff from the brigade officers. It took only a short while to contact the officers and get them on helicopters out to the battalion site. The brigade executive officer was selected to be the temporary battalion commander, and he picked his staff officers from the men already at Dak To. None of them had time even to pack a rucksack. They grabbed their weapons and ammo and left.

Hours later, Spike slipped to the bottom of his foxhole and rested his head against his helmet. He had just finished a can of C-rations and had drunk a full canteen of water. He wanted to get a couple hours' sleep during the late morning in case they had to move out later. Sol dropped down in the foxhole next to him and curled up.

"Who's on guard?" Spike mumbled, half asleep.

"The machine gun hole." Sol groaned as he shifted his position on the damp earth floor. "Move your ass over."

Spike wiggled a little closer to the wall of the fox-hole, but could still feel Sol's back up against his. He slipped into a deep sleep. Rarely did an infantryman in the field sleep deeply at night, but when given the opportunity during the daytime, he would sleep so soundly that he seemed to be dead. It was a way to catch-up on much needed rest.

1350 hours

The sound of a heavy machine gun woke Sol out of a deep sleep. He had to struggle to get his eyes to open.

Sol shook Spike's arm violently but without effect. Deep in sleep. Spike heard a pair of NVA 12.7mm heavy machine guns firing and RPG-7s exploding. He groaned and tried opening his eyes but couldn't. The dream continued. He heard men screaming and hand grenades exploding all around him. An M60 opened fire, but was quickly silenced by the heavy machine guns.

Spike opened his eyes and realized that the sounds of battle were real and not a part of his dreams. Green tracer rounds streaked over his position. He reached for his shotgun and flicked open the attached bayonet. Sol was curled up in the corner with his cheek pressed against the dirt wall. "Fuckers surprised us! Shit! Can't even look out and see what the fuck is going on!"

"Wait!" Spike braced himself just in case a stray NVA soldier decided to check inside his hole.

The heavy machine guns stopped and a volley of small arms opened up. The NVA were assaulting the paratroopers' positions. Spike waited for another few of seconds and rose out of the foxhole with his shotgun leading. He saw targets instantly and fired. Sol joined him, firing direct fire with his blooper. One of the HE rounds impacted against an NVA soldier's chest and killed his comrades on either side as well. Spike could see that the NVA were already inside of the perimeter and were fighting hand-to-hand with the Skysoldiers.

Sol pointed over at the unmanned M60. "I'm going to try to get that machine gun. This blooper can't fire fast enough."

"Go, I'll cover you . . . Try to make it to the jungle!"

Sol grabbed the weapon and a couple belts of ammo and ran toward the edge of the thick vegetation. They would be better off in the jungle, firing back at the NVA swarming inside of their position than by trying to hold their foxhole.

Seeing Sol disappear, Spike stepped out of his hole and dashed toward his partner. He saw an NVA bayonet a young paratrooper and stopped to bust a fleshette round against the NVA's face. A Chinese grenade exploded near his feet, knocking him down. Spike jumped back up almost instantly and started running to the border of their perimeter. The explosion had changed his direction and he entered the undergrowth a hundred feet away from Sol.

A sense of security came over Spike the instant he felt bamboo brush his jacket. He halted and started hunting for NVA soldiers. Each time he fired his shotgun, he reached back into his Claymore bag for a shell to replace the one he had fired. Thus he insured that there were always five rounds in his weapon, in case he ran into a pack of NVA. He turned left after penetrating a couple meters into the growth and started searching for Sol. Spike knew that he would have to be very careful because there were bound to be more paratroopers hiding in the jungle.

When the attack had begun, Captain Maynard had seen the green tracers crisscrossing his company area, and he had a couple of seconds to see the men sitting on the edges of their foxholes flip backward onto the ground. The NVA had used the early morning hours to slip into position along the perimeter and set up their heavy weapons. After that, it had been a turkey shoot. Maynard cursed himself for his stupidity: he should have listened to Lieutenant Alsop and put out listening posts. He had thought that the enemy would stay in their bunkers.

The NVA withdrew from the clearing when they heard the trumpet blowing from the edge of the jungle. A small number of men from the third platoon had rallied around a pair of M60s and were starting to change the momentum of the NVA attack. The NVA were regrouping for another attack that would totally overrun the paratroopers.

Maynard pushed the talk switch on his radio. "Sky Hawk! Sky Hawk! This is Sky Dog six . . . We have been overrun!" Maynard caught his breath and stared into the open eyes of his dead radio operator. "I need artillery and air strikes on my Defcons: One . . . five, niner and . . ." The radio went silent. A large hole had appeared in the steel case, dead center in the battery. "Shit!" Maynard pulled the radio off the lip of his foxhole. "Damn it!" He was becoming frustrated. The NVA weren't supposed to be able to kick an airborne company's ass.

An NVA gunner, seeing the radio pulled down into the foxhole, opened up with his RPD. Bullets ripped the dirt edge of Maynard's foxhole, trapping him on the bottom. One of the bullets ricocheted off a rock and hit Maynard's chest. The wound was shallow but painful. Maynard screamed and the NVA gunner smiled over at his comrade. He shifted his fire

back to the American M60 position and exchanged
fire until the American ran out of ammunition.

Lieutenant Alsop lay bleeding on the side of his
foxhole. He knew that his platoon had been wiped out
except for those men who had escaped into the jungle.
He had seen Spike and Sol make it and a couple of
men from his third squad. The NVA had made their
main attack through his section of the perimeter and
had caught everyone off guard. Alsop felt weak and
wondered if he was dying from a loss of blood. He had
been hit four times.

"Captain Maynard!" he called. He didn't receive an
answer.

Maynard had heard Alsop, but he didn't want to
risk drawing more machine-gun fire by answering him.

Alsop heard the machine gun open up on his foxhole, and he saw the dirt flying around the edges. He
removed a grenade from his webgear and struggled to
pull the pin. He was getting very weak. The RPD
stopped firing as the gunner waited for another target.
Alsop pitched the grenade out of his foxhole while he
lay on his back. He didn't get enough arch in his throw
and the grenade exploded ten feet away from his hole.

Maynard thought that the NVA were throwing hand
grenades and curled up in the bottom of his hole. He
had totally lost control of his command, and it was
now every man for himself.

Night fell, and the NVA moved back to their bunker line and waited for the American artillery and air
strikes. Sometime during the night, Lieutenant Alsop
died.

CHAPTER TEN

✪✪✪✪✪✪✪✪✪✪✪✪✪✪

BURNING BLOOD

November 27, 1967
1500 hours

Spike struggled to his feet, keeping the gold Saint Jude's medal in his mouth. The gold chain flickered in the bright sunlight that filtered through the trees, but he didn't care. The medallion was comforting and he was drawing strength through it. Captain Hanson had given the medal to him as a gift, and he knew that the captain was watching over him from wherever good soldiers went when they died in battle.

A whimpering moan brought Spike back to full alert. He listened for the sound to repeat itself. He stepped away from the tree and saw an NVA soldier holding a seriously wounded paratrooper by his hair, ready to cut his throat. Spike recognized the Skysoldier as the one whose wife had recently given birth to a baby girl.

"Hey, motherfucker!" Spike cried. The NVA turned and started toward Spike with the knife held out and a look of drug-induced hate on his face. Spike waited until he was far enough away from the wounded paratrooper so that a stray fleshette wouldn't hit him by accident, and fired. The NVA soldier fell twitching on the bamboo leaves.

Spike dropped to one knee next to the wounded man, at the same time searching the surrounding jungle for any of the NVA soldier's comrades. "Where you hit?"

"Thank God! Sergeant, he was going to cut my throat!" The wounded paratrooper closed his eyes to his pain and shook his head. "Thank God you came when you did."

"Where are you hit?" Spike's voice was soft and reassuring, but he didn't risk looking down at the man.

"Legs . . . and my side . . . A Chicom Claymore caught me and . . ." He looked over to his right side.

Spike followed his gaze and saw four dead paratroopers. "You bleeding?" Spike risked looking down for a second at the man's legs and saw field bandages.

"I'm fine. My sergeant patched me up and said he was going for help."

Spike left the paratrooper's side and scurried over to the dead Americans. He picked up one of their M16s and an ammo belt before returning to the wounded man. "Listen, I've got a couple of men waiting for me a few meters over there." Spike pointed with the barrel of his shotgun. "I know this is scary, but I've got to go get them and I promise, we'll return for you." Spike saw the fear well up in the man's eyes. "The captain is reforming the company perimeter and we'll get you back there for a Medevac. It's not as bad as it looks."

"My sergeant . . ." The paratrooper's voice reflected his fear at being left alone again.

"If he comes back first, tell him to wait for us." Spike smiled. "You've got a weapon this time. No one will fuck with you."

"You'll be right back?"

"That's an airborne promise." Spike patted his shoulder and scooped up a few handfuls of dead leaves to hide him. Mentally noting the surroundings so that he would remember how to find him again, Spike slipped away into the jungle.

Spike moved with extreme caution. Danger could come from any direction, for a jumpy paratrooper could kill him just as quickly as an NVA soldier. He paused when he saw a hand and sleeve sticking out from under a dense jungle plant. The sleeve was from an American uniform. Spike moved over and lifted the bottom leaves of the plant and stared into the eyes of the replacement's sergeant. The NCO's throat had been cut. Spike backed away and continued moving toward the spot where he had left Sol.

Hearing movement in the jungle, Sol shifted the barrel of the M60 to his left and waited. Two NVA soldiers stepped out of the jungle less than five feet in front of him, and Sol had to lift the machine gun off the ground in order to hit them. He fired a short burst and then swept the nearby wall of green jungle plants for any more NVA.

Spike hit the dirt at the sound of an M60 firing so close to him, and he watched bullets cut through the brush above his head. Moving in the jungle was always difficult, but trying to find men who were hiding was almost impossible and extremely dangerous. Ironically, if Spike had passed Sol's position only a couple of seconds earlier, he would have been killed by accident along with the pair of NVA soldiers.

"Yo! Skysoldier!" Spike whispered loudly. He didn't care anymore. Whoever had fired the M60 would certainly hear him.

There was a long pause before an answer came back across the clearing. "Paratrooper?"

Spike knew that the operator of the M60 was being extremely cautious, and what he said next would probably decide if he lived or died. "All the way!"

The reply was instantaneous. "Spike?"

Sol slipped out from his hiding place and gave his friend a tired grin. A tall black soldier followed him, staring with confusion when Spike motioned for him

to turn around and cover their rear while the two
conferred. He heard his name mentioned and glanced
back at the twosome.

"Let's get going, Dudley," Sol said, nodding for
the black soldier to take the rear while Spike took
the point. The jungle had become very quiet. The
artillery had stopped firing and Dudley felt himself
coming out of his terror-stricken daze. He focused
his eyes and saw the young sergeant pointing at
a wounded paratrooper partially hidden in loose
bamboo leaves.

"He alive?" Dudley leaned over the paratrooper,
whose eyes were closed.

"He was when I left him here a few minutes ago,"
Spike said worriedly, checking the man's pulse. He
looked up at the black soldier. "He's alive, but in a
bad way from a loss of blood. We've got to get him
back to the company and get some blood expander in
him." Just then Spike noticed that the black paratrooper's eyes had focused. "Welcome back."

Dudley blushed and was glad that it didn't show.
"Yeah, thanks."

"You carry him, Spike, and I'll cover," Sol said,
who had not ceased turning around and around with
the M60.

Spike flipped his shotgun over his back and brushed
some of the leaves off the wounded man. Dudley
helped him and they carried the man back toward the
company perimeter.

Maynard saw Spike step out of the jungle, followed
by Sol and Dudley carrying a wounded trooper. A lot
of years of experience had been added to Dudley's life
in just a few short hours. Spike helped Sol carry the
wounded man over to the old aid station and told
the junior medic what was wrong with him. Maynard
winced as he watched from his foxhole. His ricochet
wound hadn't penetrated his chest, but it was still
extremely painful.

"I've called in some Medevac ships, but the whole valley has gone crazy. I don't think anyone will get out of here today or tonight," Maynard told Spike, who was one of the few NCOs he had left. "I can't even get artillery support unless it is an emergency fire mission— same goes for air strikes."

"We'll have to make do with what we've got, but I don't think he'll make it through the night." Spike shook his head sadly. The guy's wife had just had a baby. "Who's handling the perimeter?" he asked abruptly, looking out over the empty foxholes.

"The Second Platoon sergeant." Maynard swallowed. "He's the senior NCO."

Spike didn't care who had the job, just as long as they did it. "We'd better get set up. The jungle is full of NVA."

"Did you see any while you were out there?" the captain asked, fear creeping back into his voice.

"Yes." Spike didn't bother to elaborate.

The company had reformed their perimeter inside the old, much larger, one. The distance from their new foxholes to the edge of the jungle was a lot greater and gave the men a little more confidence. Spike had them gather as much ammunition and grenades as they could off the dead troopers and NVA soldiers, figuring if the base camp at Dakto couldn't get Medevacs out to them, they sure as hell couldn't send any resupply ships either.

Sol watched as Spike tied a dark green field bandage around his head. After he tucked in his fatigue shirt, he shoved a .45-caliber pistol down the back of his pants. By the time he had stripped two pistol belts of their ammo pouches and hooked them around his waist, Sol knew Spike was planning to go back into the jungle alone.

"Spike, man, you've done enough," Sol said, biting his lip.

Spike stopped working on his gear and looked up at his partner. "When is enough?"

"Spike, stay inside of the perimeter . . . please?" Sol pleaded, knowing that he was wasting his time.

"You know, Sol, when this fucking war is over . . ." Spike couldn't look at his friend and stared up at the sky. "When this fucking war is over, I'm going to either be fucking dead, or I'm going to be able to sleep at night." He blinked back the tears that were forming from the emotion and exhaustion building inside of him. "After seeing that trooper out there" —Spike nodded at the wounded replacement they had brought back with them—"I can't stay here knowing that there might be more out there alone in the jungle."

Maynard noticed Spike slip over the edge of his foxhole and crawling toward the dark tree line. "Harwood, where in the hell do you think that you're going?" he whispered loudly.

The shadow paused at the edge of the jungle for only an instant and then disappeared. Spike wasn't going to waste his time answering the captain.

The platoon sergeant sharing the foxhole with Maynard shook his head in admiration. "That boy should get the Medal of Honor for this fight."

Maynard looked over at the sergeant's shadow. "He's going to get a damn court-martial—that's what he's going to get." It was fortunate that Maynard didn't see the look the sergeant gave him because his fear would have overwhelmed him all over again.

The paratrooper hid next to his dead buddy under a thick overhang of bamboo. He kept biting his lip to stop the sobs bubbling up his throat. It had been bad enough watching the NVA soldiers sneak past him during the daytime, but now that it had turned dark, it was horrifying. He had watched helplessly as flies landed on his friend's body, and that had nearly made him faint. Now the night sounds were starting to drive him right out of his mind.

A sudden rustle nearby made the hiding paratrooper's heart beat so loud that it echoed in his ears. Someone was was less than five feet away and coming ever closer.

A high-pitched "Aiii!" slipped past his fear-coated vocal cords when a black shape appeared out of the surrounding darkness.

Hearing the fearful sound, Spike risked whispering, "Skysoldier?"

"Oh, fuck." the paratrooper squeaked. "Oh, fuck me . . ." He felt warm liquid drench his crotch.

"You wounded?" Spike whispered. He was about to repeat the question a little louder when the man answered:

"I just pissed my pants."

Spike reached out in the dark and felt a sweat-soaked fatigue jacket. "Come on. Let's get out of here."

"Who are you?"

"Harwood. First Platoon."

Relief filled the man's voice. "Thanks for coming, Sarge. I've been thinking all afternoon that *you* wouldn't leave us out here."

Spike scowled: if the man only knew how close he had come to not leaving the perimeter. He had almost given in to Sol's plea to stay back. Now he was glad that he hadn't. Even this single paratrooper was enough reason to have come. "Let's go. And crawl slowly, we've got to get away from this bamboo. The dead leaves make too much noise."

Spike took the lead and could feel the trooper's hand touching his ankle every few feet. Realizing how scared the man was, Spike decided on taking him back to the perimeter before going back out again.

When Spike guessed that they were close to the old line of foxholes, he stopped to orient himself near the roots of a large hardwood tree. The man with him had started crawling up to his side when a dark shadow leapt from between two of the roots. Spike caught the shadowy movement out of the corner of his eye and turned over on his side to meet the attack. The heavy body hit him hard and the assailant grunted from the impact.

"Sarge!" That single word of Spike's companion saved his life.

A huge black paratrooper rolled off Spike's back. "Man, I almost wasted you!"

The sigh coming from Spike's lungs was his answer.

"Who are you with?" the paratrooper smelling of urine asked.

"Third platoon. Do you know where we're at?"

"Close to the perimeter." Spike's whisper barely carried past his lips. "Are you alone?"

"Yeah. I was with a guy named Everhart, but we got separated. I feel sorry for that dude. He got here right before noon yesterday."

"We found Dud—he's already back inside the perimeter." Spike tapped the huge black paratrooper's shoulder and pointed in the direction of the company. "Come on," he said, starting to crawl ahead.

"Glad you came along. I would have gone the wrong way for sure," the paratrooper said starting to crawl behind Spike.

Sol called for safe passage when he recognized Spike's soft whistle, and he smiled his thanks to the God his people had been worshiping for over five thousand years.

1840 hours

Spike rested his head against the back edge of the freshly dug foxhole. He had applied the last of the antibacterial ointment to his infected body, and the severe burning pain had eased up enough for him to think about eating. He opened a can of his favorite C-rations—shredded chicken in water. Using his fingers, he shoveled some of the meat into his mouth and slowly sucked the juice out of the fibers. He was too tired to chew. The pain in his muscles was gone; they just didn't work anymore.

The sound of artillery and mortars exploding was superseded by a series of tremendous explosions and an invisible shock wave. B-52s were blanket-bombing the valley to the west of Hill 875. The large bombers flew so high that they couldn't be heard on the ground as they passed by overhead and released their cargo of two-thousand-pound bombs.

Sol opened his eyes and looked up at the light blue sky. "You know something, Spike?"

"What?"

"There aren't any command and control helicopters flying around." That was a unique phenomenon in Vietnam. Usually, there were stacks of command and control choppers flying above a firefight, but not at Hill 875. Fast-moving jets roared by overhead, dropped their deadly cargo, and then hit their afterburners to escape the deadly anti-aircraft zone the NVA had established around the battle corridor.

"How long have we been here?" Spike asked around a mouthful of chicken.

"Three days?"

"Yeah, something like that." He tried swallowing the meat, but found it too dry and had to take a sip of water to get it down. "I don't know if I can handle much more of this."

Sol looked over at his war buddy. Spike's face had a number of jungle ulcers on it from the cuts inflicted by bamboo leaves, and that large ulcer at the corner of his mouth was still oozing blood. Spike kept licking the cold sore to keep it moist and prevent it from cracking and causing additional pain. "I heard that they were going to bring in another battalion tomorrow to take the hill."

"That's all we fucking need: another assault," Spike said, hurling the empty C-ration can over the edge of the foxhole without looking where it went.

All night long, artillery bombarded the upper portion of Hill 875. The paratroopers managed to sleep through most of the night, taking catnaps. The NVA would have had an extremely difficult time trying to infiltrate through the constant bombardment. The 2nd Battalion had gone from the lowest to the highest priority for fire missions in a matter of hours. Something big was in the works. Air Force flare ships kept portions of the hill lit up all night long. Paratroopers from the 4th Battalion, 503rd Airborne Infantry, and Skytroopers from the airmobile 1st Cavalry Division probed the NVA bunker lines that had been well defined during the past three days of intense fighting. All of the usual friction between the two units had been dropped during the battle. The 173rd Airborne Brigade was pissed over the Cav soldiers calling themselves Skytroopers, a nickname that was too close to theirs—Skysoldiers. Also, the 1st Cavalry Division had lost their colors during a battle in Korea and had not been allowed to return to the United States officially as a unit. But their record in Vietnam was exceptional, and all of the old sayings about their patch were rapidly being forgotten as they won battle after battle.

Thanksgiving Day, 1967
0435 hours

Spike heard the sound of the choppers just as the first rays of light entered the valley. It sounded as if hundreds of aircraft were coming all at the same time. He tried turning around in his foxhole to locate them, but they were still too far away.

Suddenly the area was filled with landing choppers and Huey gunships darting around in the sky. The few

NVA anti-aircraft positions that still existed on the hill opened fire, only to be destroyed by converging fires from the gunships.

Captain Maynard stood up in his foxhole and watched the fresh troops empty out of their choppers. He had been talking all night long to the 4th Division staff and knew that the relief force would arrive at first light. It looked as if a whole battalion was unloading in the clearing with tons of equipment.

A clean-shaven captain approached Maynard's foxhole running bent over. It looked funny to the paratroopers watching, but then again, they would have been cautious, too, if they were just landing on the side of a very hot battlesite. "I'm Captain Frazer. I've brought my company to reinforce your position."

"Aren't you replacing us?" Maynard frowned and touched the bandage that covered his wound.

"I was told to reinforce your assault to the top of the hill." The captain checked his watch. "The arty is going to start their prep fires in exactly fifteen minutes, and we kick off in thirty."

"That's not what I've been told," Maynard said angrily. "My company is supposed to be evacuated!"

"Just the wounded. Division has decided that your company, or what is left of it, is too important and will be used as guides."

"Guides!" Maynard shook his head. "I'll have my wounded Medevaced—"

"Are you going too?" Captain Frazer asked, even though he saw the blood stains on Maynard's jacket.

"Can't you see? I'm wounded . . . since the day before yesterday!" Maynard picked up his gear and walked bent over, holding his bad arm, to the waiting choppers.

Captain Frazer signaled for his men to check the foxholes around the perimeter and replace the wounded. Walking over to one of the foxholes himself, he looked down at two ragged paratroopers inside. He couldn't believe how dirty and bloodstained they were. The dark-haired one had what looked like a week's growth of beard on his face, and the other one didn't even look as if he shaved yet. "Go back to the choppers. They're Medevacing the wounded," he ordered, nodding over his shoulder.

"I'm not wounded," Sol sighed. He sure would have liked to have been slightly wounded so that he could get off the hill.

"How about you?" The captain looked at Spike.

"Me neither, sir."

"Bullshit, Spike," Sol cried. "You get your ass on that chopper."

"I'm not wounded, Sol."

"You're bad enough off . . . get! You've done enough!"

"No way. If you're staying, I'm staying." Spike looked up at the captain. "My friend gets emotional sometimes, sir. He's Jewish."

"We're going to start our assault to the top of the hill in less than fifteen minutes. Get your gear ready."

Spike nodded. He had his gear ready. His shotgun and Claymore bag of ammunition were all that he had left to carry along with his webgear. He thought for a second and then yelled over to a couple of clean-clad infantrymen, "You guys got any spare hand grenades?"

One of them looked over at Spike and slowly shook his head.

1100 hours

The remainder of the 2nd Battalion, 503rd Airborne Infantry, made it to the top of Hill 875, facing a light rearguard action by a suicide platoon of the NVA 174th Regiment. The headquarters element had slipped off the hill during the night back into Laos. The feat in itself was almost a tactical miracle, for the NVA had maneuvered through constant artillery and air strikes. The Salem-smoking colonel had lost the majority of his command during the battle for Dak To, but Radio Hanoi was already calling it a great victory.

Spike led the way for the new company as they broke through the jungle for the last three hundred meters to the top of the hill. There the foliage had been cleared almost entirely by the bombing.

Sol dropped onto a freshly downed tree and rested the M60 across his lap. "That was easy."

Spike smiled and cracked open his cold sore again. "Yeah."

"Look at this shit," Sol said, tilting the M60 so that Spike could read the lettering on its side: "CONG KILLER."

Spike shook his head.

"Fuck, I didn't even notice it until now, and I've been carrying this thing for two fucking days."

"Some things just aren't important until the battle is over, my friend." Spike slipped down on the side of the log and laid his shotgun across his lap before closing his eyes. And while the infantry company searched the NVA bunkers, finding great stores of supplies and equipment left behind, Spike and Sol rested against the log with their faces turned up toward the warm sun.

1400 hours

The landing choppers kicked up a layer of dirt and debris, forcing the soldiers on top of Hill 875 to use their drive-on rags to cover their faces. Sol watched as a pair of crew members pulled the green Mermite cans off the chopper. He struggled up on one elbow so that he could see better and nudged Spike. "Would you believe they've flown in hot food?"

Spike struggled to sit up and saw where Sol was pointing. "You're right! Let's go!"

A mess sergeant from the rear flown in to serve the food quickly set up a makeshift serving line almost before the chopper had departed. He didn't want to stay on the hill longer than he had to.

"Whatcha got in all those cans?" Spike said from the good side of his mouth.

"What do you expect?" the sergeant asked sarcastically, trying to hide the fact that he felt intimidated by the tough-looking combat vets.

"Just asking, Sarge," Spike replied softly.

The mess sergeant hadn't expected such a reply from the battle-weary paratrooper. "Sorry—I'm a little jumpy out here." His honesty brought a smile to the combat-stained faces.

"Yeah, us too." Spike nodded at the Mermite cans. "We're awful hungry," he noted, pointing at the growing line of Bravo Company survivors being drawn by the smell of the food.

"I brought out just the normal stuff for a Thanksgiving Day dinner. We didn't know if you guys were going to take the hill in time."

"Thanksgiving Day dinner?" Sol asked, pronouncing each word slowly.

"Yeah. Today's Thanksgiving. Normal stuff: turkey, mashed potatoes . . ." The mess sergeant opened one of the Mermite cans, and the smell of sweet potatoes and cranberry sauce wafted toward the line of starving men. "I even brought out some ice cream for you guys. I thought you might like it after all that sweating you've done."

"Ice cream?" Spike felt his throat get dryer.

"Yep." The sergeant lifted the lid on a nearby stack of coolers. "Different kinds too. Grab a paper plate and plasticware."

Half an hour later, Sol tried swallowing another bite of food and couldn't. "I think I'm going to be sick."

"Me too." Spike leaned back over the edge of the tree trunk they had been sitting on while they had gorged themselves and vomited up the still-warm food. It was too rich for their stomachs. When he finished, he rinsed his mouth out from a paper cup of grape Kool-Aid and smiled over at Sol. "Are you ready for some dessert? The ice cream is melting."

Sol followed Spike back over to the mess line, and they both left with a half gallon of ice cream apiece.

On the way back, Spike saw a UPI photographer squatting in front of a paratrooper who was eating from a paper plate piled high with Thanksgiving turkey and mashed potatoes. As the soldier slowly ate his food, tears ran down his cheeks, leaving clean trails in the soot that had blackened his face. The paratrooper's eyes weren't focused and snot formed a mustache around his mouth. The photographer knew that he had an award-winning photograph in the making.

"Leave him alone," threatened a voice from behind him.

"Fuck you. I've been given permission by your commanding general to take pictures up here." He turned and saw a teenage paratrooper glaring at him with a half gallon box of melting ice cream in his hand.

"Fine, but leave *him* alone."

The photojournalist sneered and went back to focusing his camera for the shot. In the next moment he felt his feet being kicked out from under him and someone tearing his expensive camera out of his hands. As he fell backward, he saw his camera flying through the air and landing in the jungle.

"I said, leave him alone." Spike took a seat on one side of the crying paratrooper and Sol sat on the other. Sol held the open ice cream container up close to his face, and Spike slapped the bottom of it with his hand. Sol's face emerged covered with ice cream from his nose on down.

"You're dead for that shit, Spike." Sol started laughing when he felt the ice cream dripping off his chin.

The photojournalist found his camera and glanced back over his shoulder to see the two paratroopers laughing hysterically, sitting on each side of the crying man. He started lifting his camera to take the shot and stopped. Some things were best left alone.

A pair of helicopters circled the top of the hill and landed. The flight of Huey gunships that had escorted the slicks into the LZ continued to circle the hill.

"Brass is landing," Spike mumbled, shoveling in another mouthful of ice cream.

Sol looked over at the lieutenant general exiting the chopper and then shifted so his back was to the officer. "Fucking brass always get here when it's all over with. You ever notice that?" He removed his drive-on rag from around his neck and wiped the snot off the crying paratrooper's face. The man continued eating slowly from his plate of food.

"Yeah. He's coming our way," Spike said, turning as Sol had. "I hope he leaves us alone."

The general paused when he reached the paratroopers. "Good afternoon, men. Enjoying your Thanksgiving dinner?"

Spike figured that being the sergeant, he would have to answer the general officer. He stood up, only to be instantly pushed back down on his log seat.

"You take a break. You've earned it." The general's smile curdled as he noticed the middle paratrooper. "What's wrong with him?

"He's crying, sir."

"Oh . . ." The general frowned for a second and then added, "What are your names?"

"I'm Sergeant Harwood, sir. And he's Specialist Levin." Spike didn't know the name of the crying paratrooper.

"Levin? Are you by some chance related to the Chicago Levins?" the general asked, almost sure the young soldier wasn't.

"Yes, sir." Sol's voice was very low.

"*Cy* Levin, the industrialist?"

"He's my father, sir."

The shocked look of surprise looked out of place on the three-star general's face. "I was a program officer and worked on a experimental-missile program in one of your father's plants."

Sol remained silent, not knowing what to say.

The general took his time studying the ragged paratroopers and then offered his hand to shake. "You men fought hard—a job well done!"

"Thanks, General." Spike clumsily shifted the carton of melting ice cream to his other hand and shook the proffered hand.

"Your ice cream is melting. You'd better hurry and finish it," the general advised, finishing on a cheery note.

Spike took a halfhearted bite from the soft ice cream while Sol shook hands in turn. Spike noticed that the general unconsciously wiped his hand against his clean fatigue jacket after he had finished. It wasn't meant to be insulting, and Spike didn't take it that way. It was just symbolic.

"He wasn't half bad," Sol said, watching the officer's party walking away.

"I've met worse," Spike snorted, watching the photojournalist running to catch up to the general.

The general glanced over at his aide-de-camp when they had gotten out of earshot of the trio of paratroopers and whispered, "Do you know who that kid is back there?"

"No, sir."

"He's the son of Cy Levin, the billionaire industrialist."

The lieutenant colonel looked back over his shoulder at Sol. "What in the hell is he doing *here*, sir?"

The general shook his head as he boarded his waiting chopper. "I really don't know."

Spike watched the chopper depart and tossed the carton of ice cream over his shoulder. He had lost interest in dessert.

Sol followed suit. "What are you thinking about?"

"He was wearing Old Spice aftershave," Spike stated illogically, looking back down Hill 875, where so many paratroopers had died.

CHAPTER ELEVEN

✪✪✪✪✪✪✪✪✪✪✪✪✪✪✪✪✪✪✪✪✪

ARMY BLUE
BLOODS

The airstrip at Dak To was so busy that some C-130s were being held in a flight pattern above the valley. Hundreds of fresh troops and artillery pieces were being rushed into the climaxing battle along the borders as the NVA withdrew back into their sanctuaries.

Sergeant Harwood and Sol Levin sat outside a large tent, wearing only cutoff shorts. Sol was going through the remains of a field sundry package, sorting out the different packages of candy from the shaving items and cigarettes.

"Do you want anything else out of here before I throw it back in the tent?"

Spike turned his head and looked down from the sandbag wall that surrounded the sleeping tent. "No, can it."

"Look over there," Sol said, his voice dropping as he pointed over to the nearby runway.

Spike sat up. He could see the detail men loading the body bags on the small airborne mobile "goats" that would haul the dead paratroopers over to the rear ramps of the waiting C-130s. Spike hadn't dreamed that there could be so many dead American soldiers in all of Vietnam. There were hundreds and hundreds of the green body bags lining the side of the runway, and teams of medics were carrying even more of them out to the waiting aircraft.

"It looks like we got our asses kicked."

"Do you think we should go over there and help?" Sol wasn't volunteering for just any detail. He knew how tough it was for replacements to handle bodies.

"If they want our help, they'll ask." Spike turned away from the airstrip, and by chance his gaze rested on the charred spot on the side of the mountain where Alpha Company had been wiped out.

"Do you think they'll send us back out there?" Sol asked, worried. He didn't want to go back and mop up. He was tired of all the killing.

"We'll see . . ." Spike pulled his waistband away from his stomach and looked down inside his pants. "That stuff the brigade surgeon gave me is really working down there. I should be ready to hump again in a couple of days."

"Let's hope that it's all over by then." Sol opened a can of warm Shasta soda and took a sip. He had been severely dehydrated when they had come down off Hill 875, but it was amazing how fast a young body could recover. He had slept for almost twenty straight hours when they returned, and that was through all of the artillery being fired and the aircraft landing and taking off.

"Sergeant Monk wanted to see me today," Spike said as he looked over the top of the artillery battery position at the Brigade TOC. He paused and watched the artillerymen humping rounds for their howitzers. The area around them was littered with thousands of empty canisters and huge piles of cardboard tubing and packing materials. Spike made a mental note to stop by the artillery position and thank them for their support on his way over to the headquarters.

Sergeant First Class Monk pretended to read the after-action report for the battle of Hill 875 while he listened to the senior officers talking. After all, he had read the report a dozen times and knew it almost by heart. It sounded like a justification for some officer to make his star, or add another one. The statistics for the month-long battle were impressive if you were sitting in a Pentagon office. Army aviation had flown over 13,000 hours of combat flights, the artillery units had fired over 170,000 rounds of ammunition, and the Air Force had flown 2,100 tactical sorties and 300 B-52 sorties in support of the battle for Dak To. The report claimed over 1,600 NVA soldiers KIA. Hill 875 had cost the 173rd Airborne Brigade its combat-effectiveness status, and the whole command was ordered to stand down and rebuild its strength before going back to the field. Monk knew that the 173rd alone had suffered 816 dead paratroopers, and he didn't know how in the hell the generals were going to hide that from the news media. But he was confident that they would find a way of breaking down their losses so that it would look like a great victory for them. Monk shook the paper in his hand and then picked up a typed intelligence report concerning an NVA courier who had been found near a bombed-out trailside bunker. The man had been carrying the loss report for the 174th Regiment back to their headquarters in Laos. The NVA commander was reporting 822 dead and missing soldiers, almost the exact number of paratroopers who had died.

Monk looked up as one of the senior officers started shouting:

"Damn it! He deserves the Medal of Honor for his actions at Hill 875!"

"I don't agree. A battalion commander is rarely exposed to the real fighting . . ."

"Bullshit! The NVA broke through his perimeter and were killing the wounded at the aid station!"

"I heard that the chaplain was the one who picked up the machine gun and drove the NVA back through the perimeter."

"A chaplain? Don't be absurd!"

The brigade commanding general ended the argument. "Gentlemen! What we need are more eyewitness statements for all of these recommendations for the Medal of Honor." Speaking to the group collectively, he said, "I agree with you, we have a number of our paratroopers who fought gallantly and with extreme valor. But any Medal of Honor recommendations coming out of this headquarters must be extremely well documented."

The brigade chief-of-staff glared at the lieutenant colonel who had spoken back to him in front of the general.

Sergeant Monk waited until the meeting was over and casually went over to the chief-of-staff's desk and placed a stack of papers in his "in" box. Pausing, he searched the top of the colonel's desk for the sheet of paper the officers had been arguing about and saw the yellow copy of the recommended awards list stuck halfway under a stack of after-action reports from the battalions. Monk pulled the paper out and looked down the list of names and units.

MEDAL OF HONOR RECOMMENDATIONS
1st Battalion, 503rd Infantry none
2nd Battalion, 503rd Infantry
LTC Elmer Yates (killed in action)
CPT Eugene K. Maynard V (wounded in action)
3rd Battalion, 503rd Infantry

Sergeant Monk's eyes went back up to the 2nd Battalion nominees. Maynard was being recommended for the Medal of Honor?

"Can I help you with something, Sergeant Monk?" the colonel inquired, coming up from behind.

"No, sir, I was just dropping off some more afteraction reports when I saw this . . ." Embarrassed, he handed the list back to the colonel.

"This is a confidential document, Sergeant," the colonel chastised.

Monk's feelings were hurt. "I have a top-secret clearance, sir."

"We're talking about a different kind of clearance, Sergeant Monk—a gossip level clearance. This recommended list could be very damaging to the morale of the brigade if it became common knowledge. A lot of people are jealous over stuff like this, and until official recommendations have been made, I don't want this list flashed around."

"Yes, sir."

"There will be more of these lists coming in, I'm sure, from the battalions," the salty chief-of-staff huffed, "probably from the headquarters elements too. Make sure they are put inside my field desk."

"Yes, sir . . . Oh, colonel?"

"Yes?" the colonel asked, pausing on his way over to the battle map.

"I couldn't help but notice Captain Maynard's name on that list. Who recommended him?"

"Why do you ask, Sergeant?"

"Everyone in the 2nd Battalion headquarters element was killed by that Air Force bomb. I was just wondering who was left who could have even seen what the captain did to deserve the recommendation."

"I don't know exactly. The recommendation for Captain Maynard just appeared in distribution with the rest of the award recommendations." The colonel gave Monk a weary look and went over to read the day's new unit locations on the main battle map.

Monk left the command bunker for his meal break a little early and walked over to the personnel tent to see one of his old poker buddies. If it was statements they needed for a Medal of Honor recommendation, it was statements he was going to get, but not for some bullshitting West Point officer.

"Hey, Monk! I thought you guys were too busy over at the TOC to take any breaks."

"Hi, Marty." Monk took a seat in one of the empty field chairs near the sergeant major's table.

"Do you think that it's about over with out there?"

"It looks like a little mopping up is about all that's left. The NVA have all pulled back to their sanctuaries across the border," Monk remarked, lighting a cigarette.

"When in the hell are we going to bomb those fucking NVA bases?" The old soldier slapped the top of his olive-drab desk with his open palm. "The governments of Cambodia and Laos have absolutely and I mean *absolutely* no control of that fucking jungle the NVA are using for their personal sanctuaries along the borders. As far as I'm concerned, it's North Vietnam, and we should bomb those fuckers back into cavemen!"

"Write the President, Marty, I'm sure he'll listen to you." Monk hot-boxed the cigarette and waited for it to cool off again before taking another drag.

"I just might do that. Those fucking NVA can cross the border anytime they want to from those sanctuaries and run back when we counterattack." Taken by a new thought, the sergeant major chuckled to himself. "We should set up our armies like the Spartans did."

"How's that?"

"Once war is declared, the senators became the generals and had to fight the fucking wars they created."

"Great, Marty! Then we'll lose for sure!" Monk shook his head. "I'm not talking about senators, either. We'd lose all of the fucking battles."

"Fuck it." The sergeant major waved his hand toward the door and looked at Monk. "What can I do for you?" He could tell by the look on his friend's face that he wanted something.

"This is going to be a tough one, Marty, and I'll

understand if you don't want to get involved . . ." Monk spent the next fifteen minutes briefing the administration man on Harwood.

"Was he the one that hopped on that forklift when that C-130 was hit?" Marty asked, tapping the edge of his desk with his ballpoint pen.

"Yes, I've been hearing good things about him ever since he was assigned to this brigade."

"Let's check his records out and I'll get back to you, but I really don't think he's been in the Army long enough to have gotten into any kind of serious trouble." The sergeant major grinned. "He's one of those Shake'n'Bakes coming out of the States."

"Maybe so, but someone must have seen something in that kid to promote him so damn fast, knowing that he was coming straight over here to Nam," Monk said, grinding out his cigarette on the matted grass floor.

"Here." The sergeant major handed Monk a stack of award-deposition forms. "See if you can find eyewitnesses to any acts of valor Harwood has performed since the battle for Dak To started." Removing one of the forms from the stack, he put it back down on his desk. "I saw him use that forklift, and personally, I think that by itself is enough of a reason to recommend him."

"Thanks, Marty. I owe you one."

"No, don't thank me. It's about time an enlisted man gets something out of this fucking war. Korea was my war and I know for a fact that the officers sucked up most of the valor awards for themselves." He tucked a pinch of Copenhagen inside his lower lip before continuing. "And I saw that list they sent to the brigade commander."

Monk was leaving the tent and when he was stopped by the sergeant major's closing comment: "Keep what you're doing quiet, or someone will stop you."

Monk nodded his head in agreement and stepped out into the hot sunshine.

He didn't have far to go to find a witness.

Hours later, Sol looked over the deposition he had written about Spike. Twenty-two pages long, it would probably be the prime piece of evidence for the Medal of Honor recommendation, he knew. What he hadn't realized was how much time he had spent with Spike and how close they had become in the past few months. After what they had gone through on Hill 875, that teenage sergeant meant the world to him. Sol was experiencing a psychological phenomenon that baffled women. Psychologists called it "war buddies." The bonds men form during battle seem to have been forged in emotional blacksmith shops of unbreakable links. Women intuitively sense the bonding between war buddies, and more than one marriage has ended in divorce because the husband would not reject his war buddy for her. Sol himself knew that when his father had returned from World War II, he had hired a number of gentiles into his industrial organization, to everyone's bafflement. Sol understood now. Those men had been war buddies and could always be trusted, no matter how much wealth or power they accumulated.

"What are you writing?"

Spike's voice snapped Sol back to the reality of the stifling tent. As Spike took a seat next to him on the canvas cot, Sol stuffed the document back into its brown envelope.

"Some shit Sergeant Monk has asked for."

"You've been acting weird as hell lately," Spike commented, crossing to his cot and stretching out on it.

"It's just a report he wants done for the brigade historian. He figures because I'm Jewish that I can write." Sol was pleased at the believable lie and smiled. "Boring shit." He waved the envelope. "I've got to get it over to Sergeant Monk right now, before the courier chopper arrives for the afternoon pickup."

Spike closed his eyes without answering.

"I hear we might be going back to Bien Hoa near

Saigon to regroup the brigade." Sol slapped the envelope against his leg. "And that means pussy!"

Spike's eyes remained closed. "What does a rich punk like you know about pussy?"

"Plenty!"

"Shit, you Jewish types only screw JAPs. You need a little variety in your puss diet there, Sol."

Sol crept up next to Spike's cot and pulled the edge of the envelope across his neck as if he were cutting his throat. " You could really get fucked up messing with a Hebrew warrior—"

Spike snatched the deposition out of Sol's hand and sat up on the edge of his cot. "Let's see what you've written about the battle." He glanced up at his buddy, grinning. "You'd better have me in this."

The sound of the incoming chopper saved Sol. "I'd better get that over to Sergeant Monk."

Uninterested, Spike flipped him the closed package and lay back down on his cot. Sol wiped the sweat off his forehead and sighed. He had damn near blown the whole plan.

Over at Brigade TOC, Sergeant Monk looked over the stack of eyewitness statements and depositions for acts-of-valor recommendations. One hundred and three soldiers had testified in behalf of Harwood, and none of the depositions were less than four pages long. Monk shook his head in disbelief. He hadn't dreamed that there would be so many witnesses to Harwood's deeds. Once the word had spread among the enlisted men, statements were coming in from all over the brigade and field hospitals where the wounded paratroopers had been sent.

Monk counted the number of enemy KIA attributed to Spike since the Dak To campaign had started and whistled softly: twenty-nine North Vietnamese regulars.

"Did you wish to see me this morning, Sergeant Monk?" the chief-of-staff asked sourly. He was in a bad mood after a full night of heavy politics. He had been visited in secret by at least a dozen of the commanders and brigade staff officers, and all of them had asked for special favors and treatment for their paperwork. The battle for Dak To had caught the attention of both the media and the Pentagon, for it was the longest continuous battle of the war. The chief-of-staff, a thirty-three-year veteran, hadn't been fooled by their requests. He knew that the recommendations presented first had the best chance of being approved.

Yes, sir," Monk said, handing the colonel the stack of statements. "I'd like for you to look at this recommendation."

Irritated by yet another request, the colonel started to turn away. "I'm very busy this morning, Sergeant. I hope you realize that the war is still going on."

"Sir." Monk's curtness stopped the tough colonel in his tracks. "Please, look at this. I think you'll be impressed."

"Impressed with what?" he sneered. "Who are these awards recommendations for?" he asked, hefting the thick stack.

"Not plural, sir. Just one recommendation."

The colonel's expression changed. "One?"

Monk waited as the officer flipped up the cover sheet and read the first paragraph. "A Medal of Honor recommendation . . . hmmm."

"There are one hundred and three eyewitness statements in that package," Monk remarked, knowing he had the colonel's attention. "And they're all for Sergeant Harwood."

"Harwood?" The colonel frowned. "I've heard that name somewhere before."

"He's a tough paratrooper, sir. Out of the Second Bat—"

"Yes!" The colonel patted the stack of papers and smiled to himself over his ability to recall an incident. "He's up for some type of drug charge, isn't he? Or did it take place back in jump school?"

"Absolutely not." Monk was shocked. "He's clean."

"Not according to his company commander."

"Captain Maynard?"

"Yes, General Maynard's son. Now I remember. Colonel Yates returned here right after he dropped young Maynard off at his new command and mentioned to the general that there might be a drug-abuse problem in Bravo Company, Second Battalion. Maynard told him that he had recognized a major drug dealer in the company who had served underneath him in jump school. A soldier named Harwood . . . I'm sure of it."

"Bullshit, sir," Monk cried, becoming furious. "I don't know what went on between him and Sergeant Harwood, sir. But read the statements in your hands before you make any further judgments about Harwood."

"That's fair. I'll get back with you soon." The colonel left Monk standing next to his desk and went over to the other corner of the TOC and sat down. Monk could see that he was smiling as he flipped through the stack of papers.

The statement the colonel had made about Harwood being involved in drugs made Monk angrier and angrier as he thought about it. Finally he couldn't stand it anymore. Storming out of the TOC, he charged over to the administration staff sergeant major's office.

"Yo, Monk," the sergeant major said, smiling, "you looked pissed about something."

"I am. The chief just told me that Harwood is under some kind of drug charge."

"Whoa!" The old NCO grinned conspiratorially. "First listen to this. We checked on what you told us about Captain Maynard's MOH recommendation, and guess what we've found out?"

"Marty, can it wait until later?"

"No, because I think it ties in with what you've just said about Harwood."

Puzzled, Monk shook his head. "Go on . . . tell me."

"We traced the recommendation back through channels and found out that it was prepared at the hospital where Captain Maynard is currently being held."

"So?"

"So, the officer who signed the recommendation is an old friend of the captain's father."

"So what?" Monk didn't understand what the sergeant major was driving at.

"So, Monk, the award recommendation is a phony one," he said, disgusted by Monk's denseness.

"Phony?" Monk started to smile. "Can you prove that?

"It's simple, my *infantry* friend. The statement was signed off by a full colonel, but his unit assignment wasn't listed on the recommendation, only his rank and branch. Which was infantry. They want the reviewing officers to assume that he was assigned to the 173rd during the battle, when in fact, he's the hospital's administration officer." The sergeant major slapped his desk as he concluded, "The whole recommendation for Maynard is phony!"

"Hot shit!"

"So you see, Maynard made the statement about Harwood being into drugs to insure that the brigade staff wouldn't approve *any* awards for the sergeant. You see, I discovered a curious thing. I checked the files and found out that Harwood had been recommended for a Silver Star by his former company commander. Oddly enough, the award had been logged into the brigade but got lost. The error that Maynard made was not checking Harwood's personnel folder for a carbon copy of the recommendation."

"Why is he riding Harwood so hard?" Monk asked, unable to understand why a commander would do such a thing to one of his own soldiers.

"Jealousy, pure and simple. I've been in the Army

too damn long, and I've seen just about every trick that can be played with a soldier's file. Maynard is jealous of the sergeant and is trying to screw him."

"Let's hope that he doesn't find out about Harwood's MOH recommendation."

"He already has."

"What?"

"Some of the soldiers in the hospital made depositions for Harwood, and the same colonel who signed off on Maynard's phony award had to sign off on their statements. I'm sure he told Maynard what was going on because in Maynard's award recommendation there are a number of identical incidents that people are writing up about Sergeant Harwood."

"Oh, shit." Now Monk understood. Instead of recommending his sergeant for a valor award, Maynard was claiming Harwood's deeds as his own.

"Don't worry, Monk. I've personally taken an interest in this case, and I promise you that he won't get away with it. I've been pushing paperwork too long to be bullshitted by a rookie captain."

"Thanks. Marty. I really appreciate your help." Monk shook his head, still unable to believe the extent of Maynard's duplicity.

"I've made copies of everything in Harwood's files, including his MOH recommendation. Nothing is going to get lost. I've already shipped a complete copy to a friend of mine in the Pentagon, with a note attached as to what I want done if the original paperwork gets lost."

"Thanks again—"

"You don't have to keep thanking me," the sergeant major said, tucking a little more Copenhagen behind his lip. "I read those statements on Harwood. That boy is a fucking American hero!"

Back in the TOC, the colonel first flipped through the depositions and then settled down to read all of them from the beginning. As he did, he flexed his jaw occasionally and felt the back of his neck getting ever warmer. He was more embarrassed than angry. It was obvious that Captain Maynard was trying to skate a phony Medal of Honor recommendation past him. The similarities between the two recommendations were obvious. The major difference was that the captain had very few eyewitness statements compared to Harwood's huge number of witnesses documenting each act of valor from numerous angles. The old colonel had even heard about the forklift incident and had tried tracking down the man responsible, but he had run into a dead end when he reached the 2nd Battalion.

Finally the colonel had read enough and reached for his field telephone. When the brigade switchboard operator came on the line, the colonel snapped, "Get me the MACV J-1's office in Saigon." The chief-of-staff drummed the top of his desk as he listened to the switchboard operator patch him through the various land lines to Saigon.

A soft female voice came on the line. "Lieutenant General Murphy's office."

"I'd like to talk to him please. Tell him Terry O'Donnell is calling."

"I'm sorry, sir. He is very busy right now and can't be disturbed."

The colonel slapped the top of his field desk. "Tell him a Rakkashan is on the line!"

"Please hold," she said, irritated.

A few seconds later a booming voice came on the line. "Terry! What can I do for you?"

"Hello, General. It looks like the fucking Army blue bloods are trying to screw up this war too."

A long laugh filled the line, and then the general coughed before asking, "Brief me on the problem." They had served together in the Rakkashan Regiment during the Korean War and had become war buddies. O'Donnell was an OSC graduate and called all West Pointers "Army blue bloods."

"If I remember right, the last time that we talked, you mentioned that the MACV command could use an all-American hero, right?"

"Yes, I mentioned that because the peace movement back in the States is kicking our asses in the papers."

The crusty old airborne colonel flashed a rare grin that showed all of his tobacco-stained teeth. "I just found you one, but he's not a fucking Army blue blood."

CHAPTER TWELVE

✪✪✪✪✪✪✪✪✪✪✪✪✪✪✪✪✪✪✪✪✪✪

RED, WHITE, AND BLOOD

A light rain had sprinkled the valley floor, leaving everything shiny. The various shades of green from the jungle plants sparkled in the midday light as Sol walked from the battalion's command bunker back to the poncho hootch he was sharing with Spike. A vivid rainbow arched across the mountains to the north, and Sol stopped to admire it.

"Nice, huh?" Spike commented, sitting on a wooden case containing hand flares.

"Yeah, Chicago has so much smog you rarely see rainbows. Even out in the suburbs, they're real pale." Sol watched the beautiful arch until a huge black rain cloud rolled in.

"What's going on over at Battalion?" Spike stirred the can of beans and meatballs he was cooking over the blue flame of a heat tablet stove. He could smell the beans burning on the bottom of the can.

"You won't believe who just came back from the hospital at Qui Nhon." Sol flipped through a bundle of letters and tossed two of them down at Spike. "Who's Kimberly?" Sol asked, grinning. "Someone I should know?"

Ignoring Sol's comment, Spike added the contents from the small can of cheese he had melting near the

fire to the beans and meatballs. He stirred the concoc-
tion until he was satisfied that they were properly
blended and sampled a spoonful.

Sol sat down and opened a letter that had the seal of
his father's company engraved in the corner.

"So who's back?" Spike asked, already knowing the
answer.

"Maynard." Sol opened his letter and started reading it. "So . . . who's this Kimberly?" Sol asked idly,
continuing to read.

Spike glanced down at the two letters lying on the
matted-down grass. "She's a good friend from back
home."

"How good?" Sol didn't look up.

"We sorta grew up together in the same neighborhood." Spike lifted the dark green can of C-rations off
the stove, using the handle he made for it by folding
back the edges of the can's top, and set it on the
ground to cool off a little.

Sol refolded the letter and stuffed it back into its
envelope. Spike didn't need to look up to know that
Sol was angry. He could tell just by the way Sol
stuffed it into his rucksack.

The letter from Kimberly was only one page long
and had been written on a piece of lined school paper.

Dear Spike,

How is it over there in Vietnam? Do you have
to fight? So what else is new, huh?

I'm pregnant. My mother is happy as hell and
she's telling me all the time how to fill out the
forms at Social Services so that we can get some
money. She hasn't even asked me if I want to
keep the baby. My dad just shrugged his shoulders and opened a beer. He didn't even care
who the father is or anything (I think it was Peter's dad who did it, because you guys always
pulled it out before you came. He liked to

come inside of me. He said that it was more
manly.)

How about that shit. I finally get nailed after
all of the sex the gang has had together, and it
has to be Peter's father. (I wish it would have been
you.)

If you ever get back to this dump, look me up.
                              Love,
                              Kimberly

Spike's face remained passive as he picked up the
second letter. He glanced at the return address before opening it.

Hi Spike!

Pete and me are doing fine. My asshole brother-
in-law was sent up to Jackson State Prison today for dealing dope.

My sister and mother decided to go live back
down South with one of her friends.

Do you remember Mr. McClure, the black sergeant from the recruiting station? Him and his
wife have taken Pete and me to live with them.
Yeah, man!

Pete really loves Mrs. McClure and it's OK for
me. Ain't any of that hitting shit going on around
here with the McClures and he, and me are
training for baseball. The sarge says that I'd be a
good baseball player for the school team. (I
don't know about that shit, but it makes him
happy.)

We were at the mall yesterday and you should
have been there. Pete called Mrs. McClure
"Ma" and everyone started staring at us! I thought
it was funny and so did the sarge. You know
how black they are and Pete's hair is almost
white.

I just wanted to tell you that we're OK. Pete

misses you (me too.) Kim is knocked up. We always told her that she fucks too much. She thinks it was Pete's dad.

Come back to Pontiac and see us. You still remember where the McClures live?

                              Your friend,
                                        Ted

P.S. Sarge told me to slip this picture in and he says hi.

Spike turned the Polaroid over and stared at the four people sitting on the long couch in Sergeant McClure's apartment.

"Snapshot?" Sol leaned over to look.

"Yeah." Spike handed the photograph to Sol. "Real good friends."

The contrast between the black man and woman and the two blond-haired boys with light blue eyes was immediate. Sol stared at the four-year-old boy with his cheek pressed tightly against the black woman's cheek and smiled. Anyone could see the love in the woman's eyes and its reflection beaming back from the small boy's.

"Harwood?" Sergeant Monk called from outside of the poncho tent.

"In here, Sarge." Spike tucked the letters away in his side pocket and picked up his can of C-rations.

"Hi, Levin." Monk squatted down in the entrance-way of the small hootch. Levin nodded back at the operations NCO.

"What can we do for you, Sarge?" Spike asked, testing the hot beans.

"I don't know if you've been told yet, but your company commander is back and has volunteered Bravo Company for a patrol."

"You mean Bravo Platoon." Sol's sarcastic comment about the size of the company wasn't far wrong.

Monk nodded and tried smiling, but it was obvious that he didn't like what he had to say next. "Whatever . . . you and Sol are detailed as the point element."

"What else is new?" Spike took a heaping spoonful of beans in his mouth. The cheese not only added just the right touch to the flavor, but also worked to bind up his loose bowels.

"I just wanted you to know that we were against the idea. But Maynard has insisted that you and Sol go along."

Spike looked up from his food. "Why wouldn't we be going out on patrol if the rest of the company is going?" He, of course, had no way of knowing that the chief-of-staff didn't want to risk his life on patrol before Spike's MOH recommendation was either approved or disapproved by the MACV commanding general for forwarding to Washington, D.C.

"You guys are on a stand down," Monk snapped, trying to control his anger. He knew what Maynard was trying to do, but he couldn't prove it. "We have three battalions from the 4th Infantry Division mopping up the border area."

"Is that where the patrol is going?" Spike felt the old sense of danger returning.

"The back side of Hill 875." Monk stared down at the tip of his unshined boots, unable to look at Spike without giving away what he was thinking. "That's why Maynard won the argument. He convinced the brass that Bravo Company had the best chance of pulling it off."

"Pulling what off?" Sol asked angrily.

"We received an intelligence report from a prisoner-of-war that the NVA left a set of battle plans back in their regimental bunker when they withdrew from Hill 875."

"I'm impressed!" Sol said.

"Those plans—if they are still there—are extremely valuable. The prisoner-of-war stated that the plans show the exact locations of major troop rest areas and depots in Laos and Cambodia."

"We've been through this before," Sol scoffed. "That's all bullshit and you know it, Sergeant Monk. The NVA rest areas are nothing more than a couple of bunkers and some bamboo huts. They can leave those areas in a matter of hours and our bombers will find nothing."

"Not this time, Levin. The plans are supposed to show the exact locations of permanent ammunition depots and resupply points. If we move fast enough, they won't be able to move the supplies in time. It took them years to haul that stuff in there."

Spike had heard enough. If what the sergeant was saying was even remotely true, it was worth the chance. The destruction of just one of the NVA ammunition depots would be worth the risk. "Let's go."

Looking over at his war buddy, Sol reluctantly agreed, even though he didn't like the idea of Maynard being involved again with the company.

The ground squished under their boots as they walked over to the small company CP, where Captain Maynard was waiting to brief the small patrol. Spike could feel the water seeping into his boots through the mesh-covered drain holes next to his arches.

"I wonder why he's back," Sol whispered so Maynard couldn't hear him. "Everyone else was Medevaced back to Japan or the States."

Maynard opened his briefing with the answer to Sol's question. "Men, I know that some of you might be wondering why I wasn't evacuated out of here. I just want all of you to know that I refused medical evacuation." Looking directly at Sol and Spike, he made no attempt to hide the hatred he felt for them. "There is too much going on right now to leave all of you to an inexperienced officer."

Glancing over, Sol saw the look on Sergeant Monk's

face, which told him something funny was going on. He sensed that it had to do with Spike.

"I would like to introduce the company's new first sergeant," Maynard said, looking at Sergeant Monk. "He's been with the Third Herd for almost two years now, and even though he doesn't have any combat time, he knows how the Brigade operates."

What a backhanded crack, Spike thought. Seeing the sergeant's embarrassment, he went over and shook his hand. Sol followed suit and stood next to Monk to show his support to the rest of the company.

"Anyway, enough of that," Maynard said, displeased. "Have your gear ready by five tonight. We're going to insert and set up before dark."

"Why not wait until first light, sir?" Spike asked, shifting his weight to his other leg.

Maynard took his time looking at his buck sergeant and then said as he turned his back, "Because I said so!"

Sol cupped his hand over his mouth to muffle his words. "That makes it good enough for me."

Maynard whirled around to see who had made the sarcastic remark, but was met by blank faces. He opened his mouth to say something and thought better of it. There was too much at stake to screw it all up now. He nodded to Sergeant Monk. "Have the men ready and waiting to load up down at the pad."

"Yes, sir." Monk's voice remained totally professional. He waited until the captain had gotten out of hearing range and then said to Spike, "Would you believe that he is going to be a general officer someday?"

"What makes you think that?" Spike asked, watching the captain walking into the Brigade TOC.

"Army blue bloods. That's what the colonel calls them and I have to agree. Maynard's father was a West Pointer and their family goes back for generations. I guess the congressmen who recommend them assume that just because one of them was an officer, they all are."

"Well, they screwed up with that one," Sol said, voicing what everyone else was thinking.

From the open door of the helicopter, Spike and Sol saw just how extensive the battle had been. Huge red clay clearings dotted the valley floor and mountainsides where artillery batteries and infantry units had established fire bases. Small circles of tank platoons were spaced out on each side of Highway 14 as it wended south to Kontum, and a long convoy of five-ton trucks were hauling in ammunition and supplies to the units conducting the mopping-up operations in the mountain ranges.

Sol tapped Spike's arm and pointed down to a small hill that would have been insignificant if not for the paratroopers who had died taking it. Spike didn't have to be told that he was looking at Hill 875: he could feel it.

The lead chopper banked hard to the right, and the nose rose slightly as the pilot changed the pitch of his rotor blades in preparation for touching down in the tall elephant grass. Captain Maynard signaled for the men to unload and scrambled off the chopper.

Spike followed Sol to the edge of the landing zone and squatted down as the sound of the choppers' engines faded away. A freshly fallen tree leaned haphazardly against a larger tree, and the air smelled of high explosives. The Air Force had been making bombing runs all day to prevent the NVA from returning to the bunker complex to retrieve the top-secret material. Having no idea why they had been conducted so many sorties against undefended targets, the pilots had finished their day making 40mm cannon practice runs against targets selected by their flight leaders.

Captain Maynard assembled his patrol and oriented himself quickly, using his pocket map. The choppers had dropped them off within a hundred meters of a large NVA regimental TOC. The captain scanned the circle of men until he located Spike and used a hand signal to tell him to take the point. Spike winked in reply and then flipped open his shotgun bayonet. Sol fell in behind him without having to be told. He was carrying an M60—the same one he had found during the battle for Hill 875.

Sergeant Monk took the position behind Sol, using his Lensetic compass to keep Spike oriented in the high grass.

A few hundred meters away, a young NVA lieutenant was pushing his men toward the same objective. He and his special reconnaissance team had been trotting all day along the secret jungle trails that fanned out into South Vietnam from Laos and Cambodia.

The lieutenant, a graduate of Hanoi Military Academy, had been sent to train in Russia with the elite Soviet Marine Reconnaissance School, and once on the battlefield he had gained a reputation in his corps as being the best reconnaissance leader in the North Vietnamese Army. He had never failed to perform successfully on a mission, and for this one his division commander had personally briefed him, explaining the importance of retrieving the top-secret plans before the Americans stumbled on them. The lieutenant had seen in the general's eyes the unwritten instruction not to return without the plans.

The sound of American helicopters landing and taking off only a short distance away forced the NVA lieutenant to push his men even harder toward their objective. He knew that he was within sight of the hidden complex, but the American bombing had erased all familiar landmarks, turning the jungle into a twisted mass of dying vegetation.

Stepping over a pile of saplings that had been leveled, Spike sensed danger, but noticed nothing out of the ordinary to reinforce his sixth sense. He risked glancing back at Sol and saw him nod curtly. Sol sensed something, too, and motioned with his palm down to move more slowly.

Sergeant Monk was the first one to see the huge NVA command bunker and tapped Sol's shoulder. They had almost walked past the torn-open side of the bunker because Spike, looking for the usual small entrance, had ignored the gaping hole in the earth.

Spike scurried up to the side of the bunker, using it as a shield before he checked the back side. As the rest of the patrol started taking up defensive positions around the huge underground structure, a pile of loose dirt the size of a pickup truck caught Spike's attention and he pointed at the new grave.

Captain Maynard nodded and used hand signals to tell one of the squad to dig up the bodies while Spike and Sol entered the dark bunker. Monk followed, holding a flashlight in one hand and his M16 by its pistol grip in the other. Following the beam of light, he saw that the walls were covered with detailed battle maps. Immediately he started removing them.

Sol pointed with the barrel of his M60 at a dark entrance that led off the main room. Spike nodded and unhooked his flashlight from his webgear. He searched the door frame for a booby trap and then entered the small room slowly. The room was bare except for a bamboo cot and a small table and chair. Noticing a leather pouch hanging over the back of the chair, Spike looked back at Sol and smiled. The pouch would be perfect for carrying his shotgun shells. He couldn't hold the flashlight and open the pouch at the same time, so he decided to take the leather pouch outside before checking the contents.

He passed Captain Maynard and several other men who had come in to remove the maps. Because the NVA symbols on the maps didn't make any sense to the captain, he wanted to make sure that he had all of them.

Monk leaned over and whispered in Sol's ear, "We fucked up. We should have brought a Vietnamese Kit Carson scout with us to read the maps."

Sol nodded his head in agreement.

Spike left the bunker and stepped out in the fading light. He guessed they had less than an hour before it got dark. Captain Maynard joined him on the side of the earth bunker and squatted down. "We've got all of the maps. I'm calling in for an extraction."

That sounded right to Spike. There was no sense spending the night if they already had what they had come for. As Sol came outside to join them, Maynard drew himself up to keep his distance from the two.

All the while, the NVA reconnaissance lieutenant had been watching the Americans crawling in and out of the bunker. Perfectly camouflaged, he felt totally confident that the stupid Americans couldn't see him. He had been on too many dangerous reconaissance missions to be afraid of a small American patrol. He watched the captain leave the bunker carrying a rucksack filled with maps and documents and almost smiled. What an idiot. Now all he had to do was wait until the Americans left, and then he would send in one of his men to retrieve the top-secret leather pouch and disappear without having to risk a fight.

Suddenly Spike turned and stared at the wall of green jungle only twenty-five meters away. He knew something was wrong, but he couldn't put his finger on it.

The NVA officer spotted the pouch hung over Spike's shoulder at exactly the same instant Spike saw his camouflaged face against the jungle background. Spike blinked to make sure his eyes weren't playing tricks on him, but he had been right. He had seen a set of white teeth that gave away the rest of the camouflaged face. It was almost like staring at one of those newspaper puzzle games with faces that blend with the leaves of the trees and buildings in the picture. Without changing his expression, Spike slowly revolved his head and saw three more camouflaged faces staring out of the jungle. He raised a hand to his jacket pocket as if reaching for a pack of cigarettes. "Sol . . . don't fuck up."

Sol looked at Spike's hand and smiled. "What the fuck are you doing?" He remained squatting down, holding the M60 by its front grip with the butt resting against his lap.

"They're watching us"—Spike smiled casually at his buddy, as if just chatting—"right over there." He nodded ever so slightly toward the jungle.

Sol kept smiling as he eased the safety off his machine gun. "You're not fucking around, are you?"

Spike's intent look was all the answer Sol needed.

The NVA lieutenant realized that Spike had seen him just as the first fleshette round tore through the leaves around his head. Spike had fired from the hip and his aim had been a little high.

Hitting the dirt, Maynard looked around to see why Spike had fired his shotgun and then saw Sol raking the jungle with his M60. In another second the NVA team began returning fire and then Maynard had his answer.

Spike heard the choppers returning and could see the red lines of tracers coming down from the sky behind his position in the fading light. Just as he started getting up to fire at a running khaki-clad figure, he felt a sledge hammer hit him twice. He felt no pain, and he could smell the sweet odor of rotting vegetation and damp earth, but he couldn't move his face out of the loose dirt. A hand grabbed his shoulder and pulled. Spike rolled over on his back. He saw Sol's fear-stricken face and heard him screaming something that didn't make any sense, but he couldn't answer. Both of his eyes were open and dirt was packed against his right eye socket.

"He's dead!" Maynard cried, pulling on Sol's shoulder harness. "Let's go!"

"No!" Sol reached down again and struggled to pick up Spike.

"He's dead!" Maynard tore Sol away from his war buddy. "The chopper cannot wait!"

Spike listened to the captain screaming and wondered who he meant was dead. He saw Sol being dragged backward out of his sight.

Sol reluctantly boarded the last chopper and sat with his legs hanging out of the open doorway next to Sergeant Monk and Captain Maynard. He was slipping into shock and so didn't resist Monk's hand on his shoulder. Spike being dead was starting to sink in. He had seen the blood covering one side of his friend's head and a large bloody splotch on his upper chest.

As the chopper lifted off and dipped its nose for takeoff, the door gunners fired into the jungle to suppress the NVA fire.

Spike heard the increased RPMs of the choppers' engines and thought, "That Sol's an asshole for leaving without me." Then he began slipping into a comfortable, warm dream world and no longer cared what Sol did.

The NVA lieutenant watched the last chopper leaving and smiled. The dead American was lying next to the bunker entrance with the top secret pouch still over his shoulder. He would wait until the chopper left and then run out and get the pouch before the American artillery started firing on the position. He was too well trained not to know exactly how the Americans operated.

Spike thought he was smiling, but his mouth failed to respond to the command. He lifted his hand to wave good-bye to the chopper.

His hand obeyed.

Sol, leaning forward in the door as the chopper lifted above the bunker, saw the arm lift about a foot off the ground and then drop back down again.

Sol instantly jumped. Monk turned in surprise when the shoulder under his hand disappeared.

Sol fell the fifteen feet and hit the soft earth on the side of the bunker. Rolling down to the bottom of the slope, he leaped to his feet in a flash. He located Spike lying less than thirty feet away and raced to his side before the NVA lieutenant realized what had happened.

"Spike!" Sol cried, brushing the dirt off his friend's face. "You're alive!"

Spike passed out.

The NVA lieutenant scampered from the cover of the jungle toward the two American paratroopers. Sol sensed someone approaching and looked back over his shoulder. He had left his machine gun on the chopper! Desperately he lunged for Spike's shotgun. The NVA officer reached Sol in time to catch all of the fleshettes in the center of his chest.

Sergeant Monk yelled above the roar of the engine and the wind, "We have to go back!"

Maynard shook his head. "No!"

The officer's words caught on the wind just as the helicopter exploded from an NVA anti-aircraft round that had penetrated the fuel pod. Monk flew out of the open door and landed on his back. Maynard did a double flip and landed in the thick bamboo face first. They were the only survivors from the crash.

As night covered the jungle, Sol lay next to Spike and listened to his friend's shallow breathing. Immediately after blowing away the NVA lieutenant, he had dragged Spike into the bunker. He had washed out Spike's eye socket with the last of the water in his canteen and had bandaged the hole in Spike's chest. The bullet had punched through his chest cavity at an angle and had exited through his side. The round that had hit Spike's head had cut a groove in his scalp all the way down to the white of his skull, but Sol hadn't seen any brain tissue and was hoping that the wound was superficial.

Frantically, Sol thought about how he was going to

get Spike to a hospital. He soon realized, though, that his only hope was that Sergeant Monk would return in the morning with a relief force. Would Spike last through the night?

As Sol kept an intent lookout through the exposed bunker wall, he saw heavy storm clouds parting over the jungle. Spike moaned as he tried rolling over on his side, and Sol felt his buddy shaking from the cold wind whipping down the valley from the north. Then Sol himself shivered and rubbed his arms. His fatigue jacket was sweat-soaked and conducted his body heat away from him. Spike moaned again and started shivering harder. In response, Sol removed a seven-inch piece of cloth tape wrapped around his left front harness and stuck it over Spike's mouth. A loud moan at night would bring any NVA within two hundred meters of the bunker.

Captain Maynard rubbed his bruised leg and gingerly touched his swelling ankle. Pain streaked up the whole left side of his body. He had severely broken his ankle in the fall from the exploding helicopter. Heat from the burning wreckage was keeping him and Sergeant Monk warm. The ammunition from the door guns had been blown out of the aircraft when the fuel pods exploded and only a burning hulk remained. Maynard closed his eyes and tried thinking about anything but the pain. He thought about the jungle. Before he had come to Vietnam he had thought that the jungle was always steamy, but had been surprised to find that he needed a blanket or poncho liner to stay warm once the sun had gone down. Jungle temperatures could vary thirty degrees at night.

"How are you doing, Captain?" Monk whispered close to Maynard's ear.

"Ugh, not very good . . . I hope they send in a rescue party at first light—"

"They will. Do you still have your pistol?" Monk asked. He himself had been thrown from the chopper without his M16. He still had ammo in his pouches, but no weapon.

"Yes." Maynard felt for the custom 9mm Browning semi-automatic pistol his father had given him when he was commissioned a second lieutenant at West Point.

"Good." Monk peered around the dark jungle for any sign of the enemy. "I'm going to leave you for a little while."

"Where are you going?" Maynard asked, wincing with fear.

"We can't be more than a click away from the NVA bunker." Monk rubbed his side to ease the pain from his wrenched back muscles. At least he had landed in a dense stand of young bamboo and elephant grass that broke his fall. "I'm going back to look for Levin and Harwood."

"No!" Maynard hissed between clenched teeth.

"Sorry, Captain, but I'm going to look for them. I'll be back way before first light," Monk said, starting to crawl away.

"Please!" Maynard's tone changed to a plea. "Please, don't leave me alone out here."

Monk almost gave in to the officer's begging before he remembered Spike's severe wounds. "You've got your pistol, Captain. Besides, there might be more of our men back there who are wounded." Monk reached up on the left side of his harness to undo the safety strap on his black-bladed K-Bar knife. He felt the cool leather handle slip down into the palm of his hand. Not looking back as he crawled away, he instantly felt the cold chill of the wind when he had gone only a few feet from the warmth of the helicopter's hot ashes.

Soon Sol heard someone crawling toward him, and felt the cold grip of fear. He wasn't so much afraid for his own safety—he could evade the NVA if he had to— but he feared for Spike, who was helpless. The sound stopped and then started again, but this time the night crawler had changed direction slightly and was advancing toward the bunker. Sol was sure that it was a returning NVA soldier.

Monk stopped at the edge of the bombed-out entrance to the large bunker. He had misjudged the distance they had flown, for the bunker was only a few hundred meters from the crash. He squeezed the handle on his K-Bar and listened to the night insects. A muffled moan reached him and instinctively he pressed his chest against the ground and tightened his leg muscles, getting ready to spring up. The moan reached him again and he risked whispering softly, "Levin?"

"In here." Levin dropped his face down against the damp earth and sighed a prayer.

Monk swiftly crawled inside.

"Am I glad to see you!"

"Yeah!"

"Where's Harwood?"

"Back against the bunker wall. He's hurting bad, but he might make it until morning."

"He's alive?" Monk asked, shocked.

"Of course," Levin hissed angrily. "Why in the fuck do you think I jumped out of the chopper? I saw his hand move."

"Shit, let me see him." Monk followed Sol over to where Spike lay moaning through the olive-drab tape covering his mouth.

Monk removed a corner of the tape and the wounded man sucked in a deep lungful of air and moaned again. Slowly Spike's hand reached up and touched the bandage Sol had wrapped around his head.

"Oh, man, does that hurt," Spike said out loud, and Sol covered his mouth with his hand.

"Shut up! The fucking NVA are all over this place!" Sol hissed before he realized, Spike's conscious! "Spike, you all right?"

"Fuck no! My chest hurts and my head feels like a tank is parked on it."

Feeling Spike's chest, Monk gently pushed in the bandage. "Does that hurt?"

"No . . . not much. It's just sore . . ." Spike said, flinching. "But my head hurts like hell and my right eye feels like someone scrubbed it with sandpaper."

Feeling tears coming, Sol reached over and hugged Spike. "Man, I thought they got your sorry ass."

"I think they did," Spike whispered, stifling a groan.

Sol released his hold. "Shit, I'm sorry."

Monk, who was now searching the jungle, said, "I think we got most of the gooks, but we'd better get the hell away from here before they come searching for their own dead. Sol, do you think you can carry him piggyback?"

"Yeah." Sol said. Why hadn't he thought of that before?

"Let me try walking on my own first." Spike rolled over on his stomach and struggled to his knees with a little help from Sol.

"Are you sure?" Sol asked, steadying his friend.

"Hot shit . . ." Spike felt his head spinning. "I feel like puking."

Monk became alarmed. A serious head wound sometimes made a person feel like vomiting.

"Ah, that's better." Spike oriented himself. "Let's go. Someone point me in the right direction."

Sergeant Monk took the lead and crept slowly through the jungle back to the spot where he had left Captain Maynard. They soon found the officer groaning in a pain-induced stupor.

Sol looked down at the captain and felt the hate bubbling up from the pit of his stomach. Spike dropped in exhaustion to his knees next to the captain and took the 9mm pistol out of his hand. The safety was off and the hammer cocked. The slightest pressure on the trigger would have fired a round.

"He looks pretty bad off," Spike whispered, flipping the safety on and tucking the pistol in his waistband. "Where's he hit?"

"He broke his ankle really bad. He won't be able to walk," Monk said, never ceasing to search the moonlit jungle.

"Fuck him. Leave him here," Sol hissed, his anger getting the best of him.

"We can't do that," Spike said, already searching the immediate area for something that could be used to carry the captain.

"Why not? He was leaving without you." Sol moved the barrel of Spike's shotgun over to point at the captain's gut.

Maynard, hearing the voices, returned to reality. "Sergeant? Are you back?""

"Yes, sir, with Harwood and Levin."

"Good. Then carry me out of here." Maynard struggled up on his elbows.

"Not exactly, sir. If you remember, Harwood is in no condition to carry anyone," Monk said, doing his damnedest to maintain a professional attitude toward an officer.

Just then a bright beam of moonlight peered from between two huge cloud banks. Spike saw the scorpion first. "Don't move, sir . . ."

Maynard froze. "Why?"

"Scorpion—on your pants." Spike pointed to the large black scorpion resting on the exact center of Maynard's fly.

When the captain looked down and saw it, he sucked in a loud lungful of air. "Oh, shit! Kill it!"

Spike looked at the mother scorpion with her colorless young still clingling to her back, and then he looked up at the bright moon above them. It was almost as if an unseen being had lit the battlefield stage for him. He looked around the area and recognized the small clearing. It was exactly the same spot he had been in during the battle for Hill 875. Was the scorpion the same one he had seen before? He looked over and saw a rotting log and smiled. He had been here before, and because of the scorpion, he knew exactly where they were located on the hill.

Spike reached in his waistband and removed the pistol. As he pushed the arachnid off the captain's crotch with the barrel, Maynard hissed, misinterpreting Spike's intentions, "Don't shoot it, for Chrissakes!"

The gold medal hanging around Spike's neck seemed to grow a little warmer against his skin. He smiled. "I'm not going to kill it. We're all God's creatures." He used the pistol barrel to guide the mother back underneath the rotting tree bark that would protect it and its young from predators.

"What in the hell did you say?" Maynard frowned. He was sure the head wound was affecting the sergeant's thinking.

Sol shook his head slowly. "Captain, you won't ever understand what he just said."

Straightening to his knees, Spike felt a severe pain flash through his head and his eyeballs seemed to send out sparks. He reached out for what looked like a tree trunk and his hand found Sergeant Monk's shoulder.

"Are you OK?" Monk asked, catching Spike before he fell.

"Dizzy . . . real dizzy . . ."

"You'd better rest for a couple of minutes." Monk helped Spike sit down next to the captain.

"Only for a second." Spike kept his eyes closed. "Sol, do you know where we're at?"

Sol looked around the clearing. "No."

"We're in the clearing where we were with Dud. Remember?" Spike opened his eyes. The moonlight was gone. "The old company perimeter is over there." He pointed down the hillside.

"Yeah," Sol said excitedly. "We can use it for an LZ!"

Colonel Terry O'Donnell and the ARVN brigadier general walked briskly down the hospital corridor toward Captain Maynard's hospital room. A special team of South Vietnamese intelligence officers and American staff planners had gone through every single map that had been extracted from the NVA regimental bunker by the raiding patrol. One of the rucksacks had been destroyed in the exploding chopper, and the consensus was that the top-secret NVA plans had been destroyed with it.

The 173rd Airborne Brigade had regained its combat strength and was ready to be deployed again as a separate brigade in the field, but the colonel couldn't help noticing that the hospital was filled with paratroopers from the Third Herd. The more seriously wounded troopers had been shipped back to Japan and the States, but every ward had at least a dozen paratroopers in them.

O'Donnell turned off the wide corridor and entered Captain Maynard's private room.

"Good morning, sir." Maynard, sitting up in bed with his leg in a cast from the knee down, was reading a book by Flavius Vegetius Renatus on the military institutions of the Romans.

The chief-of-staff got right to the point.

"Captain, we found nothing in all of the documents that your patrol brought back with them."

"I figured that, sir. I'm sure the top-secret maps were in the rucksacks on my chopper."

The old airborne colonel nodded his head sadly and looked over at the Vietnamese general. "War has a lot of luck involved in it, sir."

"Yes, but it is too bad that we were the unlucky ones this time. That information could have changed the whole offensive campaign during the dry season this year."

Colonel O'Donnell tried one last time. "Are you sure the maps were with you on the chopper?"

"Yes, sir, positive. I went to the language school at Monterey for three months and can read Vietnamese. I saw the locations of some of the depots and

NVA units on one of the maps and made sure that I personally had it with me. If the chopper hadn't crashed . . ." Maynard looked down at the sheet covering his lower body.

The colonel patted the young captain's shoulder. "Don't take it so hard, Captain. You did your best."

"I failed, sir. If only I could have grabbed that rucksack." He looked up at the colonel with hurt reflected in his eyes. "I can remember trying to grab it as we crashed, but the explosion tore it out of my hands."

Colonel O'Donnell nodded his head and changed the subject. "The brigade commander has recommended you for the Distinguished Service Cross. There's a real good chance that you'll get it."

"Great!" Maynard's face brightened. "A Medal of Honor and a DSC!" Maynard caught himself too late.

"A Medal of Honor?" O'Donnell asked, his face darkening.

"Ahh . . . ummm . . ." Trapped, Maynard pounced on the first excuse that came to mind: "My leg! Please, call a nurse. Oh, the pain!" He grabbed the cast and twisted his face in mock pain.

O'Donnell wasn't fooled. "You haven't answered my question, Captain. How did you know that you had been recommended for the Medal of Honor?"

"The grapevine, sir . . . I-I heard rumors . . ." Maynard felt his cheeks getting red.

"Very few people even knew about the recommendations except my personal staff."

"Sir, I really don't want to say who told me."

"You'd better."

"It was Sergeant Monk, sir. But please don't punish him." Maynard groaned and squeezed the cast on his leg.

O'Donnell stared at the captain for a good five seconds before turning and nodding to the brigadier general. The two senior officers left the room without looking back. When they had, Maynard smashed his bed with his fist. Shit! he thought. How could I make such a dumb mistake?

O'Donnell was livid as he walked down the long corridor towards the exit. He was positive that Monk hadn't told Maynard about the awards list, based on his own knowledge that Monk couldn't stand the captain. A screen door to an enlisted men's ward flew open in the officers' face, and a nurse carrying a hypodermic tray rushed past them. Looking into the ward, O'Donnell saw 173rd Airborne Brigade shoulder patches attached to the ends of five hospital beds.

"Excuse me a minute, General. Would you mind if I just stepped in there and said hi to a couple of my paratroopers?"

"Of course not. May I join you?"

"Please do. I want you to meet some of the finest fighting men in Vietnam."

The South Vietnamese general smiled and followed the airborne colonel into the ward. O'Donnell took his time talking to each one of the paratroopers in the long row of beds on the right. Turning to cross the aisle, he saw a paratrooper sitting at the foot of another man's bed, holding a leather pouch by its shoulder strap.

The South Vietnamese general saw the pouch at the same time and touched O'Donnell's shoulder. "Colonel, that's an NVA—"

"Trooper," O'Donnell barked, addressing the man sitting at the foot of the bed. The paratrooper under the sheet had his head and shoulder bandaged.

"Airborne, sir!" The soldier slipped off the bed and stood at attention.

"At ease. What's your name, trooper?"

"Specialist Levin, sir."

O'Donnell looked over at the patient. "And yours?"

"Sergeant Harwood, sir."

There was a long pause as O'Donnell stared at the

famous young paratrooper. The kid couldn't have been more than eighteen, yet his eyes were those of an old man. "That pouch," he said, indicating the one Levin was holding, "may we see it?"

"Yes, sir," Levin said, handing over Spike's trophy.

"It's empty," O'Donnell said in dismay.

Spike pushed his sheet back a little and pulled out the folded map and a five-page document. "It wasn't, sir. We were just going through the stuff." Spike looked at his pouch in regret. "I sort of wanted that for an ammo pouch."

"An ammo pouch?" O'Donnell asked, puzzled. The pouch wouldn't be very good for carrying metal M16 magazines because they would make too much noise.

"I carry a shotgun in the field, sir."

"Oh . . . Can we see those papers?"

When Spike handed them over, the South Vietnamese general spread open the map on the bed and gasped, "Where did you find this?"

"We were on a mission when I got hit," Spike said, worried that he might have offended the general.

"This is it!" the general cried. "This is what we have been searching for!"

Colonel O'Donnell leaned over the general's shoulder and shook his head in amazement. He looked up at both of the paratroopers. "Were you with Captain Maynard?"

Levin nodded his head.

"It all makes sense now."

Spike, thinking that they were in trouble, said hastily, "Sir, it was my fault about the pouch. Levin didn't have anything to do with it."

O'Donnell smiled slowly and then started laughing. Maynard had lied about finding the map so that he would get the credit. He obviously had assumed that they had burned in the chopper crash. "*You're* not in trouble, Sergeant. Not at all."

Spike looked up hopefully. "So I can keep the pouch?"

"It's yours, Sergeant. We just want what was inside of it." Colonel O'Donnell smiled, but this time in satisfaction. He had done the right thing when he had called Lieutenant General Murphy about the young paratrooper's Medal of Honor.

Captain Maynard drummed the hospital sheet with his fingers, deep in thought as he tried figuring a way out of his career-ending predicament. He knew that Colonel O'Donnell was too cagy not to be able to figure out what he had pulled off. Without Lieutenant Colonel Yates to run interference for him, it would only be a matter of time before the old son of a bitch discovered that all of the witnesses who had signed statements for his Medal of Honor recommendation were dead. and that the statements had been forged and back dated. Maynard shook his head, furious at himself. He had gone through such elaborate precautions! He had even used different typewriters to write the eyewitness statements.

"Captain? Are you all right?" The ward nurse stood at the foot of his bed, looking concerned.

Maynard smiled as an inspiration hit him. It was time for one of his famous end runs. He had been one of the finest quarterbacks to have ever served the Long Gray Line and he had become famous for not being afraid to run the ball against great odds. "Yes, Nurse. Could you bring me a wheelchair?"

"Do you need to go somewhere?" she asked, thinking he wanted to go to the latrine down the hall.

"Yes, I need to get to a land line and make a few telephone calls to some of my father's friends who are stationed over here."

The nurse failed to catch the sarcasm in the captian's voice.

Colonel O'Donnell stood outside of the closed door and waited until the lieutenant general's aide looked up from the paperwork he was reading. "How much longer do you think that meeting will be going on for, Major?"

The young major stuck out his lower lip and tilted his head to one side. "It should have been over with an hour ago, sir."

"I need a cup of coffee."

O'Donnell had been awakened at three in the morning and told to report immediately to the MACV Adjutant General's office. He had been led directly to a red-eye flight to Saigon. He didn't have the slightest idea why the number two administrative man in Vietnam wanted to see him, and that was making him more than a little nervous.

"Wait here, sir, and I'll find some for us." The major had pushed his swivel chair back from his desk when the door opened and a half-dozen full colonels and brigadier generals left the adjutant's office.

Two of the officers recognized O'Donnell and nodded at him, but continued walking toward their offices down the hall. O'Donnell could tell that they had received an ass-chewing for something.

A heavyset major general filled the doorway and looked over at the colonel. The expression on the senior officer's face was that of an arrogant feudal lord looking down at one of his peasants who had done something to displease him. He nodded his head for O'Donnell to follow him into his office and snapped at his aide, "Make sure no one disturbs us."

O'Donnell had had his ass chewed by experts and wasn't worried about this particular general. He knew the man had a reputation for terrorizing the officers and senior NCOs who served directly under him.

The General dropped into his leather chair and then leaned over to turn up his air conditioner. "It's miserable outside."

O'Donnell remained standing, but he was thinking that if the general lost a little weight, he might feel cooler.

"Have a seat."

"Thank you, sir."

The general looked at O'Donnell over the top edge of his glasses and smiled as he sized up his quarry. "That was one hell of a fight your paratroopers had up there at Dak To."

"Yes, sir."

"I'm going to have a tough time finding qualified replacements for you."

O'Donnell glanced at the general's chest and noticed that he wasn't wearing any jump wings above his left breast pocket.

The general smiled and continued, "I might have to fill your brigade with non-airborne qualified personnel. What do you think about that?"

"It would be a disaster, sir. The 173rd takes great pride in being an airborne unit, sir, and they fight hard to keep their reputation."

"Are you trying to tell me that the other infantry units aren't fighting hard?"

O'Donnell had been in the Army too long to be trapped so easily. "I didn't say that, General. We were talking about the 173rd *Airborne* Brigade, weren't we?"

"Yes . . . yes. Well, we've already decided to fill your units with paratroopers."

O'Donnell grinned. He knew that General Westmoreland would never allow anyone to screw with one of his airborne units.

"Let's get to the reason I brought you here." In a second the whole demeanor of the general transformed, and the black bags under his eyes accented his glare. "You have a Captain Maynard in your command."

As O'Donnell nodded, he realized instantly that the general was a friend of Maynard's father. Worse, he was probably in debt to the retired four-star general. He knew that he was on very dangerous ground. "Yes, sir. He's currently in the hospital, recovering from a broken ankle. I think he will probably be evacuated to the States soon."

"He's on his way right now," the general noted, looking at his watch.

"I didn't know that, sir."

"He called me yesterday and mentioned that you had visited him and he was very worried when you had left." The general sneered, "You don't have a very good bedside manner."

"I try and visit all of the brigade's wounded, sir."

The sneer left the general's face and an evil glint entered his eyes. "Captain Maynard is a superb officer. I used to watch him quarterback the Army team when I was assigned to West Point. A lot of people have said that he will make brigadier general before he turns forty."

Pushed as far as he was going to go, O'Donnell nodded tightly and waited for the next shot.

"He's very worried that some jealous officers will gang up on him and disapprove the Medal of Honor recommendation that his battalion commander submitted for him before he was killed in action—"

"Sir—"

"Shut up! You listen to me, Colonel!"

"Yes, sir."

"As I was saying . . . He is concerned that now Yates is dead, that certain people might consider the award recommendation in an unfavorable light because all of the eyewitnesses had been killed during the battle. Captain Maynard has asked me to withdraw the recommendation because he doesn't want it if it is going to be questioned, even by one person. I don't agree with his reasoning, but he is an officer with a very highly developed sense of honor."

O'Donnell struggled to hide the smile that wanted to break out over his face. There was no honor in the man. Maynard had been caught and he was fighting like hell to escape.

"Is there something funny about what I'm saying, Colonel?"

"No, sir."

"Enough bullshit. You're a big boy. You understand survival in the Army. I want that complete recommendation for Captain Maynard's Medal of Honor on my desk by four this afternoon. You can use my helicopter to go and get it. And, Colonel"—the general's voice lowered to a growl—"I want all of the copies and the original. Understood?"

O'Donnell nodded. All of them except the one in Washington, he thought.

"Good. I'm glad that we understand each other so well." Now that his objective had been obtained, the major general's attitude changed, and he said in a friendly tone, "By the way, your orders came across my desk yesterday."

"Orders, sir?" O'Donnell asked, becoming alarmed. He wasn't expecting a transfer for at least another five months.

"You did know that your records were reviewed by the brigadier general selection board, didn't you?"

"Yes, sir. But the results aren't due to be published until next month and besides, I've been there a couple of times before. I'm getting a little old to be seriously considered—well past forty."

"Colonel! Some of us are connected at the Pentagon." The General chuckled. "I shouldn't tell you this because Westy himself wants to frock you."

"Frock?"

"Yes, in fact, he's planning on calling you up here tomorrow and award you with your stars." The general's smile grew even wider. "You can spend the night here in Saigon when you bring that paperwork back for me."

"Yes, I might just do that, sir."

"Good. Well, I have a lot of work to do before your return at four. Have a good trip."

Colonel O'Donnell saluted and left the general's office. The aide was waiting for him outside the door. "Sir, the general's helicopter is ready for you out on the back pad." The aide was wearing the same grin the general had been wearing. O'Donnell nodded curtly and slipped his helmet on.

The wind blew in through the open chopper door and cooled off the burning sensation on the colonel's face. He had felt his blood trying to erupt through his skin. He couldn't remember when he had been so damn mad. He kept telling himself to remember the rules of the game and most of all to remember the master rule: survive so that you could strike later.

Maynard had made a deadly enemy who would be around the Army a lot longer than his father's old flunkies.

A BLOODLESS
EPILOGUE

The bugler from the Old Guard Band lifted his silverplated bugle to his lips and blew the first note to alert the rest of the Drum and Bugle Corps assembled on the White House lawn. Spike stood at attention on the raised outdoor podium and saw the people watching him from their seats on the other side of the wide border of red roses that circled the patio. He was sharing today's honor with four more recipients of the highest award the United States could give a soldier for valor in combat. The ceremony was a "rainbow" affair that had been designed to meet the political needs of the time—one black, one Indian, one Hispanic, an Oriental sailor from Hawaii, and Spike.

A rapid medley of patriotic marches filled the Rose Garden for exactly ten minutes and then there was a one-minute break. The invited guests all turned their heads toward the double French doors and watched as they opened to the accompaniment of "Hail to the Chief."

Spike found Master Sergeant McClure in the crowd and saw the pride on the black man's face as he stood ramrod straight in his dress blue uniform and held little five-year-old Peter's hand. Ted stood next to the sergeant wearing a new blue blazer and gray slacks.

Spike smiled. Ted looked extremely uncomfortable without his Levis and jean jacket. Mrs. McClure threw Spike a kiss. Then everyone stood up. Some placed their hands over their hearts and all of the military personnel saluted as the Drum and Bugle Corps played the "Star-Spangled Banner."

In the middle of it Spike became lost in thought. Yuk's face appeared, hovering over the rose bushes, and faded away, only to be replaced by the smoke-covered side of Hill 875 and the sound of F-4s making their bomb runs. Spike blinked his eyes and focused them again just in time to see a flight of F-4s streak overhead. The sound of the jet engines was real.

The President paused in front of Spike and smiled. The only teenager in the group, Spike had shaved that morning only because he figured he should before appearing in front of television cameras. A military aide-de-camp opened a leather box and handed the President the light-blue silk neck ribbon with the most coveted medal in the United States military attached to it. A hidden speaker system carried the voice of someone reading a portion of Spike's Medal of Honor, General Orders. The words were meant to describe acts of heroism, but for Spike they conjured up images of Hill 875 and the ghosts of his comrades. Sol, watching from his seat, knew what Spike was thinking and felt his war buddy's pain.

"Is there something wrong with him, son?" a distinguished older man leaned over and asked Sol.

"No, Dad, he's fine."

The billionaire industrialist glanced over at his son and saw the stream of tears running down Sol's cheek. The older man thought back in time to another continent, another war, and another group of war buddies. The father started crying, too, as he sat next to his son and listened to the martial music that stirred memories of combat in World War II.

Spike left the podium after shaking hands with the President and that day's special guests to the White

House and hurried across the grass to the McClures. He shook hands with the sergeant and picked little Peter off the ground. The five-year-old hugged Spike so hard that he could hardly breathe.

Spike turned around at a voice from his rear.

"Spike, I would like for you to meet my father," Sol said, coming up.

"It's my pleasure, Spike."

"I've heard a lot about you, sir." Spike shifted Peter to his other side and shook hands.

"All good, I hope," the man said, looking over at his son.

"Give or take a little."

The group laughed.

"Spike, I'd like a word with you in private for a minute, if I may."

"Dad . . ." Sol warned.

"Sol, I promise, only a minute." He turned back to Spike and smiled. "You can bring your little friend along."

Spike handed Peter back to Mrs. McClure and followed the billionaire over to a clump of purple azalias.

"Spike, I'll get right to the point. If not for your personal invitation I wouldn't have had the chance to be reunited with my son."

Spike saw the older man's embarrassment. "It's not that big of a deal—"

"It is to me."

"Fine. It is, then."

The older man laughed to himself. "I can see why Sol likes you so much—your honesty is refreshing." Spike really didn't understand just how powerful and wealthy the man he was talking to was. "I owe you a lot, young man."

"OK." Spike wasn't about to start arguing while everybody was watching them.

"I would like to pay your way through college—I know you can get the GI Bill, but that only pays for your tuition. I'll pay for everything, plus your spending money and a car." He raised his hand to cut off the words that were forming on Spike's lips. "Please, give me a chance to help you."

"Sorry, sir, you've got the wrong man. I don't take charity." Spike turned to leave.

"Wait, Spike! How about a loan?"

"How much interest?"

"Let's let my business manager work out the details." The older man grinned.

"Let me think about it."

"Fine, let's get back to the others. I can see Sol giving me a dirty look." He touched Spike's arm affectionately. "Thanks for getting my son and me back together again. I love him a lot."

Spike nodded.

"I really want to do something for you—and a good education is the best gift that I can think of."

"I'll think about it, sir."

"Spike, I'm used to having my own way. You don't want to shatter an old man's ego, do you?"

Spike winked at the billionaire.

Spike leaned against the telephone booth on the corner of Oakland Avenue and Baldwin Road. He watched the whores working the bars on the other side of the railroad tracks and the new breed of drug pushers hustling rich kids who had driven in from their mansions in Bloomfield Hills.

Sergeant McClure had dropped him off an hour earlier, looking worried as hell. Spike knew that he had been acting weird since he had returned from Nam. He had changed. Everything seemed different to him, as if he were looking at the same buildings and people through the eyes of another person. It had only been a year since he had left Pontiac, but Spike felt like it had been fifty.

A car honked and Spike waved at the old hooker driving past. She had been trying to get in his pants since before he had pubic hair. She had even told him that he could have it free the first time. Spike started strolling down the sidewalk toward Wisner Stadium. Using his trained recon man's eyes to scan the houses, he saw the extreme poverty and the pain etched on the kids' faces as he walked past their porches. He looked over his shoulder and jogged across the street to the front of the school. He smiled, remembering the day that Captain Hanson had come to pick him up and he had been waiting for him on the side steps. He had frozen his balls off, but when the captain had finally arrived, he had acted as if it hadn't been a big deal waiting.

Spike shoved his hands in the back pockets of his Levis as he looked over at the stairs. He could almost feel the snow and freezing wind again, even though the sun was shining and it was almost ninety degrees.

"Yo, Spike," someone called from across the road. Turning around, Spike saw a Puerto Rican wearing Aztec colors on his lime-green jacket. Spike waved, but started walking away. He needed to get away from his childhood memories for a while.

"Hey, man, wait up." The Aztec gang member dodged between the cars and crossed over to him.

"How's it going for you?" Spike asked slipping into street language almost subconsciously.

"Cool, man, I haven't seen you around much."

"Been down South, man, and then I went out of the country for a while."

"Cool. Eddie told me to tell you that he's out in the Children's Village if I see you." The Aztec started walking sideways to be cool as they passed a pair of girls watching them from their front stoop.

"When was that?"

"A couple of months ago. But like I said, man, I haven't seen you around much."

"Yeah." Spike started walking a little faster. "I think I'll go pay him a visit."

"You walking?"

"Yeah, or maybe hitchhike."

"Later, hear? I'm going back there and see if I can get laid. Those girls were giving me the eye," the Aztec boasted, swaggering away.

Spike started jogging on the side of the road and then decided to cross so that he could run on the sidewalk. The Children's Village was a couple of miles north on Oakland Avenue and a half mile back down Telegraph Road. It was a familiar route, one he had used since he was ten and had to see a probation officer once a week in the county courthouse across the street from the Village.

Coming to the corner of Blaine, he decided to take a detour. Kimberly's house was only a block away. He turned the corner, planning on just running past her house when he saw her sitting on the old metal porch swing. Using a large lilac bush as cover, he kept the shrub between the two of them until he was at the base of her porch steps.

Kimberly was crying softly. Spike heard the springs squeaking as she rocked back and forth to a sad ballad on the radio by the Momas and the Papas.

"Crying?" Spike hopped up on the porch steps. "Are pregnant women supposed to cry?"

Kimberly's head snapped up. "Spike!" As she jumped up from the porch swing and waddled over, he saw that she was very pregnant. "Oh, Spike! It's so good seeing you again!"

"It looks like I won't get laid today." He patted her firm stomach.

Kimberly smiled. "There are other things we can do—if you're that horny."

"I'll pass. How you doing?" he said softly, trying to be comforting.

Her lower lip started quivering. "OK . . . I guess."

"When's the kid due?"

"Last week."

"Really?"

"Yeah. I wish the little fucker would come out of there." She patted her belly and smiled.

"You know, they say the longer a kid stays in his mother's gut, the smarter he'll be."

"You're shitting me." She glanced over at Spike to see if he was teasing her.

"No, really."

"Then maybe I'll keep him there for another month. God knows, he's going to need all of the smarts he can get to make it in this fucking world."

"What are you going to name him?"

"I don't know . . ." Kimberly started crying.

Puzzled, Spike wondered what he had said wrong. "You OK? I mean, I don't care if it's a girl. I just said 'him' because . . . you know . . . that's what guys say."

Kimberly looked up and smiled through her tears. "You're so damn innocent all of the time. I think that's why I always liked fucking you. It was like having a virgin over and over again."

"I'm the best fuck you've ever had, woman," Spike muttered.

Kimberly's eyes lost their focus as her thoughts returned to what had been bothering her before Spike appeared. "It really isn't going to make a difference what kind of kid it is if . . ."

"If what?"

"Social Services is going to take my baby away from me if I don't come up with the name of its father." Kimberly started crying, this time harder. She choked and then caught her breath. "Spike, I can't tell them who he is! I think they suspect him and that's why they're threatening me."

Spike nodded. She had told him in the letter that it had been little Peter Butts's father, and he understood what would happen if she mentioned his name to the courts or to the Social Services vampires. "That's simple. Tell them that I'm the kid's father." Spike shrugged. "I could be, you know."

Kimberly smiled. "Only if you had some really powerful sperms."

"I've been told that before," Spike said, bowing.

"Oh, Spike, you're such a fool. You know they will make you pay child support until the kid's eighteen." Seeing that Spike's expression didn't change, she grew hopeful. "You would do that for me?"

"Of course, why not? We've been buddies for a long time, Kimberly. Ain't that what friends are for?" Spike winked. He wasn't worried about the financial responsibility. Kim had always given whatever she had, and he wasn't going to abandon her now that she needed help.

"My father will believe it too. He always thought we fucked too much."

"See? Your problem is solved." Spike looked at his watch. "Look, Kim, I've got to get. Eddie Cruz is up at the juve, and I want to see him during their supper break. They sometimes let them go out in the back basketball courts for a few minutes before they eat."

Kimberly hugged him. "I love you, Spike, and I won't forget this favor!"

"You can always find me, through Master Sergeant McClure over at the recruiting station on Saginaw Street." He kissed her cheek and eased away. "Gotta go, woman." He hopped down off the porch just as her father opened the screen door.

"You get your horny little ass away from here, boy!" the pot-bellied drunk screamed, waving his fist at Spike.

Kimberly called after him, "If it's a boy, I'll name him Spike!"

Spike sat on the picnic table behind J Building and waited for the red doors to open inside the cyclone-fenced exercise yard behind the juvenile lockup facility. He was gambling that they worked on the same schedule they had had when he was there.

A station wagon with a county decal on its door slowed nearby and then sped away toward H Building, where abused and neglected wards of the court were housed.

Seeing the vehicle, Spike sprang to his feet. He knew that the staff driver would report seeing him. The open grounds at the Children's Village were off-limits to visitors unless they were accompanied by a staff member. He knew it would only be a couple of minutes before one of the security vehicles pulled up.

The red doors opened and a few-dozen teenagers wearing blue jeans and gray sweatshirts came outside. Spike saw Eddie as soon as he stepped out of the building. Three staff members joined the prisoners on the outdoor basketball court and started yelling at the kids to play ball. Spike jogged up to the fence and waved.

"Yo, Eddie!"

The Puerto Rican fifteen-year-old smiled and waved back.

"Yo, Spike!"

"Hey you! Get the hell away from the fence!" one of the staff cried, charging toward the fence while another went back inside to call the security patrol.

While the rest of the teenage prisoners ran interference with the staff member, Spike managed to talk to Eddie for a couple of minutes. Then a pair of black patrol cars drove across the lawn and braked to a rocking halt a couple of feet away.

"Looks like I've got to be hauling ass, Eddie. You take care of yourself." Spike had his fingers laced in the fence. "Can I get you anything?"

"Yeah, you can deposit a couple of bucks in my account at the main office. That is, if you got it to spare."

"No problem. I'll do it on my way out," Spike said hurriedly, hearing men climbing out of their cars.

"You motherfucking punk!" The moment the first guard saw that he was a teenager, he swung his billy club at Spike's head. Spike caught his wrist and brought his knee up in the guard's fat-padded groin. The guard huffed and dropped to his knees.

More cautious, the second guard approached Spike in a crouch. "You had better come along peacefully . . ."

"I planned on doing just that until your friend there swung that club," Spike answered, waiting in a crouch himself to see what the guard was going to do.

A side door to J Building flew open, and four goons emerged. The guard opposite Spike smiled, showing rotting front teeth. Spike got in a couple of good licks before they all piled on top of him and shoved his face down in the thick grass. He nearly suffocated before one of the guards pulled his head back by his hair. He kneed Spike in his kidneys and shouted, "Smart-assed little motherfucker!"

To stop the goons from beating Spike senseless, Eddie jumped on the cyclone fence and climbed up high enough so that the staff couldn't reach him and started rocking back and forth. He knew that the goons would get to him later that night, but that was *his* problem. The rest of the boys in the yard followed suit, and within moments they had the whole section of the fence rocking five feet in each direction.

The senior staff member handcuffed Spike and pulled him to his feet. "The rest of you had better stop that or that fence is going to fall down!"

The Level 4 staffer glared at Spike from the other side of the gray steel desk. "Empty your pockets, Harwood." He remembered Spike from his juve days. "Who in the hell do you think you are coming back here and causing trouble?"

"I was just visiting Cruz—"

"Shut up!" The man pounded the desktop. "You know damn well that ex-internees aren't allowed to visit J Building juves."

"That's why I waited outside. I don't owe you shit anymore and I haven't broken any laws." Spike twisted violently as a pair of rough hands grabbed him from behind.

"Empty your pockets!"

"You have no right doing this to me! I'm a sergeant in the United States Army!"

"Yeah? And I'm the fucking pope!" The Level 4 staffer laughed. "Empty his pockets for him. He was probably trying to slip Cruz some drugs."

The man behind Spike tore his back pocket trying to get his wallet out and reached down in Spike's front pocket to empty it.

"You get your jollies out of playing with mens' balls?" Spike snapped, spitting in the man's face.

They stopped beating him only when the director appeared at the glass window of the in-processing room. The Level 4 staffer buzzed her in.

"What's going on here?"

"We caught this punk trying to pass drugs to one of the J Building internees and then he tried helping him escape."

The director paused before she picked up Spike's wallet. She stared hard at him, trying to recall where she had seen him before, and then smiled when she read the name printed on the military ID card. "Spike Harwood."

The guards holding Spike grinned at each other. Now they'd really give it to him.

She pulled out another card from the back compartment in his wallet as she continued to check for drugs, and held it up so that everyone in the room could see it. "What's this?"

The fluorescent lights reflected off the light blue ribbon and the gold-helmeted warrior printed on the laminated card. Reading the bold printing under the picture of the medal, she said, "The Medal of Honor Society bears greetings . . ." She glanced up and saw the look in Spike's eyes before continuing to read out loud, "The bearer whose name appears below is a member of this society and is the holder of the Medal of Honor."

The director's face turned white under her thick layer of makeup, and as she hastily put the card back down on the table in front of her, all of the goons in the room stared at it. The lights made the gold medal shimmer. The two juvenile guards released Spike, backing away from the ex-juve in awe.

The steel-walled room was so quiet that only Spike's labored breathing could be heard. As he shoved his belongings back in his pockets, he removed fifty dollars from his wallet and threw it on the table in front of the director. "Make damn sure this gets in Eddie Cruz's account. I *dare* one of you fat fuckers to steal it from him." On his way out, he paused in the open doorway and spat blood and saliva on the front of the Level 4's shirt. Poking the man's chest, he threatened, "If anything happens to Eddie because of this—and I mean *anything*—I'll put a bullet through your head. Do you hear me?" Spike poked harder and smiled. "Us Medal of Honor winners seem to suffer from flashbacks. We go nuts sometimes, if you know what I mean."

The man's eyes widened in fear and he nodded rapidly.

"That's what I thought." Spike left the room and walked unescorted over to the first locked door. The guard saw the director nod her head and he opened it. Spike wiped the blood running down his chin with the back of his hand as he turned around slowly and called back to the watching director. "Do you know where I'm going right now?"

She shook her head slowly.

"Channel Seven News wants to do a story on the Pontiac street kid who won the Medal of Honor. I'm supposed to meet them in twenty minutes at 1200 Telegraph Road." With that, Spike left.

She gasped and then reached for one of her cigarettes. She avoided looking at her goons, who were staring open-mouthed at her. They all knew that 1200 Telegraph Road was the main office for the county juvenile system.

The cars passing Spike slowed and the occupants

stared at the young man with blood on his shirt and face. Ignoring them, he jogged the half mile down Telegraph Road toward the county courthouse, where he was going to meet the reporters and take them on a tour of his neighborhood.

A large billboard on the side of the road caught Spike's attention as he jogged past it. The American Foreign Legion had rented the space, and the advertisement read in huge red, white, and blue letters: "WELCOME HOME, SOLDIER! PONTIAC SALUTES YOU!"

The second book in the Fields of Honor series, *The Distinguished Service Cross,* is due out in paperback February 1991.

GLOSSARY

AA	Antiaircraft
ABN	Airborne
ACAV	Armored cavalry assault vehicle
ACV	Air cushion vehicle
AO	Area of operations
ARA	Aerial rocket artillery
ARVN	Army of the Republic of Vietnam
AIT	Advanced Individual Training
AW	Automatic weapon
BC	Body count
baht	Unit of weight or money (Thailand)
Berm	Dike or ledge, usually used to surround an A-camp or semi-permanent military base
BAR	Browning Automatic Rifle (WWII)
BAR belt	Ammunition belt with large canvas pouches that was popular with Special Forces units because each pouch would hold four M-16 magazines

CA	Civic action or civil affairs
CAR-15	Carbine-15, short barreled/collapsible stock version of the M-16 rifle
CARE	Cooperative for American Relief Everywhere
C&C	Command and control
CIA	Captured in action
CIDG	Civilian Irregular Defense Group
CN	Type of tear gas
COMUSMACV	Commander, United States Military Assistance Command, Vietnam
CP	Command Post
CTZ	Corps tactical zone
CS	Riot-control type of tear gas
Claymore mine	Anti-personnel mine
DCO	Deputy commanding officer
DOW	Died of wounds
DSU-GSU	Direct-support, unit-general support unit
DZ	Drop zone (used for paratroopers or supplies)
EM	Enlisted men
FAC	Forward air controller
FFORCEV	Field Force, Vietnam
FOB	Forward operations base
FWMAF	Free World Military Assistance Force
G-1/S-1	Brigade and higher administrative office/battalion-level administrative office
G-2/S-2	Brigade and higher intelligence

	office/battalion-level intelligence office
G-3/S-3	Brigade and higher operations and training office/battalion-level ops and training
G-4/S-4	Brigade and higher supply office/ battalion-level supply office
GSW	Gunshot wound
GVN	Government of the Republic of Vietnam
IG	Inspector General
J-2	Assistant chief of staff for military intelligence
J-5	Assistant chief of staff for civil affairs
JGS	Joint General Staff
J Lockup	Facility at the Oakland County Children's Village in Michigan where children were secured. The most restrictive level of control for children
KBA	Killed by air
K-Bar knife	Popular knife issued to the Marine Corps infantrymen
KIA	Killed in action
KKK	Khymer Kampuchea Krom (underground Cambodian faction)
LLDB	Lac Luong Dac Biet (Vietnamese name for their Special Forces)
LN	Liaison
LRP	Long-range patrol
LRRP Ration	Special dehydrated field rations that were very popular with long-range reconnaissance teams
LZ	Landing zone

M-16	Standard American rifle used in Vietnam (5.56-caliber)
MACV	Military Assistance Command Vietnam
MEDEVAC	Medical evacuation
MAF	Marine Amphibious Force
MF	Mike Force. A special company or battalion-size unit, normally composed of Nung (Chinese) commandos and used by the Special Forces commands to support their A-camps
MG	Machine gun
MEDCAP	Medical Civic Action Program
MGF	Mobile guerrilla force
MIA	Missing in action
MIKE or MSF	Mobile strike force
MR	Morning report
Montagnard	Mountain tribesmen living in the highlands of Cambodia, Vietnam, and Laos
Nung	Tribal group of non-Indonesian stock originally from the highlands of North Vietnam who provided special units for South Vietman and U.S. Army Special Forces
NVA	North Vietnamese Army
OB	Operations base
Off	Officers
OP	Observation post
OPCON	Operating Control
OPORD	Operational order
PCS	Permanent change of station
PF	Popular Forces (Vietnamese, used locally to secure and pro-

	tect villages)
Prov	Provisional
PSYOPS	Psychological operations
PW/POW	Prisoner of war
Quad-50	Four heavy machine guns that traverse from a single pedestal and which are fired simultaneously by one gunner
RF	Regional Forces (Vietnamese)
RPG-2/RPG-7	Chinese-made rocket launcher, anti-tank
ROTC	Reserve Officers Training Corps
RR	Recoilless rifle
R&R	Rest and recuperation, normally seven days out of Vietnam (Australia, Singapore, Hawaii, Japan, etc.)
RVN	Republic of Vietnam
RZ	Reconnaissance zone
Regular Army	West Point officers and selected ROTC officer who make up the elite corp in the officers within the Army. Normally regular army officers receive the choice assignments and are protected from reductions in force, along with rapid promotions. Rarely do they serve in combat as second lieutenants
SA	Small arms
SEABEES	Naval construction engineers
SF	Special Forces
SFG/SFGA	Special Forces Group/Special Forces Group Airborne
SOP	Standing operating procedures

SPARS	Significant problem-areas reports
TAC	Tactical
TDY	Temporary duty
TAOR	Tactical area of responsibility
TOE	Table of organization and equipment
TOC	Tactical operations center
USAF	United States Air Force
USAR	United States Army Reserve. Provided the vast majority of combat lieutenants during the Vietnam War.
USARV	United States Army, Vietnam
USASF	United States Army Special Forces
USMC	United States Marine Corps
USOM	United States Operations Mission
USSF	United States Special Forces
SEALs	Sea-Air-Land, Special unit within the Navy who perform underwater missions
VC	Vietcong (Southern Communists)
VN	Vietnamese
VNN	Vietnamese Nationals
VNSF	Vietnamese Special Forces
WIA	Wounded in action